SAGE

BOB WOOD

Sylvia - you've been a great help over the years.

Bob Wood

NOTE: This is a work of fiction. Names, characters, places and incidents are the product of the author's imagination or are used fictitiously, and any resemblance to actual persons, living or dead, business establishments, events or locales is entirely coincidental.

For information about special discounts for bulk purchases, please contact Sunbury Press, Inc. Wholesale Dept. at (717) 254-7274 or orders@sunburypress.com.

To request one of our authors for speaking engagements or book signings, please contact Sunbury Press, Inc. Publicity Dept. at publicity@sunburypress.com.

FIRST SUNBURY PRESS EDITION
Printed in the United States of America
June 2011

ISBN 978-1-934597-49-1

Published by:
Sunbury Press
Camp Hill, PA
www.sunburypress.com

Camp Hill, Pennsylvania USA

"Dante Alighieri, it has always seemed to me, made the mistake of his life in dying when he did in the picturesque capital of the Exarchate five hundred and fifty years ago. Had he held on to this mortal coil until after Uncle Sam had perfected the "Gadsden Purchase," he would have found full scope for his genius in the description of a region in which not only purgatory and hell, but heaven likewise, had combined to produce a bewildering kaleidoscope of all that was wonderful, weird, terrible, and awe-inspiring, with not a little that was beautiful and romantic."

John Gregory Bourke
Captain, Third Calvary
On the Border with Crook, 1891

-1-

The six Apache boys woke up after a two-hour sleep through the darkest part of the night and continued after their quarry. The foot chase after the herd of mustangs had started back along the upper Rio San Pedro, eighty miles behind them, the previous morning.

Sees in the Night led them as the glow of the rising moon, still below the mountains to the east, added a little light to the star-choked sky. At a forty-five-hundred-foot elevation, the October night was chilly, and the warmth of exertion was welcome as he loped through the chaparral.

All of the boys were used to traveling by starlight, but the ability of Sees in the Night well exceeded that of his companions.

The boys wore only breechclouts. No moccasins could have withstood the rigors of this chase, and they had been left behind. Heavily calloused feet served them well.

Claw, an experienced warrior and their teacher, trailed behind.

The horses, exhausted and desperate to eat what little grass was available, had not moved far while the boys slept. When they saw the boys approaching, they trotted miserably on.

When the chase had started, the twelve horses had run far and fast, but the boys had followed their trail to where they had stopped, and the animals had raced off again. After forty miles the horses just moved fast enough to keep ahead of their pursuers, but they were not able to stop to feed or drink their fill at the watering places they knew.

The boys carried watertight wicker jugs for canteens and occasionally chewed on mesquite bread and a kind of parched cornmeal called pinole as they ran. The mesquite bread was hard but nutritious and durable. But now the food was gone, and the jugs were empty.

As the sun started to rise, the quarry and its pursuers were twenty miles farther, and the weakest of the horses stood exhausted with her head down and moved no farther.

Claw came up and motioned for Sees in the Night, Strong Arm, and Nantaje to kill the horse. Each boy brought up his bow and shot an arrow with pinpoint accuracy into the mare's neck.

The exercise was over. Claw had wanted to demonstrate that a human being's endurance was greater than that of any horse.

Claw disappeared while the boys cut strips of meat off the mare. They tied the ends with strings made of buckskin and draped the loops over a shoulder and under the other arm opposite their quivers.

Although they were good riders, Apaches were not horse people like the Plains Indians. For Apaches, horses were more for eating than for riding. They knew the lowlands and deserts like no one else, but they were basically mountain people.

There were a lot of barriers to horse travel in the mountains, so horses were often more of a hindrance than help. They also didn't care to waste time finding forage and waiting for a horse to eat, drink, and rest. And whenever a horse got loose, more time was wasted catching it.

The boys, ages eleven to thirteen, had been in this area, not far from Fort Bowie, before. But they hadn't yet learned all of the places where they could find water. The nearest one any of them knew of was twenty miles away. Claw knew of one five miles away and had gone there. Now the boys had to track him down before they could assuage their thirst and cook the meat.

They were confident they could do that. They had begun learning how to follow tracks when they were very young. None of them could remember when they had first begun. And all that time they had studied the natural world, what belonged where.

They started from where Claw had last been seen and spread out in a line abreast, about ten feet apart. They looked for anything out of place, and missed nothing. Strong Arm yipped when he spotted where a pebble had been rolled out of its depression in the ground, and the others shifted to place him at the center of the line.

They heard another yip where a tiny green mesquite leaf lay where it had been detached. Then a partial footprint, a few blades of flattened grass, a broken twig.

The boys studied the land ahead and formed some idea of where water might be. The occasional sightings let them know that they were on the right course.

Five miles later, they found Claw. "Too slow," he grumbled. "You need to spend more time in practice."

Sees in the Night wondered how they could squeeze any more hours out of a day.

A week later they were at a lake in a mountain range. All Apache boys were taught to swim, and here was an opportunity to practice. Claw led them into the frigid water, and they spent an hour playing games and testing their speed against each other.

Then it was back to military drills: weapon making, tracking, concealment and ambush, signaling, and coordinated maneuvers.

The fall weather began to worsen, and they made a forced march back to their rancheria in the mountains west of the Rio San Pedro, covering seventy miles a day.

-2-

Fourteen-year-old John Sage stood erect facing an outcrop of boulders in a relaxed manner with his arms hanging at his sides. He cleared his mind as he waited. For the hundredth time, a stone flew up from behind a boulder, and he reflexively drew his Colt Navy .36 and fired. To his satisfaction, the stone shattered.

There was a yelp. Then a voice called out from behind the boulder, "Damn, John, I almost took a piece of that in my eye!"

Miguel Vega walked out from behind the boulder dabbing at some blood on his cheek with his neckerchief. He crunched through a growing expanse of gravel as he approached. The boys pulled wads of cotton out of their ears, and Miguel said, "Those stones aren't getting far enough away. We've got to stand farther back when we throw.

"You're getting almost as fast as me, and you can shoot just about as straight."

"You don't count too good, Miguel," said Sage. "You missed eleven. You get to shovel the corrals today."

"Aw, John," said Vega, sighing, "why don't you ever lose count?"

"Because I'd rather ride the horses than shovel their shit."

A triangle bell rang, and the two boys, who were of the same age, headed around the corrals and into the adobe ranch house for lunch, which Blackbird had waiting for them. The horses in the corrals had been accustomed to gunfire by all the practicing, which was a desirable trait when they were sold. Not even the chickens paid attention to the frequent noise.

Blackbird, a Chiricahua Apache and Sage's mother, spooned chili into bowls and handed them out to John, Miguel, and Miguel's two younger sisters. Miguel's father Enrique had already eaten and gone out to the alfalfa fields. Gruff padded across the packed earthen floor to

Sage and rested his big muzzle hopefully in his lap. "No chili for dogs," Sage said. "You've got to wait until supper."

Consuela, Miguel's mother, finished mending a pair of pants and joined them.

After eating, the boys got to work in the corrals. Sage had a filly that needed to learn what a halter and saddle were all about, and Miguel had some shoveling to do.

The monsoon season was underway, and rain cells wandered through the Arizona skies. Great billowing white clouds and gusts of wind brought some relief from the August heat. Thunder muttered in the distance, and it was raining in the nearby Huachuca Mountains, but Sage didn't see any squalls approaching that might interrupt his work.

At the end of the next day, Sage's father, Nathan Sage, returned to the ranch. He led four packhorses. He had sold a dozen well-trained horses to the army and done some shopping in Tucson. Sage and Miguel greeted him eagerly knowing what he had set out to get.

The boys unpacked the horses while Nathan lit a cigar and watched. John was going to be fairly tall and slender, like he was. His skin was brown, but not nearly as dark as his mother's, and his hair was a sandy brown, a mix of his blond and his mother's black. He had his father's blue eyes. Miguel was a black-haired, brown-skinned, mestizo on both sides, and a little shorter and thicker than John.

In addition to bolts of cloth for the women and sacks of rolled barley for the horses, the boys unpacked a wooden box that held two new Henry .44 repeating rifles like their fathers' and Colt .44 revolvers with belts and holsters. Another box contained some tools and ammunition.

The boys had been wearing sidearms ever since they had gotten big enough to keep them from dragging on the ground. Nathan had taught them how to shoot and insisted on frequent practice. There were countless threats in this part of the world, and he wanted them to be able to handle any that required the use of either revolvers or rifles. It gave him a little peace of mind.

They had started with Smith & Wesson .22 revolvers and worked up to the cap-and-ball Navy .36. Both boys also had learned to shoot with muzzle-loading rifles and were responsible for keeping the dinner table supplied with small game and an occasional deer.

The rifles had no sights. The boys had learned to shoot shotgun style, with both eyes open and visualizing where the bullet would go. After exhaustive practice over the years, anything they shot at they hit, whether it was at rest or moving fast. No time was wasted lining up sights.

Ammunition was a big expense for the ranch, but Nathan and Enrique stood it. If the boys ever cashed in, it wouldn't be because they couldn't shoot better than anyone else.

"You've about used up those .36s," said Nathan. "Get used to these. Reloading with cartridges will be a whole lot faster than reloading those old cap-and-ball guns. Work on it. Let's get in to supper."

Sage and Miguel were almost too excited to eat and rushed to get done and try out their new weapons.

-3-

Nathan Sage had been a mountain man throughout the 1830s. When the beaver business died out, Nathan, always a wanderer, decided to see some new country. After ten freezing winters in the Rockies, he had a hankering to head south. Way south. He had heard wondrous tales of Mexico, with its huge cathedrals, Aztec and Mayan ruins, and something called a jungle, and thought he'd take a look. He was also mighty interested in seeing the ocean. Hell, both oceans.

Nathan wandered Mexico for five years, north and south, and enjoyed just about every minute, even on a few occasions when his life had a good chance of being snuffed out. Then rumors of war sent him back north. He found an army recruiter, who snapped him up as a scout.

When the Mexican War ended in 1848, he stayed on. The army was attempting to protect the mostly Mexican population in the New Mexico and Arizona territories from Apache depredations under terms of treaties between the U.S. and Mexico without a lot of success.

While scouting along the Rio San Pedro in southeastern Arizona, which had just been acquired with the Gadsden Purchase, he came across a beautiful site along the meandering stream that passed for a river in these parts. A natural dam formed a large pond surrounded by cottonwood trees. The five-thousand-foot elevation there provided a cooler climate than the low deserts to the north.

He decided then and there to quit the army and start a horse ranch. There was plenty of available flatland in the broad San Pedro Valley that could be irrigated to grow hay. However, the reason it was available was that the area was infested with Apaches. It would take a fool or a man with uncommon nerve to start a horse ranch there. Nathan had uncommon nerve.

With forty-four hard years behind him, he was getting downright ancient.

He was tall and slender but broad shouldered, and when he put a shoulder to something, it moved. His blue eyes looked out of a hawk face, and when he looked at his reflection, he could see the blond beard starting to show a little silver. Yep, time to put down a root or two, he thought. Last chance to continue his line.

One night Nathan slipped to the edge of the Apache rancheria near the land he wanted in the Huachucas. The Apaches weren't much on posting sentinels since no one had the authority to post any. He waited for dawn there so as not to disturb the dogs.

As the sun rose and as the Apaches began to stir, they were startled to see him stride nonchalantly into their midst, his rifle held by the barrel over his shoulder. He leaned the rifle against a boulder and said in their own tongue, "I have brought no soldiers. I am here to visit with you."

Apaches were prone to torturing strangers to death, especially white strangers, but they had a code of hospitality that required them not to harm a visitor—at least as long as he remained a "guest." Nathan remained for two months and convinced the Apaches that he was not only a human being, a status that non-Apaches didn't have, but that he was a human being to be respected.

The name "Apache" had been given to them by the Spanish. They didn't much like the name. They referred to themselves as "the Man" or "human beings"—Tinneh in their tongue. He cemented his new status by marrying Blackbird, the handsome daughter of a war leader.

During his service at Camp Grant, Nathan had become friends with a young Mexican couple, Enrique and Consuela Vega. Enrique was a tough, stocky young man who impressed Nathan with his friendly manner and the calm, competent way he handled himself. They had shared a ride on the stagecoach from Tucson back to the fort, and Enrique had invited Nathan to his place for dinner. The Vegas had been scratching a living on a small homestead near the fort.

After he had managed to get the Apaches to let him ranch on their land, Nathan invited the Vegas to help build and operate the ranch in a partnership. Miguel and Sage had been born in May 1854, a hard year later. Enrique followed up with two daughters, but Nathan had apparently used up whatever he had left. John Coulter Sage had been named for a mountain man that Nathan had admired by reputation, although he had lived a little before Nathan's time.

-4-

In late September the boys were doing some maintenance on the irrigation ditches when a covey of quail exploded out of the brush nearby. The boys nonchalantly wandered to where they were out of view of the spot where the quail flew from and then ducked down, dropped their hats, and worked around in a half circle to get behind whatever had flustered the birds. Vega pointed to a moccasin track on the ground. Sage nodded, and the boys settled into a quiet wait.

After a half hour, two young Apaches carrying bows and arrows moved silently into view, stealthily retreating from their failed ambush. Using hand signals, Sage and Miguel prepared an ambush of their own. Just as the Apaches passed their hiding spot, Sage and Miguel leaped on them, locked their left arms around their necks, and held knives to their throats. After a brief struggle, all four broke into laughter, and the knives were put away.

One of the Apaches shook his head sorrowfully, and in the Apache language he said, “The birds were not our friends today.”

“Nantaje, those are birds from our ranch,” replied Sage in the same tongue. “We have trained them to keep watch for us.”

Laughing, Nantaje said, “Perhaps your Apache name should be Bird Master instead of Sees in the Night. Come and train our birds for us!”

“It would be a waste of time, Nantaje,” said Sage. “You would just eat them.”

The other Apache, Hook Nose, spoke up. “You know Nantaje very well. When are you and Strong Arm going to stay with us again? You have been away for a long time. Claw says that if you tried to find your way north by the stars, you would end up in Mexico. He says you need more training.”

“Hook Nose, Claw always says we need more training. Nothing satisfies him. When Strong Arm and I tracked him for three days without losing his trail, he still wasn't satisfied. We were too slow.

"There has been much to do here for the past two months, but we will ask our fathers if we can go up into the mountains for a while."

"Good," said Hook Nose. "Nantaje and I will catch some quail to eat before we go. Next time they will not warn you."

"We have trained our quail to fly away when they see an Apache, so you will go away hungry."

The two Apache boys laughed as they trotted off. Sage and Miguel finished their work in the ditches and headed for the pond below the adobe, shucked off their clothes, and dove in. They spent an hour racing back and forth and playing tag before Consuela rang the dinner bell.

At dinner, Miguel asked if they could visit the rancheria for a while. Enrique looked around at the adults and then back at the boys.

"Well, you're not going to be able to do that," he said. "Not this winter or next. It's about time you boys got around to some schooling. Nathan and I have taught you a little reading and writing, but not enough. You know my sister down in Cananea, the schoolteacher. She's been trying to get me to send you boys down there for some time now. I sent her a letter a while back, and Nathan picked up the reply along with your new guns. We've been letting you get acquainted with them irons before you head out.

"Aunt Maria will be happy to have some help around her place while you're living with her. We'll expect you two boys to behave and pull your weight around there and learn what she has to teach you."

Miguel let out a groan and asked, "Why can't we just study some more here?"

Nathan spoke up. "Hit and miss won't cut it. You boys need to do it full time, and Enrique and I can't spend all that much time with you. And we can't teach you all the things that Maria can. Besides, you should spend some time with kids that aren't Apaches.

"A smart man keeps his options open. You know what options are? It's choices. Someday you might want to do something where you'll need to have a fair amount of education, but if you haven't got it, you won't have the option to do it. It could be a real disappointment.

"You might stay on here, might not. This piece of land ain't likely to support more families, so probably not. Enrique and I long since determined to teach you what you need to know to get on in the world, and this here is part of it. You're goin'."

Sage could see that Miguel was not at all keen on the idea, but he was intrigued at the prospect of doing something new and different. It was clear they didn't have a choice, anyway, so they might as well make the best of it.

Cananea, a silver-mining town across the border, in Sonora, wasn't a bad place, and Maria had a large adobe there. She had some horses and farm animals that she could use some help with since her husband had been killed by Apaches he had been chasing with General Pesqueira a couple of years before. The local Chiricahuas avoided Cananea out of respect for Nathan and Enrique, but there were various bands roaming around that area.

Cananea was the Apache word for "horsemeat," and Sage and Vega had found some humor in that.

"When are we leaving?" asked Sage.

"Tomorrow's as good a time as any," said Nathan. "The weather has cooled off some—down under a hundred, I think—and it'll be a good time to travel. You boys pick yourselves a couple of geldings and another to pack.

"The time to cut hay is coming up," said Nathan, "and Enrique and the women can't do it all, so I won't be riding with you. We'll miss you boys on that job, but it's best you get going. The school year is about to start. When school gets out next spring, you stay on another month for more study. Then head back up here for a couple of months before you go back."

-5-

Early the next morning, Sage and Miguel selected three geldings and saddled up. They packed some food, water, cooking gear, clothing, blankets, ammunition, a reloading kit, and a few other items on the third horse, threw a tarpaulin over the load, and tied it down with a diamond hitch. Then they headed south along the San Pedro, which flowed south to north out of the hills near Cananea.

Gruff, a big animal not too far removed from his grey wolf ancestors, clearly wanted to come with them, but he knew his job was to stay around the adobe and protect the women from whatever might come along. It was a three-day ride to Cananea, but they had been there before and knew the way.

About noon of the third day, they spotted four horsemen headed down the trail from the south. The tough-looking men in big sombreros with cartridge belts draped across their chests looked to be a mite dangerous, but they were too close to avoid.

When they got near the four, the Mexicans pulled up abreast, blocking the trail. They had been moving fast, and their horses were lathered. A big scar-faced, heavyset man said, “Well, look at this! Two little boys with big guns.”

“And fine horses,” said another man. “We could use some fresh horses. How about we swap?”

“Why swap?” asked the first, laughing.

Sage, very frightened, spoke in Apache, “These men are going to kill us. When I say ‘now,’ you take the two on the right.”

“I’m ready,” said Miguel in the same language.

“What do you say?” asked the scar-faced man.

“Now.”

The Mexicans were caught flatfooted. Bullets slammed into their chests before they even touched their handguns or brought up their rifles. They rolled out of their saddles and fell to the ground with a thud. Their spooked horses jumped around and raced back up the trail. The boys’ horses hardly flinched.

Miguel and Sage slid off their horses, .44's aimed at the Mexicans, but they were all center shot and either dead or dying.

Sage walked to the side of the trail and vomited. Miguel sat down on the trail and shook his head slowly from side to side. They had never killed a human being and didn't particularly like the hard reality even though they had both been training to be warriors with the Chiricahuas for years.

The boys gathered themselves and reloaded their handguns. Then they drug the bodies off the trail, gathered up the Mexican's weapons, and loaded them on their packhorse before continuing up the trail.

About a mile farther on, they found the Mexicans' four horses contentedly munching grass near the riverbed.

"Let's see what they had in their saddlebags," said Sage.

When he opened the first one he exclaimed, "Mother of God!" It was loaded with bags of gold coins and peso notes! Along with cooking gear and food, the other saddlebags also contained money.

"They must have robbed a damned bank," said Miguel.

"Looks like it," replied Sage. Let's take the horses along to Cananea and see what has been happening there."

They tied the lead rope of each horse to the tail of the horse in front. Sage led off with their packhorse, and Miguel followed with the Mexicans' horses.

Two hours later they spotted dust ahead. A few minutes later, a posse of ten men came galloping down the trail. They slowed when they saw the boys and got pretty excited when they saw the horses the boys were leading.

The man leading the posse, a small, wiry man with a big mustache, asked, "Boys, where did you find those horses?"

"We found them under some gents who were fixing to kill us," said Sage.

"What?" said the man. "What happened?

Sage explained. He could see the man was very skeptical but couldn't think of an alternative. The rest of the posse sat with their mouths open and shaking their heads.

The leader said, "Those men held up the bank in Cananea earlier today. These were very bad men. Very tough. How could this be?"

Sage said, "Miguel and I know how to handle our guns, and they weren't expecting it."

The man shook his head and muttered, "Four men. Jesus! Where are they?"

"Two hours back up the trail," replied Sage. "Just off it, within sight."

"Have you seen the money?" asked the leader.

"It is in those saddlebags there," said Sage, pointing at the horses. "All of it."

Two of the posse members looked in the bags, and then at the leader and nodded.

The leader said, "All right. We'll take the saddlebags back with us."

He named four men to take the bandits' horses back up the trail to get the bodies.

"My name is Jaime Corrizon," said the leader. "What are you boys doing out here?"

"My name is John Sage. My partner is Miguel Vega. We are going to Cananea to attend Maria Rodriguez's school. She is Miguel's Aunt."

Corrizon took that in. "I know Maria Rodriguez. Fine woman. Does she know you boys are out here by yourselves?"

Sage said, "We've been over this trail before. Our fathers figured that we could take care of ourselves. They have other things to do."

Corrizon stared at him for a long moment. Then he said, "Yes. We will accompany you back to Cananea. The banker and the town will be very pleased to get that money back. Losing it was a disaster.

"Three men died in the robbery. I was very much afraid that more would die if we had been able to catch up with them. It is hard to believe what you did. It was incredible! I am very grateful."

Sage didn't reply.

"How old are you boys?" asked Corrizon.

"Fourteen."

Corrizon shook his head. “What did you do with their weapons?”

“We’ve got them,” answered Sage, and he pointed at the tarpaulin-covered pack on the packhorse.

“They are yours,” said Corrizon. “I will find buyers in Cananea if you like.”

Sage looked at Vega, who nodded. “Thank you, Mr. Corrizon. “That would be welcome.”

-6-

There were forty students at the school. It consisted of one large room, which was mostly used only during foul weather. Instruction was generally conducted in an adjacent courtyard under the shade of trees, where long tables had been placed. The students ranged in age from six to fourteen and were grouped by their level of scholastic advancement, which generally reflected their ages.

Mexican children over fourteen were expected to take on the adult responsibilities of earning a living. Only the wealthy or those gifted in the arts had any opportunity for further education, which was always in far away places.

Maria had advanced only because her father had managed to convince his patron, the mayor of Cananea and owner of a profitable silver mine, that she was highly intelligent, wanted to be a teacher, and could serve the community well. The current teacher was getting on in years and wouldn't remain teaching for very long. So Maria had the good fortune of studying in Mexico City for four years after promising that she would return.

Sage and Miguel were mortified to find themselves grouped with much younger children. It was no help that they were fluent in three languages. Only the fact that the other students were awed by the story of their killing of the bank robbers saved them from derision. None of the children cared to anger them.

About a month after the boys arrived in Cananea, Nathan Sage showed up at Maria's adobe. He found the boys building a second chicken coop behind it.

Miguel said, "Aunt Maria says that at the rate we are eating her chickens, we are going to run out if she doesn't raise more of them."

Nathan beckoned them with a wave and took a seat on the patio. When the boys sat down, Nathan said, "I just heard about that fracas you two had with the bank robbers. Maria didn't write us about it, but that sort of thing has a way of getting around. Tell me how it went."

Sage explained, and Nathan asked, "When those men were lying there on the ground, how did it make you feel?"

Sage and Miguel looked at each other, and Sage ventured, "I felt pretty bad. I got sick."

Miguel said, "I felt bad, too, but I was glad that we were able to kill them. I think they meant to kill us."

Nathan said, "They called the play, put you in a spot. You did the right thing. You proud of it?"

The boys looked at each other again and nodded their heads.

Nathan fixed them with a glare and said, "Killing a man is nothing to be proud of. You didn't know them, what they went through to get to be what they were. You don't know what other people put into them. Every life is important, and damn it, don't you ever be proud of ending one! That would make you less of a man."

Chagrined and confused, Sage said, "But you said we did the right thing!"

"I did," replied Nathan. "You did what was necessary, but it wasn't something that you should have felt good about, and I'm glad you didn't. Any man that feels good about killing should be put down like a rabid coyote, and sooner or later they all are."

Miguel spoke up. "But the Apaches feel good about killing. All the men want to be warriors."

"Yes," said Nathan, "that's their culture, their tradition. They'll fight anybody that isn't in their own tribe for the glory of it, if for nothing else, and it is going to be the end of them before long.

"Our army is full of Indian scouts who think nothing of aiding the army to kill other Indians so long as it isn't their own band. Our culture prizes cooperation over killing. Which one do you think is stronger?"

The boys thought about that, and they could see the inevitable.

Nathan said, "I came down here because I don't want you to get headed off in the wrong direction. I trained you to defend yourselves and, if need be, defend others. I didn't train you to be cold killers. I'd just as soon kill you myself if I saw you head that way.

"You boys are top of the line at handling guns. That requires that you be responsible. That's asking an awful lot of someone your age. I've tried to teach you to be responsible, and if I've failed at that, then I've failed at raising you. That would be mighty hard to bear."

Nathan thought for a minute. "Don't take from this that you've got to dither if you get into another tight situation. That would get you killed. I'm just saying that you should never be the aggressor. But if someone else calls a killing play, you do what needs to be done."

Nathan visited with the boys and Maria overnight and then headed back north in the morning, leaving the boys to chew on what he had told them. Coming from a man that both deeply respected, it had an impact.

The boys anguished over the lack of time they had to spend wandering outdoors, but they tucked into their studies, and with additional tutoring in the evenings and on weekends, they gradually advanced through the groupings. Miguel struggled more than Sage, but because of their natural competitiveness, he refused to fall behind.

Miguel was uncommonly strong, and Sage never could beat him at wrestling, so he felt some satisfaction that at least he could learn more easily.

Lessons consisted mostly of reading, writing, and arithmetic, but every day Maria devoted an hour to a lecture to all the students on various subjects of history, geography, and government. Maria was an excellent storyteller, and the tales of the ancient Greeks and Romans and world explorations thrilled Sage. He was intrigued by the descriptions of the oceans, continents, islands, jungles, and all the rest.

Maria owned a globe that she kept in her home when she wasn't using it at the school, and Sage studied it for hours and pestered Maria for details. Someday he was going to see the Pacific Ocean, and maybe a lot of other places.

Sage wasn't Catholic, but on Sundays he attended mass with Maria and Miguel, and the boys stayed on for bible studies provided by a nun.

Sage tended to reserve judgment on tales of the supernatural thanks to the obvious allegorical nature of the Apache mythology, and it wasn't in his nature to accept the authority of the church without question.

Apaches were extremely superstitious. They paid a lot of attention to placating the spirits, which were everywhere and in everything. His father had cautioned the boys about that and related a very negative view of all the competing Christian denominations. Each was convinced that their way was the "only way." He found God in the wonders of nature.

After long consideration, Sage gave equal weight to the Bible and Apache mythology.

-7-

Sage and Miguel had just turned sixteen years old when they finished their time at Cananea and returned to the ranch on the Rio San Pedro. They spent a great deal of the next summer in the high mountains with the Apaches improving their skills at tracking, guerilla tactics, responding to the command of hand signals, using knives, lances, and bows and arrows, and making weapons.

More than most of the Apaches, Sage was comfortable with the night and fond of maneuvering when the moon was down and just the glittering stars provided guidance and vision. His friends and older warriors occasionally woke up to find some memento that indicated that he had visited them while they slept—even in their jacales, much to their consternation.

Even Claw found one morning during one of his marches through the desert that the arrows in the quiver that hung near his bedding had been replaced with a very agitated Gila monster.

Sage and Miguel had generally mastered warrior skills. The Apache boys of their age were about to begin accompanying the seasoned warriors on raids in Mexico. While they yearned to achieve the status of full-fledged warriors, they didn't want to fight the Mexicans and were forbidden to do so by their fathers. It was likely, though, that they would be joining in horse-stealing raids on other tribes.

A little under a year after leaving Cananea, the boys returned to the ranch after spending a month with the Apaches. Summer was underway, and waves of heat shimmered off the broad river valley floor.

As they approached the adobe, Miguel said, "Sage, I don't see anyone around, and there are no horses in the corrals! The cows aren't here. Not even any chickens."

The boys saw a lot of moccasin tracks in the yard and Gruff sprawled lifeless and covered in blood in the dirt. They drew their guns and cautiously entered the house.

What they saw made them stagger. Consuela, Blackbird, and Miguel's young sisters had been cut to bloody rags with knives. The wreckage in the room attested to their struggles. The food they had been preparing was gone, so their killers had lingered to eat.

Sage looked at Vega. "Dad and Enrique," he said, and the boys bolted from the adobe and jumped on their horses.

After searching frantically for an hour, they found the bodies two miles away in the alfalfa field along the bank of the San Pedro. The two men had been hoeing in the irrigation ditches when they had been surprised by the raiders. Both had several Apache arrows protruding from their chests and backs. They hadn't been removed as they had been from Gruff's body.

The boys sat down, and tears flowed. They were normally loathe to show anything they considered to be a weakness to each other or anyone else, but on this occasion, they just let it go. They were both bitter that they hadn't been there to help defend the ranch. After a while, they got up and studied the area.

"The Apaches crawled through the alfalfa until they got pretty close." said Sage. "Then they waited while Dad and Enrique got closer as they worked backward along the ditch before jumping up and letting loose. There is some blood around, so it looks like they got off some shots."

"Yes," said Miguel. "They must have been full of arrows when they did. Here is where two bodies were dragged toward the cliff."

The boys found where boulders had been piled in a depression beneath the cliff and rolled away the rocks until they exposed the bodies of two Apaches.

"These aren't Chiricahuas," said Sage. "Maybe out of the north."

"White Mountain, I think," said Miguel. "They favor that kind of moccasin."

The boys dragged their fathers to the riverbank, piled brush and driftwood on them, and lit the pyre with matches found in Nathan's pockets. They stood for a while with their arms behind each other's backs. Hands rested on young shoulders, and silent tears streamed.

"Dad had a good run," said Sage. "He's been where he wanted to go, seen what he wanted to see, and done what he wanted to do. I'm sorry that Enrique didn't have as long a time."

"Yes" said Miguel. "I am going to go after those who did this."

"So am I," said Sage.

The boys searched around toward the south and found where ten unshod ponies had approached from that direction. The Apaches had dismounted before coming to the alfalfa field. After the killings, they had ridden on toward the adobe.

When they got back to the adobe, they found that the pigs had been lanced in their pen. Apaches wouldn't eat pigs. They studied the ground toward the north and saw that the band had driven the ranch horses, the stallion, the mares and geldings, and the colts and fillies that way, along with their dairy cow and two steers.

"They are maybe two days gone," said Miguel. "I think that they were passing back through here after a raid in Mexico and are heading back to the White Mountains."

"I think you are right," said Sage. "Let's attend to the women now."

The boys piled all their firewood in the yard, placed the bodies on it, and sent the remains toward the heavens.

The boys packed their saddlebags with mesquite bread and ammunition. Each tied a blanket behind their cantles, which, along with their coats, would suffice for bedding. As hot as it was here along the San Pedro, nights were cool in the mountains. Each hung two one-gallon canteens on their saddles. Without looking back, they headed north.

The trail of ten ponies, a herd of shod ranch horses, and three cows was easy to follow, and they moved fast. Near the end of the second day, under circling vultures, they found a camp littered with chicken feathers. The milk cow had been killed with lances there, and great chunks of meat were missing from the fly-covered corpse. A dozen bloated vultures were barely able to fly away when they approached.

They noticed a cloud of flies over piled rocks in a nearby ravine, investigated them, and found the body of a warrior interred with his bow and quiver of arrows.

"Knife wound in the belly," said Sage. "Blackbird or Consuela got a lick in with a kitchen knife. Or maybe one of the girls. He died hard."

Miguel said, "That leaves seven."

Sage mounted up. "They're moving slow with those steers. Don't think anyone is following. They're headed for the Mule Ear Pass, only a few hours ahead of us. We can ride all night around this range, and maybe we'll be in front of them when they come out of the pass."

They pushed the geldings all night. They had the moon for a lot of it. It was a good thing they had found their chaps in the adobe, or their legs would have been torn to rags on the ride. They tied their nearly foundered mounts about a mile north of where the trail came out of the pass and gave them each a gallon of water and a quart of rolled barley. They also cut open a barrel cactus and fed them the wet pulp. They exchanged their boots for moccasins, hung their chaps over their saddles, and left their hats. In the predawn darkness, they trotted on foot back toward the pass carrying their Henry rifles. The Apaches had their father's lever action repeaters.

At first light, the boys selected an ambush site where they could fire and retreat unseen and settled down to wait. There was no sign of tracks coming out of the pass.

They watched a collard lizard pop out of the sand in front of them. It climbed up on a flat rock and nestled down to absorb the heat of the morning sun. About half an hour later, a young zebra-tailed sand lizard approached the larger predator's rock searching for insects. It stopped and did a few push-ups, trying to get a better perspective of its surroundings and looking for any threats. It failed to detect the motionless lizard on the nearby rock.

The sand lizard moved ahead and approached the rock. Now thoroughly warmed, the collard lizard moved in a flash, grabbed the sand lizard's head in its jaws, lifted it up, and gulped it down whole. The big lizard sat back on its haunches, and its stomach pulsated until the still living sand lizard suffocated.

Four hours later, dust in the pass signaled the approach of the Apaches and their herd of animals.

Sage said, "They're sure not in a hurry. When I say 'now,' you take one on the right. We'll light out of here as soon as we shoot. It'll take them a while to figure out we're gone." Miguel nodded.

The seven warriors came down out of the pass. The ranch horses, four loose ponies, two steers, and all the rest of the herd animals followed along without coercion. Four of the ranch horses were carrying packs. Although not expecting trouble, the Apaches by habit studied the area carefully. Sage and Miguel lay perfectly still and quiet in the brush with their rifles in position.

In the heat of the day, the Apaches rode bareback wearing only their long breechclouts and their knee-high moccasins.

Sage selected a warrior on the left side of the group, and when the riders were seventy-five yards away, he said, "Now."

The two rifles cracked, and Sage's target took a bullet in the center of his headband, as did Miguel's. As the two warriors slumped off their mounts, the rest vanished into the brush and boulders before the boys could get off second shots.

They instantly wriggled backward for a few yards and then loped the mile back to their somewhat rested mounts. They jumped into their saddles and cantered toward the north although it no longer mattered in what direction they headed. Now the trackers would be the ones being tracked. Sage wondered what the Apaches would make of their moccasin tracks and the shod hooves of their horses. And the ambush. Their foray was already a disaster, with three dead and now two more. The spirits had deserted them.

Their horses were about done in, but Sage wanted to make some more ground before the next confrontation. They expected that four of the Apaches would come on rapidly, while the fifth remained to bring along the stock. They didn't want to deal with the fifth too soon if they survived the four.

Miguel said, "We need a quick kill, like with the Mexican bandits."

Sage had been thinking the same thing. "Yes, but how do we get them in a bunch and get close enough to them?"

"Easy," said Miguel, laughing. "We put up a sign near our hiding place that says, 'Gather Here and Stand Still Please.'"

-8-

Uklenni and his three companions moved rapidly along the track of the two shod horses. The area they were in was flat and open—not a good place for an ambush—so they rode together at a fast pace. A little farther on he could see that the land became more broken, and much caution would be needed when they approached that area.

The four topped a low rise, and Uklenni saw a curious thing. Instantly the four stopped and tethered their mounts. They approached cautiously with two rifles and two bows held at the ready. A few low boulders were scattered around, but the area was mostly open except for a few yucca plants and saguaro cactuses.

Some object was on a chopped off yucca stalk. When they got close, they saw that it was a very large Gila monster impaled head down with the stalk through its mouth and into its stomach.

Uklenni looked around, but the boulders were too small for concealment. As the four looked at the Gila monster, Uklenni caught a movement out of the corner of his eye and swung his rifle toward it. Too late. Two torsos popped up from behind two small boulders with revolvers extended and firing. Uklenni took the first bullet in the center of his chest, and he and the other three Apaches were dead before they could fire a shot or an arrow.

Sage and Miguel shook off the sand and brush that had covered everything except their faces and guns and came up from shallow holes they had scooped with their rifle butts and hands behind the boulders. They walked over to the bodies with their guns still extended and examined the wounds. “They’re done, Miguel. Let’s find their ponies and let them loose.” He picked up their father’s repeating rifles and said, “One to go.”

They found a place with some water and grass and stayed there for a day to let their horses rest and graze. Then they circled headed back in a great arc to get behind the last Apache with the stock. and cut him off on the trail. A day later they found the track.

Miguel said, "Looks like he abandoned the steers and he's moving fast. It's going to be tough to catch him."

"Lets hold up and rest for the rest of the day," said Sage. "We'll travel at night to keep the horses cool. We can push them harder that way."

-9-

Four days later, the White Mountain Apache Big Foot was a day from his home rancheria. The evening before he had made a camp and gorged on the last of a bag of cananea, ripe as it was, and was sleeping soundly.

He had been expecting that his companions would rejoin him. He was mystified that they hadn't, but he assumed that the four had disposed of the two mystery horsemen and would be at the rancheria waiting for him.

Under that assumption, he had not traveled nearly as fast as he could have. He was the youngest and least experienced of the band and had not yet learned to avoid making assumptions.

He was startled awake by the sound of two hammers being cocked and jumped up to find himself looking in the moonlight at two revolvers leveled at him four feet away. Big Foot sat down and sang his death song.

When he finished, Sage spoke up. "You and your companions have killed our families. We have lived with the Chiricahuas. We are members of the tribe, yet you killed our families. You have to pay the price of that. You are the only one of your band that is still breathing."

Resigned to a death by torture, Big Foot stared at the two boys with big eyes, not moving. Boys. They were even younger than he was! How could they have done what they did? Big Foot and his companions had had no idea that the people of the ranch, the Mexican and the tall blond man, had been associated with the Chiricahuas even though one of the women was Apache. They had wondered about that. He shook his head.

The two boys continued to stare at him. Finally the taller one with the light brown hair spoke again. "Get up and leave. Go back to your people and tell them what has been done. We will follow you for a ways. Don't turn back."

Both Big Foot and Miguel stared at Sage in astonishment. Big Foot asked, "How are you called?"

"I am Sees In The Night. This is Strong Arm. Go on foot. Take nothing. Now!"

Big Foot disappeared in the night, heading north. Sage and Miguel did not follow. Sage said, "Let's catch up the horses and get moving. They might come after us, but I don't think they will."

"Why did you do that?" asked Miguel.

"He isn't much of a threat to us now. We didn't need to kill him. I wanted to let him live with his shame."

Miguel didn't reply, but he rightly suspected that John had his pride and wanted to let their coup be known. So did he. He hoped that Nathan's spirit would forgive them for that pride.

They returned to their mounts. The other horses had scattered to graze. They caught two of them and led them back to Big Foot's camp using their own lead ropes. While the sun was coming up, they rummaged through the packs piled in the camp but didn't find much that was useful to them other than ammunition for the rifles and four packsaddles from the ranch.

They also found a leather bag containing five twenty-dollar gold pieces that Nathan had kept in a drawer at the ranch. The Apaches knew full well what they could exchange that for at a trading post.

Big Foot's pony was picketed with a long rope. They turned it loose, packed the two horses, and led them while gathering up the other horses. There were nineteen ranch horses. They followed along with the two led horses and were joined by the pony.

They headed south at a fast clip, changing horses every two hours. They wanted to put a lot of distance between them and the White Mountains in a hurry.

The first time they stopped for sleep, Miguel asked, "Have you thought about what we are going to do now?"

"Yes," replied Sage. I want to see the ocean. I think I'll head for California. Do you want to come with me?

Miguel considered that for a long moment. Then he said, "No, that does not appeal to me. I think I will go down to Cananea for a time. Maybe I'll return to the ranch after a while and raise horses again if I can find some good help. The stallion is not here. The Apaches probably ate him. Too much trouble on the trail. I would have to find another good one. For the time being, let's sell these horses in Tucson."

-10-

After selling the horses, the boys went into the mountains to visit the Chiricahuas. Hook Nose was astonished to see them. He told them that he and Nantaje had come to the ranch and had spent part of a day working out what had happened. They had found the bodies of the two White Mountain Apaches. They had found bones in two heaps of ashes. They had seen that two shod horses had followed the raiding party but didn't know who the riders were. They didn't think the two would survive the pursuit. They had considered gathering a band and following them, but the trail was too old.

The Apaches listened to the tale of the pursuit with awe, and Claw pronounced that Sage and Miguel were warriors.

They were sixteen years old.

-11-

Three months later, Sage looked out upon the bay from the hills of San Francisco. By 1870 San Francisco was a flourishing urban center, which supplied the mining and logging operations in the interior. A large number of ships were anchored. Some were sailing ships, and some were equipped with both sail and steam. He had ridden up El Camino Real from Los Angeles, where he had first seen and swum in the Pacific Ocean.

He rode down through the teeming city and looked for a room to rent for a while. He found one for a reasonable rate near the waterfront. In the afternoon, he wandered along the docks marveling at all the activity and at the tall ships. He felt that he was a lot more than the thousand miles or so from where he had traveled from in Arizona. What a different world!

A naval officer called to him as he passed by. "Hey, kid. You looking for work? Like all the rest, my vessel is short-handed."

"Not right now," replied Sage. I just got here and want to look around. I've never been on a ship. Wouldn't know what to do. I'll probably be heading up to the mining country to maybe see the high mountains."

The seaman said, "Oh, you'd learn quick enough. Most everyone else is going to the mines or logging camps, too. Hard life in the mines. Well, if you change your mind, look up the Ocean Princess. She's a good ship with a good captain. Better than most you'd find. We're sailing in four days out to the Sandwich Islands."

That gave Sage some pause. He decided to think about it.

That evening he had another new experience: a seafood dinner. The Apaches shunned fish of any kind, but he had fished in the mountains with his father and was fond of trout. The waiter had to show him how to get meat out of the crab legs and lobster tail. It was sure worth the effort, and the slab from some great fish was delicious!

He walked to a waterfront saloon with his stomach bulging. Another new experience. He had seen the saloons by the fort in Arizona, but this one was a far cry from planks laid on barrels. It was even better than the saloon he had seen in Tucson when he was there with his father. The long, polished wooden bar and the myriad of lamps and chandeliers were a wonder.

The clientele were a poor match for the accommodations, though. The sailors and dockhands looked like one rough bunch, and the oversized, black-bearded bartender looked rougher than any of them. He found an empty stool at the bar and sat down.

The bartender came over and said, "What's your poison, kid?"

"I don't really know. Never had any. I'll try your choice."

The bartender looked Sage over and said, "Travelin' alone, kid?"

"Yep," said Sage. "Seeing a sight of sights."

The bartender said, "That's quite a hogleg you're packin'. Know how to use it?"

"Yes, I do," said Sage.

The bartender walked down the bar and took a bottle out from under it that didn't have a label on it. He poured a shot glass full and returned.

"House special," he said, and he set it in front of Sage. "You just pour it back in one swallow."

Sage would rather have nursed something while he observed the crowd but figured he could still do that and poured it down. Boy, did that burn!

"That'll be a dime," said the bartender.

Sage paid him and said, "I think I'll try some beer."

Sage was already feeling some effect of the drink when the bartender returned, and it wasn't good. He was starting to feel sick and dizzy.

The bartender sat down a mug, giving him a strange look, and said, "That'll be a nickel." Sage paid it and turned around on the stool to study the noisy crowd. After his second sip of the beer, which he didn't much like, he suddenly deposited his load of seafood on the floor and keeled over.

-12-

For the first time in his life, Sage awoke slowly with his mind groggy. He couldn't figure out what he was lying on, and the small room he was in was slightly rocking back and forth and accompanied by creaking noises. What the hell?

Something in his skull was running around with a large hammer beating it on the sides. He discovered that there was a padlocked iron band around one ankle. A chain ran from it to an eyebolt set on the curved wooden wall. He sat up and almost fell out of a canvas contraption that was hanging between another wall and a wooden framework that ran across the room. About another dozen of the canvas contraptions hung at two levels in the room under a low ceiling, all empty. His shirt and jeans were stained with dried vomit, and his boots were missing. So were his gun belt and knife.

He could hear a great deal of shouting and banging noises somewhere above. There was the great rattling of a chain, and in a few minutes the motion of the room subtly changed, and it tilted somewhat. As his mind gradually cleared, he finally realized that he must be on a ship.

After an hour, two large, burly sailors wearing red frocks and white duck trousers came into the room. Sage lay still as one of them unlocked the band on his leg, and as it came off the sailor said, "Can't sleep all day. Cap'n wants to see you."

Sage asked, "Where am I?"

"You're on the clipper Sea Star—underway to Japan."

Sage tried to digest this. Japan. In his mind he located it on Maria's globe. Clear around the other side of the world. He kept his silence, and the three went up on the deck. The tall ship was out in the middle of the great bay making way under a brisk breeze. Sage considered going over the side but decided that the shore was too far away.

The captain stood on a deck at the stern with an evil-looking man with huge forearms. He looked like he could straighten a horseshoe with his bare hands. The captain was a man of a small build who looked a bit evil in his own right.

The captain studied Sage for a moment and said, “You are the newest member of this vessel’s crew. This is your first mate, Tunney. You’ll take his orders. Ever gone to sea?”

“No, I haven’t,” replied Sage. “And I don’t recall agreeing to go now.”

“Well,” said the captain, “you’ve been ‘recruited’ by a friend of mine ashore, and it matters not at all whether you’ve agreed. You’re a sailor now and for the duration. You haul your slack and you’ll get your pay like the other hands. If you don’t, your life will be a living hell.”

Sage damped down the rage welling in him. He could see no way to get out of this situation and reluctantly decided to accept it for the time being. He was going to Japan. Well, he had wanted to see the ocean and faraway places.

Tunney spoke up. “Follow me. We’ll see the quartermaster and get you some togs you can work in. Those landlubber duds won’t do for work aloft.”

When they got to the quartermaster’s cabin, Sage was issued a red frock and a pair of tar-smeared white duck trousers. He was also issued seaman’s boots and a peacoat.

Tunney had told the quartermaster that the new hand would be tarring lines to start off, so there was no need for a clean outfit. The quartermaster told Sage he would issue him some cloth for more trousers and frocks after his watch. Some crewmate would show him how to make them along with a hat.

Tunney led Sage back out on deck into seeming pandemonium. The crew was busy setting sails and adjusting stays. Sage spoke English, Spanish, and Apache, but the orders ringing out all around didn’t appear to be in any of those languages as far as he could tell. Tunney called over three seamen and said, “This here tadpole has just come aboard. The four of you lay aloft and tar the lines, starting with the main. McGinnis, you’re the lead.”

Tunney departed, and McGinnis told the other two sailors to get the buckets. Then he turned to Sage. "My name's Andy, formerly of Boston. Where do you hail from?"

"I'm John Sage. Lately of the Arizona Territory."

"Well, now," said McGinnis, "that's some change! What made you want to become a seaman?"

Sage looked at the broad, freckled, friendly face for a moment. "Not exactly my idea. Had a drink in a saloon, and the next thing I know, I'm waking up a seaman."

"By God," said McGinnis. "Shanghaied! We're awful short of hands, and the captain ain't particularly straight. Well, you're a sailor now. Better make the best of it."

"That's what I had in mind," said Sage with a shake of his head. "I don't have any idea what to do, though, or how to do it."

McGinnis said, "What we are going to do is grease the lines to keep them from weathering. That's done about every six months. When we find any that are bad, we replace them. Just follow along with me and the lads, and you'll see how it's done. Best change your duds here and now. Leave them and the boots under that tarp there. You'll be wanting your feet to feel what they're holding on to.

"You know, this is a good job for you to learn something about the sails and rigging. Tunney's a bad-tempered ape, but he's not totally dumb."

As the great ship sailed through the Golden Gate with the tide, Sage followed his crewmates aloft. He was not unaccustomed to danger, but as they scrambled up the mast, he was terrified. His three mates were as nimble as squirrels, but McGinnis stayed back with him as the other two ascended.

Sage observed how they handled their tar buckets and moved their hands and feet and concentrated on copying them instead of thinking about the rapidly growing distance from the deck. They stopped at the main topgallant sail, which was taut in the breeze, while the other two continued to the top of the main mast and the main royal sail.

Sage, over 150 feet above the water, which was directly below at the end of a roll, looked around, and it was all he could do to keep from wrapping his arms around the mast and hugging it until he died and fell off.

McGinnis, impressed that Sage hadn't frozen somewhere along the way, stood by him for a while to let him get a little used to the lofty and undulating environment. He started pointing out the various sails and ropes and explaining their names and purposes.

Sage thought he knew a bit about ropes and knots from long days of packing horses and mules, but all of that sure did pale compared to this! There must have been at least a mile of rope up here and an unbelievable variety of knots. Each one of the fifteen or twenty sails had its own name. He had some learning to do.

The Sea Star cleared the coast and got into the offshore chop, and the ship began an agitated pitching. Up on the mainmast the motion was magnified. As the mast swept back and forth, McGinnis continued his lesson, and Sage concentrated on every word like he had never concentrated on anything else in his life. As the motion smoothed out, Sage and McGinnis got to work applying the tar until bells below signaled that it was time to eat.

Sage's empty stomach was feeling a little queasy from the motion of the ship, but the salt beef and biscuits calmed the feeling. He wasn't troubled by that again during the voyage. He felt that he was going to sorely miss tamales, frijoles, and chili, but the salt beef was a whole lot better than a lot of the Apache fare he was accustomed to.

After eating in the galley, the tarring crew returned aloft. During the day he managed to get some tar on the ropes, or "lines," as he was instructed to call them, but it seemed to him that most of it ended up on him. He had once heard a soldier refer to sailors as "tars." Now he knew why.

At the end of their watch, McGinnis found Sage a hammock in the forecastle. Something else that he was going to have to get used to. After a while he came to appreciate that the fourteen-inch-wide canvas damped the motion of the rolling ship. It eventually became comfortable even though he could never roll over on his stomach.

With added assistance from the crew, the tarring was finished by the end of the week, and Sage had pretty well learned the nomenclature of a sailing ship and was well underway to learning the language of the sea. He had assumed a squirrel's disregard of heights as well as its agility and sure-footedness. He had developed a sailor's wide gait and no longer lurched drunkenly around on the rolling deck.

Sage and McGinnis joined the regular watch. There were two watches. The crew was divided evenly into the larboard, under the chief mate, and the starboard, under the second mate. While one watch was on deck and aloft, the other was below deck in the forecastle or galley. The watches were generally for four hours, and the rotation went on through the twenty-four-hour day. The watch below could fold up the hammocks and set up tables for cards.

However, when the weather turned rough, the cry "All hands ahoy!" was shouted down, and the entire sixty-man crew went above.

Sage found that there was never an idle moment above. Every morning with fair weather, two hours were spent scrubbing and mopping the decks with seawater. The sails were constantly being furled or unfurled, stays were being adjusted, and those not aloft were kept busy cleaning, painting, and repairing just about everything. The ship never could get completely "shipshape."

The clipper was carrying a cargo of farm implements, pots and pans, iron plate, and iron bar—everything that had come to San Francisco by rail from the foundries and factories in the east. Although the holds weren't full, they certainly were heavy.

Although Japan was over seven thousand miles from San Francisco, it would only take the clipper ship, which could travel well over three hundred miles in a twenty-four-hour period, a little over a month to get there. The distance would be extended somewhat toward the south to stay in the favorable trade winds. The North Pacific at their latitude was devoid of islands, and there would be no landings before reaching Japan.

Andy McGinnis and Sage became fast friends. Andy's tales of Boston and his sailing voyages fascinated Sage, and Andy was fascinated with Sage's descriptions of the Apaches.

Their shipmates generally spent their watches below engaged in playing cards when not sleeping. Sage wanted to do some reading, but most of the hands had no education and didn't read. The only book that Sage could find was a Bible, so he read that. He wasn't much interested in cards and didn't have anything to bet except credit on pay at the end of the voyage, and he wasn't willing to risk that.

Maria Rodriguez had had him study tracts in English in the evenings, but his vocabulary in that language wasn't great. The Bible wasn't an easy read, but he made what sense of it what he could. One of the sailors was a religious man, who had read it, and he was able to explain a few things, and some of the Bible study he had done in Cananea was helpful.

In the fifth week of the voyage, near the end of September, the Sea Star was off the coast of the Ryukyu Islands, with Okinawa just visible off the port beam. Sage was in the galley consuming monotonous salt beef and biscuits and listening to the ever present grumbling about the weevils and maggots.

One of the sailors, Barney Mills, pointed at Sage and muttered, "Look at Sage over there. He don't have any problem with this swill at all! Just wolfs it down like it was fresh steak and taters."

Sage glanced at Mills and said, "I got used to eating bigger bugs than this on long marches with the Apaches. We ate anything we could catch—bugs, scorpions, lizards, snakes, whatever could keep us going. The weevils don't have much meat on them, but they won't hurt you none."

Mills stared at Sage, but before he could form a reply regarding the "heathen Injuns," the call came down. "All hands ahoy."

When the sailors got on deck, the swells were huge, but the wind was calm. There were heavy clouds above, and the sky had a yellow cast to it.

The first mate called out, "Lay aloft and reef the sails, all of them save the jibs. We're in for a big blow."

Sage, McGinnis, and others scrambled up the mainmast and began reefing the sails as a heavy rain let loose. Other sailors worked their way up the other two masts. As they worked, the wind kept picking up. By the time they reached the main skysail at the top, it was everything Sage could do to hang on, but he and Andy got it furled just as a monster wave heeled the ship far over on its beam.

The mast swung so far over that Sage and Andy found themselves frighteningly close to the foaming sea. Then the great ship shuddered as the heavy cargo of iron plate and rods broke loose from their tie downs and crashed through the side, which was unseen below the water line. Under the force of the ballast, the Sea Star righted herself, and Sage was swung back into the sky, but the ship had been stricken.

As she settled low in the water, great waves rolled over the deck, sweeping sailors overboard. Like most sailors, they couldn't swim and quickly sank from sight. Sage and Andy watched as a few men managed to free the captain's launch, but it was quickly overwhelmed by the raging waves.

As the ship settled beneath the surface, Sage and Andy clung to the mast and rode it down until they too were in the water. A large piece of the ship's siding, torn loose by the escaping cargo, bobbed near Sage, and he made for it. He saw Andy floundering and grabbed him by the collar to get him to the side of the newly made raft.

They heaved themselves aboard and looked around for others but could see no one. They were helpless in the mountainous waves and screaming wind to do anything in any case. Andy put his mouth against Sage's ear and screamed, "We're in a goddamn typhoon! This could keep up for hours."

The two hung on as best they could, but waves kept breaking over the raft and washing them off. Sage rescued Andy three times, but after the fourth time, Andy couldn't be found. He was gone.

Heartsick and exhausted, Sage struggled back aboard and managed to stay there while the raft plunged and soared. After another hour the winds decreased and the seas calmed somewhat, and Sage was able to regain some strength. Before the rain abated, he sucked up some water that pooled on the uneven surface of the raft. He slept for a while, and when he woke up, the sun was starting to break through the clouds.

He could see that the wind and current were bringing him toward land. Hours later the raft was carried onto a reef about three hundred yards from the beach. It grated about halfway across an expanse of coral, and then Sage was swept off by a foaming breaker. He struggled across the coral, which battered and abraded him, until he managed to get into the calm water inside the reef.

Sage's frock was hindering him, and he pulled it off. He made it to shore and dragged himself up on the beach. He flopped down on his back in the sand, gasping. After a while, as the sun dropped behind the land, he crossed a muddy road, taking care not to leave footprints, and walked into some low green hills above the beach. He located a concealed place to sleep. He had no idea what the people in this land were like and didn't want to contact any until he had a chance to look at them.

-13-

Lieutenant Shigura of the Japanese army led his horse-mounted squad along the road north from Nagami. The eight khaki-clad soldiers had orders to reconnoiter the farms and villages along the coast to assess damage from the typhoon. Shigura saw a lone man on foot emerge from the trees above the road and halted the squad. The unarmed man did not look threatening, and the soldier's rifles remained in their scabbards.

As the shirtless and barefoot man drew near, Shigura thought that the man looked like he had lost a fight with a tiger. He saw that he was wearing a sailor's white trousers, now mostly rags, and he had light brown hair. Some kind of foreigner. A lookout at the fort had reported seeing a sail on the horizon just before the typhoon struck. Perhaps the vessel had gone down. If so, the man's presence here was somewhat miraculous.

As the man came up to them, Shigura could see that he was quite young and taller than most Japanese. Shigura asked him who he was and where he was from and wasn't surprised that the man shook his head and replied in a language that was unintelligible.

Shigura had never met a round-eyed foreigner. He had only heard of them, and neither he nor any of his men knew a word of whatever language that was. He doubted that anyone else on Okinawa did, either.

After the American Commodore Perry had forced his way into Japan and extorted a trading treaty twenty-four years before, Japan had transformed itself. A westernized army of which Shigura was proud to be a part of had replaced the samurai. It was his misfortune that he had been sent to this backward land to enforce Japan's rule.

Neither the Americans nor any other foreigners, other than Chinese and Koreans, had established any trade here, so Shigura had no idea what would become of this young man. Not his problem.

Shigura ordered privates Hito and Naguro to take the foreigner back to Nagami and continued on with his patrol. Let Captain Homura figure out what to do with him.

Private Hito pulled his left foot out of the stirrup and motioned for Sage to mount behind him, and they trotted back to the south.

Sage had been in a quandary. He was getting very hungry, but the vegetation here was totally strange to him, and he didn't care to experiment with what was edible. By the time that he could figure out how to rig a successful snare or trap, he would starve to death.

He had just decided to try to find a farm when the soldiers had appeared down the road. He had watched them from the trees and thought that his best chance of getting back to America was to get to some port. He was hopeful that Americans traded here, wherever "here" was. Maybe the place where the soldiers were headquartered was at a port.

Sage and the two soldiers entered a substantial town that indeed had a port, but the only ships there were of a very strange construction that he wasn't familiar with. He doubted that they were of any kind of American construction, or of any European nation, either.

A massive stone fort rose above the town, and a gang of laborers was at work extending its dimensions. They didn't look like happy people. Their clothing consisted of what looked like short Apache breechclouts and sandals. Some were barefoot. What appeared to be overseers walked among them, administering occasional blows with staffs they were carrying.

The two soldiers took Sage into the fort and to a stone-walled room, where they presented him to Captain Homura.

"Wherever did you find this round-eyed bastard?" asked Homura.

Hito spoke up and said, "Sir, he was on the road to the north. Lieutenant Shigura thinks he might have washed ashore from a foreign ship that was caught in the typhoon. He doesn't speak our language."

In the hope that this man knew some English, Sage said, "My name is John Sage. My ship, the Sea Star, went down in the typhoon. Are there any American ships calling here?"

Homura looked at him blankly, and Sage repeated himself in Spanish without any better result. Sage felt at a loss for any way to communicate with the man. Maybe he would send for someone who spoke English.

Homura studied the boy. He didn't know whether he was American, English, Spanish, or Dutch. Didn't matter. The damned arrogant foreign sons of bitches had all humiliated his great nation. Japan had lost face. Well, he knew what to do with this one. Young as he apparently was, he looked big and strong and might just last a year or two on the convict crew that was expanding the fort.

Hidaka was always complaining that he was shorthanded. If he didn't beat so many to death, he wouldn't be so bad off. Homura had had to order the sadistic shit to feed the convicts well so that they had the strength to carry the stones.

Homura looked at Hito and said, "Take him to Mr. Hidaka. He's got himself a new worker."

Private Hito's eyes widened in surprise, but he saluted and obeyed.

Sage wondered what was happening as the two soldiers led him out to where the laborers were taking square blocks of stone off of a heavy wagon, putting them on their shoulders, and carrying them up a stone stairway.

A short, squat man with his long black hair tied in a knot on top of his head came over. He was wearing what looked like a shapeless brown poncho held in at the waist with several turns of a braided leather rope. Then he realized that the rope was a whip!

One of the soldiers spoke to Topknot while he looked Sage over. Then he called out, and two burly men with staffs came over. Topknot spoke with them as the soldiers left. The two motioned Sage over to them, and they walked to the wagon. One of the staff carriers pointed to the stone blocks, then at Sage, and then at the stairs.

Horrified, Sage turned to bolt, but before he could complete a step, a heavy blow across his back laid him out on his face. Sage rose to his feet, took a deep breath, and lunged at the man. He grabbed the staff and wrenched it away. He was about to see if he could drive the end of it clear through the man's gizzard when a blow to his head from the other staff carrier laid him out again.

Stupefied, Sage was dragged to a wheel of the wagon, and his wrists were tied to it. Topknot came over and unwrapped the whip from around his waist. With the first crack of the whip the pain took the breath out of him, but he endured it silently along with a further dozen blows.

When he was untied, Sage sank weakly to his knees. The two staff wielders yanked him back to his feet and held his arms as they half carried him to a large stone-walled cell with an iron bar door and threw him in.

Sage was the only inmate of the cell—at least for the time being. There were a stack of woven mats in one corner, and he crawled over, took one, and lay down on his stomach. His mind was in turmoil as he assessed his bleak situation.

He was halfway around the world from his home country in a very alien land with no friends and no known possibility of getting back. He faced the prospect of being a slave laborer until he died. His passing would be of no more consequence than that of a bug.

Aside from his mental anguish, his back and the abrasions from the coral hurt like hell. And he couldn't even talk to anyone. He had felt pretty low when he had first been shanghaied, but even that wasn't as bad as this.

Put himself out of his misery?... No. So what to do? Get past his wounds, if he could. Be a good slave for the time being and keep an eye out for any options that might present themselves. Learn to communicate with these black-haired people with the yellowish skin and strange-looking eyes.

At nightfall a dozen prisoners joined him in the cell. They brought a bucket of rice and a bucket of water with them. Sage was apprehensive about the company of criminals but surprised when they seemed to be sympathetic toward his condition.

His appearance in their cell set off a cacophony of jabbering and gesturing for a couple of minutes as they studied the appearance of this large, round-eyed stranger. Then several of them tore strips off their breechclouts, poured water on them, and set to work cleaning the blood from his back.

-14-

Sage reached the top of the new high wall at the back of the fort, lifted the one-hundred-pound stone block off the pad on his shoulder, and put it in place. Over the past two years he had added many pounds of muscle and a few inches to his height, bringing him up to two inches short of six feet.

He was now fluent in the dialect of his prisoner companions, who had turned out to be not criminals but local Ryukyu Islanders who had resisted their overlords from the main Japanese islands.

Sage had learned that no ships from America or Europe called at Okinawa, so for the time being any plan of escape seemed to be futile. But planning, or the lack of it, was overcome by fate.

It was getting dark, and he had just carried his last block of the day. Sage descended to the ground and heard a crack of a whip and a cry of pain outside the wall.

Sage was alone. For the past two years he had never attempted to escape and had shown no inclination to try. He was lightly guarded.

He looked through the open gate and saw that a cellmate, Ikawa, was getting a whipping from the ape-like Hidaka. Hidaka had his back to Sage, and no other overseers were present. Sage ghosted up behind Hidaka on his bare feet, threw his heavily muscled arm around Hidaka's neck, and pulled back until it snapped.

As the spasming body hit the ground, Sage looked at Ikawa and said, "I've got to make my run now. Do you want to come with me?

Eyes bulging, Ikawa replied, "There is nowhere to run to! I can't go home. They would find us there. Go without me. But how will you live in the hills?"

"I have no idea," said Sage, "but it is certain that I can't live here. I'll take my chances in the hills. Tell them that I killed Hidaka. It won't matter any to me."

As Sage loped off, Ikawa said, "I wish you well, Sage. You have been a good companion."

Sage was well away from the fort before shouting behind him signaled that the alarm had been sounded. He would be hunted. He didn't know the country, but the night was his element, and he was confident that he could elude the hunters. His problem was going to be figuring out how to live off this strange land.

Two days later he was fifty miles from the fort. He had had no trouble finding water, but he was starving. If he had been in Arizona, he would have thrived, but there was nothing in this alien land that he recognized as edible. Grass and bugs weren't fattening him up much. He had skirted numerous farms, not yet willing to contact anyone who might betray him to the Japanese. He was thinking about scouting a farm for an opportunity to steal some food when he caught a faint odor of smoke on the breeze.

He cautiously maneuvered upwind and saw a small, bald-headed old man cooking a pot of rice over a low fire. He approached the man, told him he was starving, and asked if he would share his meal.

The old man stared at him with wide eyes. He showed no fear, but he made no move or reply. Sage repeated his request, but the old man remained still.

Sage waited for a while and said, "I am sorry, Father, but I must have food or I will die." He walked over to the fire, reached for the pot, and was knocked senseless.

Sage found himself flat on his back with his head throbbing and ears ringing. Dumbfounded, he staggered to his feet and looked at the old man, who was standing calmly by the fire still just looking at him.

Sage lunged at the man, looking to pin him. The old man spun around and slammed the heel of a small foot with unbelievable force into Sage's jaw, knocking him flat again and leaving him barely conscious. After a few moments, Sage rolled over and sat up, staring back at the little man in astonishment.

Sage shook his head sadly and with a wry smile said, "I seem to be having a little trouble with stealing your rice. I will be on my way."

He started to get up, but the little man held up a hand, stopping him, and moved over to the fire and removed the pot. He poured off the steaming water, pulled a small bowl from a pocket in his cloak, scooped up some rice with it, and handed it to Sage. Confused, Sage let it cool a bit and then gratefully spooned the rice into his mouth with his fingers.

The old man refilled the bowl, added wood to the fire and began to prepare additional rice for himself. The fluidity of his movements belied his apparent age. As he worked he asked, "What land are you from?"

Sage said, "I'm from America. Do you know where that is?"

"Yes, but I have never seen an American. How is it that you are here?"

Sage briefly explained the typhoon and his captivity and escape, but not the killing, and then said, "How are you called?"

"I am Fisu Hiragawa, and you?"

"John Sage. Why did you refuse to share your food at first? Why the ruckus?"

"I saw that you were a being that was outside of my experience. I wished to learn something about you."

Rubbing his swollen jaw, Sage said, "I would have preferred to just tell you."

"Ah," said Hiragawa. "Words often do not convey knowledge accurately or honestly. Do you wish to tell me more about how you managed to escape the fort?"

Sage realized that this Hiragawa was uncommonly perceptive and added the details of his escape and evasion. Then he asked the question that was burning in him. "You laid me out as easily as if I were a two-year-old child, and you aren't half my size. How did you do that?"

Hiragawa said, "I am a holy man. My order forbids the use of weapons. However, there are many in this world who do not respect holy men or any others and would rob us of our few possessions and our lives. Over many generations, we developed a method of unarmed combat. It is an involved, extensive study of the way the human body moves and where its weak points are.

"We also studied how to apply maximum force to blows. If I struck you with my arm, you would only feel the weight and strength of my arm, and your aggressiveness would not be impeded. However, if I struck you with my arm with all the weight and strength of my entire body behind it plus momentum, you would cease to be aggressive, and if I so chose, you would also cease to breathe."

Sage considered that. "I'm curious. How long does one need to learn to fight in this manner?"

Hiragawa replied, "A man who trains for two years, if he is sufficiently diligent, might become competent, but not a master."

The old man and Sage conversed for some time, and then Hiragawa indicated that he was needful of sleep. He said, "I find you to be very interesting, John. I would like you to travel with me for a time."

"I appreciate that," replied Sage. "I would like to spend some time with you also, and I don't have any other place to go right now."

Hiragawa asked, "The name Sage, does that have a meaning in your language?"

"A wise man," replied Sage. "It's also a kind of bush."

Hiragawa curled up in his cloak and quickly fell asleep. Sage had nothing between him and the elements other than his breechclout, but fortunately the climate of Okinawa was fairly mild all year round, and the night was warm. He wouldn't have minded a blanket, though, and Hiragawa apparently traveled very light.

Sage found Hiragawa to be a fascinating man. Hiragawa was a Buddist monk who traveled around the countryside. He visited the farms, most of which grew rice, vegetables, and pigs, and provided counseling on everyday matters. He also gave instruction on the eightfold path to nirvana, the release from the eternal circle of rebirth. In return, the farmers provided him with food and any clothing he might need, and he didn't need much. He was also valued by the farmers for disseminating news of local events.

Hiragawa obtained a cloak for Sage and offered to get sandals for him, but Sage was more comfortable with just his heavily calloused feet.

As they traveled, Sage learned about the Buddhist fundamentals of morality, concentration, and wisdom. He had a hard time, though, getting his mind around the concept that the goal of living a good life was to end it—

permanently—and not have to live through the pain of being reborn and living another life.

Sage also learned about the art of "empty hands," or "te," also known as karate. Karate had been developed and refined on Okinawa from techniques that originated in mainland China. Hiragawa found that his new student had a talent and enthusiasm for the discipline, which motivated him in teaching it.

There were many practitioners of karate in the villages on Okinawa. Sage and Hiragawa visited numerous schools, where Sage was able to spar with other students. Sage endured many beatings from smaller, thinner students who were better trained and very quick, and they took delight in whipping the larger, round-eyed foreigner. But Sage was quick, too, and very strong. With Hiragawa's mentoring, he gradually made better showings. Hiragawa was very pleased with his progress.

Sage found it interesting that the mental disciplines required by both karate and Buddhism were so similar. Surprisingly, both emphasized nonaggression.

At first, Sage was concerned that the villagers would betray him to the Japanese overlords, but he found that the villagers were uniformly opposed to the occupiers. They had no desire to help them.

-15-

On a spring day nearly two years after meeting Hiragawa, Sage was still wandering the island with him. They were sitting on the top of a hill overlooking the Pacific and engaged in the dissection of the meaning of one of Hiragawa's anecdotes when Sage was galvanized by the sight of a white sail on the horizon. After a time, it was apparent that a schooner was approaching the island.

Sage said, "Hiragawa, you know that I've been yearning to get back to my own country. If I can manage to get aboard that ship, I'm going to do it."

"Yes, " said Hiragawa. "You have wings, but no sky in which to fly. I have valued the time you have spent with me. It has been to my benefit, but you must go."

They were not far from Nagami, and it looked like the ship was headed there. The two men reached a hill overlooking the port in the late afternoon, and there was the schooner anchored in the bay and flying an American flag!

Sage turned to Hiragawa and said, "The ship should be there at least overnight. I'll wait until late tonight, when the moon sets, and try to get through the town and into the harbor without being seen. If I can't make it and don't get caught, I'll return here."

"Very well, John," said Hiragawa. "I will wait. I would not envy anyone who caught you."

The two rested and slept until the early hours of the morning. Sage awoke by his inner alarm and lay for a while looking at the brilliant stars. He wondered for the ten thousandth time just what the hell they were.

He arose to go and touched Hiragawa on the foot. He had learned not to be in reach when arousing Hiragawa. Hiragawa came instantly awake, ready to defend himself.

Hiragawa arose and Sage said, "Hiragawa, I can't adequately say how much you mean to me or thank you enough for all you have done for me, starting with saving my life."

Hiragawa placed a hand on Sage's arm and said, "I believe that I have had the advantage in our friendship. Perhaps my assistance to you will aid me in achieving nirvana, and this life will be my last."

As hard as his life had been, Sage had never come to look at life as something that was basically undesirable. There were endless opportunities out there, and he was determined to find at least one that would fulfill him.

Hiragawa said, "I will leave you with a tale of a two samurai.

"The first was a mighty warrior, the best in the land. He was admired and feared by all, but this samurai was vain and arrogant. It was his way to travel alone and fight alone. He did not wish to share his glory. He fought many battles, overcame great obstacles, and achieved victory after victory.

"The second samurai was a good fighter, very competent. But it was his way to gather companions around him and train them all to the best of their abilities. He honored each and therefore was honored in return. His companions became very loyal to him.

"One day their master called the two samurai to him and tasked them to defeat one of his enemies, a man without honor. The first samurai said that he could do this himself. He needed no one else for this task.

"The master was in awe of this samurai and acceded to his wish.

"So the first samurai went to the village of the enemy and engaged his men, but this enemy was in great fear of this samurai, and so he had placed two archers in hiding. While the samurai fought, the archers brought him down.

"The master then sent the second samurai to defeat his enemy. This samurai took his companions with him. With two of them he engaged the enemy, but he had ordered the rest of his companions to spread out and guard against any treachery. These men found the hidden archers and slew them, and the second samurai defeated the enemy."

Hiragawa became silent for a few moments and then said, "What lesson do you take from this, John?"

Sage replied, "Preparation, cooperation, thinking ahead...these things count more than fighting skills."

Hiragawa nodded.

"Goodbye, Hiragawa."

Sage turned and immediately disappeared from Hiragawa's view in the dark of the moonless sky.

The cobbled streets of Nagami were empty, and few lamps were lit in the town. The brilliant carpet of stars overhead provided sufficient light for Sage to navigate his way to the harbor. When he arrived there, he concealed himself and waited to see if the army had posted a night watch along the lighted quay.

They had. A squad of soldiers came marching down the quay, and ten minutes later they passed back. It was twenty minutes before they reappeared. Sage wondered why soldiers both here and in Arizona stood a watch like that. Why not spread out in hidden positions and pick off any intruders that showed up?

After mentally timing the longest period that the soldiers were absent, Sage crossed the quay, shed his cloak, and went into the water in just the breechclout that he habitually wore under it. It was a quarter mile to the schooner, but he hadn't forgotten how to swim.

When he came up to the side of the ship, he called up to the deck watch, who hadn't spotted his approach. "Ahoy there! American sailor to come aboard."

The head of the deck watch appeared over the rail and asked, "Where the hell did you come from?"

"How about a line, mate? It's cold down here."

The head disappeared. After some shouting above, four heads peered over the side, and a rope ladder was lowered.

Sage climbed aboard and was confronted by four astonished hands, who all wanted to know who he was. Sage gave them a brief description of the sinking of the Sea Star four years before and said he had been living on the island with the locals ever since. And could he borrow some dry togs?

One of the sailors set off to find an officer and another to fetch some clothing.

The first mate, Steven Craig, arrived just after the frock and duck trousers, and Sage rendered an expanded version of his circumstances.

Craig was extremely interested in the fate of the Sea Star, which had become one of the mysteries of the sea.

Craig told Sage that the schooner Forthright had come into Nagami with an envoy from Tokyo to negotiate trade arrangements for American interests. They were returning to Tokyo to pick up a load of carved jade bound for New York. But before reaching that destination, they were going to be calling in Mazatlan, Mexico, to take on a consignment of silver and then in Chile to trade farming implements and steam-driven pumps for copper before sailing around the Horn. Such was the nature of maritime commerce.

Sage asked if he could leave the ship in Mazatlan, but the mate was reluctant to grant this since the ship was shorthanded. He would speak to the captain but expected that Sage would be required to stay on until they reached New York. That would be a fair exchange for his rescue.

Sage joined the crew of twenty men and was assigned to the starboard watch and a berth in the forecastle, and after three more days at anchor, his second voyage got underway.

One time before leaving Nagami, Sage encountered the Japanese envoy on deck, but he didn't attempt to talk to the man. He had explained his situation to Craig, and neither thought it would be a good idea to let the local authorities know that the ship had picked up a stranded American there.

When the Forthright reached Tokyo, Sage was granted a brief shore leave while the cargo was loaded, and he accompanied a half dozen crewmen while they wandered through shops along the waterfront. The sailors gaped at the strange architecture and wood and paper dwellings, and the locals gaped at the strange appearance of the sailors. There was some American presence in the city, but most of the inhabitants had not seen any of them.

Sage had thought that his fluency in the dialect of Okinawa would be useful but was very disappointed to discover that the main island dialect was mostly unintelligible to him.

The schooner wasn't as fast as a clipper ship, and it was seven weeks before the land at the southern tip of Baja was sighted. As they rounded Cabo San Lucas, about five miles away, a steam-powered launch appeared on their landward side and approached them.

Sage was standing near the first mate as he studied the launch with a brass telescope. Craig said, "There looks to be about twenty heavily armed men aboard. They aren't flying a flag, so I don't think they are an official party, and no one else has any business here. I believe they are pirates!"

Craig shouted "All hands ahoy!" Then he ordered the two swivel guns on the rail to be charged, and eight bolt action rifles were broken out of the firearms locker.

Sage said, "I'm a fair hand with a rifle, sir. Let me take one of those."

Craig nodded and ordered one of the sailors to give Sage a rifle.

The captain came up, and as the launch approached to within two hundred yards of the port beam, he said, "Let's see what their intentions are. Wilson, put a shot across her bows."

Wilson fired the gun, and the ball sent up a narrow spout of water about thirty yards in front of the launch. Several rifles fired in return, but there was no accuracy from the wallowing launch at that range.

Craig shouted, "Reload with grape!" Sage headed above. He climbed the mainmast to the crow's nest and told the sailor there that he was relieving him. The sailor looked reluctant, and Sage told him that he was liable to be drawing some fire. The sailor went below.

The launch was a simply constructed open skiff that was about thirty feet long and had no cabin. An exposed engine in the stern sent up a stream of smoke that was carried off in the wind.

When the launch closed to about seventy yards, Sage waited until the mast paused at the end of a roll, and ignoring the sights, fired at the pirate manning the tiller. He hadn't lost his feel for a rifle, and the man was punched over the stern. The launch was drawn away by the wind, and another pirate jumped to the tiller and began to swing the launch back on course. Sage dropped him in his tracks, and a third brave soul, perhaps goaded on by his commander, died in another attempt, and the launch continued to fall away.

The pirates were firing at Sage, and he heard a number of bullets whizzing by, but as he swung back and forth with the rolling ship, he didn't present much of a target. The pirates couldn't get a good aim from the launch, which was pitching violently in the choppy sea.

Sage had little idea of what a steam engine was. He had never seen one. But he decided to see what would happen if he put a bullet into it.

To his great surprise, the engine blew up at his second shot, from over a hundred yards away, disintegrating most of the stern.

A great chorus of cheers rang out from below, and Sage was welcomed by a lot of whooping and backslapping when he came down.

Craig came over with the captain and said, "A fair hand with a rifle indeed! You've just earned your passage to whatever port you care to debark in. But I would certainly like to have you stay on."

"Thank you, sir," replied Sage, "but I would like to leave the ship at Mazatlan and work my way up to Arizona, where I was raised and have some friends. I've lived in Mexico, and I'll make out."

Sage had spent many evening hours studying a map of Mexico with Miguel while Nathan had regaled them with tales of his travels there. He had a pretty good idea of the lay of the land.

Craig asked, "No family?"

Most of Sage's living relatives were Apaches, but he elected not to mention that. "My parents died several years ago. I have an uncle in Texas, but I've never met him."

The Forthright left the sinking pirates to their fate and sailed on. The captain said he didn't want to risk taking them on board, and he didn't particularly care to hang that many men anyway.

The Forthright got to Mazatlan the next day. Sage accompanied Craig ashore in the captain's boat, and as they parted, Craig presented him with two twenty-dollar gold coins. “This is a bit more than standard pay for your time of duty, but you have a long way to travel, and you’ve earned it.”

-16-

Sage wandered around the town and found that it was basically a fishing village, but it also did a thriving business as a port since a railroad connected Mazatlan to the hub of Durango, which lay to the east.

He relished being able to speak in what he considered to be his native language again, and the first plate of Mexican fare almost had him weeping with pleasure.

A general store provided him with the standard peasant clothing of loose white cotton shirt and pants, a serape, and a high-crowned, broad-brimmed straw hat. Although he didn't feel that he needed them, he also purchased a pair of sandals. He had worn similar clothing when he had attended the school in Cananea.

After getting his hair trimmed, he found his way to the train depot. He learned that a train would be leaving for Durango in just a couple of hours, where it would arrive by nightfall. From there he would be able to take another train north to the city of Chihuahua. It looked like it was a lot easier to get around in Mexico these days than it had been in his father's time, but he wouldn't be seeing as much of the country or its people.

Two days and 650 miles later, the train pulled into the city of Chihuahua. During the last leg of the trip, he had struck up a conversation with a vaquero, and they had had a long discussion of the various ways to train horses. Pablo Cordoba, a slender man in his thirties, worked for a Don Xavier Valendez on a huge ranch near Chihuahua, and Pablo thought that Sage might find work there if he so desired. Cordoba had been visiting his elderly parents in Ciudad Jimenez.

Sage considered it. He wasn't in any particular hurry to reach Cananea, but he was somewhat anxious to get word of the whereabouts of his friend Miguel. It would give him a chance to earn some money for a horse and guns for the last part of the journey. He still had over twenty dollars left, but that wasn't going to be enough.

As the train climbed toward Chihuahua, the land rose out of the dry country and became very attractive with trees and streams passing by. This might be a good area to stop for a while.

It was evening when they got off the train, and Cordoba invited Sage to join him for dinner at a good restaurant he knew, and they filled themselves with enchiladas, tamales, and frijoles. They found rooms above a saloon and went downstairs for a drink.

Remembering the last time he had tried drinking (his first and last drinks), Sage gingerly sipped a beer while they listened to a very good guitar player.

Cordoba told Sage he had a horse and saddle in the livery and he could purchase a horse there for a few dollars. He could borrow a saddle and bridle at the ranch if he got a job there. Sage thought he could ride bareback and use a rope halter to get to the ranch.

The music got a little hard to hear because a huge Mexican was drinking heavily at the next table, and the more he drank, the more boisterous he became. Although he was alone at his table, he was telling one and all that he was Ignacio Estrada, the best gunfighter, knife fighter, and fist fighter in all the land and that the saloon was full of mud-grubbing peons that didn't belong in his company.

Sage looked around and thought that the saloon was full of pretty tough-looking men, who were all staring at Estrada with venomous eyes. Estrada might well wind up having a very bad evening, Sage thought.

Cordoba had downed three tequilas, and he looked over his shoulder and told Estrada that he wanted to listen to the guitar, not to him.

Immediately, Estrada backhanded Cordoba across the cheek, and both men lunged to their feet and went for their guns. Estrada was faster and shot Cordoba twice in the chest. Sage had risen also and snapped a sandaled foot up under Estrada's wrist, breaking it and sending his gun flying. Sage's body continued to turn, and pivoting completely around, he slammed the rigid knuckles of his right hand into the side of Estrada's throat. It was a killing blow, and Estrada collapsed to the floor, writhing and gagging out his life.

Most of the saloon's patrons had dropped to the floor, and the guitar player had disappeared. Sage knelt by Cordoba's side and quickly determined that he was gone. The bartender came over, spat on Estrada's body, and said, "We'll bury this animal with no cross, no marker. I am very sorry about your friend." As he looked at Estrada's body he said, "That was an amazing thing you did with your bare hand—killing him like that."

Sage didn't reply. He stood up, leaned over Estrada, removed his gun belt, and strapped it around his own waist. It barely fit with the last notch. He retrieved the revolver and slipped it into the holster. He had never seen a Colt .45 Peacemaker, but it felt good in his hand. No one objected to his acquisition.

Sage addressed the patrons: "If this man has a horse outside, I'm going to claim it. Please come out with me and go to your horses."

Everyone in the saloon that had a horse there trooped outside and walked to his horse. A big black gelding stood unclaimed. Sage thought anyone staying in the rooms above would have their horses at the livery. There was a fine-looking Winchester in a saddle scabbard.

Sage returned inside and asked the bartender if he would keep the body of his friend until the morning. Receiving an assent, they carried Cordoba to a storage room. He then went through Estrada's pockets and found a few coins, including three twenty-dollar gold pieces.

The bartender said, "The bastard probably stole them."

Sage gave the bartender one of the gold coins. "For your trouble, and to get this one buried." He pocketed the other coins.

Sage was wondering why no lawmen had shown up. "What law do you have here?" he asked.

"There is a troop of Federales stationed here," replied the bartender, "but they are all off looking for a band of rustlers tonight. There will be no trouble for you over this."

Sage inquired where the livery was, went out, climbed on the black horse, and rode to it. He found the owner in an adjacent adobe, explained that one of his customers had just been killed, and said that he would be taking his horse back to his ranch with the body in the morning. Leaving the black horse there, he walked back to the saloon and went to his room.

The next morning Sage found a store that sold clothing and boots and outfitted himself in the clothing of a vaquero, including snug trousers that flared over the boots, and a grey felt sombrero. He had to try on a number of boots before finding a pair that felt anywhere near comfortable on feet that hadn't known boots for a very long time.

Sage picked up spurs, some ammunition, and a kit to clean his weapons at a hardware store and returned to the livery to claim Cordoba's horse, a decent-looking roan.

At the saloon the bartender helped Sage load and tie the tarpaulin-covered body of Cordoba over the saddle of his horse. The liveryman had given him directions to the Valendez spread, which was twenty five miles away, and he led the roan out of town. It felt good to be on a horse again.

Ten miles out of Chihuahua, Sage stopped and tried out his newly acquired weapons. After firing a box of fifty rounds, he was satisfied with the Colt. Five rounds from the Winchester were more than enough for him to be comfortable with it.

-17-

Sage rode into the Valendez ranch, the Circle V, just before dark. Two vaqueros came off the porch of a large wood-framed house, and he introduced himself and explained his burden to the shocked riders. One went to get Don Valendez. Sage introduced himself and explained again, providing some details about Cordoba's confrontation with Estrada.

Valendez said, "Poor Pablo, he was a good man. A top hand. We will bury him here, and I will send word to his parents. They will be much aggrieved." And after a moment, he asked, "What of his killer?"

"I killed him. I'm sorry that it wasn't soon enough to save Pablo."

Valendez studied Sage and then said, "Very well. You are welcome to stay the night in the bunkhouse. We eat late here, so please join us for dinner."

While the vaqueros ate in a cook shack near their bunkhouse, Valendez and his family of a wife, who would have been attractive if she had carried about a hundred fewer pounds, and five young children dined in the main house. The foreman, a tall, competent-looking man with an extravagant mustache named Francisco Baca, ate with them.

While dining on steak, potatoes, and squash, Sage was prompted to divulge some details of his life. He mentioned his origins in Arizona but left out any reference to the Apaches. He said that he had an uncle in Laredo that he had never met. He told of his brief education in Cananea. His audience was intrigued by his experiences at sea and in the exotic Orient, and there was some discussion of Buddhism, but since it wasn't the "true religion," it was dismissed out of hand.

The conversation turned to rustlers, and Valendez lamented that he was being robbed blind. He had many cattle, but they didn't command a great price in the market, and he couldn't afford the losses he was taking. It had been reported just today that a herd of fifty steers could not be located, and it was feared that they had been stolen.

Valendez said, "The Federales have been useless. They came out from Chihuahua two times and rode back and forth and here and there but found nothing. They said the whole country was full of tracks from the cattle wandering around."

Baca spoke up and complained that he was shorthanded, but tomorrow he would take six of the men and make another try at finding the cattle.

Sage said that he had some skills at tracking and perhaps he could be of assistance. Don Valendez immediately asked him if he would work for him as a vaquero.

Sage no longer needed employment to continue his journey, but he liked the look of the country and Valendez. He decided to stay on for a time. He told Valendez that he knew horses but had never worked much with cattle. He would be pleased to join the Circle V, though.

"Good!" said Valendez. "Perhaps Francisco will find a tracker to be useful."

In the bunkhouse, Sage was pressed to describe the manner of Cordoba's death once again for the twelve vaqueros there. When one of the men commented that Sage must be very good with a gun to have killed this Estrada, who already had a gun in his hand, Sage demurred, explaining that he had been unarmed at the time and had been able to kick the pistol out of Estrada's hand and land a punch to his throat that killed him. It had been a lucky blow.

The conversation shifted to rustling. Over the previous two weeks at least two hundred head of steers had vanished. The rustlers appeared to be working at night, taking a few head here and there. Two vaqueros had gone out on a night patrol, and they had been found shot to death the next day.

Sage asked what they thought the rustlers would do with the stolen cattle. Where could they be sold?

A vaquero named Fernando Jacobo spoke up and surmised that the cattle were being held somewhere until a certain number were reached, and then they would be driven south to someplace along the railroad, perhaps near Ciudad Carmago, where they would be shipped to Mexico City.

And where could they be held?

Jacobo thought that the land to the east was too dry. The rough land to the west contained many canyons, where there was water.

Early the next morning, Baca selected Sage and five other men, including Jacobo, and they headed out to where the recently missing fifty head were supposed to be grazing. When they got into the area, Sage suggested that they swing around in an arc to the west, beyond the grazing lands, and see if they could find tracks that a bunched herd would leave. Baca agreed.

At about noon, they discovered such tracks, less than a day old, heading further westward. Sage studied the ground and made out the tracks of four shod horses imprinted over the tracks of the cattle. Sage pointed these out to Baca, and the riders set out in pursuit.

Late in the afternoon they approached a canyon that the trail entered, and Baca stopped to study the terrain. He said, "That looks like a good place to get the shit shot out of us."

"That is what I was thinking," said Sage. "How about we hold up around here? Tonight I'll go up on foot and do some scouting."

Baca looked at him and said, "You are good at this?"

"Yes."

The men found a concealed location close to a small stream trickling of the canyon to camp in. They unsaddled and watered their horses, picketed them in some grass, and ate a meal of beef jerky, tortillas, and corn bread. When it got fully dark, Sage pulled off his sombrero and boots, picked up his rifle, and prepared to head out.

Baca said, "You must have some pretty tough feet."

"Yes," replied Sage.

Sage thought a moment and then walked over to his saddle and took a pigging string out of his saddlebags. Every vaquero always carried one or two.

Baca asked, "You going to catch them and tie them up for us?"

"Who knows?" said Sage. "Let me have yours and a couple of others. Might come in handy."

Baca gathered up four more and gave them to Sage, who then disappeared into the dark.

Sage worked his way up the canyon. There was a quarter moon, and he was able to travel fairly rapidly. After two hours and four miles, he caught the scent of cigarette smoke in the air flowing down the canyon. He stopped and studied the terrain ahead and saw the red glow of a cigarette above some boulders at the side of the canyon. Sage thought, "That is one dumb bastard."

He studied the terrain carefully and located a route that he thought would be out of the sentry's line of sight. He cautiously approached the man until he was just below him. He waited there for a few minutes, considering how to get to the man unseen, when the sentry stood up and stretched. He walked out on the canyon floor, unbuttoned his breeches, and began to urinate.

As he did, he turned his back to Sage. Sage laid his rifle down, stole soundlessly up to him, and struck him using the edge of his hand with a chop into the junction of his neck and shoulder. Stunned, the sentry sagged to his knees and Sage laid him out with a round kick to his jaw.

Sage used two pigging strings to hog-tie him and the rustler's bandana for a gag. Then he hid the man's knife and guns in the rocks and moved a short distance farther up the canyon.

He thought it was likely that the sentry would be relieved during the night and settled down to wait and see.

Sure enough, after an hour Sage spotted something moving down the canyon, and another rustler appeared on foot carrying a rifle. When he passed Sage, Sage stepped up behind him and repeated the maneuver he'd used with the other sentry. Then he bound and gagged this man.

Sage continued up the canyon, and after another quarter of a mile he began to hear cattle lowing. The canyon widened and flattened, and he came upon a large meadow and a herd of what looked to be about two hundred head grazing in it. Looking around, he saw the rustler's camp not far from him. Two forms lay on blankets near the coals of a fire about six feet apart.

Sage drew his .45 and quietly walked up to them until he was ten feet away. He fired a round into the ground between them. Both men jackknifed into a sitting position, and one of them grabbed a revolver lying in a holster at his side. Sage put a bullet in his chest and swung his Colt to cover the other man, who had started to reach for his gun. Seeing he was covered, he changed his mind.

Sage stepped up to him and knocked him out with a sudden kick to the chin, hog-tied him, and left him on the ground. After collecting their guns and stashing them away from the camp, he saddled a picketed horse and headed back down the canyon.

He checked the condition of the two sentries on the way, and in a little over an hour he was back at the camp of the vaqueros, careful to call out and announce who he was as he approached.

Jacobo came up to him, rifle in hand, as the others rolled out of their blankets. He looked at the horse that Sage was on and said, "I take it that you found the rustlers. They must be nice people to give you this fine animal."

As Sage slid off the horse, Baca and the other vaqueros came over, and he told them that the missing cattle and three hog-tied rustlers, and one dead, were a little over four miles up the canyon in a meadow.

Baca shook his head in wonder and decided that they wouldn't wait until dawn to go to the meadow. He was afraid the rustlers might work out of their bonds. Sage didn't think so, but he preferred to get underway also.

Sage pulled his boots on, and the men saddled up, leaving the newly acquired horse picketed, much to its displeasure. They moved up the canyon with Sage in the lead.

The first sentry lay with his britches still open and endured the derision of the vaqueros while Baca got him up, looped his riata around his neck, and told him to walk ahead of his horse.

They found the second sentry struggling. His legs were drawn up behind his back and tied to his hands with a sailor's good knots. He wasn't about to go anywhere. Another loop went around his neck, and he joined the march, stumbling ahead of a vaquero in the dark with his hands tied behind his back.

When they got to the rustler's camp, the vaqueros built up the fire, found the makings for coffee, and boiled a pot while waiting for the sun to rise. The bound prisoners sat morosely together under guard and worried about their fate. They had cause to worry.

At sunrise, Baca threw his riata over a tree limb and told Jacobo and another to get one of the rustlers on a horse, and the three shocked men began pleading for their lives.

In a venomous growl Baca said, "You sons of bitches murdered two of my men. We are sending you to hell for that."

One of the rustlers was hoisted onto a horse, which was led under the rope. Baca tightened the loop around his neck, and a vaquero pulled him upright with the rope and fastened the other end to a branch. Then, hanging onto the reins, Baca shooed the horse out from under the man with his sombrero.

When the rustler stopped strangling and kicking, Baca waited a few minutes, and then the other two followed in turn.

Sage watched stoically thinking maybe he should have killed all four quickly. This was a mighty unpleasant business.

Sage and the rest got busy rounding up the cattle, leaving the four bodies to the buzzards. Baca considered leaving the cattle there to graze but determined that the grass was pretty well used up.

The rustlers' saddled horses were herded down the canyon with the steers. As the last steer passed the camp, Sage found a burlap bag and gathered the guns into it. He picked up the ones down below when they came to them. No point in leaving them behind, he figured.

Over the next two days, the vaqueros dispersed the cattle in bunches in places that had water and forage. They would continue to graze until the fall roundup, when they had their maximum weight after the summer rainy season.

When they rode into the ranch yard in the evening, they were no longer as somber as they were for a while after the hangings. The young men whooped and hollered as they hailed Don Valendez, eager to tell him about their successful foray.

Several told the don various things all at once, and Valendez thanked them and asked Baca to come in to the house. Baca described how they had found the trail of the stolen cattle and how they had followed it to the canyon. He told Valendez what he knew of Sage's role and about the hangings. That received a gesture of approval. Valendez was greatly relieved that all of the cattle were back on his range.

Baca said, "This American, Sage, is a piece of work. He is plenty smart. He figured out how the cattle could be found, and he found them. He went out in the night by himself and captured three men and killed one. He must be able to see in the dark and move like a cat. I would not want this one chasing me!"

The don replied, "I think he said he has twenty-one years. He seems to be a very pleasant young man, but he has killed two men here—one with his bare hands."

"I don't think he is a killer," said Baca. "I do not see the aggression."

Valendez said, "I don't know how well he handles his guns, but I think if we have more trouble from cattle thieves, Sage will make their lives very difficult, if he doesn't end them. I hope he stays on here."

-18-

John Sage was an expert horseman and trainer, but so were all of the other vaqueros, and he had no particular advantage. He had quite a bit to learn about the husbandry of range cattle and went about learning it with a will. It was good to be doing something voluntarily for a change.

After two weeks, Sage asked Baca if he could ride into Chihuahua. He was in need of some chaps, another pair of britches, and a couple of shirts. Baca assented, and Fernando Jacobo overheard and asked if he might go along since he hadn't had any time off for over a month. Baca agreed to that, also.

Sage was glad to have the company. He had spent a fair amount of time with Jacobo and had learned quite a bit about his ranch duties from him. He was a couple of years older and fairly quiet but good-humored. Jacobo had very dark skin and probably a lot of Indian in his lineage. Sage envied his drooping mustache since he himself hadn't been producing much fur yet. Sage thought the mustache fit well with Jacobo's drooping eyelids.

The don owned a great many horses for the use of his riders, and Sage roped and saddled a big sorrel gelding. He had quit riding the black. The damned animal had a mouth as hard as flint, and Sage had grown tired of having to pull hard on the reins to get him turned or stopped. It was useless for roping.

Apparently the black one's deceased previous owner had been all-around mean because the black was always jumpy and in a nervous lather. None of the other riders liked him, either, so he was reserved for use as a pack animal, which seemed to suit him.

Sage climbed aboard the sorrel, which sunfished a couple of times to check him out and then settled down to a good, fast walk. They got into Chihuahua in the late afternoon, and Sage found a saddlery, where he picked a style of chaps out of a catalog. The leather worker measured Sage and told him that he would have them made up by noon the next day.

Sage found a post office and sent off a letter to Maria Rodriguez in Cananea. He hoped she knew where Miguel was these days.

Sage and Jacobo had dinner and then went to a different saloon than Sage had been in before and got a room together.

Jacobo wanted to get something to drink, and they went down to the bar and took a table. The same guitar player that had been in the other saloon was playing. Jacobo bought two mescals, and then Sage bought another round. The drinks had a smoky taste, and the second round tasted better. Sage liked the mellow feeling that came over him.

Two girls in short dresses came over and wriggled onto the two vaqueros' laps, much to Sage's astonishment and Jacobo's amusement. The girls introduced themselves, and at their urging, Sage bought another round for everyone.

The girl in Sage's lap was fairly attractive, with flowing long black hair and beautiful dark eyes, and Sage found himself becoming aroused. His girl worked her hand under her hip, and Sage found himself becoming very aroused. Then the girl whispered an invitation to come to her room in his ear.

Sage felt at sea here. He looked over at Jacobo, hoping to get some kind of instruction, and saw him getting up with his girl. Jesus, he didn't have any idea how to go about this. His girl got up and pulled at his arm, and he unsteadily followed her. He looked around the room, and no one seemed to be paying any attention, so his nervousness decreased.

They entered her tiny room, and the girl, Annetta, closed the door and immediately opened up the front of her blouse. A warm shock passed through Sage's body as Annetta unbuckled his gun belt and the other belt.

Annetta pulled him down onto the bed with her as she lay back on it. She pulled up her dress, and without either of them undressing further, Sage found himself being guided into her.

What came very shortly after astounded Sage. He had never experienced a feeling like that! He was suddenly very enthralled with Annetta, but she pushed him away, rolled off the bed, and while rearranging her clothing as he got up said, "Five pesos."

Flustered, Sage buttoned up, pulled a wad of notes out of his pocket, and took out a five-peso note. Annetta smiled as she took it and complimented him for being a real man.

As Sage replaced his gun belt, he wasn't feeling like a real man. There seemed to be a lot missing here. That was a mighty abrupt affair. But damn, that had felt good!

Sage and the girl returned to the bar together, and as they were passing a table against the wall where two men were drinking about twenty feet away, one of them called out, "Annetta, you damned whore. What are you doing with that rabbit? I'm supposed to be first."

Angered, Sage swung around to face the man and said, "Keep a civil tongue in your head, you jackass."

The man was cradling a full shot glass on the table with his left hand. He dropped his right hand to his revolver. Sage drew and blew the shot glass apart, along with a chunk of the man's hand. Shocked and splattered with glass, tequila and blood, the man looked at the .45 aimed at his head and froze, as did his drinking companion, who had also placed his hand on his gun.

Sage said, "I don't want anyone getting killed because they are overly optimistic. Put your hands on the table."

They did. Sage glanced around the room and saw that all the patrons were standing or sitting motionless, but the guitar player was beating a hasty retreat. Annette just stood there with both hands on her mouth. No one seemed to be a threat. Jacobo had just come into the room with his girl, and he was also standing frozen with his eyes not looking so droopy.

Sage sidled over to the stairs, and Jacobo followed with his hand on the butt of his gun. Sage went up the stairs and holstered the .45 as they got to their room.

Jacobo said, "Holy mother of God! You are one fast son of a bitch, and that was a hell of a shot! That shithead was dead meat, and he knows he is damned lucky you didn't kill him."

As Sage and Jacobo lit a couple of lamps, Sage said, "Didn't need to. Let's see if anyone comes a knockin."

No one did, and the two settled down for the night.

Jacobo said, "Damn, I'd have liked to have another drink or two. Don't get much opportunity these days."

"My apologies," said Sage. "We had words, and he started to draw. I wasn't sure if he was going to try to kill me or not. Maybe he just wanted to scare me with the gun. I didn't want to leave that decision up to him."

"You did the right thing. When a man pulls a gun, it is a very serious matter. But I could not have done it that way. I don't know anyone who could have. You have incredible skill."

"My father taught me well from a very young age," said Sage, and he changed the subject.

"That was the first time I have done that with a woman. I had heard about women like that when I was at sea, but I had never seen one. It sure went quickly."

Jacobo laughed and said, "It always goes quickly. The whores don't like to do it slowly. If you take too long, they start complaining. Maybe it is different with other women. I wouldn't know."

Sage blew out his lamp, lay back, and remarked, "I hope that someday I can have a drink in a saloon without any serious trouble coming out of it. That hasn't happened yet."

-19-

Sage stayed on at the Circle V for over two years. During the first year, there were a few more incidents of rustling, but Sage was successful in every case at tracking down the rustlers. He and the other vaqueros killed several of them, ending the rustling problems for the ranch.

Early on, there were a few instances of far-ranging Apaches taking a few head along with some horses, but with General Crook's successful campaign against the Apaches to the north, that problem diminished.

In the summer of 1876, the vaqueros reported that a number of Mexican squatters had moved in on the far reaches of the huge ranch, and Don Valendez dispatched Sage and five other riders to move them out.

Sage found the squatters to be hardworking families desperate to make a living, and the job troubled him a great deal. The don had more land than he could use, and it would not have been a problem for him to accommodate these people. Sage tried to get Valendez to let them return, but the man wouldn't hear of it.

Sage had been thinking about moving on and decided to ask for his pay. He considered heading up to Cananea, or maybe he'd go over to Laredo to find his uncle. He had received a letter from Maria that said Miguel had moved down into lower Mexico and she hadn't heard from him for over two years. He had been in Mexico City but hadn't kept in touch, and she had no idea where he was now.

Sage decided that he wanted to see some new country, and it would be good to meet the only kin he had on his father's side if he could find him. It was over six hundred miles to Laredo, but he could take the train to Torreon and Monterrey and ride the 150 or so up from there.

Valendez was sorry to see him leave, as were Jacobo and the other vaqueros. In addition to his pay, Valendez was happy to let him have his pick of the remuda, and he took the sorrel gelding that he usually rode.

He rode to Chihuahua, loaded the horse on a stock car, boarded a passenger car, and headed south and east.

-20-

He arrived in Monterrey on a clear May morning and spent the day riding around the city, seeing the sights, and picking up some food and coffee for his ride. Five days later he crossed the Rio Grande and entered Laredo. Benjamin Sage was known in town, and John found him living in a small house with his wife, Hilda.

Benjamin had owned a small ranch along the river to the north and sold it to retire two years before. John found that he had four cousins, two boys and two girls, who had all moved to other parts of Texas.

Benjamin and Nathan had exchanged a few letters over the years, but Benjamin hadn't been aware of Nathan's death. Aside from that, he was delighted to get caught up.

On the third day of John's visit, Mexican bandits robbed one of the two banks in Laredo. John was having lunch by himself in town when there was an uproar in the street. He was finished eating, so he went out to see what was going on.

He made out that six bandits had entered the bank, tied up the employees and a few patrons, emptied the safe and tills, and departed without being discovered. They had been seen joining two lookouts and riding across the river into Nuevo Laredo. The observers hadn't been aware of the robbery, so the alarm hadn't been sounded until another customer entered the bank.

The sheriff, Silas Hill, was putting together a posse, and Sage overheard him lamenting that he didn't have any good trackers on hand.

Thinking that his uncle's funds might well have gone missing, Sage spoke up and told Hill that he was a fair hand at tracking. The sheriff looked at the sturdy-looking young man dressed as a vaquero. He took him to be a Mexican even though he seemed to speak English well. He looked to be a serious type.

He said, "Good. Get your horse and be prepared to be out for a couple of days. We'll leave from here in an hour. You know the country around here?"

"No," said Sage. "I've been working in Chihuahua for the past two years. But if I pick up a track, I'm not likely to lose it."

Sage hurried to his uncle's home and was relieved to find that Benjamin was a patron of the other bank, but he was committed. Hilda wrapped up a package of cornbread, jerky, and a chunk of cured ham for him, and he saddled and packed his horse and said he guessed he'd be back in a day or two.

When Sage returned, Sheriff Hill had fourteen men gathered, who were apparently day drinkers from the saloons. He had already dispatched two other men to Nuevo Laredo to interview people on the streets there. He hoped someone could tell them which way a group of eight men in a hurry had gone.

In Nuevo Laredo the two riders who had gone ahead joined the posse. The bandits had been seen heading due west, and the two men guided them on to the track. They followed the trail westward at a steady trot until nightfall and then halted to rest the horses and let them graze on some grass.

Sage had been riding in the lead with the sheriff, and he told Hill that the bandits had run their horses for the first five miles and slowed to a trot and then to a walk. He thought the posse was about five miles behind them.

The trail had led into a shallow valley and was following a narrow, willow-choked stream. Sage said, "Sheriff, we might be able to move faster if we get up on the north ridge. The land looked to be pretty flat up there. There would be less chance of getting ambushed. If we keep going all night we might be able to get ahead of them and ambush them in the morning."

The sheriff thought about it and then said, "They're probably going to turn south toward Monterrey when they get past La Jarita.

"Yes, lets go up on the ridge and take the chance we'll catch up to them before they do. Yes, let's do that. They might be thinking we won't follow them far into Mexico, and maybe they'll bed down for a while."

The sheriff commented, "I don't have much problem with the law in Nuevo Laredo, but I wouldn't want to run into Federales out here. They're a mite touchy about Mexican sovereignty. Well, Laredo can't afford to lose what was in that bank, and we are going to keep going."

Sage said, "We've got a three-quarter moon tonight. We can take a look into the valley every mile or so and maybe see some sign of them."

The barflies in the posse were not at all happy about the prospect of riding all night. Sage decided that he had better be the one scouting the valley, as he didn't think that any of these people could see much farther than their horses' ears in the moonlight.

Several hours later on one of his several trips to the edge of the valley, Sage detected a scent of smoke. He could see no fire or any movement down there in the dark shadow of the moon, but he figured the bandits were down there. The other side of the valley was very steep, and he thought that the bandits would be continuing on through it in the morning.

Sage reported to Hill that he thought that the bandits were below them, and the posse continued on. At the first light of dawn they found a place that Hill figured would make a good spot for an ambush. The north side of the valley sloped steeply down two hundred yards to the stream. It was mostly open but dotted with small trees and clumps of mesquite.

Hill decided to tie the horses far away from the edge. He didn't want any horses neighing at the approach of the bandits and giving them a warning. He had the posse spread out along the slope about thirty yards from the bottom, each man taking cover in the scattered vegetation and boulders.

Hill had instructed everyone not to fire unless he or one of the bandits fired the first round. He wanted all the bandits to be in range before he started the ball rolling by demanding their surrender. If the bandits wanted to surrender, fine. If they didn't, that would be fine, too. He cautioned the posse not to smoke.

Sage dropped his sombrero on the ground and settled down behind a large boulder with his carbine and began the wait. He wasn't altogether comfortable with the situation here but didn't see any other way to do it.

If the ambush didn't work, they were going to be in a hell of a fix, having a mostly open slope above them, which offered little cover for a retreat. But the eighteen men of the posse shouldn't have a lot of difficulty dealing with eight bandits.

Two hours later Sage spotted dust up the valley to the west, beyond where it took a bend toward the south. He was wondering what the hell that was when the bandits came into view from the east.

They were bunched together and traveling at a trot. A couple of them were scanning the sides of the valley. One of them suddenly stiffened and then called out a warning as he brought up his rifle and fired at a posse member who hadn't done a good job of concealing himself.

Everyone opened up. Sage fired at the rearmost bandit, and he tumbled to the ground. The whole posse fired a volley, and two more of the bandits were knocked out of their saddles. They hadn't gotten as close to the posse as the sheriff had wanted, and accuracy suffered.

Sage brought down another bandit, and two more fell before they lost sight of the remaining four, who escaped into the willows. As Sage was thinking about going back up the slope after the horses and some of the posse were catching up the fallen bandits' horses, a large band of riders came charging around the bend from the west.

Startled, two of the posse fired at them, sending one man pitching off his horse. Not a good move. The new arrivals were a company of forty Federales, and they immediately opened fire on the posse.

Suddenly, the valley was filled with milling horses and men shooting in all directions. Sage saw an officer right below him fire his revolver at Sheriff Hill, knocking him down in a spray of blood. Sage blew the officer out of his saddle, and the officer's horse turned and charged up the slope right at Sage.

As the big blue grulla went past him, Sage lunged and got his left hand on the pommel, and the grulla dragged him up the slope. Sage dropped his carbine and managed to get his right arm around the pommel, and he held on to it with the crook of his elbow. The horse wanted out of the fight and plunged on up the slope. With bullets whizzing past him, Sage didn't try to mount. He just hung on and hoped the horse wouldn't stop.

It didn't, and when the grulla topped the ridge, Sage planted his feet on the ground and vaulted into the saddle. The grulla had broken into a full gallop, and Sage climbed up the grulla's neck to gather in the reins. He knew that he wasn't going to have time to get to his sorrel, and when he was about three hundred yards from the ridge, he stopped the grulla, quickly stripped off the heavy Mexican saddle, and jumped back on as ten Federales came over the top in pursuit.

Hanging on to the mane and spurring the big horse on, Sage fervently hoped that it was a fast runner. It was. After fifteen minutes, his lead had opened up, but the Federales kept coming after the man who had killed their officer.

The grulla wasn't only fast but had surprising endurance, and the Federales fell farther and farther behind. After another fifteen minutes, they slowed their horses, but they didn't turn back. Sage slowed the grulla to an easy canter.

He was headed due north, and the Rio Grande was up ahead somewhere. He stopped the grulla to let it blow and relieve itself and then continued on at a fast walk until he spotted the Federales in the distance and spurred the horse back to a canter. After another hour he crossed the Rio and continued north. At the top of a rise, he looked back and saw that the Federales had stopped at the river but hadn't turned back.

He reigned in the grulla and let it rest. After a while the Federales wheeled their mounts around and rode back toward the valley.

-21-

Sage was in a bit of a quandary. He had about twenty dollars in his pockets, his gun belt, and his chaps, but no saddle, no rifle, and no hat. Everything else he owned was gone with the sorrel. He figured that he was about a day and a half northwest of Laredo, and he had no good idea what other towns might be around, if any. He was going to have to get a job and get re-outfitted before he could head for Arizona.

There wasn't much choice other than to head back down to Laredo. He could stay with Benjamin and maybe borrow a saddle, and he wanted to let someone there know what had happened to the sheriff and the ill-fated posse. If they weren't all dead, the survivors would probably be starting a long stay in a Mexican prison if they weren't hung.

He felt pretty low about that and wondered what the Federales would do with the bank's money. The four bank robbers who the posse hadn't shot might well have gotten away if the Federales hadn't seen them, and they might have the money.

Sage expected that the Federales would have learned his name from any surviving members of the posse, and he was now probably a wanted man in Mexico.

Late that afternoon Sage spotted a cloud of dust ahead, and after investigating found that a large cattle drive was underway. It looked like they were bedding down for the night, and he rode to the camp.

The cowboys studied him curiously as he rode up, and an older man, tall and whip-thin, walked over to him.

"Looks like you're traveling mighty light there, pardner," he said. "I'm Lou Roeser, trail boss, and who might you be?"

"I'm John Sage, lately of Laredo. I was with a posse from there. We were chasing some bank robbers on the other side of the Rio and got into a dustup with a company of Federales. I think I'm the only one that got away. Sheriff

Hill is dead, and maybe the rest of the posse is, too. Seventeen men."

"Damn!" said Roeser, shocked. "I've got to hear more about that. Sage, you say? I know a Benjamin Sage in Laredo. Any relation?"

"My uncle," replied Sage. "I was visiting."

Roeser invited Sage to eat with them, and he gave the cowboys the details of the robbery and the pursuit's disastrous conclusion. He mentioned that he was now in need of employment.

"Well, now," said Roeser, "we're just starting our drive. Maybe the last one from these parts before the railroad arrives. We're heading for the Chisholm Trail and up to Caldwell, just north of the Oklahoma border. I could use another hand. How about you ride down to Laredo and let people there know what happened to the sheriff and the posse and then catch up with us?"

Sage immediately agreed. Roeser said, "We've got a couple of spare saddles in the chuck wagon. Take one."

In Laredo, Sage and his uncle visited the mayor, and Sage related the fate of the posse to the distraught man, who then called a meeting with the banker, a judge, and a few of the town's leaders. There, Sage told his story again.

They decided to contact the federal authorities to start inquiries with the Mexican government. It was hoped that they could recover any surviving posse members, but the prospects of recovering any of the bank's missing deposits looked to be pretty dismal.

The men wanted Sage to remain available for any further inquiries or negotiations with the Mexicans, but because there was no way of knowing how long all that would take, they spent over an hour writing up Sage's narrative and allowed him to leave after signing it.

Sage spent most of his remaining money purchasing a Stetson, rain slicker, jeans, and spare shirt, and he rode the grulla north after the herd. The mouse-colored horse, a gelding, was also the color of smoke, and Sage decided to name him Smokey. Along the way, Sage stopped the grulla and fired a couple of rounds from his Colt to see how it reacted. He was pleased to see that the grulla didn't jump at the noise.

-22-

A few days later the herd still hadn't completely settled into the routine of the drive, and the cowboys were kept busy reminding strays that they belonged with the rest. One huge mossy horn was especially missing the freedom to roam that he was used to and kept taking off for faraway places.

About the fifth time that Sage had to chase after it, he decided to rope it and maybe drag it around a bit. He caught up with the steer, and his wide loop cleared the head and horns. Sage reined Smokey to a stop as he put a dally around the saddle horn.

But Smokey was a warhorse, not a cow pony, and he got turned a little sideways and failed to brace. When the 1,500-pound animal hit the end of the rope, Smokey was jerked off his feet and laid out on his side.

The steer was spun around, and without hesitating it charged back up the rope, intent on murder. Sage had jumped clear of the horse as it went down, and flat on his back, he pulled his Colt and shot the steer between the eyes. The steer's legs folded, and the body slid into Sage head first, rolling him over on his stomach.

Smokey lunged to his feet and stood still while still attached to the steer. Sage got up, holstered the Colt, and determined that he hadn't received any damage. He walked over to Smokey as Roeser and a couple of the hands rode up and unhitched his rope from the saddle horn.

Roeser drawled, "Well, there was a sorry bit of cowboying. That's forty bucks we won't be getting in Caldwell. At least we'll be having some meat for the next couple of days, tough as it will be. Go get Cookie and help him cut it up."

Feeling a bit sheepish, Sage untangled the rope from the steer and coiled it. Smokey was looking pretty sheepish, too. One of the cowboys, Eduardo Cruz, shook his head and opined, "That was a hell of a shot!"

Sage replied, “Pretty easy when the gun is almost touching the target,” and he rode off to the get the chuck wagon.

-23-

Nearly two months and six hundred miles later, the herd was in northern Oklahoma. The cowboys had endured a number of storms and river crossings, a stampede, and seemingly endless hours in the saddle. The Indians in the territories weren't warring anymore, but they had caught on to commerce. Tribes had levied ten cents a head for crossing their lands on two different occasions, doing well from the two thousand head in the herd.

As they neared the Kansas border, four riders came up to the herd. When Roeser spotted them, he called to Sage, Eduardo Cruz, and three other riders to come with him, and they rode out to meet them.

As they approached, Sage sized them all up as hard cases. They appeared to be gunmen, not farmers or working cowboys.

With no other introduction, one of them said, "You're on our land here. We charge a toll for crossing it. We're cutting out a hundred of your steers."

Roeser said, "I don't see any fences around here. I don't see any crops. I don't see any cattle. If it's your land, you aren't using it much. Be damned if we're going to pay anything to cross it."

The gunman said, "Be damned if you don't. If we don't get the steers now, we'll be back with twenty more men tonight and take 'em all."

Roeser just stared at them, and they started to turn away. Sage spoke up. "Hey, mister."

The four stopped and looked at Sage.

Sage said, "I don't think you own a damned bit of land here, and you aren't going anywhere".

The spokesman asked, "What?"

Sage moved Smokey around to where he had a clear space between them and said, "You can try pulling your hoglegs, or you can sit there and die."

After a shocked moment, the man grabbed for his belt gun, and so did the other herd-cutters. Sage drew and shot him and one of the others. All the horses present except

Smokey started plunging, and before the other two could get a shot off, Sage shot them both out of their saddles. Sage was mighty glad he'd ridden Smokey today.

Roeser and the other cowboys had their guns out, but before they could shoot, it was all over.

Getting his horse under control, Cruz cried out, "Holy shit!"

Red faced, Roeser looked at Sage and said, "Jesus Christ, Sage, you could have got us all killed!"

"Not likely," Sage replied. "I didn't think we should wait for them to come back tonight and stampede the herd."

One of the cowboys asked, "What about the twenty others?"

Sage said, "I doubt if there are any twenty others, but I'll backtrack this bunch and see where they came from. If we've got a problem, I'll come back and warn you."

As several more cowboys came galloping up, Roeser said, "Cruz, go with him. Boys, let's gather up the horses and guns. They won't be needing them."

Sage and Cruz found where the herd-cutters had had a camp five miles away. The camp had been occupied for some time, and there was no sign that anyone else had been there.

Cruz was a medium-sized, wiry man a little older than most of the other cowboys on the drive. Cruz said, "You're really something with a gun, John. Men anywhere near that good are generally known. How come I never heard of you?"

"I've been out of the country for about the last six years, and I really don't want to be known."

"Good luck with that," said Cruz. "But I think you're going to be known."

-24-

The herd of longhorns reached Caldwell on the first day of August 1875. Roeser sold the herd and paid off the cowboys after they had loaded the last steer into the stock cars. Then, late in the afternoon, Roeser and the hands all rode into town.

Caldwell was a new town that had been built to accommodate the cattle business. It was well stocked with saloons and bordellos, and the cowboys got rooms at a hotel, cleaned up, and set out to indulge. Sage went along with them to a saloon for a couple of drinks, and then all trooped over to a bordello.

When they entered the parlor, they found a bevy of lightly clad ladies of all shapes and sizes, a few of which weren't too bad-looking. Sage walked over to a fairly young one that didn't look too hard and introduced himself.

"My name's Sally," she said. "I'll give you a good time for five dollars."

Sage said, "Five dollars? I don't want to buy you, lady. Just rent you for a while."

Sally flounced away, and with his second attempt he got a more reasonable price although the woman wasn't what he thought was attractive. But it had been a long time since his last bedding in Chihuahua, and he wasn't feeling too particular.

The Texans regrouped at a saloon and had a couple more drinks together. Lou Roeser came in and bought a round for his hands. After sharing two months of hardships, there was a lot of camaraderie among the crew, and everyone was feeling pretty good.

A big, blond, burley, red-faced Texan from another drive was standing at the bar between Sage and Eduardo Cruz. He had had a few, and he started in on Cruz.

"This here saloon is for Texans. What the hell are you doing in here?"

Cruz looked at him and said, "My family was in Texas long before any Anglos, mister, but even though you were a late arrival, I'll let you stay."

Sage glanced around the saloon and saw that several other Texans, presumably with the big one, were watching with amusement. Roeser and some of the others on his crew were also watching, and they weren't amused. The Texan rounded Cruz, and raising his voice above the piano and general babble, he said, "We whipped all you damn greasers, and I'll whip you if you don't get the hell out!"

Sage reached out with his left hand and gripped the Texan's right elbow, digging two fingers into the nerves there.

The big Texan stiffened and turned white. He tried to pull his elbow loose, but Sage gripped harder, and the Texan froze. Sage leaned over and spoke in his ear, "You and me are going to walk out front, mister, and if you speak or so much as wiggle, you won't be using this arm for a month, if ever. Let's go."

With Sage still holding his elbow, they walked across the room to the door. The Texan's friends watched them curiously, and one of them said, "Hey Chub, where you going?"

Sage replied, "My old friend Chub and I have something to talk about."

They went through the batwing doors, across the board walkway, and out into the street. Sage pulled the Texan's gun out of his holster and shoved it into his belt. Then he let go of the man and kicked his legs out from under him.

The Texan rolled over, and as he pulled his knees under him, Sage pivoted completely around and slammed the side of a boot into his head, laying him out flat and half conscious. Sage knelt beside him and grabbed an ear, twisting it with enough force to convince the man to hold still.

Sage said, "You're done for tonight. You get to where you're staying and stay there. I'll leave your gun with the bartender. You can pick it up in the morning. If you come back inside, I'll drop you before you can take a step."

Sage let go of the ear, stood up, and watched the cowboy climb to his feet.

Chub turned and walked off, rubbing his elbow.

Sage went back into the saloon and walked to the bar. Chub's friends were still curious, but no one said anything. With his back to them, he slid Chub's gun across to the bartender and told him that Chub would be picking it up in the morning, and the bartender slipped it under the bar.

Cruz came over with Roeser behind him and said, "I can fight my own fights, Sage."

Sage replied, "I'm sure you can, Eduardo, but it wasn't just you. I think that was going to turn into a gunfight between our outfit and theirs. I thought I could prevent that. Did I do wrong?"

Cruz stared at him for a few moments and then said, "I think you are going to be known." He turned back to his drink.

Roeser motioned at Sage to follow him and walked over to a table. Sage picked up the tequila that he still had at the bar and followed him.

Roeser asked, "What the hell did you do with that man?"

"I convinced him that he should get some sleep after this hard day, and he went to wherever he is staying tonight."

Roeser asked, "I mean, how did you get him to walk out with you?"

"You've got some nerves in your elbow. If the right amount of pressure is applied in the right place, you're going to get mighty docile."

Roeser took a swallow from his glass and said, "You've got some real talent, John. You're better with a gun than anyone I've ever seen or heard of, and you've got a head on your shoulders. Think you might hire that gun out?"

Surprised, Sage replied, "Never occurred to me to do that." He thought for a moment. "No. I had a teacher some time back in a far-off place. We had a lot of discussions about how a life should be lived. You have to feel good about yourself to have a good life. I wouldn't feel good about myself if I hired out my gun. I've killed men, but in each case I felt it was justified, except for one time. I wouldn't kill anyone that wasn't trying to kill me or someone I should be protecting."

Sage thought some more. "I guess if I could manage to protect myself or someone else without killing anyone to do it, I would make that choice."

"Looks to me that you made that choice just now," Roeser said.

Sage lifted his eyebrows. "That's a fact. Not something I was thinking through."

Curious, Roeser said, "If I might ask, what was the exception?"

Sage shook his head sadly. He felt comfortable enough with Roeser to answer. "A band of Apaches killed my parents and the other people on the ranch where I grew up. In the Apache culture, that was not a dishonorable thing, and I was familiar with the Apache culture. My mother was an Apache, and I was half raised by Apaches. But I had my vengeance."

My God! thought Roeser. He asked, "You killed the Apaches!?"

Sage had gone this far, so he continued. "All but one. My best friend, who I grew up with as a brother...his father, mother, and sisters had also been killed on the ranch. We went after them and killed them, except we let the last one live after we caught him. Not sure why. Wanted some memory left, I guess. Someone to know."

Roeser said, "How many Apaches were there?"

"Seven were left after the raid. My friend's father and mine killed two, and one of the women killed another."

Roeser said, "How old were you?"

"Sixteen."

Roeser realized that his mouth was hanging open. He could see that Sage was dead serious. "Well, I'd say that those killings were justified. I certainly wouldn't think any less of myself if I had done it."

"Maybe so," replied Sage. "That teacher I had was a wise man, and he said pretty much the same thing." He grinned and said, "So maybe you're a wise man too."

Flummoxed, Roeser said, "The reason I wanted to talk to you was that I've got a brother down in New Mexico. He's the sheriff of Dona Ana County, out of Mesilla. He's in need of a good deputy. You're pretty young, but I think you'd make a damned good deputy. Might you be interested?"

Now Sage was flummoxed. "That's something that never occurred to me. I've never had any particular interest in getting into other people's affairs, and I don't know anything about the law."

Roeser said, "This country is changing, John. Up until lately, people out here have all lived rough. There have always been killers and thieves around, but fortunately a lot of the honest people who have settled the land were tough enough to handle it for the most part. But we need more educated people with skills and families if we are going to achieve a civilized society, and it's sort of hard to attract them if they have to keep fighting to survive.

"We need more lawmen. Honest lawmen. Hell, there's too damned many lawmen now that are just killers and thieves with badges. My brother is one of the good ones, but he needs help. He wants people in his county to be able to go about their business without having to wear a gun to do it."

Sage grinned and said, "I'd still be hiring out my gun, though."

Roeser said, "You could look at it that way, but as a lawman, you could keep on feeling good about yourself. And I'll tell you, John, I've seen some good men that were mighty handy with a gun wind up with reputations as killers. Every one has eventually crossed the line for one reason or another, and they don't last too long after that. This society tends to weed them out although there is a lot of damage all around in the process."

Sage got another tequila and a whisky for Roeser. He sipped at it while he thought things through. He hadn't been looking at what he wanted to do with his life. During his time with Fisu Hiragawa, they had discussed "the good life," but he had had no inspiration as far as how he wanted to spend the rest of his life.

Thinking about it now, he wasn't particularly interested in spending the rest of it as a cowboy or raising horses, and he sure didn't want to be a sailor. He might just be a footloose wanderer like his father for a time.

But hell, here was an opportunity to do something that might be interesting for a while, something that was needed. He was just twenty-three, and he could take his time at coming up with long-term plans.

"All right, Lou. I'll take the deputy job if it is still there. Can you telegraph your brother tomorrow?"

"I can telegraph him now. The way your grulla steps out, you could probably get down to Las Cruces in about three weeks."

Roeser left the saloon, and a few of the hands at a card table called him over and invited him to sit down with them. Sage needed to buy a new saddle and rifle and decided that he'd better hang on to his hard-earned wages. He'd never played much poker or Monte and had no confidence in coming out ahead.

Sage had dinner with Cruz and two other cowboys and then found a playhouse where they enjoyed a melodrama. After having cigars on the porch of the hotel, they turned in. Sure beat singing to cows.

In the morning, Roeser went to the bank to arrange for a draft to be sent to a bank in Laredo and ran into the trail boss from the other herd, a man he had known slightly down in Texas named Will Hightower.

Hightower said, "Hey Lou, I've got a hand, Chub Kemp, who might be gunning for one of your boys. You might warn him to lay low."

Roeser said, "If you want to keep Kemp alive, you'd better head him off. I don't think there's a better man with a gun than John Sage anywhere in the country. He braced four herd-cutters down the trail and killed every one of them."

"The hell you say!" said Hightower. "John Sage? Never heard of him."

"That's a bit of a mystery to me, too," said Roeser. "But I saw the play. Those four were dead before I could get off a shot. Your boy won't stand a chance."

Hightower hurried out of the bank, and after finishing his business, Roeser went looking for Sage. He found him in a saddle shop.

"Mornin', John. I got the reply from my brother. His name's Jim, by the way. The job was still open, and he'll be expecting you."

Roeser handed Sage an envelope that had a wax seal on it. "Letter for Jim. I'd appreciate it if you'd give it to him."

"Sure," said Sage. "Be glad to."

Roser held out another envelope. "This here's for you. A little bonus. You saved us from a sight of trouble down the trail, and I appreciate it. We could well have lost some men and cattle."

Sage didn't reach for the envelope. "That's not necessary. I just did what needed doing."

"At the risk of your life. I got a good price for the herd. The owners can sure as hell afford it. Not that much, anyway. Take it. That's my last order for you."

Sage gave Roeser a small grin and took it. He started to turn back to his purchase.

Roeser said, "John, keep an eye out for that Chub Kemp. I got word that he was on the prod for you."

Sage said, "I was doing that, but thanks. I'll walk around him if I can. He won't have much time. I'll be getting down the trail within an hour.

An hour was a bit too long. Sage had Smokey saddled and packed and was saying good-bye to Cruz and a few of his other friends from the drive in front of a saloon when Chub Kemp stepped out through the batwings and down into the street, about twenty feet away. Kemp was a bit thick in the head and hadn't listened to his boss. A couple of Chub's friends came out on to the boardwalk behind him and moved off to the side out of the line of fire.

Sage dropped the reins and started walking rapidly toward Kemp. Kemp couldn't resist grandstanding and started jawing instead of drawing. When it dawned on him that Sage wasn't stopping, his surprise made him hesitate, and Sage was right in his face.

Sage whipped a side kick to Kemp's upper right arm, breaking it with a loud snap. Then Sage spun around and lifted Kemp up on his toes with a back-fist under his jaw, breaking that, too. Kemp thumped onto the street on his back. He was out cold.

Sage didn't watch Kemp fall. He was watching Kemp's friends, ready. But they just stood there gaping. One of them said, "Gaud damn, mister, you sure do get to business! Never seen anyone fight like that."

Sage said, "You going to buy in?"

"Hell no", said the cowboy. "The hand's been played."

"All right, said Sage. "I'll be moving on. Your friend is going to need some doctoring."

Sage mounted Smokey, lifted a hand to his friends, and rode out of town.

As the two cowboys lifted Kemp to a sitting position, Cruz pointed a thumb in Sage's direction and said, "That man just saved your friend's life. He would have had no chance with his gun."

-25-

Sage arrived in Mesilla at noon on the last day of the August. Mesilla was a farming and ranching community in the Rio Grande Valley, which neighbored Las Cruces to the north. It had been a part of old Mexico until the Gadsden Purchase was ratified in 1854. Cottonwoods near the river gave way to a pinion and juniper forest, which sloped up toward the pine forests covering the Organ Mountains to the east.

He found the sheriff's office on Calle Del Arroyo, a block from the plaza. He tied Smokey in front of the sheriff's office and went in.

Sheriff Jim Roeser's office was an adobe, as were most of the buildings in Mesilla. The office fronted his living quarters and a storage room. A stairway off to the side led to cells on an upper floor.

Roeser was doing some paperwork at his desk, and he motioned Sage to a chair in front of it. Roeser, tall and slender, looked a lot like his brother. He looked to be about forty. He had a widow's peak and was starting to go a little bald on top. He was dressed in a common black broadcloth suit with a white shirt and a black string tie. Sage thought he looked like he might be as competent as Lou.

Sage introduced himself, sat down, and handed Roeser the letter he was carrying.

"Letter from your brother Lou," said Sage.

Roeser dropped the letter on the desk. He ran fingers over his long black mustache and studied Sage. "The telegram I got from Lou was pretty brief. They charge by the word, and Lou's a frugal sort. Said you were the one I was looking for. Lou generally has good judgment, but I wasn't looking for a kid. How the hell old are you?"

As Sage was telling him, Roeser was looking out the window behind him. He stiffened and said, "Get out."

Taken aback, Sage asked, "What?"

Roeser said, "That old man out there is Jeb Cummings. Got his boy upstairs. Going to hang him. Not your fight."

Sage looked over his shoulder. Five men were tying their horses to a hitching rail across the street.

Roeser stood up and walked over to a gun rack on the wall, picked out a double-barreled shotgun, and broke it open to check the load.

Sage said, "I'm siding you."

Roeser said, "No, you're not. Get going."

Sage said, "I just rode seven hundred miles to get a job with you, and I'm not about to let you get killed."

The five men started across the street toward the office. An older man walked in the middle carrying a shotgun.

Sage drew his Colt and spun the cylinder to recheck the loads and said, "If need be, I'll take out the shotgun and the two on the left. You get the other two, and we'll walk away from this. We'd better start the play if it comes to it."

Roeser stared at him and said, "You that good?"

"Yes."

Sage and Roeser stepped out onto the boardwalk, and Sage moved to the side, away from where Smokey was tied. Roeser moved with him.

Old man Cummings stopped in the middle of the street and said, "I've come to take my boy, sheriff. You bring him out, or we'll cut you down and bring him out ourselves."

Roeser said, "There is no way I'm going to let him go, Cummings. He's a murderer, tried and convicted. If you make this play, Jeb, you'll lose everything you've got."

"Everything I've got ain't worth spit without Samuel. I'm taking him."

Sage could see that the hard old man wasn't going to back off. Cummings started to raise the shotgun, and Sage drew and put a bullet in his forehead, and in an instant he center shot the two on the left as they were bringing up their handguns. Both barrels of Roeser's shotgun let go, and the two on the right were rocked back. They were both still on their feet and holding their guns, so Sage put a bullet in each, laying them out on their backs.

Sage stepped down off the walk with the Colt cocked and made sure all five men were out of action. Roeser walked up beside him and said, "I'd say you're old enough. My God. I've never seen shooting like that! I can't believe I've never heard of you."

As Sage reloaded, Roeser turned and trotted over to the store across the street, where some pellets had taken out a window. People were picking themselves up from wherever they had dropped flat and walked over to look at the bodies.

Roeser came back and announced to the gawkers, “This here’s my new deputy, John Sage. Thought I’d break him in easy.”

-26-

The town barber was also the undertaker, and he took over the job of getting the bodies off the street. Sage and Roeser went back into Roeser's office, and Roeser went upstairs to let Sam know he was now an orphan.

When he came back down he said, "I was going to have to be dealing with Jeb Cummings before long. His herd has been growing at a rate that's a mite faster than nature allows, and I've been getting complaints from some of the other ranchers. He isn't going to be missed.

"Where do you hail from, John?"

"I grew up in Arizona. My dad raised horses on a ranch along the Rio San Pedro, southeast of Tucson."

Roeser said, "That must have been some chore, seeing as how the Apaches were so fond of stealing horses."

Sage hesitated and then said, "My mother was an Apache. My father was adopted by the Chiricahuas. So was I."

Roeser considered that for a few moments. "I'll be damned. You're a bit dark. Thought you might have some Mexican in you. All the Mescaleros that were around here have been moved onto a reservation northeast of Alamagordo, so you won't get much use from speaking Apache.

"You speak any Mex? More than half the population around here is Mexican."

Sage said, "I grew up with Mexicans on the ranch, and I've lived in Mexico for four years. Went to school in Sonora for a couple of years, and worked as a vaquero near Chihuahua. I speak Spanish maybe better than English."

Roeser lapsed into Spanish. "Good. I guess that explains why I've never heard of you, being that you were in Mexico."

Sage said, "Well, I was also at sea and spent four years in the Japanese islands. An island called Okinawa."

Roeser went back to English. "You're getting more and more interesting. What the hell were you doing in Okinawa?"

"Shipwrecked," replied Sage. "I spent the first two years there as a slave. Then I traveled with a holy man for the next two before I was picked up by an American vessel."

Roeser stared at Sage. "I'll be wanting to hear more about all that. But let's get you sworn in and settled. I don't suppose you've ever done any law work?"

"Never carried a badge. Helped catch a few rustlers down in Chihuahua. Learned about tracking from the Apaches."

"Well, that could be useful," said Roeser.

"There's a widow woman in town that has a room for rent. Ten dollars a month, I think. She could use the money and maybe some help around her place. You be interested in that?"

"Yes, I would," replied Sage. "What's a deputy sheriff make?"

"Fifty dollars a month," said Roeser. More than a cowhand for less hard work. A bit more risk sometimes, though."

Sage swore to protect and uphold the law, and Roeser gave him a badge. Then they walked up the street to meet the widow.

Mrs. Maggie Morris looked Sage up and down and then said, "I just heard that you are one hell of a shooter, but you don't look all that evil."

Sage blinked and replied, "I don't usually shoot that many men before lunch, ma'am, but the circumstances were a mite dire there."

Maggie looked at Roeser and said, "I'm mighty glad to see you standing there still alive, Jim. I heard you wouldn't be if this young man hadn't been hellish quick. Why in tarnation didn't you just let that Sam Cummings go? You could have taken a posse and rounded him up later."

"And maybe gotten some of the posse killed," said Roeser. "But aside from that, it just wasn't in me to let Cummings trample on the law."

"Even if you died for it," Maggie spat.

"Yes."

Maggie said, "Well, speaking of lunch, you boys had any yet? I've got a pot of chili on the stove. I was making enough for a couple of days."

Roeser said, "That'd be kind of you Maggie. I'd never pass up your chili."

Sage soon saw what Roeser meant. "This is the best bowl of chili I've ever had, Mrs. Morris. And I've had a lot."

"Buttering me up will get you anywhere," replied Maggie. "And call me Maggie. So what brings you here, Jim?"

"You said that you were thinking of renting out a room, Maggie. John here needs a place to stay. You in the market?"

"Well, I could use a fast gun around here. There's a coyote that's been killing the chickens." She looked at Sage. "How about ten dollars a month, plus twenty five cents for any meals I cook? This one's on the house. You can cook your own meals if you want."

"That sounds fine, ma'am. Maggie. Could I see the room?"

Sage was pleased to see that the room on the side of the adobe had its own door leading outside, and although it was small, it looked plenty comfortable. There was a dilapidated corral behind the house with a lightly populated chicken coop next to it.

As they walked back to Roeser's office, Sage commented, "I like her. Pretty salty. I'm surprised she hasn't remarried. She's a fine-looking woman, and I doubt that she is fifty yet."

Roeser chuckled. "Her husband was a lot older. He sold his dry goods store and decided to take up drinking in his retirement. Drank himself to death. Maggie's still enjoying the peace and quiet around the place. Been enjoying it for three years."

Sage said, "I'd like to spend the afternoon fixing up that corral. You mind waiting to start teaching me about the deputy business until this evening?"

"Sure," Roeser said. "I'd give you a hand, but I've got to ride out to the Cummings' place."

The cook from Paddy's Restaurant came in and gave Roeser a sandwich wrapped in a sheet of newspaper. Roeser took it and handed it to Sage. "For the prisoner. How about taking it up while I read Lou's letter?"

Sage came back down, and Roeser finished the letter and put it in a drawer. He sat back and considered Sage for a few moments. Then he said, "I'd have felt a lot more confident if I'd read that before our run-in with the Cummings bunch. He was mighty impressed with your shooting skills, and I can sure see why. But he was also impressed that you managed to get the crew out of a shooting fix. I like that just as much, if not more. A cold killer makes a pretty poor lawman, and I was somewhat concerned there. I suspect that you are going to make a pretty good lawman."

-27-

The coyote came up from his lair by the river in the dark of the night, ready for a chicken dinner, and there was a nice fat chicken all by itself behind the house. He looked around to check for any threats. The horse in the corral was something new, but although the horse was watching him, it didn't appear to be threatening. No dogs or humans were around.

The coyote stealthily crept up on its prey, pounced on it, and grabbed it in his jaws, crushing it with a startled squawk. As he lifted the chicken to make his escape, there was a snapping sound, and something fastened around his neck, choking him as he was hoisted into the air.

Maggie was awakened by the sound of a maul splitting wood behind the adobe. She got up and dressed. She found Sage converting a pile of dried rounds into stove wood. A chicken had been plucked and gutted and was laying on one of the rounds. A dead coyote was hanging from a wire noose suspended from a greenwood pole near the corral.

"Mornin, Maggie," said Sage. If you can use the fur, I'll skin that coyote for you."

"Well, now, aren't you a handy one," said Maggie as she inspected the coyote. "That some kind of Indian snare?"

"Yep, only they don't use wire. Had to use up one of your chickens for bait. It's got a few holes in it, but the meat's fine."

Maggie picked up the chicken and started back to the house. She turned back and said, "I could use a fur hat this winter. You know how to tan a hide?"

"Sure," said Sage. "I'll get it done."

"Fried chicken for dinner tonight. No charge. Breakfast will be ready in about twenty minutes." Maggie went into the house.

The next Saturday night, Roeser and Sage were at a table in the Catamount saloon smoking cigars and nursing cold beers. The saloon's icehouse was apparently still in business for the season. Sage looked at a stuffed lion above the mirrors behind the bartender. He'd seen better taxidermy. The cat looked a bit too long and narrow.

The place had a lively business this evening full of cowhands, farm hands, and miners. Two girls were working the crowd for drinks, and occasionally they would disappear to a room in the back with one of the men.

Roeser commented, "Bless those girls. They say the West is wild, and I guess it is, but it would be a lot wilder without 'em. Just not enough women to go around. Maybe if we hang enough badmen, more women would be willing to move out here.

"Speaking of hangings, Sam Cummings is scheduled for Monday morning at sunrise."

Sage shook his head. "I've seen hangings. Mighty unpleasant business."

"Yep," said Roeser. "But it's necessary, and it falls to us."

A group of miners across the room seemed to have an interest in Sage. They were having an animated conversation and kept glancing over at him. After a while, the biggest one stood up. He came over and stood in front of their table, hands on his hips, and gave Sage a belligerent stare.

"Hear you're really something with a gun, Mr. Deputy. Well, without a gun, a gunman ain't worth shit. You think you could handle a man without it?"

Roeser sat back without commenting, and Sage thought that maybe a little demonstration might be useful. "I don't fight for fun, mister. If you mean to push one, you're going down hard."

Grinning, the miner stepped back and raised his fists in front of him. "Like hell."

Sage stood up, unbuckled his gun belt, and laid it on the table. The miner stood six inches taller and was twice as wide.

The room grew silent as Sage held both hands open in front of his chest with his palms turned in. The miner stepped forward and led with a punch with his right hand, throwing his body behind it. Instead of ducking or trying to block it, Sage guided the punch past his head with the back of his right wrist, and as the miner lunged by, Sage spun around and slammed his right elbow into the man's kidney.

The miner sagged, and Sage spun again and swept his feet out from under him with the side of his boot, and the man dropped flat on his face with a heavy thud.

The miner scrambled to his feet, enraged. He charged, trying to wrap his burly arms around Sage. Sage grabbed his wrist and pivoted, and the miner found himself hurtling over the top. Sage applied leverage to the arm and the miner crashed to the floor on his back. He lay still for a moment, stunned.

One of the bystanders called out, "Hey Sully, how you going to fight if you can't stay on your feet?

Stung by the laughter, Sully scrambled to his feet and made another try at landing a punch. Sage decided to end it. He spun and landed a crushing back fist under the man's jaw without aligning his knuckles to break it. Sully was lifted to his toes. Half unconscious, he staggered, and Sage spun and whipped a round kick to the side of his head. Sully crashed to the floor and lay unmoving.

The room went into an uproar as Sage stepped over to his table and buckled his gun belt back on. Roeser looked at him with his eyebrows lifted and shook his head. "You're a wonder," he said in a low voice.

Sully's companions hauled the unconscious man to their table, sat him in a chair, and worked for a while to revive him. Sage picked up his beer, went to the bar, and bought a shot of whiskey. He took it over to the miner's table, pulled a chair over from another table, and sat down next to Sully.

Sully gaped at him blearily, and Sage handed him the whisky. He wasn't sure the man would take it and was relieved when he did. Sage said, "I expect you could whip any other man in here. I just had a lot of training that you didn't. I hope you won't hold it against me."

Sage held up his mug, and after looking at him for a moment, Sully grinned and said, "It was my play. You warned me, deputy." He tapped his shot glass on the mug and downed it. Sage took a couple of swallows and stood up. One of the miners said, "Where in hell did you learn to fight like that? Never seen the like!"

"From a priest," said Sage, and he left the miners muttering that maybe they should get some religion.

Sage rejoined Roeser and relit his cigar.

Roeser said, "Where in hell did you learn to fight like that? I've never seen anything like it."

Sage explained in more detail about his experience on Okinawa and then said, "I'd like to take a few days to ride around the country. I need to see the lay of the land and meet some of the farmers and ranchers around here. I'd hate to be chasing anyone and not know what was out there."

Roeser said, "I was fixing to suggest that same thing. You can head out on Monday after the hanging. Get your mind off it. When you get back, I'm going to ride up to Rincon, at the north end of the county. I've been hearing some things about my deputy there that need looking into. The main reason I wanted a deputy here was so that I could get loose and move around some.

I've got two deputies over in Las Cruces. You haven't met them yet. Saul Espinosa and Jesse Mendez. You need to get over there and meet them. They have their hands full there, so I didn't want to bring one of them over here. By the way, since the railroad was built through Las Cruces, the county seat will be moving over there soon, and so will I. The good people of Mesilla didn't want railroad traffic through here.

Roeser finished off his beer and said, "Things are settled down in here for the time being. Let's see what they're up to in the in the Rio and the Cattleman."

When they were about to enter the Rio Saloon, a shot thundered inside. Roeser and Sage drew their guns and went in low through the batwings. They flattened themselves against the wall on either side. A drunk standing in front of the bar was re-holstering his sidearm. Staggering slightly, he roared, "I'm Curly Bill Jebson. It's Saturday night and I'm lookin' to fight! Any of you ladies here ready to take me on?"

Sage and Roeser looked at each other and holstered their guns. With a little grin, Roeser said, "Curly Bill is disturbing the peace. You're warmed up," and with a sweep of his hand he motioned for Sage to take the lead.

With Roeser at his back, Sage walked up to the big burly man, who was apparently another miner. He held his hands together in front of his chest as if in prayer, and said, "You're done for the night, Curly Bill. Let's head over to the lockup."

"Jest startin'," said Curley, and he threw a roundhouse punch at Sage's jaw. Sage stepped slightly to the side, gripped Curley's wrist with his right hand, and fastened his left hand on Curley's upper arm. He pushed down on the arm and twisted the wrist with the arm held straight out.

Curley found himself unable to move without getting his shoulder dislocated. Sage was applying enough force to make that plain. Curly made a try to get loose anyway. He felt his arm start to come out of the socket and quickly changed his mind. Tears of pain squeezed out of his eyes.

Sage eased the pressure slightly and said, "Let's go."

Roeser pulled Curley's gun and knife out of his belt, and Sage walked Curly out the door and down the street to the sheriff's office on the same block with Roeser at their side. Roeser opened the office door, and Sage walked Curly up the stairs and into an open cell. Roeser carefully frisked the man and stepped out of the cell.

Sage let go and warily stepped out of the cell, but Curly was rubbing his shoulder. All the fight had gone out of him. "Damn," moaned Curly. "Man can't have any fun around here."

As he locked the cell door, Roeser said, "Yep, we're pretty mean." He turned to Cummings' cell and said, "Brought you a little company, Sam. Probably be some more before the night's over."

He turned back to Sage and said, "Let's try that again," and they headed back to the Rio.

As they walked Roeser said, "I surely do like working with you, John. You'll have to show me that move. It beats laying them out with a gun barrel. Hard on the gun."

-28-

When Roeser returned from Rincon, he found Sage up to his bare shoulders in a pit he was digging behind Maggie's adobe. Roeser noted that Sage was pretty damned muscular. He also noted a network of scars across Sage's back.

Sage climbed out of the hole and picked up his shirt. "Privy was plumb full. Thought I'd dig a new pit and move it over."

Roeser commented, "Looks like you've had some hard use. Those whip marks?"

"'Fraid so. The Japanese overseer thought I needed some convincing to be a good slave. I hauled rocks for two years before I broke his neck and managed to escape." He added, "Might have done it sooner, but I didn't know the language at first, and I couldn't see where there was anywhere to go. Damn near starved to death as it was."

Roeser took off his coat, and the two of them tipped over the wooden privy and drug it over to the new pit.

Roeser said, "Come over to my office after dinner. I need to talk to you about Rincon. Got a situation there."

In the office Roeser said, "My deputy up in Rincon is Julio Sanchez. I inherited him from the previous sheriff. I never trusted him much, but he kept the lid on. Thing is, it looks like there's a can of snakes under the lid, and they're getting out.

"The owner of the Emperor Saloon is a man named Jeremy Lugo. He took over there about a year ago. Some men I talked to say that the place has become a magnet for gunmen. Lugo has a man name of Bart Waco working for him. He mainly keeps order in the place, and he's a man that can do it. He's a known killer who's damned fast with a gun.

"He's been involved with one of the rings up in Lincoln County. They've got a bit of a war going on up there between different rings all trying to get on top of whatever makes money. The law there is a part of one of the rings.

Bunch of crooks themselves. I think Waco wound up on a loosing side and got out.

"Before that, he was down in Old Mexico for a time. Their new president, Porfirio Diaz, is all for American investment and development. Risky place to work, and one of the railroad outfits hired Waco to handle security. I never heard why he left.

"Anyway, people I talked to think that a whole lot of rustling and robberies around the country are directed by Lugo. They also believe that Sanchez is taking money to look the other way, and by damn I won't abide that.

"Hiram Cawthon, the mayor, is a mighty worried man. He sent me a letter a while back asking me to look into things, but I couldn't get loose from here for long enough to do much good.

"I thought I'd leave you here and move up there for a while, but I've got responsibilities here with the court and all, and I might not be able to spend the time in Rincon that's needed.

"So here's what I'm thinking. I'm thinking that you've got the ability to take this thing on. It's a tough situation up there, and I won't order you to do it, but I'm asking you to."

Sage thought for a minute. "I'm paid to do what needs to be done, and I take it that needs doing. Sure, I'll go."

Roeser had been sitting tensely, and he sat back in relief. "Good. You won't be paid enough for this one. I'll give you a letter for Sanchez telling him he's fired. You take over the office there. It's set up like this one here, with living quarters.

"You talk to Mayor Cawthon, and you talk to a man named Vern Summers. He's a retired rancher, an old friend of mine. I think you'll find him to be helpful."

Sage said, "If need be, what are the chances of me hiring another deputy or two there for a while?"

Roeser replied, "Well, since the county won't be paying Sanchez, there might be a little room there. I'll check with Mort Spencer tomorrow. He's a county supervisor. There's a number of tough men around Rincon—honest men—but they're all working men. You might pay a couple of them for part-time work if you can get any to do it. I'll delegate to you the authority to deputize them.

"You might be up there for some time. Maggie's going to miss you. She tells me that she should be paying you ten dollars a month to stay at her place.

Roeser handed Sage a stack of papers. "I've told you some about procedures for handling prisoners and getting them tried. Here's a summary of territorial laws and county ordinances. Better study up some."

The next day, Roeser told Sage that he had a budget of fifty dollars a month for any deputy work. He could draw it at the bank along with his own pay on the first of the month. He could head out the following morning.

-29-

When Sage neared Rincon near the end of the day, he decided to camp along the Rio Grande. Best to get the ball rolling in the quiet of the morning.

When Sage rode into Rincon, he put his badge in his shirt pocket and rode through the length of the town. The town was up against some hills on a bench above the Rio. There were two saloons, the Emperor and the San Diego, and two churches, the usual Protestant and Catholic. Rincon was the southern terminus of a branch of the Santa Fe Railroad that ran down from Santa Fe and Albuquerque.

While he was thinking that it was kind of funny to name a saloon after a saint, he spotted a restaurant and decided to have breakfast. The jerky he'd had the night before was all used up. With the habit he was starting to get into, Sanchez probably worked late and was a late riser, and Sage figured that he would take his time.

He went into the Pot Belly and looked it over. A half dozen men, mostly Mexicans, were filling their briskets at the counter and tables. He picked a table near the window and sat down. A white-haired man in a broadcloth suit sipping coffee over a newspaper studied him for a bit, but the rest paid him no attention.

The elderly waitress smiled and said, "Don't recall you being in here before."

Sage replied, "I don't recall being in here before. Can I get a couple of eggs scrambled with jalapenos?"

"We can handle that. Want some taters fried and jalapenos and onions with that?"

"Sounds good," said Sage, "and some bacon and coffee."

When he paid his bill Sage said, "That was mighty fine, ma'am. I'll be in again. Where might I find the mayor?"

Raising her eyebrows at this unexpected request, the waitress said, "Over at the bank. Mayor Cawthon is also the banker. They open at ten."

She was obviously curious about what his business with the mayor was, but he just thanked her and left. The clock on the wall had the time at nine o'clock, so he fished a cigar out of his saddlebags and took a chair on the boardwalk in front of the restaurant. He spent half an hour watching people go about their business and then got on Smokey.

The white-haired gentleman came out of the Pot Belly, looked at Smokey, and commented, "Fine looking animal. Nice coat and conformation. Got a pedigree?"

"Not that I know of," replied Sage. "Got him from an officer in Mexico. He didn't tell me about his heritage. What counts is he gets me there and back with no time wasted."

"Harrumph", said the man, and he walked off down the boardwalk."

Sage tied Smokey in front of the sheriff's office, pinned his badge back on, and went in. Sanchez had his boots up on the desk. He was sipping a cup of coffee and reading a newspaper.

Sanchez was a medium-sized man with a mustache over a three-day beard. He looked to be in his mid-thirties and a bit overweight. Sanchez didn't get up. He looked at the badge pinned on Sage's shirt and said, "Well now, you must be Roeser's new whizbang deputy from who knows where. What brings you here?"

"Delivering the mail," said Sage. He handed Sanchez the envelope from Roeser and took a seat in a chair in front of the desk.

Sanchez opened the envelope and pulled out the letter and fifty dollars. "What the hell's this?" asked Sanchez.

"Severance pay," said Sage. Sanchez's dark face grew darker and darker as he read the letter.

Sanchez said, "Son of a bitch. The bastard didn't say anything about this when he was up here!"

"He wanted to be sure I'd take the job," said Sage. "It was going to be either him or me."

Sanchez said, "You're taking my job? I hear you're damned fast with a gun, but you're just a kid. They'll eat you alive here."

"That's my and Roeser's concern. Not yours." Sage held out his hand. "I'll take the badge."

Sanchez dropped his boots to the floor, stood up, and came around the desk. Sage stood up also.

Sanchez said, “Get the hell out of here! I’ll go when I’m ready.”

Sage said, “I was going to give you until this evening, when I’ll be moving in. But you’re not a deputy anymore. You’re leaving now, and I’ll take the badge.”

Sanchez threw a sucker punch at Sage’s belly, but Sage was ready. He tensed his abdominal muscles, and the fist landed with no apparent effect. It felt to Sanchez like he had slugged a rock.

Startled, Sanchez froze for an instant, and Sage jabbed the rigid fingers of his left hand into a nerve center in Sanchez’ chest just inside the right shoulder. It was immediately followed by a jab with his right hand to the other side. Sanchez grunted in pain, and both of his arms went completely numb. Sage then grabbed his nose and jerked down hard. Sanchez felt like his whole face had been lit on fire, and he stumbled backward. His arms hung loose and he blinked tears from his eyes.

Sage stepped up, pulled the gun from Sanchez’ holster, and slid it into his belt. Then he ripped the badge off of Sanchez’s shirt. Stepping back, he said, “You keep coming, I’m going to do some real damage. Now you gather your own personal gear and put it on the floor right here.” Sage pointed at the floor in front of the door.

Sage kept close to Sanchez as the thoroughly cowed ex-deputy rubbed some life back into his arms and gathered up his possessions. He didn’t have much. It all fit into a big canvass bag.

Sage pulled out Sanchez’s .45 and unloaded it. He handed him the shells, and Sanchez stuffed them in his pocket. Then Sage gave him the gun. Sage opened the door and asked, “Where are the keys kept?”

“Top right desk drawer. My horse and saddle are out back.”

“Pick them up when you get settled in somewhere,” said Sage, and Sanchez hoisted the sack over his shoulder and walked off.

Sage went out to unload Smokey and eased the cinch. He didn’t own much, either.

After carrying his gear inside, Sage poured himself another cup of coffee. When he finished it, he locked up the office and went to find the mayor.

-30-

A teller brought Hiram Cawthon out, and Sage introduced himself. Cawthon ushered Sage into his office and asked, "What can I do for you, Mr. Sage?"

Cawthon was a small man with thinning hair. He looked to be pretty sharp.

"What can I do for you"? replied Sage.

Cawthon moved his reading glasses down on his nose, peered over them, and said, "Not much, so long as Julio Sanchez is the deputy here. You reporting to him?"

"Sanchez isn't a deputy anymore. I just gave him a letter from Sheriff Roeser firing him. I'm the deputy here now."

Cawthon raised his eyebrows and said, "You don't say! He just took it and he'll be leaving?"

Sage said, "He took it. He needed a little convincing to leave, but he left."

Cawthon's eyebrows remained up, and he gazed at Sage, reappraising him. He thought the man looked pretty young, but he had a steady, self-confident look. Well put together. Maybe a little Mexican in him, but his hair and eyes were light.

He'd heard about the shootout with the Cummings bunch. Perhaps this young man would be of some use.

Cawthon said, "You asked what you could do for me. What I need is for you to do something for the town, but it's going to take more than a fast gun. I talked some with Sheriff Roeser, and he was pretty damned noncommittal. Said he was tied to Mesilla most of the time, but he said he might have an idea about how to go about helping us out. Guess you're it. I doubt that any one man can do much, though.

"I thought about hiring a town marshall and a bunch of deputies, but the town council didn't want to tolerate the expense. We'd have had to build a place for them, and I don't know where we would have gotten them. No one qualified around here has time to take on something like that full time or wants to take on the tough nuts that hang around the Emperor.

"Thanks to Jeremy Lugo, Rincon has become a haven for murderers and thieves. They don't generally shit in their own lair, though. Most of the killing and thieving takes place in other towns and counties, although some cowboys and farmers have ended their days in the Emperor. Julio Sanchez seemed to be mighty easy to convince that Lugo's boys were acting in self-defense.

"You might have noticed that the farming and ranching land along the river is pretty prime. Probably the most valuable land in the state. Lugo has been buying it up when any has come available. Apparently not enough has, though. Not for him. What has me worried is that three owners have disappeared in the past six months. Flat out vanished. When the families tried to sell, any prospective buyers were warned off. I think it was Lugo's people, but Sanchez said it wasn't.

"Anyway, Lugo bought two of them farms for a song. The third place, a small ranch with some nice pastureland ten miles up the river, hasn't been sold yet. The widow, Mrs. Nancy Martin, has gotten an offer, but she's been a bit stubborn about hanging on to it. A damned shame there. She's a young thing. They hadn't been married a month. Her husband, Jeffrey, disappeared right after he had been in to see me about a loan for some improvements out at his place, the Rocking M. Never made it home. Just his horse showed up there with a lot of blood on the saddle.

"Then her hands started getting some threats, and one of them lost a gunfight with Bart Waco. Waco was apparently hard-pressed to defend himself against a kid who probably couldn't hit the side of a barn if he was standing inside of it. The dumb kid shouldn't have been wearing a gun. I guess he thought that was being grown up. Two of her hands quit, so she's only got one left. Jed Peters is a feisty war vet, but he's no gunman."

"When did Martin go missing?"

Cawthon thought for a moment and then said, "That was just over two months ago."

"Sanchez look into it?"

"Oh, he rode out and back. Didn't do any good."

Sage said, "Tell me about the other saloon, the San Diego."

Cawthon said, "That's the Mexican saloon. Man name of Benito Alvarez owns it. Lugo's been putting some pressure on Alvarez to sell that, too. Alvarez is a hard man but a good one. I'd hate to see him go."

"I'm surprised that a saloon would be named for a saint," said Sage.

"There's a mountain peak near here by that name," replied Cawthon. "Couldn't say why Alvarez picked it."

Sage said, "I'll need to get to know the people around here and the lay of the land before I can do much. I need to get some support. Maybe a couple of part-time deputies. Like you said, a fast gun isn't going to be enough."

Cawthon sat back and said, "I'm starting to think that maybe you've got a head on your shoulders, Mr. Sage. Sheriff Roeser wasn't the one that hired Sanchez, but I think any man he'd hire and send up here now would be at least competent."

"Where might I locate a man named Vern Summers?" Sage asked.

"He'd be a good one to start with," replied Cawthon. "Civil War veteran. Officer with the Union. He sold his ranch a few years ago and lives over on Olivera Street. His adobe has a cannon in the front yard. Don't think it works, though."

Sage stood up and said, "Thank you for your time, Mayor Cawthon".

Cawthon said, "Please call me Hiram. How about having dinner at my place tonight, Mr. Sage? May I call you John?"

"Of course," said Sage. "Thank you."

Sage got directions to Cawthon's residence and decided to go back to his office, go through the desk, and clean the place up. Sanchez was a pig.

He rode around behind the office and found that the corral there was empty and that there was no hay or grain anywhere around. He rode down to the feed store and got two bales of alfalfa and a sack of grain. He tied the bales loosely together with his rope and hung them over the saddle. He put the sack on top and led Smokey back to the corral.

The feed store owner was standoffish until Sage managed to loosen him up with some pleasantries, and people who saw him on the street looked at the badge and avoided him. Apparently Sanchez had given the law a bad name here.

Sage started looking through the papers in the desk and found a Colt Peacemaker in a holster with the cartridge belt wrapped around it in a bottom drawer. While wondering what that was doing there, he heard something banging upstairs, and a muffled voice called out, “Hey, how about some food up here?”

“Oh, shit!” breathed Sage. He hurried up the stairs and through a heavy wooden door into the cell area. One cell was occupied.

Sage approached the man standing in the cell, apparently a cowboy in his mid-twenties, and asked, “Who might you be?”

“Cody Miller,” said the cowboy. “And who might you be?”

“John Sage. I’m the new deputy sheriff here. I notified the old deputy sheriff that he was fired this morning. We had some difficulties about that, and I’m afraid I didn’t think to ask if anyone was up here. And Sanchez didn’t mention it. What are you in here for?”

Miller said, “If you don’t know, I don’t know if I should tell you about all them dead and dying out there.”

Sage looked at him, and Miller said, “I was in the Emperor last night playing cards. I was sitting to the right of the dealer and saw him deal three cards off the bottom of the deck to a player when there was a big pot. The gent took the pot with three aces. I stood up and laid the dealer out, and before I knew it, there was a gun muzzle poking me in the back of the head. Sanchez was holding it.

“Sanchez appeared to be a friend of both the dealer and the guy that took the pot, and he arrested me for battery.”

Sage said, “I’ll check to see if Sanchez did any paperwork on it. But first, I owe you a lunch. Be back in a minute.”

Sage got the key out of the desk and opened the cell. He said, "Let's hike over to the Pot Belly."

Surprised, Miller said, "You don't think a desperado like me will take off on you?"

Sage gave him an even look and said, "You wouldn't get two steps."

Miller decided that the deputy wasn't just woofing. He didn't look like he'd go down easy. Might try him, though, if need be.

While waiting for plates of enchiladas and refried beans, Sage asked, "You from around here?"

"Nope," said Miller. "I've been working on a ranch near Taos. Seasonal work. Been keeping an eye out for work as I move south. I heard a while back that the sheriff in Mesilla was looking for a deputy. Thought I might try lawin'. No offense, but I wasn't too impressed with my first look at the Sheriff's Department in this county."

"I filled the job," said Sage, "but since the other position just went vacant, there might be something. Not sure what Sheriff Roeser's plans are. The sheriff's a good man, but I wasn't too impressed with Sanchez, either. Ever do any law work?"

"You recruit out of your jails here?" said Miller.

"I'm not sure you belonged there yet," replied Sage. "I'll be looking into that."

"I never carried a badge," said Miller. "But I'm handy in any kind of a fight. I grew up in the hills of Kentucky. Fightin' was the main form of recreation around there. Fightin' and shootin'. My pappy made sure I knew how."

The waitress showed up with the enchiladas. After seeing his badge, she didn't look as friendly as she had that morning.

After the meal, Sage paid, and they went back to the office. Sage went through the desk more thoroughly while Miller read the weekly paper from Mesilla. Sage was glad to see he could read. After a while, Sage pulled the Peacemaker out of the bottom drawer and held it up. "This yours?"

"Yep" said Miller.

Sage laid the belted gun on top of the desk and said, "I don't find a thing in here about your arrest. There's a logbook, but nothing's been entered for the past week. You're a free man. If I find out later that I made a mistake, I'll rectify it.

Miller said, "I guess maybe I'd better light out."

"I'd guess maybe you'd better stick around. I might have a job for you. I want to talk to some people before I offer it, though, if you still think you'd be interested in some lawin'. Are you staying at the hotel?"

Miller chewed on that for a minute and then replied, "Yes. And yes, I'd be interested."

Sage said, "You might not be so interested once you understand the situation here. Don't fully understand it myself yet. But you might check around for something cheaper than the hotel. Maybe someone's got a room.

"I've got a couple of people to see. How about you come back in the morning?"

Sage found Olivera Street and the adobe with the cannon in front. It looked like an old piece, but maybe it was serviceable. He knocked on the door.

The white-haired gentleman he'd seen at breakfast came to the door, and when he saw the badge he said, "Well, now."

Sage said, "Mr. Summers? My name's John Sage. I'm the new deputy here. Sheriff Roeser suggested that I look you up."

Vern Summers might have had white hair and was probably in the mid-sixties, but he looked damned fit. He also looked like he might be pretty intelligent.

Summers invited Sage to come in. Sage turned down a coffee, and they sat on cowhide-covered chairs in the front room. Summers said, "Call me Vern. I read about the fracas with the Cummings bunch in the Mesilla Crier. When Jim was here he spoke highly of you. Said you handled tough hombres like they were babies if they got out of hand. Jim's a hard man to impress, but you sure did impress him. If you hadn't, you wouldn't be here."

Sage said, "I talked to Mayor Cawthon this morning. He told me some about Jeremy Lugo and his bunch at the Emperor. Lugo seems to be an ambitious sort—maybe to the point of murdering folks to get what he wants."

"I'd put that a mite stronger than 'maybe,'" said Summers. Circumstantial evidence, but circumstantial is still evidence. You've got yourself a real problem there, and you aren't going to get any help from Julio Sanchez. He's part of the problem. Jim should have fired him."

Sage said, "He did. Brought a letter to that effect with me and gave it to Sanchez this morning. He's not a deputy any more. I've moved into the office."

Summers raised his eyebrows. "Well, well. He go peacefully?"

"Not particularly, but he went," said Sage. "I'm looking to get some help. The problem with Lugo isn't just my problem. Looks to me like others are affected. I'll be looking for some of them to step up. I need some backup."

Summers said, "I'd say you're more mature than your age, which is what Jim said. Any ideas on how you're going to proceed?"

"Well, I'm sure not going to storm the Emperor," said Sage. "I expect that it will take me a while to figure out what to do. Get a better understanding of what is going on to start and who's who.

"I was thinking about hiring a couple of part-time deputies for evening work, but now I'm looking at hiring one man full time. That won't leave me funds for any part-timers. You think there would be anyone around who might be willing to wear a badge on a volunteer basis?"

Summers said, "You got someone in mind for the full-time job?"

"Yes, man named Cody Miller. Found him this morning. He's not from around here, though, and I need someone around who is familiar with Rincon."

"Cody Miller. You didn't by any chance find him in a cell at your office, did you?" asked Summers.

Surprised, Sage said, "As a matter of fact, I did. He claimed that Sanchez railroaded him. I tend to believe him, but I'll be asking around about that."

"Ask no further", said Summers. "I was there. I like to keep my eye on what the Emperor bunch is up to. I was having a drink at the next table. I've seen that dealer, Barney Sipe, and his partner shear the sheep before, and that's what they were doing. Miller wasn't too keen on being a sheep, though."

"That eases my mind," said Sage. "What do you think about volunteers?"

Summers sat back and thought for a few moments. "Actually, there are several men that might make good candidates. How about if I got them together here so that maybe you could talk some of them into it?"

"That would be very good," said Sage. "Maybe tomorrow evening."

Summers said, "Some are on nearby farms and ranches. Might take a little time to gather them. This is Tuesday. How about Friday?"

"That'll do," replied Sage. "Maybe I'll know a little more about the situation by then. I certainly appreciate your assistance, Vern. I'm very pleased to have met you. I've got to be going. Mayor Cawthon invited me to dinner."

They stood, and Summers said, "Not as pleased as I am to have met you, John. Rincon might be in for some renovation."

-31-

Sage had an enjoyable dinner with the Cawthon family. The mayor's wife, Susan, was lively and personable and made him feel right at home. Afterward, he and the mayor had some additional discussion about Rincon's problems.

Sage asked Cawthon if Lugo banked with him, and Cawthon replied, "Lugo doesn't do any business with my bank other than some mortgages on his properties. But ethically and legally, I am not at liberty to discuss any financial affairs of any of my clients without a court order. I can't help you in that area."

"I understand that," replied Sage. He was glad to learn, though, that it wasn't likely that the mayor might have conflicting interests here.

After leaving Cawthon's home, he walked over to the San Diego. He went in through the batwings and stood to the side for a moment, looking the place over. Tuesday nights were apparently pretty slow here. Two vaqueros were sharing a bottle at their table, and a woman was seated on a low stool on the other side of the room picking a few notes on a guitar. Two men were on tall stools at the far end of the bar talking to the bartender.

The room was spacious but simply furnished with a dozen tables. Colorful Mexican blankets hung on the walls, and a large pair of bull horns hung over the mirrors behind the bar.

Sage took a closer look at the woman, and a shock coursed through him, leaving him weak in the knees. He had never seen a woman anywhere near that beautiful. Her long, black hair was held in a band on one side and draped down the front of one side of her white blouse. The blouse, which hung loosely off bare brown shoulders, appeared to be abundantly full. She was wearing a colorful skirt that draped to the floor. She looked like she might be around sixteen or seventeen.

Sage realized that he hadn't been breathing and filled his lungs as he gathered his addled thoughts and walked to the bar.

The bartender, who he assumed was Benito Alvarez, came down the bar, and Sage ordered a beer in Spanish. When it arrived, the bartender placed it in front of him, gave him a hard look, and started to walk back toward the other patrons.

Sage pulled a silver dollar out of his pocket and asked, "How much?"

The bartender stopped, turned, and gave Sage a surprised look. "You want to pay? The other deputy never pays."

Sage said, "The other deputy isn't a deputy any more. Why in hell wasn't he paying?"

The bartender came back and said, "Sanchez explained to me one time that because he was here to prevent trouble for me, it was in my best interest to support the law by providing drinks without charge. He hinted that trouble might increase here without him being around to prevent it."

The bartender started to walk away again, and Sage said, "I believe that the San Diego is in Dona Ana County. I'm paid by the taxpayers to prevent trouble here. I expect that you pay taxes. I don't expect anything extra. How much?"

The bartender looked at Sage appraisingly and said, "Sanchez is not a deputy any more?"

"Apparently Sanchez wasn't particularly good at preventing trouble," said Sage. "Sheriff Roeser fired him. I gave Sanchez a letter to that effect this morning, and I took his badge."

"That is right," said the bartender. "When there was trouble here, Sanchez was always over in the Emperor. I sent for him a couple of times, but he didn't come. There were other things he was busy with." He spat on the floor.

Sage looked him in the eye and said, "I'll come. Or another deputy will.

"My name is John Sage", and he held out his hand.

The bartender hesitated. He took it and said, "I am Benito Alvarez, at your service".

Sage said, "Mayor Cawthon spoke well of you. I am at your service. The mayor told me some about the situation here in Rincon. A little about Jeremy Lugo. Maybe you could tell me some more. Apparently the man is ambitious about acquiring property and may be a little forceful in going about getting it."

Alvarez spat on the floor again. "A little forceful. My friend Pedro Martinez owned a farm down the valley. Lugo offered to buy it, and Pedro refused. Then Pedro disappeared from the face of the earth. He had a wife, Louisa, and four children. One of Lugo's men came to her and offered her what was less than half the value for the farm, and she refused. She found another buyer, but the man backed out. She said the man looked frightened when he told her he had changed his mind. Then the same with another man.

"Louisa couldn't pay the mortgage. I wanted to help her, but I just barely make ends meet for my family. Hiram Cawthon gave her extra time, but she could see that there was no way she was going to be able to work the farm, and she sold it to Lugo's man. She has since moved to El Paso."

"Do you know the name of Lugo's man?" asked Sage.

"His name is Jack Palermo," said Alvarez. "I understand that he hangs around the Emperor. A gunman. I do not think he would have the money or the desire to buy a farm, even a cheap one."

Sage said, "Hiram told me that Lugo had approached you about buying this place."

"That is so," replied Alvarez. "I told him not only no, but hell no. Since then, men—gringos—have been coming in here on Saturday nights and picking fights with my customers. Two have been killed. It is very bad for business. Most of the men who come here are workingmen, not fighters. This has always been a good place for these men to come to relax, talk over their drinks, and play some cards. I am very afraid that is changing.

"That damned Sanchez would do nothing. He said the killings were self-defense even when I said that I would testify that they were murder. Those men who were killed were not gunfighters. He said that it was my word against theirs, and I am afraid of what would happen to any of my other customers if they were called to testify in a trial."

The woman with the guitar started playing a tune that caught Sage's attention. It was a beautiful piece. Sage looked at her and then back to Alvarez and said, “That is a very beautiful woman.”

Alvarez replied, “Yes. Lupita Calderon. Her family was taken by cholera when she was twelve. I have raised her since then. She is now eighteen. She has been a blessing and a curse.”

Sage said, “A curse?”

“Yes,” said Alvarez. “Men see her and loose their senses. They do not always behave well. Do stupid things to try to get her attention.”

“I can believe that,” said Sage. “Is it wise for her to work here?”

“No, it is not wise,” said Alvarez. “But Lupita has a mind of her own. She enjoys entertaining and the attention of men. For the most part, she handles them well. One of the gringos—a troublemaker—began to pester her. I told him to leave and that if he came back I would kill him at the door. I was holding a shotgun against his belly when I told him. He knew I meant it. But I am afraid there will be more trouble from them.

“It is my hope that she will pick a good man and settle down. But she has not met anyone that interests her very much. She seems to be content with things the way they are, and she is good for business. Men like to hear her play and look at her even though she will not let them get close.”

Sage changed the subject. “Mr. Alvarez, I intend to take on Lugo, but I can’t do it by myself. He appears to be troubling many people, and I expect some of those people to step up. I wouldn’t expect them to confront Lugo or any of his men. I’ll be doing that. But I need people at my back. Do you know any men who might be interested in volunteering as deputies? I don’t mean full-time, just when they have some time.”

Alvarez studied Sage and considered the idea for a few moments. “This is a new idea to me. I’ll have to give it some thought. There may be a few men that might ‘step up,’ as you say.”

Sage said, “Friday evening I will be meeting with some men at the home of Vern Summers. Do you know him?”

"I know who he is," replied Alvarez, "but I do not know him very well. Few men come in here that are not Mexican. He appeared to be a good man."

"Summers lives on Olivera Street," said Sage. There is a cannon in front of his adobe. If you find anyone who is interested before then, have them drop by. Or they can come by my office anytime.

"I'm getting tired of holding this dollar." Sage placed the coin on the bar. Alvarez took it to a drawer, came back with the change, and laid down ninety cents.

"You took the badge from Julio Sanchez? He wasn't willing to give it to you?"

"Not particularly," replied Sage. "Had to use a little force."

Alvarez looked thoughtfully at Sage as he took a seat at a table to finish his beer. He thought that he would liked to have seen that.

Sage nursed the beer and listened to the guitar. Looking at Lupita Calderon felt better than the beer, but she didn't seem to notice him. When he finished he touched his hand to his the brim of his hat as he passed her. He bowed slightly and said, "You play very well. Thank you."

The smile she gave him almost made him wobble as he went out through the batwings.

-32-

About ten the next morning, Cody Miller came to the office and hesitated when he looked through the window as he approached the door. He knocked twice and then entered.

"Don't need to knock", said Sage. "It's a public office."

Miller looked at Sage quizzically and said, "Mind if I ask what you were doing there?"

"It's an exercise," replied Sage. "Loosens up the joints, stretches the muscles, improves balance, and concentrates the mind.

"I'm offering you that job now if you haven't come to your senses."

"Never been too sensible," replied Miller. "I'll take it."

"Good," said Sage. "You find a place you can stay?"

"I did," replied Miller. "There's a boarding house in town. Got a room for fifteen a month. I can use the kitchen and front room. What're you paying?"

"We deputies make fifty a month," replied Sage.

"Sounds good," replied Miller. "That's better than what I was making as a nursemaid to cows."

"A bit more dangerous," said Sage. "Let me fill you in on what I know so far about what we'll need to be doing."

Sage spent a half hour explaining what he knew and then said, "Sounds like Lugo's got a large crowd over there. I've been looking into getting some more help. I'm hoping to get some men to volunteer to be part-time deputies. I've got a meeting set up for Friday evening to meet a few candidates. I'd like to have you there."

"How many you want to get?" asked Miller.

"As many as I can," replied Sage. "I'm hoping a show of strength will discourage gunplay. But when we start cramping Lugo's operation, there may well be some. Anyway, the more eyes and ears the better, and if it comes to it, it would be good to have some friends around. I wouldn't much want to get shot in the back while I was busy with someone in front of me."

Sage swore Miller in as a deputy and gave him the badge he'd taken off Sanchez. He hadn't found any other badges around and hoped he could get some from Roeser.

"Let's take a ride out of town," said Sage. "I want to see how you shoot. Might have to take the badge back."

Miller grinned and said, "I shoot pretty good. Let's go."

Sage gathered up some tin cans and put them in a sack, which he tied to Smokey's saddle. When Miller came back they rode up into the hills above Rincon.

Sage placed six cans on a log and stepped back about thirty feet. He said, "When I say 'draw,' go after 'em. See if you can hit any."

Miller grinned, stepped back another ten feet, and stood with his arms at his sides.

"Draw!"

Miller was fast and accurate. He only missed one can.

"You can keep the badge, Cody. You might try moving your body less; it wastes a little time. Just move the arm."

Miller walked over to the log and replaced the cans.

He walked back and said, "Your turn."

"Draw!"

Miller gaped at the speed at which Sage drew and cleared all six cans off the log.

"Holy shit!" exclaimed Miller. "I've never seen anyone that good!"

"My pappy made sure I knew how," replied Sage. "Taught me how to throw a knife, too. I'll show you a little trick I've been working on."

Sage reloaded and holstered his gun. He carried a sheath knife on the left side of his gun belt. He reached across with his right hand, whipped the knife out, and threw it by the handle at a nearby tree. While the knife was in the air, he drew and fired at the tree.

The knife stuck in the tree, and the two walked over to it. Miller looked at the knife and said, "I'll be damned. The knife is stuck right in the bullet hole. That's some trick!"

"I picked a mark on the tree and aimed at it with the knife and the gun," said Sage. "Might be useful to impress the natives sometime. Make them somewhat reluctant to try me and get themselves killed".

"I think that would do it," said Miller. "I think I'll avoid trying you. I surely will. And I'd been thinking I was about top of the line."

Sage said, "I actually haven't seen all that much gunplay, but I expect that your chances would be pretty damned good against anyone."

"Maybe so," replied Miller, "but I wouldn't try you unless I'd decided that living was unbearable. You really haven't seen much gunplay?"

"I've killed some people", said Sage. "I didn't like doing that. I would like to never have to do it again, and I've gone out of my way to avoid killing some others. Always will if I can.

"No, I haven't seen a lot of gunplay. I was out of the country for a long time, and there haven't been many situations I've been in, or seen, that have called for it."

"You're in the wrong line of work," said Miller.

"That crossed my mind," replied Sage. "But I've come to believe it's needed."

Miller said, "Well, you go out of your way to avoid killing someone, that could get you killed."

"I'll accept some risk," said Sage," but not to the point of being foolish, and I can handle some situations all right without using a gun. I'll tell you, though, if it comes to gunplay, I wouldn't want you to do any dithering.

"Let's get fed and go take a look at the Emperor."

While they were eating, Sage said, "What do you know about cards and cardsharps?"

"Plenty," replied Miller. "A friend of my father ran a game in Kentucky. He ran an honest game. I think mostly that's because he figured he'd live longer in that business if he did. But he knew all the tricks just so he wouldn't get skinned. He took a liking to me, and when he wasn't busy he spent a lot of time showing them to me. I learned to spot about anything."

Sage said, "Well, you're still alive, so I take it that you followed his example. You don't appear to be unusually rich, though."

Miller grinned and said, "Well, I've skinned a few skinners just for fun. I never was interested in playing cards full time. Not enough action, and I didn't feel too good about taking money off folks that couldn't afford it even though they were dumb enough to put their money down. I've always liked work that got me outdoors."

-33-

The Emperor was a very large, two-story adobe building. Sage was impressed with the southwestern decor. Stools made out of sections of logs that had been barked and lacquered fronted the long, polished wooden bar. Large arrays of lamps were mounted on wagon wheels suspended from the ceiling. Navajo blankets hung on the walls, and shelves were loaded with Indian artifacts. Maybe they were Navaho or of those who had inhabited the area before them.

The room had about thirty tables in it, and an area at the far end contained half a dozen card tables. One of those had a dealer at work with four players. Only a few men were at the other tables at the mid-morning hour, and three men were seated on the stools along the bar. One of them was Julio Sanchez. Sanchez was sitting alone, and he was apparently fascinated with his mug of beer because he kept his attention focused on it.

There was a small upright piano in the center of the room, but the piano player wasn't around.

Sage and Miller took the stools closest to the door. In a low voice Sage said, "I doubt that any of the men in here other than Sanchez are locals—unless the locals tend to be hard cases."

After a long delay the bartender came down to them. A picture of an unhappy rat came to Sage's mind. The bartender looked at Miller with a frown and did a double take when he saw the badge on his shirt.

He started to say something, thought better of it, and said something else: "What'll you have?"

Sage said, "My name is John Sage. I took over from Julio Sanchez. This is Deputy Cody Miller. We came by to pay our respects to Mr. Lugo. Is he in?

The bartender didn't reply or introduce himself, but he came out from behind the bar and went upstairs.

A few minutes later he came back down and said, "Mr. Lugo would like you to come up to his office. First door on the left at the top of the stairs."

The door was open, and Sage and Miller went in. Lugo was an enormously fat man seated at a large desk facing the door. Lounging in a chair to the side of the desk was another man. The man looked to be tall and well formed and was wearing a broadcloth suit and string tie. He had a smug look on his face and a .45 Peacemaker on his hip. The gun looked to be comfortable on him.

Lugo motioned to a couple of chairs in front of the desk, and Sage and Miller sat down. The fat man studied Sage for a few moments. Then he spoke up and said, "I'm Jeremy Lugo. This is my assistant, Bart Waco. What can I do for you, Mr. Sage?"

"This is my assistant, Cody Miller," replied Sage. "Sheriff Roeser sent me to replace Julio Sanchez. Since my job is to uphold the law and protect people in Rincon and this part of the county, I'll be doing business here in the Emperor from time to time. Thought Cody and I should introduce ourselves."

Waco spoke up and said, "Last I knew, Miller here was in jail. It's a mite surprising to see someone who assaulted one of our dealers wearing a badge. What's that about upholding the law?"

Miller leaned forward and started to speak, but Sage gave him a slight shake of the head, and he sat back in his chair. Sage said, "Sanchez neglected to file any charges. Cody knows a bottom deal when he sees one. I checked around and was satisfied that the party at fault there was your dealer, which gives me some concern about the way you operate here, Mr. Lugo."

Waco tensed, and Lugo's face turned red. He said evenly, "I run an honest business here. Never had any complaints."

Sage said, "I might believe that if you fire that dealer.

"Mr. Lugo, I'm not ready to pass judgment. I want cowboys, farmers, and miners, whoever your customers are, to be able to enjoy themselves without getting either skinned or shot. I'm willing to assume that you see that that's in your best interest, too. When Cody and I and other deputies are in here, that's what we'll have in mind."

Lugo raised his eyebrows. "Other deputies?"

"There'll be some more," said Sage.

Lugo's face stayed red. "Bart here keeps the peace, and I've hired Sanchez to help him out. We don't need you and a bunch of deputies wasting your time hanging around."

"I'm new here, Mr. Lugo. I'll make up my mind as to what's needed after a while."

Waco spoke up and said, "I hear that you're mighty quick with a gun. Read about that fracas down in Mesilla. Heard some about some shootings along the trail, up in the Nations. That you?"

Sage said, "Some gents figured on cutting the herd. I didn't want them to do that."

"Four men," said Waco. "Never heard anything else about you. Where the hell you come from?"

"I've been herding cows in Chihuahua," said Sage. "Pretty quiet there."

Waco stared at him for a moment and then said, "You a Mexican?"

"Nope," said Sage.

"Got some kind of mix in you. Indian?"

Sage ignored him. He stood up and said, "Good day, Mr. Lugo. Pleased to meet you."

Waco rose, but Lugo remained seated. No one offered to shake hands as Sage and Miller left the room.

When they got out on the street Miller said, "Whew! That sure laid it out. What happened in Mesilla?"

Sage looked at him and said, "I think you're the only man in this part of the world that didn't hear about that."

Miller listened with no little amazement as Sage related the details about the gunfight with the Cummings outfit.

Miller said, "If I hadn't seen the way you handle an iron, I'd have found that a little hard to believe." After a moment he said, "So, what do we do next?"

"We sit in front of our office and have a couple of cigars. Might as well relax while we have the chance. Chances might get to be scarce after a while. Then I have to write a letter to let Roeser know how things stand and that I want him to send up some deputy badges.

"You can get yourself moved into your room and come back in the morning. I'm just going to walk around a little tonight. Get a feel for the town. I still haven't seen everything."

As they finished their cigars, Sage said, "You might stop by the San Diego and introduce yourself to the owner tonight. Benito Alvarez. There's a guitar player there you might enjoy listening to."

Sage smiled at Miller and said, "Try to remember that you're a gentleman and an officer of the law."

As he rode to the boarding house, Miller wondered why Sage would say something like that.

-34-

Sage and Miller went over to Vern Summers' adobe on Friday evening after dinner. Summers had four men gathered in his front room. They all eyed the deputies as Summers introduced Sage.

"John Sage here is the new deputy. Sheriff Roeser sent him up here to look into the goings-on with Jeremy Lugo at the Emperor. I'll let him fill you in on what he's got in mind."

Sage said, "It appears that Lugo is an ambitious sort. Looks like he wants to make his fortune here—and not necessarily by honest hard work. Some things going on, and the kind of company he keeps leads me to believe that he intends to get whatever it is he wants by force, so I'd say Lugo is a threat to Rincon. What I've got in mind is getting in his way.

"He won't like that, so I want some force of my own. Cody and I will be up front, but we'll get our heads handed to us unless we have some help. You're all citizens here, and I'm asking you to volunteer to be deputies. It would be good to have people watching our backs."

A leathery cowboy with grey in his mustache spoke up. "My name's Calvin Call. I nursemaid cows for a livin', but I been through the war, and I'm no stranger to gunplay. I'd volunteer to jest go over there to the Empire and show that bunch out of town. We could probably round up another dozen hands and do it all at once. Maybe apply a little tar and some feathers to help get our point across."

Sage tapped his badge and said, "Mr. Call, I've sworn to uphold the law. You're talking about a vigilante action here. Vigilantes operate outside the law. I won't abide by that. We watch Lugo and his crowd, and if any of them break any laws, we arrest and prosecute. We'll see how much arresting and prosecuting they can take before the rest become upstanding citizens or get the hell out."

A heavyset man dressed in overalls said, "I'm Bill Rogers. I have a farm up the river. Lugo's people seem to have an unholy interest in my place, and it has me a bit nervous. A couple of my friends have disappeared, and I'd like to help out there. I can handle a rifle and shotgun, but I'm no gun hand."

Sage said, "I wouldn't expect any of you take on the likes of Bart Waco by yourselves. In fact, I don't want anyone to put on their badge or confront anyone unless there are at least two of you together. I expect Waco would be downright peaceful and polite if two men had shotguns ready. I know I would be.

"We won't get it done if we go out with guns blazing anyway. That isn't what I want to do. I want to avoid gunfights. Why risk the wrong people getting killed if you don't have to? If a man needs to be taken down, I want him surrounded with no chance to draw. That's part of why I want all the deputies I can get."

A short, wiry cowboy spoke up. "I heard about that shootout in Mesilla, and some more about how you handle yourself with your fists. Sounded like you could take care of anything that came up. When Mr. Summers here invited me over, I was thinking that there wouldn't be much point in being a deputy. But the way you put it, it makes sense to kind of discourage folks from getting violent by having a lot of badges around. I'm Chance Slade, and you can count me in."

Heads nodded all around, and Sage said, "I don't have any badges to hand out yet, but I'll get them soon. I'll go ahead and swear you in tonight, though."

Before Sage could proceed, there was the sound of horses approaching the adobe followed by a knock on the door. Summers opened it up to find three vaqueros outside, complete with tall, wide felt sombreros, short jackets, string ties, and huge spurs on their boots. He spoke in Spanish to invite them in.

A tall, whip-thin man with a large mustache and long sideburns looked around at the gathering and said, "Señor John Sage?"

In Spanish, Sage said, "I'm Sage. Did Benito Alvarez tell you to come?"

"Yes," said the man. "I am Ernesto Robledo. These men are Manuel Vasquez and Pablo Peron. We ride for the San Andres Ranch. Mr. Alvarez spoke with the owner, Mr.

Ortega, who is a friend of his. Mr. Alvarez is also a friend of ours. We enjoy the San Diego and are not happy that Mr. Alvarez is having troubles there. Perhaps we can help. We could come in on Friday and Saturday evenings".

"Very good," said Sage. "How is your English? I would like to include everyone in this conservation."

Robledo replied in heavily accented English, "Our English is not too bad. We are citizens of New Mexico."

Sage had Summers do introductions all around. The fourth deputy candidate in the first group was a sturdy-looking man about Sage's size who worked on one of the nearby ranches named Charlie Rupp. There weren't enough chairs for ten men, so they went out onto the patio behind the adobe, and Summers lit several lamps. The men pulled rounds off a woodpile and sat down. Summers had ten glasses, and he passed them around and filled them with a generous helping of tequila from a clay jug.

Sage outlined the situation and his plans for the newcomers and swore in all but Summers. Summers said his fighting days were over and he would content himself with providing eyes and ears.

With the help of the tequila, Cody Miller displayed a talent for getting the men talking, and by the end of the meeting, everyone was on a first-name basis. Cody thought he'd like to listen to some guitar music and suggested that Robledo, Vasquez, and Peron join him at the San Diego.

Sage, Summers, and the other four new deputies decided to go to the Emperor. As they were leaving the adobe, Miller looked at Sage and said, "That Lupita is really something. I had a near overpowering urge to just scoop her up and carry her off, but I remembered what you told me just in time."

Sage grinned and said, "That thought crossed my mind, too. But Alvarez might have had some objection to that. We want him on our side. If you're interested, you'll have to do it the hard way. But I'll tell you, that woman could take up all of a man's time and then some. And all of his mind. I'd like to have you paying attention to business. I decided not to go that way."

Miller left with the three vaqueros with a bemused look on his face, and Sage headed for the Emperor with the rest.

The Emperor was busy, and they didn't draw much attention when they took a table at the side of the room. But Waco and Sanchez were standing together at the far end of the bar, and they sure drew their attention.

Summers started to order a bottle of tequila and some glasses from a bar girl but hesitated and looked inquiringly at Sage. Sage told him that nobody but him was on duty yet. Sage was still feeling a slight buzz from the drink earlier and asked her if she could manage to rustle up some coffee. She said she could put a pot on the stove in the back, but it would take a while.

The patrons in the saloon were a mix of farmers, cowboys, miners, and two young soldiers at a table next to theirs. A piano player was making a lot of noise without seeming to manage any particular tune. Sage preferred to listen to a guitar. Three women were working the crowd, occasionally heading upstairs with a customer in tow. Two other bartenders were assisting rat face.

After an hour, Sage was about to call it a night when something said to the soldiers from the table on the other side of them caused one of the soldiers to jump up and swear at the speaker, who also jumped up. A ripple of silence spread out from the two men as they squared off.

The civilian was a lot larger than the soldier. In a low voice, Summers said, "That's one of Lugo's boys, Saul Snead—a real troublemaker."

Sage looked over at Waco and Sanchez, but they weren't moving. The soldier started swinging but didn't have much luck getting through the beefy arms of his opponent. Then Snead threw two punches that doubled the soldier over and exploded his nose. He clubbed the soldier in the side of the head with enough force to drop him cold and proceeded to kick him. The other soldier looked to be mighty scared, but he jumped up and started for Snead. The other three men at Snead's table jumped up, and the soldier backed off.

Waco and Sanchez still weren't moving, so Sage told his companions to watch his back and stood up to face Snead. He said, "That's enough; he's through."

Snead's blood was up, and he swung a big fist at Sage's face. Sage guided it past his head with the heel of his left hand, spun around, and landed a crushing back fist under Snead's jaw, lifting him up on his toes and spinning him completely around. Sage followed up with a front kick to the jaw, which knocked him unconscious before he landed on the table.

Snead's three companions weighed in, and with a flurry of kicks, jabs, and chops with the edges of his hands, Sage took all of four seconds to lay all three of them out on the floor.

There was a stunned silence in the room for a few moments, and then it erupted into a bedlam of hoots and shouts, including from his own table.

Sage snapped at them, "Watch the room!"

A bearded miner yelled out, "Whooee, we've got a new deputy in town. How-de-doo!"

Bart Waco walked up to Sage and said, "Hell of a job of keeping the peace."

"Didn't see any laws being broken," replied Sage. "You want peace in here, you tell your boys to keep it. In fact, I thought that was your job. Where the hell were you?"

"Thought I'd watch the deputy at work," said Waco. "Sure did. I don't think I'll be throwing any punches at you. Just blow your head off if it comes to it."

Sage looked at him evenly and said, "A couple of those gents have bones broken. You might want to get them to a doc."

He turned back to his table and motioned for the men to follow him outside. On the walk, he said, "Since you don't have badges yet, you weren't on duty tonight, but when you are, I need you to keep your mind on business, no matter what. Consider the Emperor to be hostile territory and stay alert. Not too much to drink. If you all hadn't been there, one of Lugo's hard cases might just have decided to end it and taken a shot at me. Probably not tonight. They aren't really riled up yet, but they will be before long."

Cal Call spoke up and said, "I seen what you meant, that you'd be up front. That was the up frontest thing I ever saw. Whew! We'll sure watch your back, but it'll be hard not watching your play."

"Amen," muttered a couple of others.

-35-

Monday morning Sage was doing exercises in his office when a stage up from El Paso and Mesilla rolled in and stopped in front of the stage station down the street. Sage hoped that a dozen deputy badges were on it. As he stepped out on the walk he noticed that the left lead horse was missing from the team.

As he approached, there were some shouts, and several bystanders ran to the stage. The driver was yelling, "We've been held up! Where's the sheriff?"

"Right here," said Sage.

The driver said, "Got a man killed here. Shotgun rider."

The station keeper and relief driver had come around from the corral, and the station keeper and Sage climbed up next to the driver and saw a man curled up on the floor in front of the driver's seat lying in a pool of blood.

"He sure is dead," said Sage. "What happened?"

"Got jumped about five miles out. Ambush. Two shots out of nowhere, and the shotgun rider and one of the lead horses were dead. Four men stepped out of the brush and had us covered. Hell of a mess, what with the rest of the team spooked and jumping around all tangled up. Lucky there weren't any legs broke. We were moving slow up a grade, or we would have been wrecked.

"The bandits lined us up and took everything we had on us and strongbox out of the boot. Shot the lock and cleaned it out. I was bringing the payroll for the Twin Peaks mine to the bank here."

Three shaken men had climbed out of the stage and were standing by it talking to the onlookers.

Sage said, "I'll get you a horse. I want you to show me where it happened. I don't expect they headed down the road to Mesilla. Which way did they go?"

"They headed toward the hills to the east."

"What's your name?" asked Sage.

"Isaac Hooker," replied the driver.

Hooker studied Sage skeptically. "Know anything about tracking?"

"Yes, I do," said Sage. "How do you want the body of your shotgun rider handled? Where's he from?"

"El Paso," said Hooker. "Best bury him here. Company will pay for it."

The station keeper said, "We've got a horse here that Isaac can use."

One of the onlookers was the owner of the general store, Milo Hawkins. Sage jumped down and walked over to him.

"Mr. Hawkins, would you give me a hand? I need you to get the names of the passengers and where I can locate them. I expect I'll be needing them to testify in court after a while. Please make a list of what they lost."

Hawkins said, "I'll do that. Think you can catch those bandits?"

"Yes," replied Sage. He gathered up the passengers and Hawkins led them off to his store.

Cody Miller appeared, and Sage explained briefly what was going on. "We're going after them. Get the undertaker over here. Then get your horse. We may be out a day or two. Maybe more."

A few of the bystanders volunteered to join the posse. Sage addressed them and said, "Thank you, men, but we don't need a posse on this one. Cody and I will earn our keep."

Hooker and the station keeper took the body into the office and came back out.

Sage said, "By the way, did you have a package for me?"

"Matter of fact, I do," replied Hooker, and he walked back to the boot and pulled out a bulging brown envelope.

While Hooker and the other driver pulled the stage around behind the station to change teams, Sage went to the telegraph office and sent Roeser a short message:

STAGE HELD UP
IN PURSUIT

Sage went to his office and opened the envelope. It contained a dozen badges, and a note:

Had to get these made up. What are you doing up there, building an army?

Sage saddled and packed Smokey and led him around front, where Miller soon joined him. His packing included half a dozen pigging strings. While they waited for Hooker Miller said, "Sure we don't need a posse?"

Sage said, "Don't know them. Don't know how they'd handle themselves. I don't want to have to worry about them. I learned something about posses a while back when I was in one in Laredo. That posse got the sheriff killed. If we get into a fight, I'll just sic you on 'em."

Hooker led them to the scene of the holdup. Sage quizzed Hooker about the description of the robbers. They had all worn bandanas over their faces, but Hooker gave a good description of sizes, shapes, and clothing. He also commented that one of the men had a long scar on the left side of his forehead.

Sage rode around and studied tracks for a while. Then he said, "That will do, Mr. Hooker. Thank you for your help. I'll be getting in touch with you through the stage line."

The tracks were pretty plain, and the two men followed them at a fast clip. When they approached the hills, Sage reined up and said, "Three riders came in from the north here yesterday and headed up the valley. No tracks coming down, and I don't know of anything of interest out this way, so I believe that we're going to have seven men to deal with."

Late in the afternoon, while they were resting their horses, Sage said, "We're only a few minutes behind them. Under a mile. I don't want to catch up to them just yet."

Cody said, "How the hell do you know that?"

Sage replied, "It's there in the tracks. They haven't been traveling fast. They aren't interested in covering a lot of distance. I think they're intending to ambush whoever comes after them. They might have a good spot picked out.

I wish I'd been able to spend a couple of weeks scouting the country around Rincon. I've got to do that before long."

"But how do you know how fast they're traveling and where they are?"

Sage said, "When I was growing up I spent a whole lot of time learning to be a tracker. I'd follow someone on horseback close enough to watch him and see what the tracks looked like at different paces. Then I'd go back and look at them again after an hour, again in two hours, and so on. Then I'd do all that again and again in all kinds of terrain and weather.

"I did all that with a man on foot. For weeks at a time.

"I'd watch a pile of horse shit for days to see how it changed over time. I'd do that when it was hot, and again when it was cold, and when it was wet. Same with human shit.

"I learned to follow a man on foot who didn't want to be followed. You try to figure out where he wants to go. Something like an overturned pebble, a green leaf on the ground, or a bent twig is enough to let you know you're getting it right. I had training in all that from the best."

"Who are the best?" asked Miller.

"Apaches."

Miller stared at him a moment. Then he said, "That brown hide of yours—you got some Apache in you?"

"My mother. She was a Chiricahua. Me and my blood brother spent about half our time with the Chiricahuas."

Sage watched Miller as he chewed on that and was pleased that he showed no sign of disapproval.

Sage turned Smokey back on the trail and set off at a walk, studying the terrain ahead carefully.

Just before sundown Sage said, "I think we hadn't better push it any further. They probably won't be traveling in the dark. Let's tie up here and eat. I'll scout up the valley on foot when it gets full dark.

After they had eaten a cold meal, Miller pulled out a short cigar, and Sage held up a hand. "No smoke. The breeze is blowing up the valley. That could be smelled for a mile. And no loud noises."

Sage pulled a pair of knee-high moccasins out of his saddlebags and pulled them on.

Miller said, "Where'd you get those?"

"Made them up when I was in Mesilla. Hard to be quiet in the dark wearing boots."

The two stretched out for a few hours. Sage learned something about life in Kentucky, and he answered a lot of questions about Apaches. Sage dozed a bit and then got up.

"I'll take a look up the valley; then I'll come back. Hold Smokey's nose for a while. He might take to whinnying when he realizes he's getting left behind."

"Jesus," said Miller "It's dark as a cave. How you going find your way around?"

"What do you mean?" replied Sage. "The stars are out. Any more light than that and I'd get nervous about being seen."

Sage disappeared into the dark.

Two hours later, Sage touched Miller on a foot. He snapped awake and reached for his gun.

"Easy, Cody."

Miller saw that a half moon had come up over the horizon to the east, and he was able to make out Sage in the dark.

"They're up there a little over a mile. It's straight all the way. If we'd gone any farther they'd have spotted us. They're camped in some rocks in a natural little fort that overlooks the valley. They had a sentry, but I got in close. Here's what we're going to do."

-36-

Cole Bailey woke up at first light and checked the sentry, Tom Abbot. The dumb bastard was sitting with his back to a boulder sound asleep. Bailey walked over and kicked him in the side. Then he rustled up a fire and put on a pot of coffee. The other five were starting to stir awake when Bailey filled a tin cup and lifted it to his lips.

The cup exploded in his face, splashing it with scalding coffee as he heard the roar of a rifle close by. He blindly reached for his belt gun but discovered that he didn't have much of a hand left to reach with.

A voice rang out off to his left side from the slope above the circle of rocks. "You're covered. Get your hands on top of your heads—now!"

Still being dumb, Abbot swung his rifle toward the shooter. Two rifles rang out this time, the one from above and another from rocks up a slope a little above their level down in the valley. Abbot took one in the back and another in the head.

As he blinked his eyes clear and raised his hands, Bailey saw that three of his men were sitting up in their blankets with their hands on their heads but that two had pulled their revolvers from somewhere and were looking around wildly for a target. The rifles spoke again, and one of the men took both bullets. That convinced the other one to drop his gun and slap both hands on top of his head.

When Bailey realized that the mangled hand was bleeding all over him, he moved it out to the side and held it higher hoping the shooters would cut him some slack.

The first shooter stood up and approached. When he got close, he shifted the rifle to his left hand and drew his handgun. He drew it awful quick. He must have waltzed right past that goddamn Abbot while he slept to get to where he had been.

The second shooter scrambled up from below with his rifle held ready. Both the shooters were wearing stars. Jesus, there were only the two of them. One of them had to be the new deputy up from Mesilla that Waco had wanted taken out. Waco had told him about the shootout down there. He had said the man was real trouble and figured they had better get him sooner rather than later.

Sage lined up the five surviving bandits, made them lie spread-eagle on the ground, and held his gun on them while Miller checked them for weapons. Sage said, "You're all under arrest for robbery and murder. Anyone does anything that scares us, we're taking you in dead."

He had two of the outlaws use their bandanas to bandage Bailey's hand. He showed Bailey where the big artery ran in his upper arm and had him keep it up high while he maintained pressure on the artery with his left thumb.

Sage picked out the least intelligent-looking one and asked casually, "Does Lugo pay you wages or a cut of the take?"

The man said, "A cut...." Then he snapped his mouth closed.

Sage said, "What's your name?"

The man just glared at him, and Sage said, "Not too proud of it, I guess. I can see why."

The bandit flared, "Billy Fine!"

While Miller had the prisoners take their spurs off, Sage located the cash in the strongbox and the items taken from the stage passengers. Then he had the prisoners saddle their horses one at a time, leaving the bridles off. After each horse was saddled, Sage had the prisoner lead his horse back and forth in front of him.

One of them said, "What are you doing?" But Sage just told him to button it.

Sage had Fine and another prisoner load the bodies of the two dead on their horses, belly down, and tie them in place with the pigging strings he had brought along. They both gagged at the sight of Abbot's body. The bullet in the head had made both eyes bulge clear out of their sockets. They gagged some more at the smell of the shit-filled pants. The horse shied at the scent of blood, and they had a time getting him on it, but they got it done.

Sage tied the lead rope of each horse to the tail of the horse in front of it with the two burdened horses at the rear and got each man mounted. Since the horses were tied in line and without reins, Sage didn't think he needed to tie their hands.

After they got the five men mounted, Sage pulled Miller aside, and in a low voice he said, "We're going to take them down to Mesilla. I don't want them anywhere near the Emperor. I don't want us to have to spend all our time guarding them. Lugo might have a mind to either break them out or kill them. We can make Mesilla before nightfall."

Sage pointed out two of the men and said, "Those two and one of the dead were the ones that rode up here yesterday. The rest did the stage."

It dawned on Miller why Sage had held the little parades: he'd wanted to study the tracks!

Sage picked up the lead rope of the first horse and started walking down the valley with Miller walking behind. After picking up their horses, Sage continued to lead the procession down to the Rio Grande and turned downriver.

Bailey said, "Hey, where the hell are we going?"

"Mesilla," replied Sage. "You got some objection?"

Bailey opened and closed his mouth a couple of times, but nothing came out.

As they rode into Mesilla, Sage saw the barber sitting in front of his shop and stopped. "Evenin', Lucas. Got some business here for you. Might as well just untie the last two horses and take them."

Lucas walked over and looked at the bodies. He took off his hat, scratched his head, and said, "Yep, they sure was killed."

People along the street had come over, and Sage asked one of them to get Doc Carroll over to the sheriff's office. They continued on with Sage hoping that Roeser was in.

He was. Roeser came out of his office as Sage was getting the bandits off their horses. He drew his gun and casually held it down at his side. He looked at the prisoners and then at Sage and said, "I figured these gents would rue the day they robbed a stage in your part of the country. Let's get them upstairs."

After installing the prisoners in their cells, the lawmen returned to the office. Roeser said, "You sent the posse home?

Miller said, "John needed a posse like he needed a third leg. We took care of the business."

Sage said, "This here is Cody Miller, lately of Taos and Kentucky. Sanchez caught him for me and I put him to work. He works good."

After a pause, Roeser decided not to get into that and shook Miller's hand. "John said in a letter that he'd hired you. Welcome aboard."

He looked at Sage and said, "You caught up with them near here?"

"No," said Sage. "Up closer to Rincon. But they're Lugo's people. I was afraid Lugo might try to get them busted out or maybe killed. Didn't want to spend all my time guarding against that."

Roeser thought for a moment. "So, I'll spend all my time guarding them. Thank you not too much. How do you know they're Lugo's people? Can we nail Lugo's hide to the wall for ordering the holdup?"

Sage said, "I haven't seen them around the Emperor, but one of them made a little slip. We can't nail Lugo unless one of them confesses and agrees to testify to that. Not too likely. I could get one of them telling us whatever we'd like to hear in less than five minutes, but I don't think he'd repeat it in court, and I don't think any judge would much appreciate that kind of confession.

"I think it will be less likely that Lugo will make a move down here. I think it would be very likely if I was holding those folks in Rincon. Sorry about that, but maybe you could get some extra help here."

Roeser said, "I'm not faulting you. Judge Bennet is up in Santa Fe. He'll be back in two weeks. I expect that the county will be willing to let me hire a couple of guards for at least that amount of time, and I'll get a deputy over from Las Cruces. We'll have Isaac Hooker and his shotgun rider, Shorty Williams, for witnesses along with the passengers."

Sage replied, "We won't have Williams. He was shot out of hand when they stopped the stage. They stopped it by shooting one of the lead horses."

Roeser shook his head and said, "Goddamn! I knew Shorty. Good man. That sure changes the picture". He gestured upstairs with his thumb. "We'll be hanging those bastards."

Sage said, "Three of them. Four pulled off the holdup, and three others were waiting at the spot where we caught up with them. They would have come in the day before. One of them is dead, and so is one of the holdup crew. I dropped them off with Lucas Riley on the way into town."

Roeser stared at Sage and then said, "OK. Fill me in on everything on the holdup and the capture. I don't suppose you know which ones did which?"

"I know. I brought them all in because I didn't want two of them running loose while I was bringing in the rest. We'd better cut those two loose. They didn't commit any crime."

Roeser rubbed his forehead and said, "That's a fact. How do you know which two weren't at the holdup?"

Sage replied, "Horse shoes all wear differently. When I saw the day-old tracks, I looked at them. They had some distinctions. When I got the riders and horses matched up after we caught them, two men were on horses that had gotten there the day before."

"You can tell when tracks are a day old?" asked Roeser skeptically.

"Pretty well," said Sage. "And I can tell when horse shit is a day old even easier."

"Were the bandits wearing masks?" asked Roeser.

"Bandanas over their noses."

"Well," said Roeser, "If the three we put on trial all claim they weren't at the holdup, you might have to spend some time explaining all that to the judge and jury."

Sage said, "I'll bet Isaac Hooker could pick all the ones wearing bandanas out of a crowd. Maybe the passengers could, too. One by the name of Fine upstairs has a big scar on his forehead. Hooker described that."

Before Sage could continue, Doctor Carroll stepped into the office carrying a black bag. He said, "I was told you had a wounded prisoner."

"How bad was that hand?" Roeser asked Sage.

Sage looked at Carroll and said, "You're going to have to trim off what little bit is left."

"In that case," said Carroll, "You had better bring him down and over to my office."

Roeser stood up and said, "I'll do that. John, point out the ones that weren't at the holdup. I'll turn them out. Then you and Cody go get something to eat and come back in the morning. You can get a room at the Catamount. Bill it to me."

"Maggie got that room rented yet?" Sage asked.

"No, she doesn't, and I expect she'd like to see you."

Sage said, "I think I'll go by and visit after we eat. We've got the stuff the bandits stole on our horses. They had the payroll for the Twin Peaks mine and what they took off the passengers. Hold on a minute and I'll bring it in."

Roeser looked at the bundles of bills and odds and ends that belonged to the passengers and said, "I'd better hang on to the belongings here for evidence. You can take the payroll up to Rincon after I count it for the record. I assume the loose bills and coins belonged to the passengers, but we'll keep track. You know how to get a hold of the passengers?"

"I had a man getting their names, where they could be located, and a list of what was taken from them. Haven't seen it yet."

Roeser said, "Let's get the wounded man and the other two down here."

The two extra prisoners claimed their horses, bridles, spurs, and guns and rode off. Sage and Miller were about to take the outlaws' three remaining horses to the livery, but Sage stopped and beckoned Roeser to step outside.

"Might be a good idea to take the prisoners' shirts for evidence before the trial. They are all three kind of distinctive. They were wearing them when we caught them, and they were probably wearing them during the holdup. Identifying them in court might carry a little weight."

"Couldn't hurt," replied Roeser.

The went back in, and Roeser and Doc Carroll left with Bailey.

Sage turned to Miller and said, "Let's go to the Catamount. We can get a decent bowl of chili there. I expect that I'll spend the night at Maggie Morris' place. That's where I was living when I was here.

After eating, Sage left Miller at the mercy of a lot of curious patrons in the Catamount and rode Smoky over to Maggie's.

At the door, John was startled when Maggie threw her arms around him and said, "John! Good to see you. What brings you down here?"

Sage said, "Business. Just handed off some gents that robbed the stage up near Rincon yesterday to Jim. They had the payroll for the Twin Peaks mine, and they'd killed the shotgun rider, Shorty Williams."

"Good Lord!" exclaimed Maggie. "Come on in and sit. You had anything to eat?"

"Yep. Bowl of chili over at the Catamount. Theirs sure don't beat yours."

"Of course not," said Maggie. "Why in tarnation didn't you come over here?"

"Had a deputy with me. He took a room at the Catamount."

Maggie said, "Well, I hope you're staying here. Room's still empty, and I'd love to have some company."

Sage said, "I was kind of hoping I could. Been missing your conversation. I'll go and put Smokey in your corral."

Sage spent the rest of the evening filling Maggie in on doings in Rincon, the details of the holdup, and the pursuit of the bandits. Maggie kept him talking until he held up his hand and said, "Maggie, I've had a long day. I've got to turn in. I'd appreciate it if you'd let me sleep a bit late in the morning."

He slept until nine. Maggie fixed him a breakfast of eggs scrambled with jalapenos and fried potatoes. Maggie commented, "Now that I can let the chickens run loose, they're doing a pretty good job of laying eggs. And there's more chickens. Been selling eggs and chickens around town.

"Sounds like you've got your hands full up there in Rincon. Jim says something about being grateful that you're up there about every time I see him."

"He's not too grateful right now," said Sage. "I just dropped a load on him. Lugo is going to be mighty worried that his boys might tie him to the holdup. He overstepped a bit pulling something like that close to home. He might well try to break them out or kill them to keep them from talking."

Maggie fretted about that for a few moments and then said, "I wish you could take them somewhere else."

Sage's eyes widened. "Now that's a thought," he said. "I've got to get over to the office. Thanks for the good bed, good food, and good company."

-37-

Cody Miller got to Roeser's office at nine. Sage wasn't there yet. Roeser quizzed him about the capture, and Miller related the details.

Roeser said, "I'm not that good at tracking or night scouting. I'd have taken a posse, rode right up that valley, and probably gotten shot to rags. I expect they were figuring on doing that to you."

"He uses that Indian in him," said Cody. "Uses it good. But he sure don't shoot like an Indian—or fight like one. The man's a demon in a fight. Last Friday night he took on four of Lugo's toughs in the Emperor, and they were all laid out cold on the floor in not any more than six seconds, according to Vern Summers. Vern said he'd never seen anyone fight like that. Couldn't hardly believe what he'd seen. I've been crying in my beer that I'd missed it. I was over at the San Diego with three of our new volunteer deputies."

Roeser grinned and said, "I've seen John in action. I'm not all that surprised—but four men? Wheu! He's lucky nobody put a bullet in him while he was fighting."

"Not all that much luck involved," said Miller. "Aside from Vern, he had four deputies with him. Only they didn't have badges yet. John told them to watch his back and went at it."

Roeser sat back in his chair and rubbed the side of his head. "The light dawns. I was wondering what he was doing asking for twelve badges. He doesn't just use his fists and guns. Got a damned good head on his shoulders. Thinks ahead of things."

Miller said, "I'll tell you, sheriff, I've got a few years on John, and I've seen some elephants, but I feel like a tenderfoot kid when I'm around him. We had a meeting with Jeremy Lugo and Bart Waco. Those two are pretty formidable, but John told them how things stood and didn't take any of their guff. Not a bit."

In a low voice Roeser said, "I wrote my brother a letter, telling him I owed him. I'm going to write him again."

Doc Carroll came in the door and said, “Mornin’, Jim. I need to check Bailey’s hand.”

Roeser saw Sage approaching from across the street and sent Miller up with the doctor.

Sage sat down and said, “Jim, how’s your relations with the sheriff over in Deming?”

“Hector Lopez? Pretty good. We’ve worked back and forth some. Why do you ask?”

“Maggie said something that got me thinking. If Lugo’s boys show up after the bunch upstairs, I’m thinking it would be a good thing if they weren’t here. That would sort of defuse the situation. How about we put them on the train over there and bring ‘em back when the court convenes?”

Roeser snapped his fingers and said, “By damn! I was just saying you had a head on your shoulders. We’ll do that. The westbound train comes through Las Cruces tomorrow morning. I’ll telegraph Lopez. You can take them over, and Cody can take the payroll up to Rincon. The railroad doesn’t charge us for using it. You’ll have a day layover until the eastbound train runs.”

Sage said, “I think I’ll take Smokey along to look around some there. I’ll tell you about how we got the bandits.”

Roeser held up his hand, “Cody already did. He’s upstairs with Doc Carroll. Nice piece of work.

“Robbing the stage where they did, and set up like they were, they probably figured to take you out in the bargain. In fact, that was probably the main objective. They’ll have to figure again, and I’m sure they will. Better be careful.”

Sage gave Roeser a level look. “I’m careful.”

Doc Carroll and Miller came down the stairs and pulled up a couple of chairs. Carroll looked at Sage and said, “I told Bailey that he was lucky that he hadn’t bled out. Artery in his wrist was cut. He said you showed him how to use the pressure point in his arm. How’d you happen to know about that?”

Sage said, “Doc, I know about every artery, every muscle, every bone, and every nerve in the body. And I know the best ways to damage every one. Unfortunately, I don't know the best ways to fix them for the most part. But I knew that one."

The three men stared at him. Carroll said, "That sounds rather chilling. You've studied anatomy and physiology?"

Sage replied, "I'm not sure what those are. I've studied how to defeat a man using only my hands and feet under a master. Studied hard for two years at least half a day everyday."

Sage grinned ruefully, "You know? I know the names of all those parts, but not in English. So I couldn't explain them to anybody."

Carroll looked at Roeser and said, "I'm glad he's wearing a badge."

"Amen," said Roeser.

Carroll turned back to Sage and said, "If I might ask, Mr. Sage, what language?"

"Japanese," replied Sage. "The Ryukyu dialect. I was stranded on Okinawa for some time when my ship went down in a typhoon."

Carroll blinked. "My word. You've gotten around. I'd like to hear more about that. Perhaps we could have lunch together?"

Sage said, "Looks like I'll be in town all day."

He glanced at Roeser, who nodded. He continued, "Sure, doc. Where do you eat?"

"The Dona Ana Cantina is as good as any. See you there at noon."

The doctor left, and Miller said, "Be in town all day?"

Roeser said, "John will be. He's moving the prisoners to Deming tomorrow. Don't tell anyone that up in Rincon. You head up there now, and get the payroll in the bank.

Miller said, "OK, I'll light out. By the way, a fellow by the name of Smith came into the Catamount last night looking for me or John. Said he was with the Mesilla Crier. Pumped me pretty good about the holdup and the capture. I hope we didn't have any secrets there."

Roeser sat back and thought for a few moments. "Bob Smith owns the Crier. No, no secrets up to this point, but that will make it harder to get an impartial jury. I'd just rather not have Lugo know where we are taking the prisoners for as long as possible. I'm glad you let me know."

"You say anything about the bandits being Lugo's people?" Sage asked.

"No," replied Miller. "Couldn't really back it up."

"That's good thinking," said Sage. "We don't need to be stirring things up that don't need to be stirred yet."

-38-

The train from Deming pulled into Las Cruces in the late afternoon. When Sage got off, he saw two Apache scouts sitting on the top pole of the holding corral watching the comings and goings. They were wearing blue army shirts and campaign hats. Their shirts hung loosely over their long white breechclouts, and their moccasins came up to the knees of their bare legs. Probably from Fort Seldon, he thought.

He walked back and unloaded Smokey from a boxcar, slipped his Winchester into the saddle scabbard, and led the grulla past the scouts.

As he went by them, he said in the Apache tongue, "It is not every day that I see the Tinneh wearing blue shirts."

The scouts sat up straight, and one of them said in the same language, "It is not every day that a lawman speaks to us in our language."

Sage tied Smokey to a hitching rail, rummaged in his saddlebags, and pulled three cigars out of a new box. He drew his knife and whittled the ends off the cigars as he approached the Apaches.

He stopped in front of them and said, "This must be a special day. Let's smoke on it."

He handed each of them a cigar and matches, lit his own cigar, and climbed up on the pole beside them. They smoked in contemplative silence for a while, savoring the smoke.

Still speaking in Apache, the scout next to him said, "How is it that you speak the language of the Tinneh?"

"I have Apache blood. I grew up with a Chiricahua band near the San Pedro in Arizona, but I haven't been in that country for eight years. I no longer know where my family and friends are. I take it by your moccasins that you are White Mountain."

Both of the scouts grunted their assent, and the speaker said, "Most of the Tinneh are on reservations now. The Chiricahuas and White Mountain people are all on the San Carlos Reservation."

They were silent for a while, and then Sage said, "Two of my friends were Hook Nose and Nantaje. Do you know of them?"

The scout next to Sage said, "Hook Nose has passed on. He fought the blue coats of General Crook and was killed in battle."

He sighed and then went on. "We fought well, but there were too many soldiers wherever we went. Crook followed us everywhere. He had many Apache scouts, and we could not lose them. We had no time to hunt or gather food. The soldiers burned our corn. We could not bake mescal for three days without the soldiers coming. Crook had hundreds of mules carrying food, so the soldiers never got hungry. We forgot what it was like not to be hungry."

The other Apache said, "Crook could never have found us without those scouts. We were defeated by our own people."

After a series of whistles, the engine roared to life with a cloud of smoke. And venting steam, the train chuffed out of the station.

Sage mulled over his thoughts until the noise receded. Then he said, "Americans do not live in bands or tribes. They are all the same band, even if they live thousands of miles apart and do not know each other. If people who are not Americans attack one American, they have to fight them all. A few Americans may help them, but very few. That makes the Americans very powerful. The Tinneh have no loyalty beyond their own band, so even if they are better warriors, they are weak."

After some time the first Apache said, "What you say is true."

"The other one, Nantaje, is with the police."

"With what?" asked Sage.

The scout said, "At San Carlos, the laws of the reservation are enforced by police. All the police are Tinneh."

"That is interesting," said Sage. "I mourn for Hook Nose. He and Nantaje were blood brothers to Strong Arm and me. We trained to be warriors together."

The two scouts jerked straight up and stared at Sage. One said, "By what name are you called?"

Among Apaches, asking someone their name was considered to be very impolite, but the man had been startled into asking.

"Sees in the Night," replied Sage.

The scout's eyes widened, and the questioner said, "I know of you! The tale of the vengeance of Sees in the Night and Strong arm has been told many times in the rancherias. Uklenni and those with him were strong warriors. All were amazed that they were defeated by two very young warriors. We know how five were killed, but we do not know how you were able to defeat Uklenni, Strong Bow, Blue Hawk, and Slow Foot."

While they finished their cigars Sage described the ruse with the Gila monster and the short final fight.

"I did not know their names," said Sage. "I only know that they killed our parents and sisters. We lived in peace with the Chiricahuas and belonged to a band. To lose them to Apaches was a bitter thing."

The scout said, "Uklenni had not been that way before. The Rio San Pedro. He did not know the Chiricahuas there. It was not a fortunate thing."

"No," said Sage, "it was not fortunate. It set me on a different path. Perhaps a better one. I don't know yet.

"How is it with the Tinneh now?"

The scout shook his head sadly. "We cannot fight the Americans anymore. We would be content to live as in the past, without fighting them, but they want us to become like white men. They put all the children in schools and teach them the ways of the Americans and the Americans' religion. They are told to forget their language.

"The rules of the whites are strange, and the children are not learning the rules of the Tinneh, so many have no rules to live by. They are confused and lost. They do not see how they can make their way in the white man's world, and they are forgetting how to live as Tinneh.

"Many warriors have taken to whisky, and now they are no longer warriors. They are not even men.

"General Crook has gone to the north to fight the Sioux. He was a fair man who respected the Tinneh. He honored the treaties and made sure we had food and blankets. Now that he is gone, the Tinneh are starving again. The Indian agents and contractors are stealing most everything that Washington sends out.

"The contractors in Tucson do not want peace. That would end their business to be ended by any peace. We hear they have friends in Washington who work against any efforts to bring peace.

"Nantaje and his police are busy keeping the young men on the reservation. They have been successful so far, but Geronimo has been gathering followers, and I think he will take them out. He is one bad Apache, but I am tempted to join him. The soldiers do not respect us. Call us 'red niggers.'"

"I have heard of Geronimo," said Sage, "He is a Chiricahua, but he operated mostly in Mexico and New Mexico. I've never seen him. I think that going out with him would be a dead end. You have seen how strong the Americans are. You would not last long."

"The scout said, "Yes, but I would die a warrior, a man. I feel shame for what I am doing now."

"Are you good at what you do?" asked Sage.

"Yes."

"Then you should feel no shame," said Sage. "You do not need to feel the insults. That would be respecting those who insult you. What do you care what they think? I would be surprised if the soldiers that know you don't respect you."

The scout looked at Sage and said, "The ones who make the insults are not the ones I ride with."

Sage said, "If you feel good about yourself, that is all that counts."

Sage was quiet for a while. Then he said, "The Americans will not teach the Tinneh children in the schools how to feel good about themselves. They wouldn't know how.

"The schools will teach the ways of the whites, but the children will always know that they aren't white. They will know that they are Tinneh, but they won't know how to live as Tinneh or what the Apache values are. Every Apache I've ever known had much higher standards of honesty than many of the whites I've met.

"The traditional stories that are told to children in the rancherias provide far more instruction in how a life should be lived than the white man's Bible. Some of the stories in that are good, but many are terrible, and they are confusing.

Sage tilted his Stetson back on his head and rubbed his forehead. "I am afraid that the Tinneh are going to be left with nothing."

After a few moments the scout said softly, "What can we do?"

Sage thought about that for a while and replied, "Learn all the ways of the Americans that you can. But don't forget the ways of the Tinneh.

"The whites have feared Indians for a very long time. At least a couple hundred years. It's the nature of people to hate what they fear, and they aren't going to forget that fear and hate for a long time. Not in our lifetimes. All you can do is live in a way that makes you feel good about yourselves.

"Scouting for the army is a good thing. Keep on being good at it."

The scout thought that over and then said, "Sees in the Night, I believe that what you are saying is wise. I will think on it."

It was starting to get dark, and Jim Roeser rode down the street to the depot. He did a double take when he spotted Sage and the Apaches sitting on the corral pole. He rode over.

"Thought you'd be on that train, John. You know these scouts?"

"I do now," replied Sage. "We were talking about going out on the warpath. You whites have been getting too full of yourselves."

Startled, the two scouts sat up straight and shook with repressed laughter. One of them pointed at Roeser and said in a serious tone, "Can this be our first scalp?"

Sage said, "Well, it would be a start, but he doesn't have a lot of hair, and he wouldn't pay me any more."

The scouts and Sage broke into laughter. After a hesitation, Roeser joined in.

The three jumped to the ground, and one of the scouts turned to Sage and said in Apache, "I am Blue Sky, and this is Red Feather. We are pleased that you have spoken with us, and the smokes were good. We will be at Fort Seldon for some time, and we would welcome you there.

"We came in with some soldiers who went to the saloons. We wanted to watch the fire wagon. We will ride back with them in the morning."

Red Feather spoke up and said, "The soldiers will probably need us to show them where the fort is in the morning."

They chuckled some more, and Sage unhitched Smokey and rode back to Mesilla with Roeser.

As they started out Roeser said, "Never seen an Apache laugh before. Didn't know they ever did."

"You haven't spent much time with Apaches, then," Sage said. "They have as much a sense of humor as we do. Maybe more."

-39-

It was dark when Sage got back to Rincon, and he stopped off at the Pot Belly for a steak. His reception there was a lot warmer than it had been when he had first pinned on the badge. A couple of men congratulated him for capturing the bandits, so he knew the word was around. The waitress was all smiles.

He found Miller at the office. He was studying the summaries of the county and territorial laws that Roeser had given him.

Sage said, "I'll bet the stage company was glad to get that payroll back."

"You'd win the bet," said Miller. "Caused quite a stir when I brought it in. Ran into Waco just after. He's one smug son of a bitch, but he didn't look too smug when he saw me. He looked like someone that had just seen a ghost. Didn't say anything; he just kept going. A little later, I saw those two we let go head over to the Emperor, so I guess they let Waco and Lugo know what happened."

Sage said, "Cody, I think I'll ride out for a while, take a look around the country, and visit some farms and ranches. Maybe be out a week or a little more. I think you can hold down the fort. I'll leave Monday morning."

It was Friday evening. The four Anglo deputies came in. Sage gave them their badges and asked them to drift over to the Emperor. He told them that he and Cody would stop by later.

After they went out, Miller said, "Looked kind of proud of themselves when they put those badges on. Had a couple of others come by that were interested in being deputies, too. Seemed to think that working for you would be a good thing. Not sure we should pick up anyone that foolish."

Sage grinned and said, "Obviously, they were men of intelligence and discernment. I'd like to have Lugo's people seeing badges everywhere they look. If we see them this weekend, I'll put them on. Let's go over to the San Diego. I haven't seen Alvarez for a while."

Sage put three more badges in his pocket in case the vaqueros showed up, and the two men walked down to the saloon at the other end of the town.

Sage looked around the room as he stepped in. He was surprised to see three tough-looking Anglos sitting at a table by the side wall. As he understood it, Anglos didn't go in there much, if ever.

Alvarez flashed a grin when he saw Sage and Miller, and he hustled down the bar toward them.

"Mr. Sage, I am very glad to see you! I was about to send someone to look for you. Those three gringos over there have been here before. They are troublemakers. They have been making rude comments to Lupita, and I think that Robledo and Vasquez are about to start something with them."

Robledo and Vasquez, two of Sage's new deputies, had been poised to stand up, but they relaxed slightly when they saw Sage and Miller.

Sage looked at Miller and said, "Stay here. I think I'll introduce myself."

Sage walked to the middle of the room, across from the gringos where there was a clear space between him and the men. He turned back so that his right side was toward the table. As soon as he stopped, he reached across his middle and pulled the big knife out of the scabbard on the left side of his gun belt and threw it at the roof support post behind the table. While the knife was in the air, he drew and fired, hitting the post a foot above the table and six inches from the nearest man.

As the knife thumped into the post he kept the gun leveled at the three shocked men. They had all jumped but hadn't reach for their guns, and they slowly put their hands on the table. Miller had drawn and was aiming at them with his Colt held in both hands. Sage glanced over his shoulder and saw that Robledo and Vasquez had also drawn.

Sage looked at the man closest to the knife and said, "Pull it out."

The man reached over and yanked on the handle. "Holy shit!" he said. "Knife's stuck right in the bullet hole!"

Sage said, "Lay it on the table. You three can't seem to behave yourselves in here, so you are no longer welcome. Haul your freight outside. Now!"

The three got up and walked out through the batwings, careful to keep their hands away from their guns. Miller walked over to the doors and watched them walk cursing back through the town.

The room erupted with exclamations and chatter. Sage saw Lupita Calderon retrieving her guitar from the floor. She'd let out a yelp when his gun fired, but she hadn't screamed and didn't seem to be too shaken.

The two vaqueros came up to Sage with their eyes wide, and Ernesto Robledo said, "Holy mother of God! I can't believe what I saw! We were going to meet Pablo here and then come looking for you. Pablo is going to be very sorry he was late."

Vasquez said, "You have incredible speed! No one could take you with a gun."

Sage said, "I could get a bullet in the back from anyone. That's why I need you. If I'm making a play, you watch my back. Your action was good there."

He reached into his pocket and pulled out the badges. "These are yours. Give one to Pablo when he shows up."

Sage looked around the room. All eyes were on him, and all were wide. He spoke up and said, "Sorry about the disturbance, folks, but I take a dim view of troublemakers. Let's all settle down now."

Sombreros bobbed all around, and the Mexicans got back to the business of drinking and talking, although now at an excited pitch.

Sage's four other deputies came in cautiously with hands on their guns and panting from a run up from the Emperor. They came over to Sage, and Chance Slade said, "We heard a shot. Thought we'd better get down here."

Sage said, "I was doing a little demonstration. Thought it might help keep the peace. Glad you showed up, though. While you're here, I'd like to introduce you to Benito Alvarez, the owner, if you don't know him."

They didn't, and they all walked over to the bar. Sage paused by Lupita, touched his hat brim and said, "Good evening, Miss Calderon. Why don't you show these gringos what you can do with a guitar? It would help get the place calmed down."

She flashed a smile that triggered his nerves from head to toe and began to play.

Alvarez lined up six mugs full with beer on the bar. "For these I will not allow you to pay," he said. "Eight deputies in here when I needed them." He shook his head. "Incredible!"

Sage grinned and picked up a mug. He said, "Just this once, Mr. Alvarez. Thanks."

Sage introduced the four deputies. Cal Call took a sip, looked at Lupita, and listening to her play, said, "I like this place. I've never been in here all this time."

In a low voice Sage said, "Prejudice never pays."

Call frowned and said, "I like Mexicans, OK? Just didn't think I'd fit in."

Sage said, "A man can fit in about anywhere if he's got a mind to. A friendly approach is welcome by anyone. White, brown, red, yellow...anyone. Except maybe by some at the Emperor."

Alvarez had gone down the bar to serve some customers. He came back and said, "Mr. Sage, I have been around. I have seen many things. I have never seen anything like what you did there. I had no idea that such a thing could be done."

Sage said, "I've done a lot of practicing. I hope that if people know I'm good with a gun, they won't try me. I'm not fond of killing people."

Alvarez said, "The danger is that they may try other ways."

"That is so. You've noticed that I've got a lot of deputies. When I need some help, maybe it'll be there.

"And Mr. Alvarez, my name is John."

"And mine is Benito."

-40-

On Sunday afternoon Sage was sitting on a chair on the walk in front of his office smoking a cigar and watching the comings and goings along the street. A medium-sized man with some gray hair curling out from under his narrow-brimmed black hat crossed the street and stopped in front of him. He was wearing a black suit and a black shirt with an upturned collar that had a white section in the front of it. His coat was hard-pressed to contain his belly.

The man spoke up and said, "Good afternoon, Deputy Sage. I am Reverend Charles Burns. I don't believe that I have seen you at our services."

"I haven't been there," said Sage.

The reverend asked, "Are you a Christian, Mr. Sage?"

"No, reverend, I'm not."

Burns lifted his eyebrows in surprise and then lit up at the prospect of a new soul to save. He stepped up on the walk and held out the Bible he was carrying.

"Please take this, Mr. Sage. You will find it to be uplifting. Particularly the New Testament."

Sage stood up but didn't reach out his hand. "Thank you, reverend, but I've read it."

"I beg your pardon?" said the reverend.

"Cover to cover."

Burns lifted his eyebrows again and said, "And you're not a Christian?"

Sage motioned to another chair and said, "Have a seat, reverend. Can I get you a cigar?"

"No, thank you," said Burns. "Healthy body, healthy mind, healthy soul."

Sage sat back down, wondering what the reverend meant by "healthy body." While he was gathering his thoughts, a sparrow landed on the hitching rail in front of them.

Sage said, "When I was growing up, I had more experience with nature than most kids—even the ones on farms. My teachers taught me to observe every detail of every plant, every insect, every bird, and every other every animal we knew of. I learned how a lot of things in nature worked.

"Reverend, I am in absolute awe of nature. That sparrow over there is an incredible accomplishment for the Creator, as are human beings and every other living thing. I came to realize that the Creator had to have a level of intelligence and understanding that we could hardly imagine. Hell...pardon. I can't imagine it."

Reverend Burns was beaming with a smug little smile on his full face and nodded for Sage to go on.

"And then," said Sage, "I read the Bible. The Bible describes the God of Adam and Eve, Noah, Moses, David, and everyone else as an absolute tyrant, devoid of fairness —the ultimate being that only minds in a society that knew tyrants could dream up.

"The Apaches may have a savage culture, but their idea of the Creator didn't hold it to be as primitive as the one described in the book. It didn't slaughter multitudes of innocents. It didn't demand absolute obedience. It didn't inflict immense suffering, or instant death if it didn't get it. It didn't create a place to torture anyone for all time because they had never heard of this creator."

The smug smile was gone, and the reverend's face had gone dark red.

Sage gave him a level look and said, "Reverend, neither the Jews nor the Christians have got it right. I've got a mighty high regard for the Creator, but it appears from their book that they don't. I don't believe that it could be anything like what is in there."

Reverend Burns rose to his feet spluttering.

"That is a very pretentious thing to say! How can you deny the beliefs of millions of people over the last three thousand years?"

Sage said, "I can only go where reason takes me. It shouldn't have taken all those people three thousand years to figure out that primitive tribesmen had got it wrong."

Burns raised his voice and said, "I will not listen to heresy! You will learn to fear God or you will burn in the fires of hell!"

Heads turned along the street. Sage just looked at Burns until he turned and stepped down off the walk and strode stiff-backed across the street.

Sage sat back and took a pull on his cigar. Hell, he thought, he'd just told Alvarez that he didn't make enemies he didn't have to, and here he probably just did. Maybe a bunch of them.

Sage's varied experiences had not yet taught him to avoid discussing religion if he wanted to be in government service.

-41-

Jim Roeser was about to turn in on Tuesday night when he heard a number of horses in the street. He looked out and saw six riders getting down off their horses in front of his hitching rail. They had three extra horses with them.

Roeser grabbed the shotgun off the rack, hurried out the back door, and sprinted two buildings down. He went around to the front and peeked back toward his office from around the corner of the building.

The men had drawn their guns and were rushing inside. After a few minutes they came back out with their guns in their holsters and found Roeser standing in the street with a shotgun casually pointed at their feet.

"Got business that needs some sheriffing?" asked Roeser.

The flustered men looked at each other, and then one of them said, "Thought we'd pay a visit to your prisoners. Where the hell are they?"

"Lost 'em," replied Roeser. "Sort of wandered off when I wasn't looking. I guess I'll have to do something about that. Friends of yours, are they? And who might you be?"

One of the men said, "What? How could you?..."

"Shut up, Luke," one of the other men said. "He's blowin' smoke. We're leaving."

The man looked at Roeser and said, "Got any objection?"

"Nope," replied Roeser. "Haven't seen any particular laws being broken. Have a good ride."

It was dark when Sage approached the Rocking M. He had been looking over the country for over a week when a rare storm had blown in. A heavy rain sluiced off his hat, slicker, and chaps.

The ranch house looked like a serviceable mix of logs and stonework. Sage pulled Smokey up in front of it and called out, "Hello, the house. Deputy Sheriff Sage here."

The door opened slightly and a woman's face peered out.

Sage said, “A mite damp out here, ma’am. Would you mind if I laid up in your barn tonight?”

The door opened a little wider, and the woman said, “Go up to the bunkhouse and see Jed Peters. You can put up there. You’re welcome to put your horse in the barn. Come in with Jed for breakfast. I’m glad you’re here.”

She did seem to be gladder than what would be natural, and Sage wondered why. “Thank you, ma’am. I’m looking forward to talking with you.”

Sage rode around to the bunkhouse and hailed it. Peters opened the door and looked out. He said, “Well, now, a deputy sheriff. We just happen to be needing one. I hope you’re better at it than Sanchez.”

Sage said, “I’ll put my horse in the barn. Mrs. Martin suggested that I bunk here. That all right with you?”

“Sure,” said Peters. “There’s grain in a barrel by the stalls.”

When he got back to the cabin, Peters said, “Have a chair.” Sage hung his wet hat, slicker, and chaps on pegs on the wall and introduced himself. They sat down.

Peters said, “Didn’t know there was another deputy around. We just had some stock rustled, but we didn’t think it would do any good to get Sanchez out here—if he would even come, which he probably wouldn’t have. Pardon me for speaking against a fellow lawman, but that is one useless son of a bitch.”

“You’re pardoned,” said Sage. “Sanchez isn’t a deputy any more. Sheriff Roeser fired him. Roeser sent me up to replace him about three weeks ago.”

“You don’t say!” said Peters. He looked at Sage appraisingly. He thought the man looked to be pretty young, but he had a steady, confident look about him. “How do you happen to be out this way?”

“I’ve spent the last week looking over the country around here. Figured I’d better get familiar with it, and I wanted to see Mrs. Martin. I heard about her losing her husband and wanted to talk to her about that.”

Peters sat back in his chair. He was a tall, lean man. He had some years on him, maybe a little more than fifty, but he had the fit look of a man that did a lot of hard work outdoors. His forehead was white from being under his hat, but the rest of his face had a dark tan.

"That was a hard thing," said Peters. "Jeff was a damned good man. Had to be to catch a woman like Nancy. They hadn't been married a month. He apparently got bushwhacked when he was coming back from Rincon. They must have buried him deep. We sure couldn't find him.

"Later on, man by the name of Palermo came by. Made Nancy an offer for the place. A ridiculously low offer. She turned him down cold. He just laughed and said, 'we'll see.

"A week after that, Billy McQuade and our other two hands were in the Emperor. Billy went to the bar to refill his mug, and Bart Waco picked a fight with him and shot him dead. Billy wasn't no damned good with a gun. Shouldn't have been wearing one.

"The other two stood up, but Waco looked to be itching to kill them, and he had some men behind him. Sanchez was there and didn't lift a finger. Joe and Will wound up having to crawfish out of there. They came back here and picked up their pay.

"Ever since, we've been hard-pressed to get work done around here. Nancy put on a pair of britches and pitched in. Works as good as any man, too, now that she's getting the hang of it. She was raised on a ranch, so it didn't take her long. That is one determined woman, and she's mighty fit.

"This afternoon, Nancy and I went out to round up thirty steers and get them into a holding pen. We needed to take them down to Las Cruces and sell them. Nancy's got to put something on the mortgage. We found that a lot of steers had gone missing. We think about forty head. Rustled.

"We didn't have any luck finding them. Rain came in hard, and we didn't find their tracks. Mr. Sage, we're in trouble here."

Sage said, "The steers are about twenty miles south of here."

"What!?"

"I noticed tracks just before it started to rain. They were headed south toward Las Cruces, and they were half a day old. I figure they would have made about twenty miles by now. Three men driving the herd. Two of them were on horses that I tracked last week, so I was some interested in those tracks."

Sage grinned ironically, "I'd caught those two riders and let them go. I won't let them go this time."

Peters stared incredulously at Sage. "You can pick out a particular horse by its tracks?"

"Not all that hard with some practice. There are usually some nicks, and the shoes on different horses wear in different ways. You just have to look carefully and remember what you see. It helps to name a horse for some characteristic of its shoes. Those riders are on Right Forefoot Turns In and Two Bent."

Peters stared some more and then jumped up. "We've got to tell Nancy about this!"

When they got outside, the rain had let up to a light drizzle, and there were some breaks in the clouds where stars were shining through.

Mrs. Martin came to her door and let the men in.

Sage recounted what he'd told Peters and said, "I'm in need of some sleep, but if I start out at about three in the morning, I can beat them down to Las Cruces. Then Sheriff Roeser and I can give them a warm welcome. I'll be going by Rincon, so I'll get another deputy, too."

Mrs. Martin said, "I'm going with you. Jed, you'll need to stay here and take care of the feeding."

Sage said, "Ma'am, I'll be traveling fast. My horse really steps out. And there's liable to be some gunplay. It won't be any trick to identify branded cattle. It would be best if you stayed here."

Nancy Martin lifted her chin and said, "Those are my cattle, and I intend to see to their disposition. I would prefer to ride with you, but I'll just follow behind if I have to. I'll take two horses and change off."

Sage knew determination when he saw it and gave in. He decided to borrow one of her horses. No use being hard on Smokey if he didn't have to.

-42-

Sage, Martin, and Miller caught up with the herd ten miles north of Las Cruces the next day in the mid-afternoon. When they had left the Rocking M, the clouds had gone on to wherever clouds went, and a waning moon was in the sky, so they had been able to travel fast. Sage was impressed that the woman had not voiced any complaints or showed any signs of fatigue. She rode a horse like she'd been doing it all her life.

The tracks of the cattle and riders had appeared in the road early on. "They were taking the chance that the steers wouldn't be missed just yet or couldn't be found," commented Sage.

"Lost those bets," said Miller. "If they'd known you were in the neighborhood, they wouldn't have made that second one."

The pursuers left the road and passed the herd, giving it a very wide berth, and rode down through Las Cruces and on to Mesilla.

Jim Roeser was in his office, and Sage introduced him to Nancy Martin. Sage quickly filled him in on what was going on.

Roeser showed some surprise at seeing a woman wearing pants but didn't comment on it. He said, "I heard about you losing your husband, Mrs. Martin. My condolences. My deputy up there at the time said that there wasn't any way that we could find out who did it in his report, so I didn't go up there."

Sage said, "Mrs. Martin was planning on selling thirty head before she found that they were missing. Looks like those rustlers have done some work for her.

"Jim, two of the rustlers are the men we turned loose a while back. I recognized the tracks of their horses."

Roeser said, "You don't say! Well, now, those boys are going to see some justice done after all.

"I think I'll round up a posse for this. I should be able to put one together and have it ready within half an hour. I think we can afford that much time. If we can spot the herd without the rustlers spotting us, we can surround them. Maybe save us a chase.

"You're welcome to wait in here, Mrs. Martin, or you might want to go to one of the restaurants."

Martin looked at him and said, "Not on your life. That's my herd out there, and I'll see this through."

Roeser looked at Sage for some help, but he just sat there with an amused look on his face.

Not wanting to waste time, Roeser stood up and said, "John, you head over to the Catamount. I'll go to the Cattleman and the Rio if need be. Look for men along the street, too. I'd like to round up about ten men. We'll meet back here."

After Sage and Roeser left, Martin said, "Cody, Mr. Sage was dead on about where we'd find the herd. That was remarkable. All he did was look at some tracks two days ago."

Miller said, "John reads tracks like you or me read a book. He's half Apache, but when he's on a trail, he's all Apache. And he doesn't just read the tracks; he figures things out."

Martin's eyebrows shot up. "Half Apache?"

"His mother was a Chiricahua. He spent half his time growing up being an Indian, half on his father's ranch in Arizona. I take it that his old man was a piece of work. Made sure John learned to shoot. I think he shoots better than any other man alive."

Martin said, "I'd say that you're pretty impressed with your boss."

Miller looked at her. She was a fine-looking woman no more than twenty, but something about her looks had struck him as odd. Then he noticed that she had one blue eye and one brown one, and her nose was a little crooked. It all worked to give her face some character.

"I've never met a man that impressed me more. There is no one I'd rather work for."

Men on horseback started showing up in front of the office, and Miller went out followed by Martin. Every man looked startled by the appearance of a woman in jeans and a man's boots, but no one said anything.

Sage and Roeser returned with some more men, which made eleven in all. Miller and Martin mounted up, and a couple of men grumbled their disapproval of a woman coming along.

Roeser said, "It's a free country. That's her herd out there, and she's going to see this through." The grumbling stopped.

After they'd passed through Las Cruces, Sage said, "Jim, I doubt the rustlers figure on bringing the herd into the rail yards. They'll probably hold it along the river, send a man in to find a buyer, and take him out there. How about sending a man ahead? A lone man won't look suspicious, and he can get a drop on whoever they send. The rustler might recognize you or me or Cody."

Roeser thought for a moment while he looked over the posse. "Jethro, how about you do that? Don't ride all the way to the herd if you don't see anyone."

Jethro Morgan touched his hat, wheeled his horse, and cantered up the road.

Roeser looked at Sage and said, "Jethro's handy with a gun."

After a few minutes, the posse followed Morgan north on the road.

Two miles out of town, the posse caught up to Morgan, who was holding a man at gunpoint. Sage didn't know the man, but he had seen him in the Emperor.

Morgan said, "Man says he doesn't know anything about any cows, but he doesn't strike me as an honest sort. Thought I'd hold on to him."

Nancy Martin spoke up and said, "He didn't strike me as an honest sort, either. Hello, Mr. Palermo."

Sage stepped down off Smokey, drew his Colt, and walked up to Palermo. He reached up and pulled Palermo's gun out of its holster.

"Get down," he ordered.

When Palermo was on the ground Sage said, "Put your hands on top of your head, and lock your fingers."

Sage patted Palermo's pockets and pulled out a leather billfold. He stepped back, looked in it, and pulled out a folded paper.

Sage looked at the paper and said, “Well, Mrs. Martin, looks like you sold Mr. Palermo here a herd of forty steers. How about that?”

“What?” said Martin. “Let me see that.”

Martin looked at the bill of sale and said furiously, “That is not my signature!”

Roeser said, “Well now. Rustling and forgery. Jethro, you and Bob take this man back to town. Keys to the cells are in the top left drawer of my desk.”

Sage pulled the bridle off of Palermo’s horse, hung it over the horn, and tied the reins up with the saddle strings. Roeser tossed him a set of handcuffs, and Sage put them on Palermo and got the heavily sweating man mounted. He handed the lead rope to Bob.

Roeser said, “Nice work, Jethro. Have any trouble getting the drop on him?”

“No trouble at all, sheriff,” replied Morgan. As I went by, I tipped my hat and said, ‘Howdy.’ Then I turned and drew. Had him cold.”

Bob led Palermo off with Morgan following.

Roeser turned to Sage and said, “There are only two of them, but I’ve been thinking that if we charge in, we’re liable to lose somebody. How about you ride a ways ahead of us and try to spot them before they see you? Get the lay of the land.”

Sage nodded and rode off.

After two miles, Sage spotted a couple of steers by the river in the distance and slid off Smokey. Leaving the horse tied, he climbed a low hill and bellied forward to where he could see ahead. After looking things over, he returned to Smokey and rode back down the road.

Sage rode up to Roeser and said, “They’re just ahead. The rustlers are sitting by the river like they’re on some damned picnic or something. Pardon me, ma’am.”

Martin said, “Don’t ‘ma’am’ me. We’re old friends. My name is Nancy.”

Sage looked down and grinned briefly. Then he said to Roeser, “I’ll show you where to tie up. I can get up on a rock outcrop, and then you can all work your way in on foot. When they spot you, Jim, call out for them to surrender. If they go to shooting, I'll let loose and keep them pinned until you're on top of them."

When the posse got near the herd, Sage stopped them and pointed at the outcrop. "Tie up here. I'll get on up there."

Roeser said, "Hell, that's almost two hundred yards from them. Can you do any good from there?"

"Yes."

Sage tied Smokey and put his spurs in the saddlebags. He took out a box of shells and pulled his Winchester out of its scabbard. He told Roeser to give him ten minutes and disappeared into the brush.

Martin slid a carbine from the scabbard on her saddle, and Roeser said, "Mrs. Martin, enough is enough. You will wait here with the horses, or you will ride back to town."

Martin froze for a moment. Then she replaced the rifle and found a seat.

Up on the outcrop, Sage removed his hat and settled into position behind a boulder. He emptied the box of shells onto a flat rock and laid them out in a row. Then he levered a round into the chamber, thumbed a replacement into the magazine, and waited.

Roeser was fifty yards from the two rustlers when one of them noticed one of his men. After a startled exclamation, both of the rustlers drew their sidearms and Roeser yelled, "Drop your guns; you're covered!"

Both rustlers fired, not hitting anything at that range. One of them was immediately knocked off his feet in a spray of blood as Sage's rifle thundered in the distance. The other rustler jumped behind the trunk of a cottonwood about two feet wide. A rain of bullets from the rock outcrop blew chips off both sides of the tree as the posse sprinted forward, firing a few shots at the tree themselves and taking care to stay out of the line of fire from the outcrop.

Jesus, thought Roeser, those shots are coming hellishly fast and hitting where they are needed!

Running with spurs on wasn't easy, and four of the men had gotten their feet tangled and gone down. Roeser and those still with him were about to dive around the side of the tree when a revolver came flying out from behind it and the rustler screamed, "I quit! I quit!"

Roeser turned toward Sage and held up his hand, and the firing stopped.

The rustler came out from behind the tree with his hands raised and blood leaking from several gouges and splinters in his hide. He looked around at all the guns leveled at him and said, “Holy shit! What have you got up there, a Gatling gun?”

Roeser handcuffed the prisoner, whose name he knew was Willis Farley, and Miller used Farley’s bandana to bandage the worst wound and the dead man’s bandana to bandage another one. Two of the men loaded the body of the dead rustler on his horse, and everyone walked back to their horses.

Martin was on her feet holding her carbine at the ready, but she relaxed when it was obvious that the fight was over. She eyed the prisoner and the body coldly but made no comment.

Sage came running up looking distraught, but he regained his composure when he saw that all the men were apparently unharmed.

With his eyes on the prisoner he said, “I saw men going down and thought this bastard had managed to shoot them.”

Still looking at Farley, he said, “I’m starting to get tired of catching you. This time, you’re staying caught.”

Roeser looked around at the posse and said, “There’s cows running all over the place. How about rounding them up and helping Mrs. Martin get them to the corrals by the depot? My deputies and I are taking in the prisoner.

Heads nodded all around, and a few “sure ‘nuff’s” were voiced.

Roeser said, “Thanks for stepping up, men. I appreciate your help.”

He turned to Martin and said, “I’ll get Sam Larsen over there. He’s in the business of buying livestock. You want to sell all of them?”

Martin said, “We’ve done business with Sam. I was only figuring on selling thirty head, but I’ll sell all of them. No point in driving ten back. I’ll put the extra money into buying some calves.”

-43-

When the lawmen got into Mesilla, they stopped at Doc Carroll's place. There was a note on his door that he was making calls and would be back at about six o'clock. Roeser checked his pocket watch, and it was five thirty, so he told Miller to wait there with the prisoner. Then he and Sage took the corpse to Lucas Riley's shop.

Afterward, they stopped by Maggie's place to see if her room was available for Sage, and she insisted on feeding them.

Maggie said, "You're having a hard time staying away from here, John. You bring in more badmen?"

"Yep. Rustlers this time."

Over chicken and dumplings, Maggie learned all about Nancy Martin's problems and the recovery of her stock.

Maggie said, "That's a terrible thing about Mrs. Martin losing her husband like that so soon after being married and all. You said this Palermo had offered to buy her place, and now he's found rustling her cattle. Jim, do you think he killed her husband, too?"

Roeser and Sage both nodded their heads, and Sage said, "That crossed my mind, but we can't be too sure. At the bottom of this is Jeremy Lugo, and he could have had anyone kill Jeff Martin. That was about three months back, and we don't even have a body."

Roeser changed the subject. He looked at Sage and said, "I had some visitors a few nights ago. Six fellers showed up to visit our holdup men along with three extra saddle horses."

Sage said, "Well, I see you're still alive. What happened?"

Roeser described how he'd handled it. Then he said, "I'm mighty thankful that the stage robbers were stored over in Deming. I'd have had a hell of a situation if they'd been here.

"By the way, the judge will be here next Wednesday. He's been riding circuit. How about you stay on here and head over to Deming Monday and bring them back? I'll be needing Mrs. Martin to stay on here, too, to testify against Palermo and Farley. The county will stand the cost of a room and meals for her. Cody will probably need to do some testifying, too."

Sage said, "I'd better telegraph a message to Vern Summers. He could get someone to ride out to the Rocking M to let Jed Peters know what is going on. He could pass the word to our volunteer deputies, too.

"Maggie, I'd better get on a paying basis with you. Looks like I'll be bedding here for a while."

Sage and Roeser walked back to the office, and Miller was just arriving with the prisoner.

Sage stopped Roeser and said, "I just had an idea. Let's have Cody wait down here with Farley while you and I have a talk with Palermo."

Roeser gave Sage an inquisitive look, and Sage said, "I'm going to try something. Just follow along."

Palermo stood up in his cell and gave the lawmen a puzzled look when he saw that they were alone. He asked, "Where's my men? You kill them?"

"Killed one of them," said Sage. "Let the other one go."

"What?"

"Yep," said Sage. "He said he had some information we could use, and we worked out a deal. That information was mighty interesting. He told us all about how you ambushed Jeffrey Martin and buried him out there."

Palermo turned white and stood there without protesting, the lawmen noticed.

Roeser glared menacingly at Palermo and said, "You sign a confession and plead guilty, maybe you can avoid a noose, but I'd just as soon do a bad job with that noose. Let you strangle slow."

Palermo went from white to gray, gulped, and then nodded his assent. Roeser turned around and bounded down the stairs. Two minutes later, he was back with a short handwritten confession, and Palermo signed it.

With the confession in hand, Roeser said, "Where's Martin buried?"

Palermo's eyes widened and then narrowed. "You weren't told?"

"Didn't think to ask, but I'll be doing that. How about saving me the time? Mrs. Martin will want to know."

Palermo was starting think maybe he'd been played for a fool. He was done with saying anything. He couldn't care less what Nancy Martin wanted.

Sage and Roeser went back down to the office. Sage looked at Roeser and then at Farley and said, "We had cause to believe that Palermo murdered Jeffrey Martin, and we're pushing him pretty hard on it. He told us that you did it."

Farley flared red and jumped to his feet. "That's a damned lie! Palermo and Strange did the ambush."

Sage recalled that the name of the rustler he'd killed was named Leonard Strange.

"That so?" asked Sage. "Where'd they do it at?"

Farley looked at the floor and didn't respond.

"Lugo put them up to it?" asked Sage on an off chance, but Farley clamped his lips together and wouldn't say anything else.

Roeser took Farley upstairs. When Palermo saw him, he went back to looking gray. Then he erupted with an impressive string of curse words. Roeser put Farley in a separate cell and locked the door. Then he had Farley hold his hands through the bars while he took the cuffs off.

Roeser gave Palermo a level look. Then he went back down the stairs.

Roeser grinned at Sage and said, "Your parents failed you. They raised a miserable, scheming, lying human being."

Sage hung his head and said, "I'm guilty, but I'm not feeling too miserable."

Roeser said, "I've got to go find Sam Lawson and get him up to the rail yard. That herd should be showing up about now. Why don't you head up there, Sage?

"Cody, how about you get something to eat and pick up some grub for the prisoners?"

-44-

When Sage got to the rail yard in Las Cruces, the posse was just getting the last of the steers into the corrals. He told Martin that Roeser should be along shortly with the buyer and thanked the men again. So did Martin.

Jethro Morgan had come to the corrals to help out and find out how the posse had fared. Sage called him over.

Sage said, "Jethro, you didn't just catch a rustler out there. You also caught a murderer."

Martin had started to walk toward the corral, and she spun around and stared at Sage.

Morgan said, "What?"

Sage looked at Martin and said, "I had my suspicions. I tried a little deception with Palermo, and it worked. He wound up signing a confession to murdering your husband."

Martin put a hand over her heart and said, "My God. I had my suspicions, too, but couldn't see any way to pursue them. Did he tell you where Jeff is buried?"

"No, ma...Nancy, he wouldn't say. We'll be needing you to stay here or in Mesilla for the trials next week. The judge will be convening them on Wednesday. You can room and eat at the county's expense. I can get word to Jed about what is going on.

"Another thing—the other rustler, Willis Farley, told us that Leonard Strange, the rustler I shot, was with Palermo when he killed your husband."

"That's good to know. It brings some closure. I don't suppose that I'll ever be able to mark the grave," she said sadly.

Martin said, "I've got to have some clothes for the trial. I can't go wearing jeans, and I'd like to tell Jed myself what is happening. I'll ride up and be back by Wednesday."

Sage said, "Nancy, that's a long ride. I'd go with you, but I'll be needing to bring in the prisoners from the stage holdup."

Martin said, "I'm quite capable of making the ride by myself, John."

Sage started to reply, but Morgan spoke up. “I’d be pleased to ride with you, Mrs. Martin. I haven’t got anything going on right now.”

Martin started to repeat what she’d told Sage but hesitated and said, “Are you employed at the present time, Mr. Morgan?”

“No, ma’am,” Martin said sheepishly. The outfit I was packin’ for went out of business. I haven’t looked too hard for anything else yet, but I will before long. I’m a top hand.”

Martin said, “I’m in need of a hand. Forty and found. Would you be interested?”

Morgan hesitated, and Sage figured he had misgivings about working for a woman. Sage said, “The Rocking M is a nice spread. You’d be working with Jed Peters. He’s a good man, and he needs some help.”

Morgan said, “Why, yes I would be. Where is your place?”

“The Rocking M is about ten miles up the river from Rincon. Would you be able to ride up with me in the morning? I have two extra horses, and we can change off. Be there by dark or soon after if we leave at dawn.”

Morgan touched his hand to the brim of his hat and said, “Yes, ma’am.”

Martin asked, “Is there someplace open early for breakfast?”

Morgan told her, and they agreed to meet there in the morning.

Martin went over to the corrals as Roeser arrived with Larsen.

Morgan looked at Sage and said, “That’ll be a hard ride for a lady.”

Sage said, “She can handle it. Tell you what, Jethro, when you get north of Rincon, keep your eye out for good spots for an ambush. Jeff Martin was bushwhacked somewhere along the road to his ranch. He probably isn’t buried too far off the road. There aren’t a lot of places where the ground is soft for digging along there.

“If you see any likely spots, take a look around. Look for any place where coyotes have been digging. I was going to do that when I got back, but I won’t have a chance before the trial. It would be good to be able to prove that there was a death. We've got a signed confession, but even that might not be enough to get a conviction for murder if we can't prove that a murder was done. The odds of finding him aren't too good, but you could give it a try."

Martin and Larsen agreed on a price, and Larsen gave her a check. She came over to Sage and said, "I'm going to get something to eat and then find a place to bed down. It's been a long day, and tomorrow is going to be another one. Care to join me for dinner?"

Sage said, "I've eaten, but I'll have some coffee with you. Maria's Cantina has some pretty good food."

When Sage and Martin entered the cantina, the men there looked at her jeans and frowned. Then they looked at the rest of her when she took off her floppy wide-brimmed hat, did a reassessment, and looked more approvingly.

When they were seated and had given their order, Martin said, "John, you are one mighty fine deputy. You just saved my ranch—not to mention nailed my husband's murderer."

"Doing what I'm paid for, Nancy. I'm feeling good that it's working out for you. You've had a hard time."

"I'm actually glad that I've had to keep busy," she said. "If I had just sat around the house moping, I'd have gone crazy with grief. It was bad enough as it was. I miss Jeff so much. He was the love of my life. Life with him was a joy, and I expected it to last all our years."

She teared up and then angrily said, "His life was so short! I never wanted to see a hanging, but I want to be there when the sheriff hangs Jack Palermo."

For the first time, Sage studied her in an appraising mode. She was a tall woman—nearly as tall as he was with her riding boots on. Her long auburn hair was coiled on top of her head, and her face, grimy as it was at the moment, was interesting. Kind of spunky. He realized that her wide-set eyes were different colors, which added to the interest, as did the slightly crooked nose.

She had the body of an athlete, but it had some attractive curves. In fact, she was just plain attractive, Sage decided. He thought she'd make a lot more comfortable and reliable partner than Lupita Calderon.

With his brief acquaintance with Lupita, he'd had the impression that life with her would be a life of servitude, not partnership, or even friendship.

But he wasn't in the market for a partner right now. His job required his full attention if he was going to get it done and survive it.

Sage said, "He needs to hang, all right, but so does Jeremy Lugo. I think that he was behind it calling the play. Palermo was just a hired gun. I doubt that he had the kind of money it would take to buy your ranch, even at reduced price."

Martin said, "What are you going to do, John?"

"Not sure yet," he replied. "Keep the pressure on, keep looking for my chance, and move hard when I see it.

"You look like you've been riding for a long time, not just for the past couple of months. And I suspect that you know how to use a rifle since you've been packing one."

She said, "I grew up on a ranch near Santa Fe with five brothers. No sisters. I've always done boy things. I liked to ride, and I learned to shoot a rifle."

She raised her chin and said, "I'm not too ladylike, I guess. I was surprised Jeff would have me."

Sage gave her a level look and said, "I'm not surprised at all."

Martin colored. She said, "Cody said that your mother was a Chiricahua Apache. You must have had an interesting childhood."

Sage studied her, but there was no hint that she disapproved. "I had a childhood that not many Americans have had. I grew up with three cultures: American, Mexican, and Apache. Then a fourth—Japanese. I learned things from each one that have been of considerable value."

It took Sage an hour and three more cups of coffee to recount some of his life and answer a hundred questions from the fascinated woman. Finally she said, "I'm about to keel over. Where can I get a room here?"

Sage suggested the Amador House. He bid her good night after taking her there and went back to Mesilla.

-45-

On Saturday afternoon a passenger on the eastbound train had Las Cruces in an uproar. Big Bill McClusky, the world champion bare-knuckle prizefighter, was passing through on his national tour. He had fought a very short fight in San Francisco and was on his way to New Orleans for another match. He was going to stay overnight in Las Cruces.

Big Bill got off the train with his retinue. He waved his bowler hat and pranced around, grinning and throwing a few air punches in front of the admiring crowd.

One of the retinue, who looked like a carnival barker in a checkered suit and straw hat, called out, "We're staying at the Wild Horse tonight, folks. You can meet Big Bill there this evening," and shepherded Big Bill off.

Sage and Roeser had come over to watch the excitement. Roeser had had to explain to Sage what a prizefighter was, and Sage had been impressed. Sage looked at Big Bill and commented, "Now, there's a man who is mighty fond of himself."

"He's got a right to be," said Roeser. "He's been knocking out all comers for about four years now. Mostly in New York and Chicago. And they've been coming from all over.

That evening when Roeser, Sage, Miller, and the two Las Cruces deputies got to the Wild Horse Saloon, the place was packed, and it looked like they were going to have to stand along the wall with a lot of the crowd.

Then Sage heard a man call his name, and he saw the miner Sully waving him over to his table. Roeser and Miller followed him, and Sully greeted Sage like a long lost friend and invited the lawmen to sit down. They located five empty chairs and packed them in around the table two deep.

Sage nursed a beer and chatted with the miners and deputies for an hour before Big Bill came down the stairs with his retinue of trainers, sparring partners, and the barker. As he came down, he waved both arms to the crowd, who roared their approval.

Big Bill worked his way across the room shaking hands and throwing a few more air punches. The man really was big, about six and a half feet tall, thought Sage. Maybe about 250 pounds, and a lot of that was in his chest and arms.

When Big Bill got two tables away from where Sage was sitting, a young freckle-faced cowboy of about eighteen jumped up, pranced around in front of the prizefighter, and playfully jabbed at him. The kid had obviously had some drinks, and one of the jabs inadvertently thumped Big Bill in the chest.

Instantly, Big Bill threw two punches, left and right, and the kid dropped like a stone, out cold.

Men at all the tables around the scene let out a shocked gasp, and a couple said, "Hey now! That weren't fair."

Two of the kid's friends glared venomously at McClusky as they hovered over the unconscious boy.

Sage stood up and walked over in front of Big Bill. Roeser looked at Miller apprehensively and said, "Oh... shit."

Sage faced the prizefighter and said, "You son of a bitch. The kid was just funning. That wasn't called for."

Big Bill smirked at Sage and said, "So the hick deputy is going to arrest me? That badge isn't big enough, you ass."

Sage unpinned his badge and slipped it into his shirt pocket. Then he laid his hat and gun belt on the nearest table. Jaws dropped and the room in the area went silent as people caught on to what was happening.

In an awed low voice Sully said, "Oh my God. Sage is going to fight him. And I'm right here to see it!"

Sage said evenly, "I'm not going to arrest you—just lay you out."

McClusky barked an incredulous laugh and took a fighter's stance with his huge fists held up in front of him. His retinue looked on in amusement.

Sage held his hands up and open with the palms facing in, and Big Bill threw four quick jabs at his face. Sage deflected two of them, but two were only partially deflected and connected, rocking him. Sage was amazed at how fast the man was. He hadn't been hit like that since he had participated in village contests on Okinawa.

The prizefighter had maintained perfect balance, so Sage wasn't able to take any advantage. He brought a boot up from the floor with blinding speed and landed a solid front kick to the man's jaw, and McClusky staggered two steps backward.

As big as he was, Big Bill was stunned, but Sage was surprised that he was still on his feet. McClusky lunged forward and launched a big fist, but this time he was a little off balance. Sage deflected it, spun completely around, and hammered a back fist into the side of McClusky's head. He immediately spun back around the other way and slammed a round kick to the other side of his head, and this time, it was Big Bill that dropped like a stone.

The barker let out a shriek and ran to Big Bill, and the two sparring partners rushed at Sage, who squared off, but Roeser, Miller, and the other two deputies were there with their guns drawn.

"Fight's over!" yelled Roeser, and the two backed off and went to help the downed man.

The room went into a frenzy of shouting and hooting.

Sully looked wide-eyed at his friends and said, "I saw that. I saw that. I would have paid anything to see that, and I saw it. For free! Jesus Kee-rist! What was I ever doing fighting that deputy?"

Sage belted his gun back on, mopped a split lip with his bandanna, and went over to the fallen cowboy. His friends had him sitting up, but he wasn't there yet. The cowboys looked at Sage, and one said, "Mister, I've never seen anything like that in my life. Jody here's my best friend, but I'm not sorry at all he got laid out. He'll have something to talk about, and I wouldn't have missed that for anything."

Another cowboy said, "Yeah, but Jody's sure going to be upset that he missed it."

The sparring partners had McClusky sitting up, and the trainer was checking him over. The trainer looked at the barker and told the horrified man, "Godammit! His jaw's broken!"

The sparring partners half carried the dazed prizefighter up the stairs to their rooms followed by the barker and trainer while the room buzzed with the chatter of those who had seen what had happened explaining it to those who hadn't had a view.

Roeser looked at Sage's mouth and said, "I think you had better have Doc Carroll tie a couple of knots in that lip."

Bob Smith of the Mesilla Crier came over and said, "I'm starting to get mighty fond of you, Deputy Sage. You keep providing great copy. This one is going to be picked up all over the country. Maybe the headline will be 'Hick Deputy John Sage New World Champion.' They'll be reading and weeping in New Orleans."

Sage shook his head slowly from side to side and said, "Oh, my God. Jim, can I just shoot him?"

Roeser grinned and said, "'Fraid not. We've got a free press. Says so right there in the Constitution."

Sage looked at Smith and said, "I'm no world champion. If I'd had to fight him with those Queensbury Rules Jim told me about, that would have been me lying there on the floor."

"Yes, that was quite unconventional," said Smith. "But nevertheless, an extraordinary accomplishment. I am in awe of your abilities. Where did you learn to fight like that?"

"From a priest," said Sully.

Sage had to fill in some details on that before he could escape back to Mesilla and Doc Carroll's office. In the background, Jody Wilson was wailing about missing the fight.

-46-

Sheriff Hector Lopez greeted Sage with some relief. "When you told me that Lugo might try to break the prisoners out if he found them, I put on some extra deputies. We have been guarding them day and night. No try was made, but I think his men know they are here. There have been five gunmen hanging around town, and one was seen at the back of the jail talking through the window."

When it came time to board the train to Las Cruces, Lopez and three of his deputies put the handcuffs and leg irons that Sage had brought on the prisoners for the ride to Deming. The prisoners and Sage rode in a wagon to the depot, which was a mile out of town, while the other lawmen followed along on their horses. They all kept an eye out for the gunmen but didn't spot any of them.

The prisoners were seated in the back of the third coach in line, two in one seat and one in the back seat. A chain that Lopez provided was run under the seats, and the leg irons were locked to it. Sage took a seat across the isle from them. Sage thought they looked a little too relaxed for men headed to a hanging, and he was regretting not bringing Miller along.

There were a number of passengers in the coach, but there a lot of empty seats, and Sage had everyone move to the front, leaving several empty rows in front of him when the train pulled out of the station.

Halfway to Las Cruces, the door to the coach ahead opened, and Saul Snead and two other men that Sage had seen in the Emperor rushed in with their guns drawn.

It took them a moment to get a fix on where Sage was located, and in that moment, Sage drew and center shot two of the gunmen. Snead grabbed a young girl who was screaming instead of ducking and jerked her up in front of him. He held his gun to her head.

Snead yelled, "Drop your gun, Sage, or she's dead!"

Sage, still seated, had his elbows on the back of the seat in front of him and kept his Colt aimed at Snead with both hands.

The prisoners all lunged at Sage but were caught short by the chain and tripped in the isle. Sage didn't react to the disturbance and kept his attention focused on Snead, but Snead moved his aim toward Sage. Sage fired.

The bullet struck the bridge of Snead's nose and blew the back of his head open.

Sage waited until the three prisoners had gotten unscrambled and regained their seats. Then he started forward just as the conductor came through the door. He decided to stay with the prisoners while the conductor got the hysterical girl and her parents calmed down.

With the help of two passengers, the conductor started dragging the bodies down the isle toward the empty seats. While the third one was being dragged, Cole Bailey lifted his cuffed hands and reached for the emergency stop cord, but Sage instantly whipped out his Colt and held it cocked at Bailey's head. Bailey lowered his arms.

Sage looked out the windows and saw two men and eight saddled horses standing at the side of the tracks. He gave them a friendly wave as the train barreled by.

Bailey and the two other prisoners now looked like men headed for a hanging.

-47-

When the train got into Las Cruces, Roeser and Miller were waiting for it. As they waited while the excited passengers debarked, Miller glanced at Roeser and said, "Uh oh."

Roeser saw Sage and the prisoners in the last coach, and as he and Miller climbed aboard and walked down the isle, Roeser remarked, "Looks like it's been a bad day for Lugo's people."

Miller said, "You sure sicced a demon on that man."

The unhappy conductor helped them unload the bodies and lay them on the platform. Then he and the train's fireman went to cleaning while the lawmen got the prisoners off.

The conductor looked at Roeser and said, "You ought to be paying double for using this line!"

They got the prisoners installed in the local holding cell, and Miller left to get the Las Cruces undertaker over to the station.

Sage told Roeser the details of the trip from Deming, and Roeser said, "Those two will be getting word to Lugo, but I don't see where he's going to have time to do anything before the trials. At least I hope not. I deputized two men to help guard the rustlers, and I'm going to deputize four more. I'll keep them on until we get this over with.

"Nancy Martin is back in town. Jed Peters came with her. John...Nancy and Jethro found where some coyotes had been digging near the road to her ranch. They went back with shovels and dug deeper. They found Jeff Martin."

Sage shook his head and said, "That poor woman. That must have been a damned unpleasant job. At least she'll have some closure. That will do it for Palermo. It would be good to be able to get him for the two farmers who disappeared, but I guess we can only hang him once."

Roeser said, "None of the prisoners have hired a lawyer, and Lugo won't be admitting his connection by hiring any for them. Leonard Horn, a local lawyer, takes on these cases for the county. I've written up the charges for him, and I'll be doing the prosecuting. Judge Bennett is taking the train down from Santa Fe to Rincon and will be here on a stage tomorrow at noon. The trials will get underway on Thursday. Now there are going to be three of them."

-48-

A one-story adobe on the corner of the Mesilla plaza served as the courthouse. After hearing the prisoner's not guilty pleas, Judge Bennett spent Thursday morning getting a jury selected. He called the first trial to order after lunch. He'd had to interview a lot of prospective jurors to find twelve that hadn't read the Crier's account of the stage holdup and capture of the robbers. Most of the jurors selected couldn't read.

Jim Roeser laid out the charge that Cole Bailey, Billy Fine, and Willard Peterson had robbed the stage and murdered Shorty Williams.

Roeser called Isaac Hooker to the stand to describe the holdup and murder and identify the prisoners as the bandits.

The attorney for the defense, Leonard Horn, objected because since the bandits were wearing bandanas over their noses and another three men had been found with the bandits, a positive identification could not be made. He asked the judge to dismiss the trial.

Roeser stated that he would be able to prove through the course of the trial that he had the right defendants here. Bennett overruled.

"Mr. Hooker, you seem pretty sure it was these men. Why are you so sure?" Roeser asked.

"Well," said Hooker, "the bandanas didn't cover their eyes or their size and shape. Their hats didn't cover all their hair or the scar on Fine's forehead. Nothing covered their voices."

Roeser removed the three shirts worn by the defendants at the time of their arrest from a bag and entered them as evidence. He draped the shirts over the railing in front of the jury and turned to Hooker.

"Mr. Hooker, do you recognize these shirts?"

"I surely do, sheriff. Those three were wearing them during the holdup."

Horn objected: “Your honor, those might be store-bought shirts, and any number of men could be wearing them.”

Judge Bennett addressed the jury: “It is established that the perpetrators were wearing shirts like these. You can give some weight to the odds.”

On cross examination, Horn asked Hooker if he had heard the defendants speak at any time since the holdup.

“Why, yes,” replied Hooker. “While we were waiting for you and the judge to come into the room, Deputy Sage told them that they had been easier to catch than a bunch of puppies in a pen, and they spoke plenty—mostly cussing him out.”

Roeser looked over at Sage, stared at him for a moment, and then looked down and grinned as he shook his head slowly from side to side.

The two stage passengers that Roeser had been able to find were called, and they also identified the defendants and the shirts. They then identified their personal belongings that had been in the possession of the bandits.

Roeser called Sage to the stand, and Sage described the pursuit and capture. He was careful to explain how he had matched the tracks of the horses to the riders to determine that the defendants were the ones who held up the stage.

On cross examination, Horn asked, “How can you expect us to believe that you could tell which horses were which by their tracks? You some kind of Indian?”

“Yes,” said Sage. “But blood doesn’t matter. What matters is that I had years of training by experts. Those experts were Apaches.

“Horse shoes all wear differently. I’ve learned to spot the differences. Same goes with boots. I was behind you when we walked over here from Sheriff Roeser’s office. I noticed from your tracks that the heel of your left boot is worn more on the inside than the inside of your right heel. Your right heel has a nick in the back. If I saw your tracks out on the street, I’d know whose they were.”

Horn didn’t look like he was convinced. Judge Bennett said, “Len, take off your boots and bring them over here.”

Bennett studied the soles of the boots and then held them up toward the jury.

"For your information, Deputy Sage's description was correct."

The people and the defense rested their cases and then made their closing arguments. Horn did his best to cast doubt on whether they were trying the right men.

Bennett gave the jury their instructions and then cleared the room of everyone except the jurors.

They all had to return in just half an hour. The jury was composed of no-nonsense western men, and it only took that long for them to find the three defendants guilty. Bennett sentenced them to hang.

The second trial, with a new jury, would convene the next morning.

-49-

It was a short trial. Jack Palermo and Willis Farley were found guilty of rustling and sentenced to fifteen years each. Palermo got another two years for forgery. The third trial got underway that same afternoon.

In his opening statement, Jim Roeser accused Jack Palermo of murdering Jeffrey Martin in an ambush for financial gain. He entered the confession signed by Jack Palermo as evidence and then called Nancy Martin to the stand.

Martin described the disappearance of her husband after Palermo had offered to buy their ranch and described how Jethro Morgan had located the remains of her husband.

On cross examination, Leonard Horn asked, “Mrs. Martin, your husband has been missing for about three months. I appreciate the distress that you must have gone through in identifying the remains, but I have got to ask, how could you be sure they were those of your husband?”

Martin glared at Palermo and said, “Jeff's wedding band was gone, but he had two gold teeth. He missed those.”

Another short trial. Judge Bennett didn't even clear the room while the jury huddled for a few moments before announcing their verdict.

Before the Judge pronounced sentence, Jim Roeser asked if he could approach the bench.

“Your honor,” Roeser began, “we believe that Palermo was hired to do that murder. I would surely like to see the man that did the hiring brought to justice. Would you consider offering some leniency if Palermo would help convict that man?”

Judge Bennett declared a recess before sentencing and cleared the room. Roeser, Sage, Martin, and Horn remained. Roeser had Deputy Saul Espinosa, who was acting as bailiff, sit with Palermo at the far end of the room.

Judge Bennett was a tall, slender, and very distinguished-looking man with a mane of white hair and a flowing white mustache.

Bennett said, "Please repeat what you asked, sheriff."

Roeser did, and Nancy Martin flared, "Palermo has got to hang!"

Roeser said, "Mrs. Martin, this might be the only way we can get to Jeremy Lugo. He is even more responsible for your husband's death than Palermo. This could be a powerful incentive for Palermo to give up Lugo. I doubt that he loves the man."

Bennett said, "Too powerful. I suspect that his kind would give up his mother if it would keep his neck out of a noose. The law must remain credible, sheriff, and Palermo's testimony in these circumstances would not be credible, even if accepted by a jury. As much as I would like to see justice done completely here, I will not consider leniency."

Sage spoke to Martin. "Lugo has a lot going on. I'll nail him for one thing or another eventually. I'll do everything I can to bring that about."

Bennett turned to Sage and said, "You appear to be an exceptionally competent young man, Deputy Sage. Take care not to diminish your value by acting outside the law."

Sage looked Bennett in the eye for a long moment and nodded his head.

After the court's participants and the spectators refilled the room, Judge Bennett pronounced sentence: Jack Palermo was to be hung by the neck until dead.

-50-

Roeser had Deputy Espinosa haul Willis Farley off to the territorial prison in Albuquerque by coach and train on Saturday, and at dawn on Monday morning, Roeser and his two deputies from Rincon hung the four killers. The hangings were well attended.

As Roeser, Sage, and Miller walked back to Roeser's office, Sage remarked, "I just don't understand why anyone other than Nancy Martin would have wanted to watch that. Ugly business."

Roeser said, "People like drama, I guess. That was dramatic. Public executions always draw a crowd."

"I like my drama to be a little more pleasant and uplifting," said Miller.

"Amen," replied Sage.

Roeser said, "Well, it has been quite a week. Glad it's over and that we made it without getting shot up by Lugo's people. I'm kind of surprised that they didn't try something."

"Yep," said Miller. "Maybe that bunch will lay low for a while now. Maybe even abide by the law. They really suffered some damage."

"I don't think they are about to become law abiding," said Roeser. "I think they will lay low for a while because John has become a monumental threat to them. I don't see Lugo and Waco tolerating that for long.

"John, I think that you and Cody are in for some lethal attention. I wouldn't fault you if you decided to pack it in."

"I'd fault me," Sage responded. "I wouldn't feel very good about myself if I quit. What kind of lawman would back off when things got dangerous? You weren't about to back off when the Cummings bunch showed up. I'm going to see this through."

"Me too," said Miller. "John would fall flat on his face if I wasn't holding him up and telling him how to get things done."

Roeser chuckled and said, "Well, John, if you weren't such a marvel in any kind of a fight, I wouldn't be sleeping much at night. How about I get you another dozen badges?"

Sage said, "It would get to a point where all I had time to do was manage deputies. I think the seven volunteers I've got plus maybe three or four more will serve their purpose. Eyes and ears and backup. I haven't spent much time with them yet, but I feel pretty good about those men. They appear to be steady."

-51-

Sage and Miller rode back to Rincon with Nancy Martin and Jed Peters. When Miller and Sage got to their office, they found Bill Rogers there wearing his badge.

"How do, Bill?" said Sage. "I'm surprised to see you here on a Monday evening."

"We all decided to put in some extra time while you two were away at the trials, and we had a little work to do," replied Rogers. "We heard that you got the goods on Jack Palermo for killing Jeff Martin. Palermo was interested in buying my farm, and I'd been expecting trouble from him. Was he found guilty?"

"Hung him this morning," said Miller.

"That's a relief," said Rogers. "I knew Jeff. We were friendly. I was afraid that I might go missing, too.

"A few days ago, Vern Summers got in touch with all of us deputies and told us that he had picked up some talk in the Emperor that a party would be going down to Mesilla to break out the prisoners there. So we all came in and took turns keeping an eye on the place full time.

"Wednesday morning, eight of Lugo's gunmen had a meeting there with Bart Waco. After the meeting, they left the Emperor, got on their horses, and started to head south. They were somewhat surprised to see a dozen deputies drift in around them. I was holding my double-barreled ready across my lap."

"A dozen?" asked Sage.

"Yep. The four of us gringos, Ortega's three riders, and five other men that had been telling us they wanted to be deputies, too, were there. They didn't have badges and weren't sworn in, but they sided with us.

"Waco wasn't with the bunch. One of them asked what the hell we were doing, and Cal Call told them that they looked like fellers that could use some guidance to keep them off the sinful path to perdition.

"Chance Slade said, 'Yep, we take it as our sacred duty to follow along and make sure all our brethren make it to the Promised Land...if it became apparent that they might stray.

"Well, things were a mite tense there. Those gunmen were having a hard time deciding whether to back down or let loose. Then Charlie Rupp suggested that they go back in the Emperor and reconsider their path for a while, and that's what they did. Once they started to move, Chance Slade put in that if anyone looked like they'd be drifting south, we'd all ride down to Mesilla and get together again there."

"Whew!" breathed Miller. "So that's why none of Lugo's people showed up."

Sage said, "You deputies really came through, there. I'm beholden to you."

"You've been doing a lot," said Rogers. "We all appreciate it. We weren't about to stand by and leave you the full load."

"How about passing the word to those new men to get in here?" said Sage. "I'd like to meet them and swear them in. No, tell you what—if everyone is still around town, let's all get together at the San Diego tomorrow at noon. Talk some more about how we are going to work."

-52-

After having a late dinner, Sage and Miller went over to Vern Summers' place. He was still up, and Mayor Cawthon was with him.

After catching each other up on events, Vern Summers said, "John, there's a new player in town. Man name of Ephraim Colwell. He was pointed out to me in the Emperor. He used to be a Confederate sharpshooter and buffalo hunter. He's a long-range killer that is rumored to hire out. The man I was talking to said Colwell could pick off a squirrel at a thousand yards, and he packs a long-barreled .50 caliber that could do it."

Sage thought about it. "I guess I'd better not be telegraphing where I'm going to be riding to for a while. Maybe you could point him out to me."

"Sure. Let's go over to the Emperor. He might well be there."

"All right," said Sage. "Vern, Hiram, we're having a meeting with all the deputies over at the San Diego at noon tomorrow. You might like to sit in. I'd like to get a little bit organized. Figure out who is going to be where and when."

Both men said they'd be there, and Sage, Miller, and Summers walked over to the Emperor.

When they went in, Sage saw Bart Waco sitting with another man at a table. In a low voice, Summers said, "That's Colwell there with Waco."

Waco said something to Colwell, and Colwell fixed a pair of reptilian eyes on Sage. The eyes followed the three men as they went over to the bar and ordered beer. Waco stood up and went up the stairs.

Sage led the way over to the table next to Colwell's, and they sat down. Sage openly studied Colwell. If that made the man nervous, he sure didn't show it. He just sat there and studied back. Sage thought those eyes belonged in a lizard.

Colwell was maybe in his early fifties. He was fairly short and wire thin, and the beard and hair sticking out from under his floppy hat were partly gray. A very long bolt-action rifle leaned against the chair next to him. The rifle had a hell of a big bore.

After the men finished their drinks, they got up and left the Emperor.

The next morning Sage went over to the livery. The owner, Phil Emory, was forking hay into the occupied stalls.

"Morning, Phil," said Sage. "You got a horse here that belongs to a man named Ephraim Colwell?"

"I do at that," replied Emory. "That bay gelding over there at the end."

Sage walked down the stalls and looked at the horse. Emory came over, and Sage said, "Could I get you to take him out of the stall and lead him around a bit?"

Emory said, "That Colwell looked like a real hard ass. He might take exception to anyone fooling with his horse."

"I don't see him around," said Sage. "I have a need to see that horse."

"You're the law," said Emory. He put a lead rope around the bay's neck and led him out of the stall.

Sage had Emory lead the dark brown horse back and forth a couple of times. It was a magnificent animal. Tall and built for speed.

"New shoes," remarked Sage.

Sage picked up a file from a jumble of tools on a bench and walked over to the bay. He lifted the right forefoot and, with two strokes, filed a shallow notch on the inside bottom of the shoe.

"You can put him back in the stall, Phil. I'd appreciate it if you wouldn't mention that I was here."

"I sure as hell won't," replied Emory. "Wouldn't want that man to know I'd touched his horse. He gives me the willies."

-53-

As Sage had thought it would be, the San Diego was about empty when he went in with Miller a little before noon. Sage told Benito Alvarez that he was going to be meeting with about another fourteen men there shortly and that he would probably be able to do a little business in food if he made some up. Alvarez delightedly went to work slicing up some beef for fajitas.

As the men drifted in, they moved several tables together. Vern Summers and Mayor Cawthon arrived after the dozen volunteers, and Sage got the meeting underway by welcoming the five new men. After chatting with them for a few minutes, he had them stand up and swear to uphold the laws of the land and handed out their badges.

Sage reviewed what he expected of them and thanked everyone for putting a lid on Lugo's bunch the previous week. Mayor Cawthon stood up and thanked them some more and expressed how proud he was to be the mayor of a citizenry that stepped up like they had done to serve the community.

"I've heard immigrants in this country state that this is a free country and that they can do what they want. They don't understand at first that for every freedom, there is an obligation. They have an obligation to get whatever education they need to hold jobs so that they can contribute to our society instead of being a burden. They have an obligation to obey the law, to pay taxes, to vote intelligently, to serve on juries, and to raise their children to be good citizens.

"The best citizens go the extra mile and serve in the military and law enforcement and do other public service. The very best citizens become mayors."

After the hoots, catcalls, and laughter died down, Cawthon said, "We've had an ugly situation here in Rincon. Lugo's gang has been a threat to the community, and the law enforcement we had was part of the threat. Lugo is still a threat, but I am greatly relieved that John Sage has turned the law enforcement situation around. I am in awe of his abilities."

Heads nodded all around. Cawthon thanked them all again and sat down. The rest of the meeting consisted of lining out a schedule.

-54-

Thursday morning Sage tied Smokey to the outside of his corral and set about putting on a new set of horseshoes on him. The grulla was cooperative and the job went smoothly. He trimmed the last hoof and flattened the surface with a rasp. He was in the process of nailing on the cold shoe when a buggy pulled up in front of his office. A moment later he heard a woman's voice call his name from inside.

"Out back," he called.

A heavyset woman in a voluminous dress and bonnet came out the back door. Sage could see that she was distraught.

She trembled as she said, "Deputy Sage, I'm Anna Rogers. Bill has been killed. Murdered."

Shocked, Sage dropped Smokey's hoof and went to her.

"What happened, Mrs. Rogers?"

"I was cleaning up with the girls after breakfast," she explained. "Bill was out at the corral. I heard horses on the road and then two rifle shots, so I ran out. Bill was lying on the ground. He was already dead. Two men on horses were beating it down the road."

Her face crumpled, and she convulsed into tears. "My two daughters are in the buggy. My two boys will be coming in. They'll be bringing Bill."

Sage awkwardly embraced her and said, "Mrs. Rogers, I can't say how bad I feel. Bill was a good man. The best. Did you get a look at those men?"

She shook her head. "No. Just that one was kind of heavyset. I just saw their backs."

"You notice anything about their shirts? Their hats or their horses?"

Rogers scrunched her face up and closed her eyes for a moment. She shook her head. "Why would they do that to Bill?" she sobbed. "He was a kind man. I don't think he ever had an enemy."

"I couldn't say," said Sage. "I'll be asking them."

Sage asked "How about we go over to Mayor Cawthon's place? You can stay with Susan Cawthon until you're ready to get back to your place. I'll be heading out there shortly. How old are your boys?"

"Eleven and thirteen," replied Rogers.

Sage drove the buggy over to the Cawthons'. The two Rogers girls were younger than their brothers. Susan quickly took charge of the Rogers women when she heard what had happened.

Sage hurried back to his office, finished nailing the last shoe on Smokey, and trimmed the hoof to the shoe. He saddled up and cantered down to Miller's boarding house and found Miller. Then the two of them rode over to Summers' place.

Sage told the shocked man that he and Miller were going out after the killers and to let the other deputies know what was going on.

Outside of town they met the Rogers boys driving a flatbed wagon. Bill was wrapped in a blanket and tied down on the bed. It must have been a job for the young boys to get him up there.

Sage asked them what they'd seen, but they had both been in the barn and hadn't seen anything more than what Mrs. Rogers had. He told them to drive over to Mayor Cawthon's house.

The killers' tracks left the road and headed east toward the San Andres Mountains, and the lawmen followed at a trot. After a while, Sage remarked, "We're going to find those two with dead horses before long if they don't ease up. They've really been moving."

"You think one of them might be Colwell?" asked Miller.

"Neither of these horses is his," replied Sage. "I expect that the man works alone."

Miller had to ask, "You'd know his horse's tracks?"

"Yep," replied Sage. "Made a point of it."

Miller shook his head.

Farther on, Sage pulled up and said, "The game just changed. Colwell's out here."

"What?" said Miller. "How in hell do you know that?"

Sage pointed at the ground. "See that hoof print there with the nick in it? I put that nick in with a file a few days ago. Those tracks were made a while before the men we're after came along.

"I'm thinking that Bill Rogers died to get us out here."

Sage studied the country. They were out in the wide open sage. About half a mile ahead the foothills of the San Andres began with a rugged escarpment that rose above the flats.

Sage said, "The tracks are all heading toward that notch. It's very likely that Colwell is right in there. If so, he's watching us right now, and here we are without a thing to hide behind. Lucky we're still out of range.

"Well, we're going to do something that will surprise Colwell."

"What would that be?" asked Miller.

"Leave. Colwell hasn't broken any laws, and I'm not about to play any cards that he's dealt. What I want to do is get those two that got Bill.

"I scouted this area a while back. On the other side of that notch is a valley. They can get back to Rincon that way. Let's head back toward Rincon and swing around to where that valley comes out. They've got to be resting their horses, and maybe they're waiting for Colwell to pick us off before they head back to town. We might be able to get in front of them."

They turned their horses and cantered back toward the Rio. After they had moved about a hundred feet, there was a noise like an axe smacking into a side of beef. Smoky's hind legs folded, and Sage rolled off the big horse. Smoky screamed as he went down on his belly and rolled over on his side. The boom of a heavy rifle came from the distance.

Sage instantly jumped to his feet and moved to Smoky's side. The horse's right hind knee had been blown apart, and the lower leg flopped sickeningly as the other legs thrashed.

Sage whipped out his Colt and put a bullet in Smoky's head. Then he dropped to his belly and worked his Winchester out of its scabbard as another bullet snapped through the air where he'd been.

Miller rode up to him. Sage jumped up and vaulted onto the horse behind Miller.

"Go!" he yelled, and Miller went as another bullet kicked up dust in front of them.

After a quarter mile Sage looked back. A plume of dust indicated that a rider was following them.

Sage yelled in Miller's ear, "He's coming, and he'll catch up. He can get us in his range well before he's in ours, and he'll have us!"

Sage studied the flat ground ahead and all around.

"Cody, go through that tall sage up there and slow down. I'll jump off, and you keep going. Go far. Maybe he won't see you're alone in the dust."

Miller didn't argue. Sage swung off the back of Miller's horse and rolled. Then he wormed around in the brush until he had a good view of their back trail.

He levered a round in the Winchester and waited. Sage was amazed that the son of a bitch had been able to hit anything from the distance he was at. They must have been just outside the range where he was really accurate. Maybe Colwell was just hoping to goad them into coming on and got a lucky shot. Not so lucky for Smokey. God damn that man!

Colwell was coming on at a dead run. Sage fervently hoped that Colwell hadn't seen him drop off. If he had, he was in for a hot time. The brush here wasn't all that thick. He'd know in a minute if Colwell stopped before he got there.

He didn't. When Colwell was two hundred yards away, Sage figured that he was liable to be spotted in the thin brush if he waited any longer. He took his shot and Colwell jerked back. Then he bent foreword over his saddle horn and rolled off.

Colwell's horse came to a stop and stood ground tied. Apparently, it was well trained. Sage stood up and fired three more rounds into the prone body. The horse flinched at the first one but remained standing. That first shot made Colwell writhe some.

Sage jogged up to the body. Colwell had taken the first one high in the stomach. Sage was glad that he hadn't taken the top of the horse's head off.

A half hour later, Miller came pounding back and was greatly relieved to find Sage waiting for him with a whole hide. Miller looked at the body and said, "Damn, John, you must have been really mad."

Sage said, "Let's go back to Smokey. Stirrups are too short on this saddle, and I want my gear back anyway."

Sage picked up his hat from the ground near Smokey and put it on. Then he pulled his saddle off the grulla and put it on Colwell's horse. Miller asked Sage what they were going to do next, but Sage didn't reply at first. He was too choked up.

"That horse saved my life right at the start and carried me for a hell of a lot of miles. I'll miss him.

"I'm thinking that I like the idea of going around to the end of that valley. Those two probably couldn't make out what's been happening here even if they climbed up high. But if they saw us coming on they might well try an ambush of their own. They might be looking at us right now."

-55-

Late in the day Sage was about to give it up. He and Miller had taken up positions hours before at the bottom of the valley. There hadn't been any fresh tracks coming out, and Sage figured that they had gotten there in time. But now he figured that the killers had returned to the flats instead of heading down the valley.

He'd just have to go back to the flats and see if he could pick up their tracks before nightfall, but the killers were probably back in Rincon by now.

He was positioned beside a dry streambed, where the walls of the valley closed to within twenty-five feet of each other. He stood up and was about to get the bay and ride up to where Miller was waiting when several pistol shots rang out up that way.

Moments later two riders came galloping through the gap. Sage had his lariat strung across the gap between two trees two feet off the ground. The horses hit the rope and somersaulted, throwing the riders to the ground. They struggled to get up, dazed, and found Sage standing over them with his Colt drawn.

Miller rode up with his handgun drawn, looked at one of the captives, and said, "My turn, Sanchez."

Sage rode back up the valley a small distance and confirmed that the tracks of the horses ridden by ex-deputy Julio Sanchez and the other man, who he remembered from the fight with the soldiers in the Emperor, were the tracks he had followed from the Rogers' farm.

-56-

Sage and Miller stepped into the Emperor and stood to the side of the batwings to look over the crowd. Sage was pleased to see Chance Slade and Calvin Call seated at a front table along the wall across from the bar. He nodded to them, and they nodded back. Call waved them over, but Sage shook his head.

Three men that Sage thought were Lugo's people were seated a few tables in front of the deputies.

Bart Waco was sitting alone at a table at the far end of the room near the card tables. He was smoking a cigar and keeping an eye on the room. Waco spotted the deputies and stiffened with shock.

Miller followed Sage as he walked up to Waco's table. Sage stopped in front of Waco, pulled an object out of a stained white cotton bag he was carrying, and bounced it off the table onto Waco's lap.

With a strangled cry, Waco jumped to his feet, and the head of Ephraim Colwell rolled onto the floor.

Sage and Waco stood frozen for a moment. Then the room reverberated from two gunshots behind Sage. Miller drew as he spun around, but Sage figured that since he wasn't dead, he'd keep his attention on Waco.

Unnerved, Waco reacted to Miller by grabbing his gun, and Sage drew and fired four bullets into Waco's chest in a continuous roar.

Sage spun around as Miller fired a bullet into the rat-faced bartender, who had brought a sawed-off double-barreled shotgun up from under the bar. Another bartender farther down lifted his hands in the air.

Sage faced the room. Just about everyone except Slade and Call, who had their guns trained on one of Lugo's men, was on the floor, including three screaming bar girls. The other two were stretched out on the floor in widening pools of blood.

Sage moved over to his deputies. Slade said, "Never shot a man in the back before, but they'd pulled their guns and were lining up on you. Guess they'd forgot about us back there or hadn't noticed."

"You did good," said Sage.

He faced Lugo's man and said, "You get upstairs and tell Lugo this place is closed for tonight. We'll get the undertaker over here. Leave your gun on the floor there for the time being."

As the man went up the stairs, Sage wondered if Lugo was too fat to get through his office door. Seemed like he never left his desk.

Sage turned back to the room, lifted his voice and said, "The Emperor's closed for tonight. If you're in need of a drink, head over to the San Diego."

It looked like they were all in need of a drink.

Sage asked Slade and Call to get the undertaker. He pointed at Colwell's head and said, "Tell him to pick up that head while he's at it."

The deputies looked at the head and walked a little closer to it.

"Jesus Christ," said Call. "That that Colwell feller?"

"Yes," said Sage. "He was lying in wait for us out there while we were chasing Bill's killers. They were leading us to him. I guess that's why they killed Bill."

Call stared at Sage. "How come you ain't dead? I heard Colwell was really something with a long gun."

"John is really something with a Winchester," said Miller. "That and some smarts saved our bacon. He almost had us. Shot John's horse out from under him."

Slade looked at Waco and said, "Man, you sure did him. I'm surprised he went for his gun. He was fast, but he'd have known it was suicide."

"Had a guilty conscience," said Sage.

"I've got to get over to Mayor Cawthon's place, see if Mrs. Rogers is still over there, and let them know what is going on. How about you all go over to the San Diego as soon as you can? I expect there is a crowd over there now."

Miller said, "I'll do that as soon as I get something to eat."

"Better get something for the prisoners, too," said Sage.

"Prisoners?" asked Call.

"We got the two that did Bill," said Sage. "We'll tell you about it later."

-57-

The next morning Sage went over to the telegraph office to send a message to Sheriff Roeser:

VOLUNTEER ROGERS MURDERED
2 IN CUSTODY
1 IS SANCHEZ
BART WACO DEAD

The telegraph operator sent the message and then said, "Got a message for you, too. Came in earlier this morning."

He handed Sage the handwritten message:

4 MEXICANS HEADED YOUR WAY
ASKED AROUND ABOUT YOU
HARD MEN

Sage pondered that as he walked back to his office. He couldn't think of why any four Mexicans would be interested in him. Federales, maybe? Something to do with that officer he'd killed? He didn't think the Federales would come north of the border officially. Maybe unofficially? The message had said "hard men," not "bandits" or "gunmen." He wondered if Roeser had talked to them. Probably just heard something. There was nothing in the telegraph about their intentions.

Silas Green, Rincon's undertaker, came down the street on his wagon. He had two helpers on the seat with him.

Green stopped the wagon near him and said, "Mornin, deputy. We're heading over to Boot Hill with your evening's work here. Busy day today. We'll be burying Bill Rogers this afternoon. Shame about that.

"Nobody will be up there for these four except Reverend Burns. I take it you didn't bring in the rest of Colwell?"

"No, I didn't," replied Sage. "I had to be moving fast. Left it for the vultures and coyotes. I brought in his guns. You can pick them up along with the ones the other two had to cover your costs. I'm claiming Colwell's horse, though, since he shot mine."

"Fair enough," said Green. "I expect there will be a lot of folks out this afternoon. Bill was well liked around here. Sure glad you caught the ones that done him in. Sorry I won't be the one planting them. Wish I had all the business you've been providing for Lucas Riley down in Mesilla."

Sage gave Green a long look and then said, "Do you know what time the service is this afternoon?"

"They want the grave ready by three o'clock, so I suppose that's when it is," replied Green.

Sage went into his office and found Cody Miller there. Sage showed him the message from Roeser.

"I've got no idea what this is about," said Sage. "But keep an eye out for them."

Miller said, "Benito had a hell of a lot of business last night. He says that you should close the Emperor more often. I got the impression that after getting a look at Lupita and hearing her play, most of them will be going back there anyway."

Sage grinned but then sobered up. "Let's go over to Mayor Cawthon's house. I want to check on what's planned for Bill's service.

"You get Sanchez and Kegler fed?"

"Yep," said Miller. "Those two are looking mighty down."

"They've got cause," said Sage. "I wouldn't want to be in their boots when Mrs. Rogers shows up at the trial with her kids. Or for what comes later."

The whole Rogers family was staying at the Cawthon's house. Anna grabbed Sage's hand and thanked him again for catching the murderers.

"Did they say why they killed Bill?" she asked.

"I didn't ask them," replied Sage. "Didn't need to. They had it set up to lead Cody and me into an ambush. I'm afraid Bill died to make us chase them. I wouldn't be surprised if Jeremy Lugo had designs on acquiring your farm to boot. Those two in the lockup and Ephraim Colwell, who was going to do the ambush, are all tied in with him."

Susan Cawthon and Hiram had come up.

"That Lugo is a monster," she said. "Can't you arrest him?"

"I don't have anything I can use in court," replied Sage. "Not yet. But I'll be putting pressure on him."

"You've been doing that already," said the mayor. "Lugo's troops are getting pretty well thinned out."

"There are plenty more where they came from," said Sage. "I'm surprised that I haven't been seeing new faces showing up."

"I'm not," said Cawthon. "I expect the word is out that Rincon is no longer a town where it is safe to break the law. Far from it. Bart Waco was probably the only reason why Lugo's men that were already here weren't drifting away. Now that he's dead, Lugo might wind up pretty much alone. Lugo is feeling pressure, all right. The man must be getting desperate.

"Well, we have the business here. Vern Summers is out spreading the word about the burial service this afternoon. I expect that you and most of your deputies will want to be there. It's at three o'clock."

-58-

The service drew a crowd. Sage was surprised at how many people knew and liked Bill Rogers. All the volunteer deputies were there, including the three vaqueros from the San Andres Ranch.

Nancy Martin had come in with both Jed Peters and Jethro Morgan. Before the service began, she went over to Anna Rogers and hugged her, and both women teared up.

Anna said, “I knew it was bad for you when Jeffrey disappeared. Now I know just how bad.”

That set them to some serious weeping. Morgan was standing nearby. He came over and put an arm around Martin’s shoulders and gave her a hug.

Sage was astonished that the move sent a wave of jealousy coursing through him, and he reassessed his feelings about Nancy Martin. He realized that respect and admiration didn’t quite cover it.

Reverend Burns conducted the service. He droned on and on about forgiveness of sins and about how poor Bill would be getting his rewards in heaven. Sage doubted that Rogers had many sins that needed forgiving, and to his way of thinking, there was no hereafter. You got one shot at life, so you had to make the best of it to get any rewards. His mind held extra grief for Rogers because that life was cut so short.

After the service Burns circulated the crowd, commiserating with some and inviting others to his Sunday services if he hadn’t seen them there.

He stopped in front of Sage and, frowning, he said, “I suppose that your sins are an especially heavy burden since by your lights, you don’t believe in the God of the Bible, and so they can’t be forgiven.”

“That is exactly right, reverend”, responded Sage. “Nothing and no one can forgive my sins. So I do my best to avoid sinning. I don’t want to have that burden.”

Burns raised his eyebrows. “But you’re a gunfighter! You’ve killed a number of men since you’ve come here. That isn’t a burden?”

"Sins are relative, reverend. No one has any authority that I recognize to dictate what sins are. Cultures pretty much establish what sins are, but different cultures establish different sins. What is wrong for one is right for another. I pretty much boil it down to what does harm and what does good. I killed those men to stop them from doing harm, and I'm satisfied that it wasn't a sin."

Burn's voice elevated. "God commanded that thou shalt not kill. Killing is a sin!"

"You're living in the wrong culture, reverend. But whatever you believe, I take responsibility for my own actions, and your beliefs are not relevant to me."

Sage left Reverend Burns red-faced and spluttering as he turned to walk away. He and the reverend just weren't destined to get along.

He almost walked right into Nancy Martin, who had come up behind him.

Martin turned around and walked with him. "Wow," she said. "No one I know would face off with Reverend Burns like that. He's pretty forceful."

"I don't have much reverence for the reverend," said Sage. "I appreciate that he gets out and marries them and buries them and maybe provides some comfort when he isn't preaching at people. But I'd be surprised if much of what he does is actually beneficial. I wouldn't be surprised if it was harmful."

Grinning, Martin said, "You're going straight to hell."

"I don't believe there is any such thing," replied Sage. "What advanced, all-powerful intelligence would create such a place?"

Martin blinked and stopped walking. She said, "You're pretty deep. How did you get to be so self-assured in your beliefs?"

Sage thought for a moment and then said, "I spent two years with a wise teacher. He didn't teach me facts for the most part. He taught me to reason. We spent countless hours trying to work our way down to basic things: why we do things, why we feel things, and what kinds of things really matter. Actually, we didn't arrive at many of the same conclusions. Different experiences tended to head us in different directions, but both directions were reasonable.

Maybe if we could have achieved 'pure reason,' we would have gotten to the same place, but we didn't. Anyway, he was just pleased that I could reason."

Martin looked at him for a moment. "The man you told me about over on that distant island?" she asked.

"Yes."

"Perhaps you're a wise man, too," she said, grinning.

"I'm a deputy sheriff," he said. "Is that wise?"

Before they could continue, Cody Miller came up and said, "The womenfolk are all headed over to Mayor Cawthon's home. Vern suggested that the menfolk head over to the San Diego. So that's where we're headed. This is turning into quite a social gathering."

"How social is it if we're splitting up?" asked Martin. "We women are going to be holding a wake and crying all over each other while you boys are having a party! I'd rather go to the San Diego."

Sage mulled over getting everyone over to the San Diego and then said, "That wouldn't be wise. Nancy, would you have dinner with me again? I could meet you at the Steak Parlor at eight."

"I'd like that," smiled Martin. "You'll be able to eat something this time."

-59-

When Sage and Miller entered the San Diego with the large group of mourners, Benito Alvarez surveyed them with wide eyes and motioned Sage over to where he was already lining up glasses and starting to pour drinks.

In Spanish, Alverez said, "Once again I am overwhelmed with business. I wish I could know when this is going to happen. But it is a good kind of problem to have."

"It tends to be sort of spontaneous," said Sage. "But I suggest you put on some extra help. I think the Anglo community is taking a liking to this place."

"Yes, many are coming in here now. My regular customers were a little wary of that at first, but they seem to be getting along."

Alvarez got too busy to continue talking. He hurried to the back rooms and returned with Lupita Calderon, whom he pressed into serving at the bar.

After most had obtained drinks, Mayor Cawthon asked Sage for his knife and rapped the handle on the bar a few times for attention. The room quieted down, and Cawthon gave a moving eulogy for Bill Rogers. He followed that by saying that the Rogers family would be in a bind without Bill and suggested that folks stop by the farm and give them a hand from time to time, especially when the crops needed harvesting.

Heads nodded and Sage made a mental note to get out there himself. He didn't see how the family could stay out there for long, but he expected that Anna Rogers would make every effort to keep the place out of Lugo's hands.

Afterward, several men stood up and spoke of their memories of Rogers.

Sage stepped forward and praised Rogers for stepping up as a citizen and putting on a badge even though he wasn't skilled with guns. He credited Rogers for standing with the other deputies when they faced down Lugo's men at great risk to his own life.

After he finished, one of the men opined, “We ought to finish that job. String up Sanchez, Kegler, and Lugo to boot. Give poor Bill a memorial hanging.”

That drew a number of assenting murmurs.

Sage flared up. “There will be no more of that! Cody and I caught them, not you, and we'll be the ones that hang them. Bill put his life on the line to uphold the law, and he would demand that we abide by it. This is not a lawless town anymore.”

Chastened, the group settled down. Lupita walked over to a corner of the room and picked up her guitar.

“I will play a song for Señor Bill Rogers,” she announced.

And she did. It was a song from Mexico about brave men who did their duty and lost their lives for their country. Since she sang in Spanish, most of the men didn't understand it, but they greatly appreciated the music and the performer just the same. Everyone relaxed and turned to drinking and talking.

Later, Jed Peters walked over to Sage and said, “Nancy told me she was having dinner with you. I've got to get back to the ranch and do some feeding, but Jethro will be staying overnight and driving her back in the morning. They came in the buggy.

“I'm glad you are spending some time with her. She's been sort of moping around. I got the impression she thought you were kind of standoffish on the ride up from Mesilla.”

Taken aback, Sage said, “I had things on my mind that she wasn't a part of, and I was feeling a bit low after hanging four men. But I'm a mite surprised that would matter any.”

Peters said, “I think it mattered. I think she's taken a real interest in you. Been talking about you a lot. Seems to think you might be of some use. Women get fool notions sometimes.”

Sage chuckled and then asked, “How's Jethro working out?”

“Good hand. Good as they get. We're putting a real dent in the work needed around there. I thought we'd be needing another hand, but Nancy is still putting in saddle time, and we're getting along all right without one.

"That place could carry a lot more stock than what we've got now. Jeff was working to expand when he was killed. If we can get ahead of things, Nancy will be wanting to add cattle and get more hands.

"Jethro wasn't too sure about working for a woman at first, but now he's saying she's turned out to be a hell of a good boss. Got a head on her shoulders and pulls her weight, even though she doesn't know everything about cows and is kind of sorry with a rope. Good cook, though."

"If you're getting well fed, things can't be all bad," said Sage. "Well, it's getting on toward eight. I've got to be meeting up with Nancy."

"And I've got to be getting back to the Rocking M," said Peters.

Lupita Calderon stepped in front of Sage before he got to the door. She placed her hands on her hips and said with a frown, "Why do you not like me?"

Flummoxed, Sage asked, "Why in the world would you think such a thing?"

"You come and you go, and you never talk to me! You must think that I am very ugly."

"I just happen to think that you are very beautiful. I've never seen a more beautiful woman in my whole life."

"Then why do you not talk to me?"

Sage had to chew on that for a moment. "Because I think you are the most dangerous woman I have ever seen in my whole life."

The frown was replaced with a wide-eyed look of incredulity.

"Dangerous!? Why do you say dangerous? No one has ever called me dangerous."

"Lupita," said Sage, "I am a weak man. You would have the power to make me do whatever you wished."

Lupita gave him a wry look and said, "And this would be a bad thing?"

"Very bad," replied Sage. "Perhaps you respect me for what I am. The danger is that you would change me from what I am. I am content with what I am. I don't think I would be content if I changed into anything else."

Lupita looked at him solemnly for a long moment and then said, "I do not believe that you are a weak man. We would just fight and then make up." She gave him that heart-stopping smile and said, "And then things would be good."

Sage was sweating. This had gotten too deep too fast. He thought of Nancy Martin and calmed down.

He looked Lupita in the eye and said, "Fighting with a woman does not appeal to me. There shouldn't be any need to fight. A man and a woman should be a better fit.

"You are quite a woman. I admire your beauty, and I have seen you step up twice now to calm things down in here when it was needed. I admire that, too.

"But we wouldn't fit."

Lupita stared at him. Then, frustrated, she turned and walked quickly back behind the bar.

Sage went outside, stopped, and drew in a deep breath of the cooling air while he looked at the setting sun. Then he walked over the Steak Parlor.

He was a little early, and Martin hadn't arrived yet. The Steak Parlor was a small, homey affair run by an immigrant couple named Krantz. Paul Krantz worked in the Twin Peaks mine during the day, and the restaurant was only open five evenings a week. His wife, Brigitte, did the cooking. Sage had only eaten there once, but he'd liked the food and the comfortable atmosphere.

Seven of the eight tables were occupied, and Sage felt lucky that there was one still available in a corner. He should have stopped by for a reservation before going to the San Diego.

Several of the customers gave Sage a friendly greeting, and Milo Hawkins, owner of the General Store, invited him to sit with him and his wife, Meg.

"Thank you, Milo," said Sage, "but I'm meeting a lady here shortly."

"Well," said Milo, "you'd both be welcome to join us."

"Milo," said Meg, "perhaps Deputy Sage would like to be alone with the lady."

Both Milo and Sage were a little flustered. Just then, Paul Krantz arrived with the Hawkins' dinners, and Sage said, "Looks like we'd be a bit behind you, but thank you anyway."

As he laid down the plates, Krantz said, "Deputy Sage, I can't thank you enough for recovering the mine's payroll. Most of the miners live month to month on their pay, and I don't think the Twin Peaks would have made up their loss right away. You prevented a lot of suffering."

Sage said, "My name is John. I can't say that I was thinking about the miner's situation. I just wanted to do my job: catch the bandits and recover what they'd stolen. Thank you for reminding me that some more good came of that. I like to feel that I am doing something worthwhile."

Meg said, "John, you are among the blessed."

Sage said, "That's kind of you. You might pass that along to Reverend Burns." He walked over to the empty table.

Martin came in the door, looked around, and came over to Sage's table. He stood up and pulled out her chair.

She was wearing the floor-length tan skirt and long-sleeved, high-collared white blouse she had been wearing at the burial service, but she had redone her hair and added a necklace and earrings, and her lips had more color. Sage thought she looked pretty damned good.

"What a pleasant place this is!" she said. "I've never been in here."

"I think you'll be able to choke down the food, too," said Sage.

Krantz came over to take their order, and Sage introduced him to Martin.

Krantz said in an accented voice, "I heard about how you lost your husband. My heart goes out to you. I am very glad that Deputy Sage brought his murderers to justice."

Martin said, "The badmen have been having a very hard time around here lately. John is their worst nightmare come to life. I am grateful that he is here."

Martin looked at Sage, and seeing that he was looking uncomfortable, she smiled at him and said, "Come on John. If you have a compliment coming, take it."

Her smile had about the same effect as Lupita's but was more welcome.

While they were waiting for their meal, Martin said, "I was right. It was pretty dismal over at the Cawthons'. I was jealous of you boys over at the San Diego. I made excuses and left early. How did it go?"

"Mayor Cawthon gave a good eulogy," Sage replied. "Several men spoke well of Bill. Benito Alvarez had quite a lot of business.

"A few of the men wanted to string up Sanchez and Kegler in remembrance, but I put a stop to that talk. That is not going to happen here. Lupita Calderon got everyone calmed down with her music. She plays the guitar well and has a good voice."

"I've heard of her," said Martin. "Jeff was in there once."

Her eyes narrowed. "He said she would make Helen of Troy look like a wallflower. Are you friends with her?"

Uh oh, thought Sage. Maria Rodriguez had spent several hours describing the siege of Troy. Why would the damn fool say something like that? Nancy had probably fried him in his own oil.

"Friendly. Not particularly friends."

Martin looked at him closely. "I would think she might take an interest in you," she probed.

"Well, she did express an interest," Sage said carefully. "That ended when I told her that we wouldn't make a good fit." At least he hoped it had ended.

Martin raised her eyebrows and asked, "How might that be?"

Sage leaned back and looked down at the table, thinking. "If I took to courting, I would want the woman to be someone I would be comfortable with, someone I could trust and had the same values. I'd want to have a little room, not have to be on my toes all the time."

"But she's a real beauty!" said Martin.

"She is. But I wouldn't be comfortable with her. We wouldn't fit."

Martin's face softened somewhat. "You must have had a lot of experience with women. Not many men can see beyond a pretty face."

Surprised, Sage said, “Hardly any at all. But I know myself pretty well. Fisu Hiragawa had me doing a lot of introspection. He taught me how to meditate and look inside myself, to get to know myself, and what my foundation is made of. From there I can figure out what is of actual value.”

Her face softened further. “You are quite unique,” she said in a low voice.

They were halfway through their steaks when Martin asked, “Do you plan on staying in Rincon for the rest of your life?”

Sage shook his head. “I like what I’m doing. I feel that I’m doing some good, and I’ll keep at it for a while. But I don’t see myself spending my whole life being a lawman. There are a lot of places that would be worth seeing that I haven’t seen yet or even heard of. My father did a lot of wandering, and I guess that’s in my blood.

“When I was in a school, there was a globe of the world that I studied. It fascinated me. So much out there. I saw a part of it that was a lot different than here. I told you about that. I had some hard times there, but I count the experience as valuable. I’d like to see more.”

“I was going to ask you if you had considered ranching,” said Martin. “I take it that ranching wouldn’t fit your needs, either.”

“I’ve worked with cattle. I’ve met a lot of good men who liked doing that and wouldn’t care to do anything else. Good thing. I like steak. But I didn’t find working with cattle to be... *jyuu bun*.” He searched for the word in English.

“Fulfilling.”

Martin thought for a moment and then said, “I found raising cattle with Jeffrey to be fulfilling.”

She teared up for a moment. Then she shook her head and said, “But with him gone, it is not so fulfilling. But it is challenging, and it’s a living. And I like steak, too,” she grinned.

She tapped her steak with her fork and said, “I like this steak in particular. I’ll be coming back here.”

“I don’t know what Mrs. Krantz does to it, but it sure is savory,” said Sage. “Mighty tender, too.”

While they were eating apple pie for dessert, Milo Hawkins came over to their table and introduced Meg to Nancy. Milo had known the Martins as customers. They commiserated with Martin, and she invited them to have a seat, but they wanted to get home and make sure the kids hadn't torn their place down.

When they finished, Sage and Martin went back to the kitchen to thank Brigitte for the good dinner.

Brigitte was a large, pudgy woman with blond hair and a reddish face. Her mouth and eyes reminded Sage of a carp he'd seen pulled up on the bank of a pond on Okinawa. Her round mouth gasped and her hands flew to the sides of her face.

She looked at Sage with the huge eyes, and said with a thick accent, "So you are the deputy John Sage. I've heard men talking about you. They say they would rather take their chances riding through a Texas tornado than have you come after them. But you don't look like you're fierce at all!"

"Oh, don't be fooled by the innocent face," said Martin. "He's fierce. But your excellent dinner calmed him down for now."

Sage just shook his head and thanked Mrs. Krantz for the fine dinner. Then he wrapped his fingers around Martin's upper arm and walked her out of the kitchen.

When they were out in the dining room, he let go, and Martin said, "Why John, how rude!"

"Didn't know what you were going to say next," said Sage.

She fluttered her eyelashes innocently and said, "I was just going to tell her about your pets. The grizzly and the cougar."

"That's what I was afraid of."

When they got outside, Sage surveyed the dark street. The street was empty, but he could faintly hear the piano in the Emperor, and voices from the San Diego in the other direction. The "wake" was still somewhat underway. Martin told him she was staying at the same boarding house where Miller lived. As they walked, she slipped her right hand around his upper left arm. That startled Sage, but he thought it felt good there.

She said, "John, traveling around the country or the world doesn't leave a lot of room for a family. Are you planning on having one?"

"I haven't really thought much about that," said Sage. "I'm just twenty-four. I haven't settled on what I might do in the future just yet. I was satisfied to get along until I found something to do that would be...fulfilling. I haven't seen my way to what that would be yet."

"Was satisfied?" said Martin. "Not so satisfied now?"

Sage stopped and turned toward her. She maintained her hold on his arm. What a large, hard bicep, she thought.

"I hadn't been thinking about finding a partner," said Sage. "I'm realizing that I might be missing something. Something I didn't realize I needed."

Martin looked into his eyes for a long moment, which were barely visible in the night. Then she said, "A partner is a good thing to have."

She released his arm and faced him fully. Then she put her hands on his shoulders.

"The custom is that I mourn Jeffrey for a year. Well, I'm going to mourn him for the rest of my life. But I'm going to live my life. Jeff would have expected that. Wanted that."

Sage placed his arms around her and drew her close.

"Nancy, I think we would fit."

She tightened her arms around his neck and lifted her mouth.

"Yes," she said. "Yes."

After a long kiss, they tilted their heads back and said, "Whew!"

With his head swimming, Sage said, "We'll be needing to spend some time together and work out what we want to do. Things are coming to a head here with Lugo, and I've got to stay around town. Maybe you could ride back in and stay a while."

"I'd like to stay right now," said Martin. "But people would frown, wouldn't they? Can't have them frowning. You're a respected public official, and I'm a respectable widow. But we're damned well going to get together!"

"I'll get you to your room," said Sage. "Then I've got to check whether anyone has fed my prisoners. I'm being derelict in my duty."

They pressed together and kissed again by the door, and it took all of Sage's self-discipline not to go in with her.

-60-

Just before noon the next morning, Sage and Miller were sitting in chairs in front of their office savoring cigars and solving a few of the territory and the country's problems. A man walked toward them that Sage recognized as one of the bartenders at the Emperor.

The bartender handed Sage an envelope and stood by with a smug look on his face while Sage tore it open and read the note inside.

Deputy Sage:

I have a business matter that I would like to discuss with you. Please do me the kindness of meeting with me in my office at 1:00. I would appreciate your individual attention.

Jeremy Lugo

Sage wondered why Lugo hadn't just waddled down here. Maybe he couldn't walk that far. He looked at the bartender and said, "I'll be there."

The bartender nodded and walked back to the Emperor.

Sage handed Miller the note. Miller read it and said, "He hasn't had much luck with killing you off. Maybe now he wants to buy you off."

"I'd be surprised if he thought he could," said Sage. "I can't imagine what he's got on his mind. I'll just have to let him tell me."

Sage and Miller entered the Emperor at one. Since it was known they were coming, they went in low and fast and jumped to either side of the batwings. The bartenders looked at them with astonishment and then smirked. There weren't many patrons.

Two bar girls lounged at the empty card tables.

Sage said, "Wait down here, Cody. I take it he wants to see me alone and might not say what's on his mind if you're there."

"Careful you don't walk into a shotgun blast," said Cody.

Sage went up the stairs and stood to the side of Lugo's door when he tapped on it.

"Come in," called Lugo.

Sage turned the knob and pushed the door open. But he remained where he was for a few seconds before entering. He saw Lugo behind his desk, apparently alone, and stepped quickly through the door and to the side. He froze.

Four Mexicans were standing along the side wall. Four hard men. But they didn't have their guns drawn. Sage looked at them, and a sick feeling washed through him from head to toe.

In the Apache language he said, "I thought that seeing you again would be a thing of joy, Strong Arm. But I'm not feeling any joy. I feel like I just got my guts cut out. This means that you have forgotten everything our fathers stood for.

"I'm not going to try to kill you. Just go ahead and finish it."

In the same language Miguel Vega said, "I did not come to kill you, Sees in the Night. I came to see the men who wanted you killed."

Alarmed, Lugo said, "What's going on? Kill him!"

In accented English, Vega, looking at Sage, said, "This morning, Mr. Lugo gave us a great deal of money to make you dead. Is this not illegal?"

Lugo's jaw dropped in horror as he leaned back in his chair.

Sage gave Vega a penetrating look and then turned to Lugo. "Yes, it is illegal. Jeremy Lugo, you are under arrest for the attempted murder of a peace officer."

Lugo's open mouth closed and opened again, but nothing came out.

"Stand up, Lugo," ordered Sage.

Trembling and sweating profusely, the white-faced man struggled to his feet. Sage stepped around the desk and made sure Lugo didn't have a weapon hidden in his clothing.

"Let's all go downstairs," said Sage, and he watched curiously to see if Lugo could make it through his door and down the stairs. He just barely could.

The two bartenders looked at them incredulously as they descended. Sage kept an eye on them.

Miller was startled by the appearance of the Mexicans, but he relaxed when he saw that Sage wasn't in any distress.

Sage said, "Cody, Lugo is under arrest. Get this place closed up and stick around. I don't want any money or papers walking out of here. After I jail Lugo, I'll talk to Hiram. I think the bank has a mortgage interest, and maybe he'll take over things here.

"Careful with those bartenders. I think they knew what was going on."

"What was going on?" asked Cody.

"Lugo had a trap set up. I'll tell you about it later."

Mystified, Miller went to work, and Sage and his prisoner walked over to the office with Vega and his companions.

While they were walking, Sage said, "Miguel, I've got to take care of this business. There is a saloon here, the San Diego, that I think you will find pleasing. Would you wait for me there?"

"Of course, John," replied Vega. "We have seen the San Diego."

Sage took Lugo up to the cells. Lugo had to pause to rest several times, so it was a slow process.

When Sanchez and Kegler saw Lugo, they jumped up.

Kegler, not the brightest of people, said, "You come to get us out, Mr. Lugo?"

Lugo exploded. "You incompetent bastards!" he screamed. "None of you could do your jobs. You can go to hell! Sanchez, I don't know why I ever paid you a single goddamn dime, you worthless shit!" he raged.

Sanchez stiffened, and his obsidian eyes glittered with hate. Sage held his breath.

Sanchez bit off his words as he said, "You son of a whoring pig, you paid us to kill, and we killed. Now we are going to hang, and so are you. I hope I can watch you go first."

Sage grabbed Lugo and nearly lifted the huge man off the floor as he flung him through the door of an open cell. He slammed and locked it behind him.

He opened Sanchez's cell and said, "Let's go downstairs."

When they were half way down, Lugo screamed, "Sanchez, I'll get you the best lawyer in the country!"

"Lot of good that would do," said Sage. "You're caught too good."

Sage wasn't completely sure about that.

"I take it you are willing to make a statement against Lugo?" asked Sage.

Sanchez was. He dictated a statement that Lugo had paid him and Kegler two hundred dollars each to murder Bill Rogers. He also detailed the payments for the murders of Jeffrey Martin and the two missing farmers, Pedro Martinez and a man named Michael Hall.

He went on to state that Lugo had ordered the stage holdup and attempted ambush as well as the rescue attempt for the bandits.

Sanchez paused and said, "Damn, Sage, if I'd had any idea of what you could do, I sure would have kept on going when you kicked me out of here. I can't believe you got Colwell and Waco."

"I got 'em," said Sage. "Can I put down that Lugo hired Colwell to ambush me and Miller?"

"Waco hired him for Lugo."

Sage finished up, and Sanchez signed the statement. He took Sanchez back up the stairs keeping far enough behind him to avoid a possible kick, but Sanchez wasn't about to try him.

Lugo was sitting on the edge of the cot with his face in his hands. He didn't look up. Sage could see that Lugo was going to have to sleep on two mattress pads on the floor.

As he went downstairs, Sage thought he should have been feeling elated. But he wasn't.

Hiram Cawthon was at the bank, and Sage asked him to sit down with him in his office.

Sage got right down to it. "I've arrested Jeremy Lugo on several counts of murder. He's in a cell, and the Emperor is closed."

"Good Lord," said Cawthon. "What murders?"

"He paid for the murders of Jeffrey Martin, Bill Rogers, Pedro Martinez, and Michael Hall. He also ordered the stage holdup and the attempt to ambush me, and later on he paid Ephraim Colwell to ambush Cody Miller and me. He also hired four other men to kill me."

Sage paused. "The man sure wanted me dead."

"He certainly did!" said Cawthon. "I find it astonishing that you aren't. You are very lucky to have such incredible skills."

"Luck wasn't involved," said Sage.

"Cody is over at the Emperor making sure nothing leaves the place that shouldn't. Do you hold the mortgage for that place?"

"I do," replied Cawthon. "I'm going to have to get some legal work done before I can proceed with its disposition. In the meantime I'll have to keep it closed. I'd better get over there with one of my clerks and secure the papers and any cash. I don't suppose Lugo would be so cooperative as to open the safe."

"I don't suppose he would," said Sage. "I suggest that you secure the liquor, too. Maybe wholesale it to Benito Alvarez. I think he'll be needing it. Lugo is not in a position to object."

"That's a very good idea," said Cawthon. "I'll keep a record of the transaction and let the lawyers work it out later.

"I'll need you to accompany me so that you can attest to what goes where."

"Cody can do that," said Sage. "I've got to meet with a man on some other business."

"Well, John," said Cawthon, "you have done a remarkable job. Do you have good evidence against Lugo?"

"Yes."

"You said that four other men were hired to kill you?" said Cawthon.

"That's the other business," said Sage.

-61-

Sage went to the telegraph office and sent a short message to Sheriff Roeser:

ARRESTED LUGO FOR MURDER
EMPEROR CLOSED
NEED YOU HERE

Sage went into the San Diego. Vega and his companions were sharing a bottle of mescal at a table. Sage nodded toward them and went over to talk to Alvarez. He didn't see Calderon in the room.

As usual while in the San Diego, Sage conversed in Spanish. "Benito, the Emperor is shut down. I just arrested Lugo for murder, so it is going to stay shut down for a while. Looks like you're going to have to shoulder the load."

Wide-eyed, Alvarez said, "My God! Murder?"

"Several murders," said Sage. "One charge is for Pedro Martinez."

Alvarez reached over the bar and gripped Sage's left arm.

"Pedro. You got the son of a bitch for Pedro?"

Sage nodded. "I got him."

Alvarez's eyes watered. He blinked and said, "John, you are doing miracles here! Sheriff Roeser can't be paying you enough."

"Enough to eat on," smiled Sage. "What more can I ask?

"I just talked to Hiram. He'll be getting in touch with you. You might want to pick up some merchandise from the Emperor. Liquor and maybe some other things."

Sage gave Alvarez a wry look. "There will be three ladies from over there looking for work."

Alvarez looked shocked. "I do not do that business!" he exclaimed. "What would my wife think? What would Father Lopez think? What would Lupita think?"

"Well, what I think," said Sage, "is that they'll go on working somewhere, and they'd be better off with someone watching out for them. They'll probably move on, and that's too bad. There's a need for that service."

Alvarez stared at Sage incredulously and shook his head. "Not in here, my friend."

"Just a thought," said Sage. "Now I have an old friend to see." He nodded his head toward the four men seated across the room.

"You know those men? They do not appear to be vaqueros. When they came in, I thought I would not want to have trouble with these men. They have the look of those who hunt other men, they way you do."

Sage gave Alvarez a inquisitive look and said, "I know one of them, not the others. I haven't seen him for about eight years, and I don't know what he has been doing."

Alvarez nodded at another table where four Mexicans were sharing a bottle of mescal and said, "Tough crowd in here today. Those men have been in here several times. One of them is obsessed with Lupita, but Lupita wants nothing to do with him. She says he is evil. I think he is going to be trouble."

Sage looked at the men at the table and thought that they did indeed look evil. They didn't look like working vaqueros but rather like off-duty bandits.

"Excuse me."

Sage walked over to one of the empty tables and sat down. He looked at Vega, and Vega stood up, walked over to Sage's table, and took a chair.

Before Sage could ask, Vega said, "I am a member of the rural police, the Rurales. Do you know of them?"

Sage shook his head.

"When Porfirio Diaz became the president of Mexico, he said that Mexico needed more railroads, not more cathedrals. First he broke the hold of the church over the government. Then he went looking for investors to build railroads—foreign investors.

"But the investors would not come because all of Mexico was overrun by bandits. So Diaz created the Rurales. He did this by hiring most of the bandits. With an income and an honorable position, these men were no longer bandits, and they quickly captured or killed all those who did not come in."

Vega spread his hands. "Poof. Overnight, no more bandits, and the investors came from America and Europe."

Sage said, "So, Miguel, you were a bandit?"

Vega gave Sage a long, serious look. "John, Enrique and Nathan did not raise us to be bandits. Diaz could not rely entirely on such men. During the revolution I sided with Diaz against Lerdo. They noticed that I was proficient with guns. I became a member of Diaz's personal guard. Now, I have some rank in the Rurales."

Sage thought for a moment and said, "Miguel, I've got to hear how it was that Lugo hired you."

Vega grinned. "Bart Waco knew a man who worked for the railroads in Mexico. Waco asked this man if he knew of people there who were exceptionally good with guns and willing to eliminate a certain deputy John Sage in Rincon for a large sum of money.

"This man knew of my reputation with the pistol and the rifle and that I was in the Rurales, but he did not know that I had not been a bandit. When he approached me and I heard who Waco wanted killed, I immediately accepted the job. The request was for four men, so I selected three from my troop who were happy to see some new country, took my leave, and here I am."

Sage said, "Miguel, I owe you an apology."

Vega held up his hand. "No. What else could you have thought?"

Sage stood up and came around the table as Vega also stood.

Sage said, "Damn, Miguel, it is very good to see you!" He wrapped his arms around Vega and hugged him.

Lupita Calderon walked into the room at that moment and was startled to see Sage and a tough-looking stranger in that position.

Vega said, "Come and meet my companions."

Vega's companions had bolted up in their chairs and were looking at Calderon. In a low voice one of them said, "Mother of God! That woman makes me want to go home and throw stones at my beloved Rosa."

Vega introduced Sage. Sage told the men that he needed them to stay until Lugo's trial was held in Mesilla.

He would know soon when that would be. He explained to them that now he had murder charges against Lugo, so it was not so important that they stay, but he wanted to hit Lugo with everything he had. Vega said that they would stay.

"Just how much were you paid to take me on?" Sage asked Vega.

Vega grinned and said, "You were worth four thousand American dollars dead. We have it right here in our pockets. We have never had so much gold in our pockets. It is very heavy."

"I'll lighten your load," said Sage. "It is now officially evidence. I suppose it will be up to Judge Bennett whether you will be able to keep it. Maybe it will be considered to be an illegal transaction, part of Lugo's estate. I don't really know."

Vega looked at his three companions and said, "Perhaps we cannot stay."

Sage considered his reply for a moment and then said, "Perhaps not."

"I've got to be getting back to the Emperor. Let's get together for dinner. Come on over to my office when you are ready."

Calderon sang a song about a suitor named Miguel who won the heart of a maiden, which delighted Vega's companions and got Vega's complete attention. It also apparently delighted another man at the table Alvarez had pointed out.

The man walked over to Calderon, spread his arms wide, and said, "Lupita, I would put Miguel to shame. Come and sit with me."

"I would be ashamed to sit with you, Zimorrow." spat Calderon.

Zimorrow cracked an open hand across Calderon's face.

Sage and Vega lunged to their feet. Zimorrow started to draw, but Vega and Sage had their guns up and cocked before he cleared leather. Zimorrow froze. Vega walked up to him and drove his left fist into Zimorrow's nose with enough force to cave it in along with teeth and facial bone, laying him out on the floor.

Zimorrow's companions had jumped up from their table, but Vega's men were covering them, and they stood still.

Alvarez hustled over carrying his shotgun. He looked at Zimorrow's companions and said, "Get this garbage out of here. Don't any of you come back here again."

Vega fussed over Calderon while Zimorrow's men carried the stupefied man outside. Sage and Vega's men followed them out, and Sage pointed out where the doctor's office was.

"Do you work around here?" asked Sage.

The three men looked at each other and shook their heads.

"As far as I'm concerned, you're a threat to this town," said Sage. "If I see you again, I'll remove the threat."

Sage went back inside. Calderon was sitting with Vega. She looked composed. Aside from a slightly reddened face, she wasn't showing any damage.

Sage said, "Allow me to introduce my friend, Miguel Vega. We grew up together. Miguel, this is Lupita Calderon."

Calderon said, "I am very pleased to meet your friend. He is very handsome and very strong."

She looked at Vega and said, "Thank you for helping me. Whenever I sing that song I will think of you."

Vega's face got as red as Calderon's. "I can't believe any man would hit such a beautiful woman."

"Neither could I," she said. "He was not much of a man. Where are you from, Miguel?"

Sage left them talking and went back to the Emperor.

Someone had painted CLOSED in large letters across the batwings, but the inner doors were unlocked, and Sage went in. No one was in the room, so Sage went up the stairs. He found Cawthon, Miller, and two other men from the bank sorting through piles of papers they had stacked on the desk and a table.

"Turns out Lugo's got a little problem with his temper," said Sage. "He tore into Sanchez. Sanchez took some exception to that, and I wound up getting Sanchez to dictate a statement that pretty well wraps up Lugo.

"Cody, Hiram, we've got him."

Miller raised both fists over his head and pumped them up and down. Then he said, "Who are those Mexicans?"

"I grew up with one of them," said Sage. "Miguel Vega is my oldest friend. We went through a lot together. He and the others are all Rurales now. Mexican rural police."

"I haven't heard of them," said Miller. "They come up to visit you? What were they doing with Lugo?"

"They came up to kill me," said Sage.

Sage chuckled at Miller's expression and then said, "Miguel and I learned to handle guns together. He's at least as good as me. He had some reputation down there, and most of the Rurales are ex-bandits, so when Waco asked an acquaintance of his to recruit some firepower, the man approached Miguel.

"Miguel doesn't hire out his gun, but the man didn't know that. When Miguel heard who Waco wanted killed, he signed up pronto.

"When I found Miguel in Lugo's office, it was the worst moment in my life. But then Miguel sided with me, and Lugo probably had the worst moment in his life. Probably had one that was even worse when Sanchez turned on him.

"I'm wondering if Lugo was even still interested in taking me out. Things have developed here to the point that if I went down, Lugo wouldn't have lasted a day. I guess he just couldn't resist the opportunity when he thought he had it. Maybe figured that with the four new guns, he'd be protected."

"That sounds about right," said Cawthon. "The way you went about developing support for the law here, he wouldn't have lasted a day even if they'd nailed Cody in here."

Miller's eyebrows lifted.

Cawthon waved a hand at the stacks of papers. "We'll be taking all of this to the bank. It's going to take some time to make some sense of it all. At first look, there are some papers that I think will be of interest to the prosecution, and I'll be working on figuring out the financial status of both Lugo and the Emperor."

"I sent a message to Jim Roeser asking him to come up," said Sage. "I expect that he will be working on those papers with you."

"Lugo has a large safe here," said Cawthon. "I'll be applying for a court order to open it. Have to break it open unless you can get the combination from Lugo."

"I'll give it a try once you get the order," replied Sage.

"By the way," said Sage, "what's become of Lugo's employees here?"

"I informed them all that they are no longer employed," said Cawthon. "The bartenders, the dealers, the girls, and the swamper."

-62-

"Good steak," said Vega after the first bite. "Now I would like to hear what you have been doing for the last eight years."

Sage spent the rest of the meal describing his getting shanghaied, his life on Okinawa, the trip back to Mexico, and the years on the Valendez spread. When he spoke of his experience with the Federales near Laredo, Miguel's eyes widened.

"I heard something of that!" he said. "A Lieutenant Garcia was killed. He was from a very prominent family aligned with Lerdo de Tejada. Diaz led the revolution against Lerdo and became president.

"I heard that an American killed the lieutenant, but I did not hear the name of the American. I think it was known, though. Lieutenant Gabriel Garcia's father, Adolpho, is the family patron, the leader of the extended family and those who are aligned with them."

"The name of the American was John Sage," said Sage. "Garcia killed the sheriff I was with. We were fighting for our lives. I was the only one that managed to escape thanks to Garcia's horse. Very fast horse. A lot of endurance."

Vega gave Sage a long look. "The Garcias are not so powerful now, but I would not go near Veracruz if I were you.

"So, how did you come to be a deputy sheriff?"

Sage went on to the end of his story and said, "I have met a woman—a young widow. She has a ranch near here. Perhaps I will marry this woman although this is something new. We haven't worked through things yet."

"You will become a rancher?" asked Vega.

"I'm not too interested in being a rancher. Not too interested in being a deputy sheriff for a lot longer, either. As I said, we haven't worked things through. Haven't even started. But I want to be with this woman."

Vega said, "You're ahead of me. I have not met a woman that I want to marry. That is a good thing. I am busy with the Rurales. I am a lieutenant—second in command of a company. If I was older or was a member of one of the important families, I think I would have had a higher appointment.

"But the man interested in my career and who got me into the Rurales is Diaz himself. Over time, I think I will do well."

"I expect you will," said Sage. "I doubt that there are many men who are as capable as you."

"In Mexico," said Vega, "'capable' is about the last thing that gets one a promotion. But Diaz is a great man, and he appreciated some of the things I did during the revolution. I don't think he will forget."

With the dinner over, Sage and Vega rode down to the river, built a fire, lit up cigars, and reminisced through most of the night.

As they rode back into town, Vega said, "I think we will leave today. You will not need our testimony now to hang Lugo."

"No," said Sage. "What you did put him on the edge of a cliff. I gave him a little push, and over he went. I don't need more."

Sage reached across and gripped Vega's hand. "I hope it won't be another eight years before I see you again," he said.

-63-

The following evening, Sage was having a beer with Hiram Cawthon and Cody Miller at the San Diego when Sheriff Roeser came in with Vern Summers.

Roeser and Summers visited with Alvarez for a few minutes. Then he brought a couple of mugs over to the table and sat down.

Roeser looked at Sage and said, "When I didn't find you at the office, I went over to Vern's. I'll be staying with him while I'm here. Vern's been telling me you've been up to no good as usual. Bothering the likes of poor Jeremy Lugo and all."

"I'm guilty," said Sage. "You can go over to his cell and let him cry on your shoulder if you want."

"Pretty hard on a gent named Ephraim Colwell, too," said Roeser. "You cut off his head?"

"He didn't need it any more," said Sage, "and I did. It got the result I was looking for."

Roeser tipped his hat back on his head, looked at Mayor Cawthon, and said, "I was worried that the situation here would be too much for a green deputy when I sent him up. I'm realizing that Lugo and his bunch never had a chance."

"Amen," said Cawthon. "It's been like watching the seven plagues all landing on a disfavored tribe."

Uncomfortable, Sage said, "I've had good help."

"Yes, because you had the foresight to go out and get that help," said Summers. "You're intelligent. You think ahead. Men want to follow your lead. We could use a man with your abilities representing us in Albuquerque. Right now our man there isn't worth spit. He did good in the war, but he hasn't done anything since. Have you ever thought of running for office? He'll be up for reelection after another year."

Astonished, Sage said, "Not even once. Hell, I don't have hardly any education. I don't know anything about government."

"There's a cure for that," said Summers. "It's called books. Between Hiram and me, we've got a pretty good library. I think we'd both be happy to let you have at it."

Cawthon nodded and said, "I think we'd both be happy to give you some tutoring, too. I agree with Vern. I think you'd make us an excellent representative. Thanks to you, the law enforcement workload in Rincon has decreased considerably. You'd have some time for study."

Sage was reeling. He said, "I like the idea of getting some studying done. I'm not so sure about being a representative. I don't know what that is all about."

Summers said, "The people of Dona Ana County have needs that the territorial government can help with. Sometimes other counties have interests that compete with those needs. We need a representative that will work for the people here. Think about it."

Sage said, "Hiram, I'm half Apache. How do you think that would play in an election?"

"Well," replied Cawthon, "if this was Texas or Arizona, that would be insurmountable. In New Mexico, not so much, even though the Apaches terrorized this area for over two hundred years. Now that the Apaches have been mostly subdued, the newer population doesn't have those memories—at least not at the gut level. I think that for the most part you would be judged on your character and abilities."

Roeser said, "Hiram, you're right that the deputy workload has gone down. I don't really need two deputies here now. I've been looking at moving John to Mesilla and leaving Cody in charge of the office here. But maybe it would be best if Cody came to Mesilla.

"I can't say that I'd like to lose Sage as a deputy, but I think that it would be good for him to look at other opportunities."

Cawthon said, "You wouldn't be losing him. Legislators aren't paid, and they only meet for one month in a year, and three months in the next year."

Sage said, "I'd be in favor of staying here.

"Cody, what do you think about moving to Mesilla?"

"I like working with you, John." He looked at Roeser. "But I might find Jim to be tolerable."

Roeser grinned and said, "Don't count on it.

"All right, Cody, when I go back to Mesilla, you can help me move the prisoners down there, and then you stay on. I'll take them down on the stage, and you can follow along with my horse."

Roeser turned to Sage and said, "I contacted Judge Bennett when you arrested Sanchez and Kegler. He'll convene the court on Monday, two weeks from tomorrow. I'll let him know there will be another defendant. Has Lugo or the others made any arrangements for representation?"

"Not yet," said Sage. "We can talk to them about that tomorrow."

"Hiram, how fast do you think you can get a court order for opening Lugo's safe? If Lugo needs to get into it for funds for a lawyer, maybe we could just clean it all out then?"

"Good thinking," said Cawthon. "Jim and I can draft a message for Judge Bennett first thing in the morning."

Sage said, "Vern, I'm thinking I need to have a meeting with the volunteers. They can pretty much stand down, but it would be useful to keep them deputized and on call in case anything comes up."

Summers said, "They're kind of fond of those badges. You could let them come in and wear them once in a while. How about getting together at my place Friday evening for a barbeque?"

"That will be good," said Sage.

"The deputies from the San Andres were in here last night," said Summers. "And a few others came by when they found the Emperor closed. I caught them up on what has been happening, and they won't be surprised by the changes."

A girl came to their table and asked if they wanted another round. They did. Sage noted that she had been formerly employed at the Emperor and wondered if she was just serving drinks.

Alvarez had put on two new bartenders, both Mexican. Alvarez had told Sage that he'd been approached by Lugo's bartenders and dealers but that he didn't want anything to do with those people. He thought he might get a couple of card tables going if he could find some suitable dealers.

The San Diego was about half full, busier for a Sunday evening than it had ever been. About half of the customers were Anglos. Sage hoped that it would stay that way whenever the Emperor reopened. He thought it would. Everyone was enjoying Calderon's music. The place quieted down when she played.

Roeser looked at Sage and said, "Let's take a walk."

As they walked, Roeser said, "That play with Waco took out a threat and weakened Lugo. Waco certainly had it coming, but I wouldn't want you to be too quick to resort to your fast gun to solve your problems."

Sage thought for a moment and then said, "My father told me once that I should never feel good about killing a man. He said he'd rather kill me himself than see me turn into a cold killer.

"Well, when I killed Ephraim Colwell and Bart Waco, I felt good about it."

Sage stopped and faced Roeser. "I don't feel good about that at all. I can see that I'm getting close to crossing the line. I don't want to do that. Maybe this job provides too many temptations."

"That's what the devil is all about," said Roeser. "Providing temptations. I've said before—this is a devil of a job. I guess that's about right.

"I've admired your restraint as much as I've admired your fighting abilities. It is good to know that you're concerned. That's what will keep you from crossing the line. I'm confident of that."

-64-

On Tuesday Roeser and Cawthon got the court order to open the safe in the Emperor. Lugo wanted to hire a law firm in Albuquerque, so Roeser took him over to the telegraph office to make arrangements. Then he took him to the Emperor to withdraw funds from his safe in order to wire a draft.

Roeser didn't let Lugo close the safe. To Lugo's dismay, he was shown the court order and marched back to his cell.

With Roeser and Cawthon continuing to work on Lugo's papers, Sage decided to ride out to the Rocking M.

Sage saddled Colwell's bay just before dawn. He wondered when he was ever going to pay for a horse. The tall gelding didn't like to follow any other horse. He was always trying to get in front of anyone he was riding with, so Sage decided to name him Leader.

When he got to the ranch house, no one was around. The fresh tracks of three horses led Sage to where Martin, Peters, and Morgan were repairing a pole holding corral a few miles out.

As he rode up, Martin called out, "John! You beat me to it. I was going to come into Rincon tomorrow. We've just about got to where Jed and Jethro can keep the place from falling apart without me for a while."

Peters said, "Oh, no. If you're gone for two hours, we're staring ruination in the face."

"A little ruination builds character," said Martin. "And yours could use some building. I'm going to head back to the house and spend some time with John. We have some things to talk over."

Sage swung down off of Leader and said, "I wanted to let you all know what has been going on in town. I've got Lugo jailed for murder. I've got a witness to say that he ordered the murders of four men, including your husband, Nancy."

Martin gasped and said, "Thank God! Who is the witness?"

"Julio Sanchez. Lugo said some unkind things to him, and Sanchez took enough offense to give me a signed statement. Lugo is a dead man."

Martin's eyes closed for a long moment. "This brings final closure," she said. "I can say good-bye."

She buried her face in Sage's chest and let the tears flow.

Startled and moved, Sage held her tightly until the sobbing quieted. She stayed in his arms for a little more and then stepped back, grasped his arms, and said, "You're the best damned lawman anywhere! Thank you."

Sage demurred but then remembered her remark about compliments and said, "I appreciate that."

Morgan said, "Looks like we'll be heading back to Mesilla for another trial and, I assume, a hanging. When is it going to be?"

"The trial starts a week from Monday," said Sage. "I don't know which trial will go first. Probably Sanchez and Kegler. That will sort of pave the way for Lugo."

"Let's ride," said Martin.

They stopped on a knoll about a quarter mile from the ranch house where a wooden cross marked the grave of Jeffrey Martin.

They got off their horses and Martin said, "We brought him home."

Sage didn't want to think about what that had entailed and didn't speak.

She stood straight with her eyes closed and tears streaming down her face. She didn't indicate that she wanted Sage to hold her, so he stood by her side silently until she was ready to go.

"Good-bye, Jeffrey," whispered Martin.

The early fall day still had some heat in it, and they sat in chairs on the front porch feeling somewhat subdued.

Sage told her about the new arrangements with Cody in Mesilla and Summers' suggestion about running for the territorial legislature.

"Why John!" exclaimed Martin, "What a fascinating idea. But I won't vote for you. I don't want you moving to Santa Fe."

Sage grinned and said, "That's only part-time work—and a mighty small part. I'd still be here most of the time. You can't vote, anyway."

"Yes, it's a man's world," said Martin. "That's why you are all still carrying guns. Someday maybe you'll get some sense and give women the vote."

"It would be good not to have to carry a gun," said Sage. "But I think I'd tip over if I didn't have that weight there. Maybe we can find a place where they aren't needed."

Martin put a hand on Sage's forearm and said, "We?"

Sage looked at her. "I want to get moving before long. I don't know where yet or what I'll do. But I do know that I want you with me."

Martin stood up and said, "When I'm in Mesilla for the trial, I'm going to stay at the Amador House up in Las Cruces. I want you to stay with me."

Sage stood up, and they came together. After a long while, Sage started to pull her toward the door, but Martin held back and said, "Not yet. Jeffrey is too close. Let's wait until Las Cruces."

-65-

Sage rode down to Las Cruces with Martin. She had come into Rincon just after dawn wearing a divided skirt and sitting astride on her horse. Extra clothing was rolled up in a canvas bag and tied behind her saddle.

They got to the Amador House just before sunset, and, famished, they ate in the dining room before registering. Sage had not been in the Amador before except to drop off Martin when she stayed there. He didn't see anyone there that he knew. He'd slipped his badge into his pocket before entering, thinking that might be the case. They registered as man and wife.

Sage was feeling a little awkward, but as soon as they got into their room and set their baggage down, Martin moved toward him, wrapped her arms around his neck, and kissed him hungrily.

Sage didn't feel awkward anymore. He felt like he'd been lit on fire. He brought up his right hand and cupped a breast, and Nancy put her hand over his and pressed it tighter.

Not enough time later, Nancy said, "You were telling the truth. You haven't had hardly any experience with women."

Crushed, Sage started to apologize, but Nancy put a hand over his mouth and said, "It's like anything else. It takes practice to get it right; we're going to practice and practice, and it will be right."

Her hands stroked his bare back, and then she stiffened. She sat up and climbed over him to look at his back.

"Oh, John!" she wailed. "They hurt you!"

"Yes, that did hurt," he said. "Another experience in life. Not a good one."

"Who did that?" she snarled. "I'll kill him!"

Amused and deeply touched at the thought that she would fight for him, he said, "Can't. I already did—a long time ago and far, far away."

She climbed back over him and lay down to face him. She looked into his eyes.

"I should have known. You can be quite lethal—maybe the most lethal man on earth."

"Not even close," said Sage. "There are societies in Japan and other places that dedicate their whole lives to martial arts. I wouldn't stand a chance against those people unless I had a gun."

After a moment she said, "The man was on that island?"

Sage told her more about his two years of slavery and escape.

"It wasn't a total loss," said Sage. "My cellmates were interesting people, I learned the language, and I put on some muscle."

"Did you ever!" said Martin.

They got back to practicing. By morning he was getting it a lot more right than wrong. He was a quick study.

As they rode the four miles down to Mesilla, John thought about his experiences with whores in Mexico and Kansas. At the time he'd thought that something had been missing. He'd had no idea how much.

-66-

Judge Bennett had been in a bit of a quandary. If he tried the Jeremy Lugo and the Sanchez and Kegler cases separately, either trial could be construed as prejudicing the court against the other. He decided to try all three men together.

Then Leonard Horn, who was representing Sanchez and Kegler, informed the judge that his clients would be pleading guilty and that Sanchez intended to testify against Lugo.

Bennett decided to handle the Lugo case first.

In his opening statement, Roeser recounted the disappearances of Bill Rogers and Jeffrey Martin and the murders of the two farmers. He described the stage holdup and murder of the shotgun rider as well as the ambush attempt on Sage and Miller. He also described the assault on Sage while he was transporting the prisoners from Deming and the attempted ambush by Ephraim Colwell.

Roeser stated that all of these crimes had been ordered and paid for by Jeremy Lugo.

Sheriff Roeser called Anna Rogers and all four of her children to the stand to describe the circumstances of Rogers' murder.

Julio Sanchez, sitting next to Deputy Miller in the back of the room in handcuffs and leg irons, listened stone-faced. Then he was called to the stand and made to swear on the Bible.

Judge Bennett said, "Mr. Sanchez, do you understand that you have a constitutional right to remain silent and give no testimony that would incriminate yourself in any crimes?"

"Yes, your honor," said Sanchez. "But Sage has my goose cooked to a turn, and I'm ready to testify. Mrs. Rogers deserves it, and so does Lugo."

Sanchez testified for over an hour, and despite the best efforts of Lugo's two lawyers, he thoroughly cooked Lugo's goose.

After the jury delivered verdicts that Lugo was guilty of four murders, accessory to the murder of shotgun rider Shorty Williams, and several counts of attempted murders of peace officers, Judge Bennett pronounced sentence.

"Jeremy Lugo, normally, I would sentence you to hang by the neck until dead. But since I observe that you have no neck, I sentence you to death by firing squad. This sentence will be carried out tomorrow morning at dawn."

The judge rapped his gavel and then waited while Deputy Espinosa from Las Cruces removed the distraught prisoner from the room.

He turned to the jury and said, "Thank you for your service. You are dismissed. You may leave or remain seated while I take up the case involving Julio Sanchez and Robbie Kegler.

The jurors remained seated.

Miller brought Sanchez and Kegler forward, and Sheriff Roeser read the indictment.

Bennett said, "Julio Sanchez and Robbie Kegler, how do you plead?"

"Guilty," they both said.

"Julio Sanchez," said Bennett, "I might have granted some measure of leniency for your testimony against Jeremy Lugo and the fact that you once were an officer of the law. Deputy sheriffs put their lives on the line every day to protect our citizens, and special consideration would be justified.

"However, you didn't do that. While you were wearing a badge, you were protecting Jeremy Lugo, enabling his depredations. You brought shame to the profession.

"The man you murdered, William Rogers, put on a badge and did his utmost to uphold the law even though he had a wife and four children to support. He is sorely missed by the community.

"I sentence you, Julio Sanchez, and you, Robbie Kegler, to hang by the neck until dead. The sentence will be carried out tomorrow morning at dawn following the execution of Jeremy Lugo."

Bennett brought down his gavel and adjourned the court.

Bennett said, "Deputy Sage, a word with you in my chambers please."

Nancy Martin was seated beside Anna Rogers. When all stood as the judge departed the bench, the two women hugged each other and sobbed quietly.

Benito Alvarez, who had ridden down for the trial, walked over to Sage and shook his hand.

Alvarez said, "You have done wonders, my friend. I thank you for my friend Pedro. If he were seeing this, he would be pleased. I am going to El Paso to see his wife now to let her know."

Sage touched Alvarez on the arm, and said, "That's good of you, Benito. I hope she is doing all right."

"If she isn't," said Alvarez, "I will make it right. I am better able to do that now."

Martin had come over, and as Alvarez left, Sage said, "How about waiting for me in the plaza? I shouldn't be long."

Judge Bennett's chambers consisted of a small room with a desk and four chairs facing it. Bennett stood up from a large chair behind the desk. He had just lit a cigar and offered Sage the box. Sage took one, cut off the end with his knife, and got it going with a match from a container on the judge's desk. It was the best cigar he'd ever had.

Bennett motioned him to one of the chairs and said, "Sit down, John.

"Congratulations are in order. It didn't take you very long to clean up the situation in Rincon. I'm quite impressed. I've never met a man with your array of fighting and tracking skills, and brains to boot. Are you going to be content now with life as a deputy in a small, quiet town?

"Thank you, your honor. I didn't do it by myself. I had a lot of good help."

"That's where the brains came in," said Bennett, "and my name is Wilber. Please call me Will. Are you fixing to stay on up there?"

"I don't have a lot of education," said Sage. "I'm fixing to work on that. Hiram Cawthon and Vern Summers have offered to lend me books and help me with tutoring. They think I should make a run for the legislature."

Bennett leaned back in his chair and took a long pull on his cigar while he contemplated Sage.

"How do you feel about hitting the books?" he asked.

"I can hardly wait to get started," said Sage. "I've never had any opportunity to do much reading since I was in school. That was just for two years in Mexico when I was a kid. But I learned then that there was a whole lot more to learn, and it's always been in the back of my mind to tuck into it someday. I just haven't had the chance until now."

"I served with Vern in the war," said Bennett. "We're good friends. Don't see enough of him. I know Hiram, too. They are discerning men. I take it that they are interested in your future. They wouldn't be if they thought that your sole value went no further than your guns and fists."

Another pull on the cigar.

"When I was up in Santa Fe I ran into an old friend from the army. He's in Washington now. He wanted to know if I knew of a deputy sheriff down here named Sage.

"When I said that it just happened that I did, he got as eager as a kid. Wanted to know all about the man that whipped Big Bill McClusky and mowed down the Cummings Gang. Luckily, Vern had filled me in on the McClusky fight, and I'd talked to Jim about the Cummings affair. You sure carried Jim through there."

Sage shook his head, appalled. "I didn't want to lose my job before I even started.

"That wasn't a gang. Old man Cummings was a rancher who brought in his hands.

"Your friend heard about that in Washington?"

"You've gotten some play in the eastern papers," said Bennett. "Actually, I'm surprised that no one has been out here from the east to interview you. People back there take an interest in those kinds of things. Hell, everyone takes an interest in those kinds of things. You're getting to be pretty well known."

Now Sage took a long pull on his cigar. He wasn't sure what to make of being that well known.

"My friend, Andrew Pike, works in the Foreign Service in the Hays administration," said Bennett. "He was visiting kinfolk in Santa Fe. Next year he is going to be posted to Mexico City.

"Working in Mexico can be a little rough," continued Bennett. "Andrew remarked that it would certainly be good to have someone with your fighting skills around during that posting, and I said, 'Why not? The man knows the language and works pretty damned well with people. He knows when to shoot, and when not to.

"John, Andrew jumped at that. He'd like to have you visit him there in Washington, if you'd be interested."

Sage was floored. And intrigued.

Sage said, "Well, judge...Will, that's a bolt of lightning out of the clear sky. I am interested. Very interested. But I've got to discuss this with a friend. A lady friend."

With a slight grin, Bennett said, "Mrs. Martin?"

Sage blinked.

Bennett Said, "I face everyone in the courtroom. Looked like a little silent communication going on there between you two. She hardly ever took her eyes off you."

"It is sort of a new thing with us," said Sage. "I'm not sure where it is going yet, but I feel that it will be going a long way."

"Maybe all the way to Mexico City," said Bennett. "Wives are welcome at the embassies."

Jesus, thought Sage. When things moved in his life, they really got up and went.

"I'll talk to you again before I leave town," said Sage, "after I've talked some with Nancy and Jim Roeser."

Bennett said, "How about the two of you coming over to my place this evening after dinner? Meet the wife and talk things over. I'd invite you to dinner, but I've learned to give her a little more warning about dinner guests."

"Thank you, Will," said Sage. "We'll be over. I really enjoyed this cigar."

-67-

When Sage left the courtroom, he spotted Nancy Martin sitting alone on a bench in the plaza across the street.

She stood up as he approached and took his arm as they started walking to Roeser's office. They had left their horses in his corral. She was puzzled by his expression and silence.

"Well, what did the judge have to say?" asked Martin.

Sage stopped and turned toward her.

He put his hands on her shoulders and said, "Nancy, I've just been handed an opportunity that would take my life into a whole other place. But I won't go there without you.

"Judge Bennett has a friend in Washington in the Foreign Service. He's being posted in Mexico City next year. It turns out that I've been noticed outside of Dona Ana County. Would you believe that this man heard about me in Washington?"

"I could believe that," said Martin.

"Bob Smith of the Crier here wrote some articles about the shootout with the Cummings outfit and the fight with McClusky. They were picked up by newspapers in the east.

"This man, Andrew Pike, wants me to go to Mexico City with him, be on his team to provide security. Pike wants me to go to Washington to meet with him."

Martin thought for a moment. "Let's go," she said.

Sage looked into her eyes, and gripping her shoulders tightly, he said, "I want you to be my wife. Will you marry me?"

"Yes. Oh, yes!"

-68-

Jim Roeser was in his office when they got there. They pulled up chairs in front of his desk and sat down.

Roeser looked inquisitively at Martin and then at Sage and said, "John, you got it done. You're going to have some quiet time now up there in Rincon. You deserve it."

Sage and Martin glanced at each other. Sage said, "Something's come up. I'm going to be turning in my badge.

Roeser sat up straight and said, "What?"

Sage explained about the opportunity with Pike in Mexico City. He would need a month or more off to travel to Washington. At this point, he didn't know how things would shake out after that.

And by the way, he and Nancy were getting married.

Roeser's mouth opened and closed a couple of times as he stared at Sage. Then he stood up and came around the desk.

Sage and Martin stood up, and Roeser grasped Martin's hand in both of his and said, "And here I've been thinking you were a pretty sensible lady."

He looked at the floor and thought for a moment. Then he looked Martin in the eye and grinned.

"But congratulations. I think the two of you are going to get where you want to go, and heaven help anyone who tries to get in your way."

He gripped Sage's hand and said, "I think you are doing a good thing here. Not so good for Mrs. Martin, but maybe she can make something of you."

Martin said, "My name is Nancy, and John is John. I don't want him to be anything else."

Roeser said, "When are you planning to head east?" "I don't know yet," said Sage. "I've got to talk to Judge Bennett some more."

He looked questioningly at Martin and said, "Nancy and I will be getting married in Rincon...shortly?"

"Shortly," said Martin.

"Well," said Roeser, "don't turn in your badge just yet. Keep it until you get your plans set. You have a week's leave coming, and the county just might have some business that you could do in Washington."

"That's good of you," said Sage. "We're going to see Judge Bennett now and stay up in Las Cruces tonight. I'll come back in tomorrow for the executions, and maybe I'll have some more information."

Sage and Martin rode out to Judge Bennett's home on the outskirts of Mesilla. The judge's Mexican housekeeper answered the door and invited them in. Bennett and his wife, Estella, were in the living room.

The judge introduced his wife, and she said, "I'm pleased to meet you both. I've been hearing a lot about you. Mrs. Martin, I was so sorry to hear about your loss. I'm certainly glad that justice is being brought to Jeremy Lugo and the rest."

Martin said, "I've been able to say good-bye to Jeffrey. He'll always be in my heart, but I'm moving on. I'm going to make a new life now with John. We're going to be married."

Mrs. Bennett put a hand over her heart and blinked while she digested that. Then she said, "My goodness! Well, congratulations. I think you will be a fine couple. Are you going to wait for a few months?"

"I know that would be customary," said Martin. "But events in our lives are taking precedence over custom. John and I are going to need to be working together as husband and wife—and soon."

"Will, Nancy and I are going to Washington together," said Sage. "We're both interested in seeing that, and I'd want Pike to meet her."

"Good," said Bennett. "I'm pleased that you decided to do that. How soon will you want to be going?"

"Right after we're married," said Sage. "I'd think in about two weeks. That will be our honeymoon."

"Will, would you be willing to perform the ceremony up in Rincon? We're not religious people, and I'm not on good terms with Reverend Burns up there."

Sage realized that he didn't know if Martin was religious or not at this point. He looked at her, and she wasn't objecting.

"I would be proud to do that," said Bennett. "How about two Saturdays from now?"

Sage and Martin looked at each other, and they both nodded.

"I'll send a telegram to Andrew to let him know that you are coming," said Bennett. "I'll follow that up with a letter."

"I'll pay for the telegram," said Sage.

"No, you won't," said Bennett. "Andrew will. He'll be reimbursing you for your travel expenses, too. He's got a budget for that.

Sage and Martin rode up to the Amador in the moonlight.

Along the way Sage asked, "Nancy, just what are your religious convictions? I kind of got ahead of myself there."

"Oh, I believe there is a God," she said. "I've just never felt that I needed to go to a church to sustain that belief. I never had much opportunity to do that anyway, although I did attend a few of Reverend Burn's services. He married Jeffrey and me. Those services weren't particularly satisfying."

Sage changed the subject. "If we wind up going to Mexico, what do you intend to do with the ranch?"

"I was thinking that I could have Jed manage it for me, but it looks like ranching isn't really in our future, so I expect that I'll sell it. I'd probably get a couple of thousand dollars out of it after the mortgage is paid off. Maybe I could sell it to Jed if Hiram would let him take over the mortgage. He could pay me in installments over time.

"Would we be needing a couple of thousand to live on?"

"I haven't spent much of what I've earned since I got back to the States," said Sage. I have enough saved up to get us through to when I'd start earning an income from the government."

Nancy talked about her family up in Santa Fe. Three of her brothers had gone to California. She expected that her parents and other two brothers would be coming down for the wedding.

After Sage and Martin arrived in their room at the Amador, they got back to practicing.

Afterward, Martin said dreamily, “You don’t need any more practice, John. Now we can do the real thing.”

“Not tonight,” said Sage. “I’ve got to get some sleep. We’ll be up very early.”

“I’m not going to go in to Mesilla with you, John,” said Martin. “I don’t have any need to see those executions. It’s just good to know that Lugo is finished.”

-69-

The wedding took place in an alcove of cottonwoods along the bank of the Rio Grande. The southwestern weather was cooperative, and the mid-October day was clear and warm.

Nancy's father, Carl Leatherby, gave the bride away, and the Rogers girls served as bridesmaids. The younger Rogers boy had served as ring bearer. Sage wore a new broadcloth suit with a new black flat-brimmed hat. It was the first time he had owned either.

It looked to Sage like most of the town had turned out—Anglo and Mexican. Roeser had apologized to Miller, who had moved back up to Rincon, and told him he'd better stay in town. Anyone who came in could waltz right out again with about anything they took a liking to.

An entire steer was being barbequed over a large fire pit under the supervision of the Krantzes. Benito Alvarez had set up a bar on planks with one of his bartenders.

After Sage had kissed the bride, Lupita Calderon sang a Mexican wedding song. While she was singing, Nancy looked at Sage and whispered in his ear, "Jesus Christ! How did I beat her out?"

During the ceremony, Sage was astonished to see Blue Sky and Red Feather, the two Apache scouts from Fort Seldon, standing off to the side of the group with a couple of soldiers.

After the ceremony was over, Sage took Nancy and walked over to them as they were about to ride off.

Sage addressed them in the Apache tongue. "I am pleased to see you. You are welcome here. My wife Nancy and I would like you to stay and eat with us."

Sage turned to Nancy and said in English, "I met Blue Sky and Red Feather in Las Cruces a while back. We spoke of times in Arizona."

"I am pleased to meet you," said Nancy. "I hope you will stay and share the food."

Blue Sky said, "We would be pleased to share your food.

"You have married a great warrior. He is known to our people as Sees in the Night. He will provide well for you and kill all of your enemies. You will have many children, and all the boys will be great warriors."

Nancy looked at Sage with an amused expression and her eyebrows raised high. "Yes, he is a great warrior. He has already killed all my enemies, but I'll keep him around in case I get any more."

The two soldiers shook Sage's hand. They were the two that had gotten into the fight in the Emperor with Saul Snead and his cronies.

Vern Summers came over with Jim Roeser, Judge Bennett, and Hiram Cawthon.

Summers looked at the soldier that Snead had knocked out and said, "Last time I saw you, you were being carried out of the Emperor. That Snead was a nasty customer. Looks like you've healed up OK."

"What hurt worse," said the soldier, "was that I didn't see Deputy Sage here take those gents out. I heard it was really something."

Roeser said, "Later on, Snead made the mistake of trying to take some prisoners away from John on the train from Deming. That was his last mistake. Snead isn't with us living anymore, and the two that were with him aren't either."

The Apaches grunted and nodded their heads.

"I hadn't heard that," said the soldier. "I think I'll drink to that."

After Sage thanked them for coming, the soldiers headed for Alvarez's crowded makeshift bar.

Judge Bennett addressed the Apaches. "I hear that Geronimo has gone off the reservation again. Will you be getting into that?"

"Yes," said Red Feather. "We will be going to Arizona with the Buffalo Soldiers soon."

"The what?" said Sage.

"We have two companies of Buffalo Soldiers at Fort Seldon now," said Red Feather. "These soldiers have black skin and strange curly hair, like buffalo. I think that they will be good fighting men. They are very serious when they are training. They ride well, do not tire easily, and do not complain all the time like the white soldiers."

The group moved over to where the beef was being served up along with side dishes.

Sage spoke with the Apaches, telling them that he had seen Strong Arm recently and what he had been doing.

They told Sage that Nantaje had not gone out with Geronimo. He was still at San Carlos. If they got up that way, they would speak of Sage to him.

There weren't nearly enough tables to seat everyone, so the men sat on the ground in groups and talked while they stuffed themselves.

Judge Bennett said, "John, I got word back from Andrew Pike. He will be expecting you and Nancy around the first of November."

Bennett handed Sage a couple of sheets of folded paper. "The name of the hotel where you will be staying is in there. Show that to the desk when you check in, and they will bill it to the U.S. Government.

"Andrew is looking forward to meeting you. The information you will need to find him is there, too."

Hiram Cawthon said, "It sounds like you've been handed quite an opportunity. Probably a lot better one than if you had managed to get elected to go to Santa Fe. You might find that working for a federal bureaucracy, especially that one, will suit you better than being a politician.

"Politicians make the laws and policy, but it's the bureaucrats that carry them out. I still think you'd make a good politician in the future, but in the meantime, there is no one that I would rather have carrying things out."

"Amen," said Summers. "Anything they turn him loose on is going to get done."

Sage said, "I appreciate your confidence, but I really haven't got much idea of just what it is that I'll be doing or what I'll need to do it. But I'm looking forward to trying something new."

"Vern and Hiram and I put together a little wedding present for you," said Bennett. "You might find it helpful."

He got up and went to his buggy, which he had come up in with Estella and Maggie Morris. He pulled out a bag and brought it back. He handed the heavy bag to Sage, and Sage opened it.

"Books!" said Sage.

"Yes," said Bennett. "You'll find information there on how the government works and some history of the country, and there's a good treatise on our foreign policy. Aside from these, you will find that there are fine libraries in Washington."

Maggie Morris came over with Jed Peters at her side. Sage had noticed that the two had been having an animated conversation.

Nancy had finished eating and came over with them.

Maggie said, "John, I hear you're going to be leaving us. I'm going to miss you. You've been a good man to have around. You kept your bed made and were good for the chicken business. And you did a few other things that were of some use to folks.

"Too bad Jim won't have time now to make something out of you like he thought he might."

Roeser laughed and said, "Maggie, John came made of something right out of the store. I learned real quick to just get out of his way."

Maggie turned to Nancy and said, "Mrs. Nancy Sage, congratulations! I don't think you did too badly here. You might just have something to work with."

Nancy smiled and said, "Mrs. Nancy Sage. I do like the sound of that.

"Thank you, Maggie. I will always count you as a friend."

The reception wound down, and Sage readied Nancy's buggy for the ride to the Rocking M. Benito Alvarez and Lupita Calderon came up to them as they were about to climb on.

Lupita said, "Señora Sage, I wish you happiness. I hope you never fight with him. He does not like to fight with his woman."

She looked down and took a deep breath. Then she said in a small, choked, voice, "I would not have fought with him very hard."

Nancy glanced at Sage and then said, "Lupita, thank you very much for your song. It was beautiful, and you are beautiful. If you make good decisions, you will do very well."

Alvarez said, "John, I have done very well since you came to Rincon. I did not come to your wedding to make a profit, only to provide refreshments. The profits that were made are a wedding gift to you and Nancy from me and all those who enjoyed those refreshments. Many added something extra when they heard of this. You have many friends here, and I am proud to count myself among them."

Alvarez placed a bag he was carrying in the back of the buggy.

Sage said, "Benito, that's very generous of you. I didn't expect that. I was happy to see you doing a good business. I've been very glad to have you on my side while I've been here. My friend, it was a help.

All the volunteer deputies were gathered around. They were wearing their badges.

Chance Slade said, "This being a deputy isn't going to be as much fun with Lugo and Waco out of it and you gone. But we'll be backing Cody."

"That's good," said Sage. "I expect that things will blow up now and then. Cody will need your help when it does."

He looked around at them. "You all stood up when the town needed you to. Lugo and Waco sure wanted to put my lights out, and they might have been able to do that if you hadn't been there. Thank you."

-70-

Nancy's family was staying in Rincon for a couple of days so that Sage and his bride could have the house to themselves. Peters and Morgan were steering clear.

When Sage unloaded the buggy, he glanced into the bag that Alvarez had given them and said, "Whoa!"

After they got inside, Nancy counted up the contents. There were a lot of coins, and it took some time. She said, "Sage, there is nearly six hundred dollars here!"

Sage shook his head and said, "That's a year's pay. Mighty good of Benito and the rest."

"You were worth it to them, John," said Nancy. "To all of us."

Two days later, Nancy's family returned. Her younger brothers stayed in the bunkhouse with Peters and Morgan. They stayed for two more days.

The Leatherbys were fascinated by Sage. Carl quizzed him for hours about his life with the Apaches, his time on Okinawa, and ranching in Mexico. The boys pestered him about his shooting skills that they'd heard about until he showed everyone the trick with the knife.

The boys gaped at the knife sticking in the hole in a tree, and Carl said to his wife, "Jesus, Catherine, we sure don't have to worry about Nancy being safe in Mexico!"

The Leatherbys had to get back to their spread near Santa Fe. After they left, Sage and Nancy rode into Rincon with Jed Peters to talk with Hiram Cawthon.

As they rode through the town, Sage noted that the Emperor was open but that the name had been changed to the San Andres Saloon.

They went into Cawthon's office in the bank, and Sage mentioned the Emperor.

"Lugo's papers had the address of a brother in New York," said Cawthon. "I got in touch with him. He's got no interest in coming out here. He just said to liquidate Lugo's properties and send him whatever funds were coming. I got a good fee for that.

“Jacob Wheeler is the new owner of the San Andres. He’s up from El Paso. He appears to be an honest businessman, but he’s got a hard edge. He needs it in that business. He owned a saloon in El Paso with a brother.

“I told him that Rincon wouldn’t tolerate a dishonest operation and mentioned that the previous owner had just been executed. I think Mr. Wheeler got the message.

“Now, what can I do for you?”

Cawthon was very helpful in arranging for Peters to take over the mortgage. Peters would draw a salary of sixty dollars a month from the profits. Everything beyond that would be banked for the Sages until the equity of two thousand dollars was paid off. Sage and Nancy were willing to risk the equity if the ranch didn’t turn a profit, but the Rocking M was on prime land, and Sage didn’t think Peters would fail. Neither did Cawthon.

Peters had decided to rename the ranch. It was now the Circle P. He drew the brand on a piece of paper: the letter P inside a circle.

“Can’t wait to see that on the next new calf,” he said.

Out on the street, Peters said, “I won’t be riding back to the ranch with you. I’m going to ride down to Las Cruces and look up a couple of hands that Jethro gave me the names of.”

His dark face took on a little more color, and he said, “And I’ve got a little courtin’ to do.”

Nancy said, “Why Jed! Maggie?”

“Yep,” said Peters, “we kind of hit it off.”

“You’ll like her chili,” said Sage.

Nancy raised her eyes to the sky and said, “I think he’ll like more than that!”

Nancy had some shopping to do for their trip east, and Sage went to the saddlery. He wasn’t sure what the customs were in the east or if people went around armed. He wanted to get a shoulder holster made up to go under his broadcloth coat.

While he was waiting for that, he walked down to the San Diego and thanked Alvarez for his generosity.

He found Nancy, and they went over to the sheriff’s office. Miller was there talking to a man dressed up in a bleached deerskin outfit with fringes and beadwork all over it. He was wearing an oversized white broad-brimmed hat with a big feather in the hatband and Indian moccasins of a style he wasn't familiar with.

Miller said, "John, we were just talking about you. This here is Jeremiah Nash. He..."

The man jumped up to grabbed Sage's hand and pumped it up and down.

"Jeremiah Nash, with the Ned Buntline Shows of the American West," he said. "I'm very pleased to meet the man who saved Mesilla from the Cummings Gang and whipped Big Bill McClusky to claim the title of World Champion Prizefighter."

Sage gave the grinning Miller a wide-eyed look and said, "Hold on, Mr. Nash. Mesilla didn't need saving, and there was no 'Cummings Gang.' My fight with McClusky was in a saloon. No title involved. If we'd met in a ring under rules, he'd have wiped me out."

"You didn't gun down seven men in Mesilla?" said Nash.

Sage looked at Nancy, who had a wry grin on her face.

"A Peacemaker holds six rounds," said Sage. "I shot three men and then two more that were already full of buckshot. Old man Cummings and his ranch hands were trying to save his son from a hanging.

"Five men!" chortled Nash. "We could bill you as the fastest gun in the West. Maybe faster than Bill Hickock. We could find that out."

Sage asked, "What in hell are you talking about?"

Nash said, "We do Wild West shows all over the east and in Europe. We'd like to have you in our troop.

"How much are you making now as a deputy sheriff?"

"Fifty dollars a month," said Sage.

"We'll pay you fifty a week to start," said Nash. "I'm thinking of billing you as the Apache Kid. Mr. Miller here says you could shoot the eyelashes off a gnat before it could blink. You could do shooting demonstrations, and we'd stage showdowns where you cut down six outlaws at a time and save a beautiful heroine to boot. Audiences will love it!"

Sage glared at Miller and then looked at Nash and said, "Mr. Nash, I'd have about as much interest in that as being staked out on an anthill.

"I've just been married, and I'm taking a job with the government in Washington. I want to do things that are useful."

Nash's expression became serious. He said, "Mr. Sage, show business is useful. We're developing a country here. People back east need to be interested in the West. If they aren't, they aren't going to be supporting their congressmen when they want to pass bills that aid that development.

"There's nothing like a real western hero, a deputy sheriff out here that has taken on badmen at great odds and beat them—not to mention whipped the best prizefighter in the country. That will get their interest."

Sage said, "Mr. Nash, you've just changed my viewpoint. I appreciate what you are saying. I just don't have any interest in being an entertainer for any amount of money. It's not in me."

Nash said, "Well, give it some more thought. I'll be here for another day in case you change your mind."

"It seems like I've already drawn too much attention. It has resulted in another opportunity for me, but it could be a problem if it gets out of hand. I'm not about to go out and draw anymore. Don't wait around just for me."

Nash studied Sage for a long moment and then looked at Nancy and said, "Is this lovely lady your bride?"

"Yes, she is," said Sage. "My wife Nancy."

Nash took her hand in both of his. "Nancy Sage, I'm pleased to meet you. You'd make a great heroine in need of rescue from vicious brutes with evil intentions. You could be a star! Have fame and wealth. See the world. Talk some sense into this man."

"Give it up, Mr. Nash," said Nancy. "We have other plans."

Nash shook his head. "Very well. Mr. Sage, it was an honor to meet you. From what I've heard, you are a remarkable man."

-71-

When they left the Circle P for the ride to Mesilla and Las Cruces, Sage said, “Well, we’ve burned that bridge. If we come back, we’ll have to stay somewhere else.”

“As you’ve said, we probably won’t be coming back,” said Nancy. “We can afford to stay in the east until we leave for Mexico. We’ll have the opportunity to look around that part of the country, and you’ll need to be doing a lot of studying back there.

“If the job falls through for any reason, Jim would hire you back in a heartbeat. Or we might want to do something totally new. My place is with you, wherever we go and whatever we do. It doesn’t matter to me where we wind up.”

Touched, Sage said, “OK, partner. I’ll do everything I can to make that a good place.”

“I know,” said Nancy. “I’m not worried at all.”

While they waited for the eastbound train, the Buffalo Soldiers were boarding the westbound train. The soldiers were loading their horses onto the stock cars under the shouted orders of black sergeants and white officers.

Sage studied the soldiers with interest. He’d seen few negroes in his life but had never talked to one. They looked like they were well put together, and they appeared to be competent as they got the loading done.

Sage walked up to a couple of black privates. “Ever been to Arizona before?” he asked.

“No suh,” said a soldier. “I hear it’s hot.”

“Depends on where you are,” said Sage. “But yes, a lot of it is hot. Pretty comfortable this time of year, though. There’ll be some snow in the mountains later on.”

“Never seen no snow,” the man said.

“How do you like being a soldier?” asked Sage.

The soldier gave him a steady look and said, “Been pretty boring, lately, but anything beats being under a slaver’s whip. I guess you wouldn’t know about that.”

Sage and Nancy exchanged a look. Sage said, "I guess not. Good luck out there. You've got a hard job ahead of you. The Apaches are as tough as they come. It's their land, and they know every lizard by its first name."

"We'll get 'em," said the soldier. We're pretty tough our ownselves."

Sage looked him in the eye and said, "I can believe that."

They walked back toward where Jim Roeser was sitting on a bench smoking a cigar.

Nancy said, "I've never seen a negro before. They sure look different."

"In those uniforms, they all look like Americans to me," said Sage.

Sage spotted Blue Sky and Red Feather, and he and Nancy walked down to where they were squatting on the platform. The scouts rose as they approached.

Out of deference to Nancy, Red Feather spoke in English. "Do you travel today, John?"

"Yes, but in the other direction," said Sage. "Nancy and I are going to Washington."

The Apaches grunted. "Huh. The home of the Great White Father. Tell him that there are Tinneh on his side going out to fight his enemies. Maybe he will order his agents to stop stealing the supplies of our people."

"Perhaps I will have a chance to do that," said Sage. "At least I will attempt to talk to those who are responsible for providing those supplies and tell them that they are failing."

"That is all that I can ask," said Red Feather. "You are known for succeeding in what you attempt.

"We are going to be riding on the firewagon. We have been wanting to do this for a long time. Even our horses are doing this. It is a great event."

The eastbound train pulled into the station with steam venting and brakes squealing. As soon as it cleared the switch from the side track, the westbound engine's whistle blew, and the conductor yelled, "All aboard."

"Farewell, my friends," said Sage.

"Farewell, Sees in the Night," replied Red Feather and Blue Sky, and they shook hands.

"Farewell, Nancy Sage," they said. "May the good spirits stay with you."

Nancy said, "Thank you for coming to our wedding. It was very good to meet you."

Sage and Nancy returned to where Roeser was sitting. A few minutes later the engine emitted clouds of smoke and steam, and with a farewell blast of the whistle, the westbound train left the station.

Roeser stood up and said, "Well, John, I sure do hope this isn't the last I see of you. You've always got a job here if you want it. At least as long as I'm sheriff, and I expect that I will be for some time yet."

Sage had given Roeser his badge in Mesilla, telling him that he wasn't expecting to return anytime soon. They had dropped the idea of Sage doing any lobbying for the county, and Roeser had given him his final pay.

They had sold Nancy's horse along with the packhorse they had brought down, and Sage had given Leader to Roeser. Leader was a lot faster than the horse Roeser had been riding. They were taking their saddles along with them to Washington. Roeser had driven them up to Las Cruces in a buggy.

A half hour after the train had come in, the whistle blew and the conductor hollered.

Sage shook Roeser's hand, Nancy kissed him on the cheek, and they said their farewells.

-72-

Sage and Nancy arrived in Washington early on a Sunday morning and checked into their hotel, which was near the Capitol building.

They hadn't slept much on the train during the night, so after washing off the soot from the train, they bedded down until noon. Then they decided to look around.

Sage hadn't seen anyone wearing guns on their carriage ride from the station, so he left his Colt in a drawer in their room when they went downstairs. Not wearing a gun was going to take some getting used to. The concierge suggested that they take a tour of the city. Tourist carriages operated out of a stand just down the street.

The streets in Washington were mostly unpaved, but some were surfaced with paving stones, and some were paved with a material that Sage later found out was macadam. Some of these streets had iron tracks imbedded in them for sizable trams pulled by horses.

They spent the afternoon gawking at the magnificent buildings and monuments like the tourists they were with, and they took note of many they would return to visit at greater length. The tour guide pointed out that the Capitol, treasury, post office, and other buildings were of Greek revival architecture.

If the Greeks had had buildings like that two thousand years ago, Sage wondered what civilization had been doing ever since.

They marveled at all the greenery. In fact, they had been marveling at that ever since they had crossed into eastern Texas. They were astonished at the Mississippi River, and the bridge across it had been astonishing, too, as had a lot of other sights, and they had hardly noticed the discomforts of riding a train.

On Monday morning Sage and Nancy found their way to the office of Andrew Pike.

Pike was a short, thin man with a full black beard. He looked to be in his mid-fifties.

Pike studied Sage with lively gray eyes as Sage introduced himself and Nancy, and he invited the couple to take chairs. He took a chair near them instead of sitting behind his desk.

"Willard spoke highly of your capabilities, Mr. Sage," said Pike. "You don't appear to be as old or as big as I had pictured the man who whipped Big Bill McClusky to be. You must be incredibly skilled with your fists."

"Actually, I mostly used my feet," said Sage. "We weren't in a ring, and that wasn't a sporting contest. I don't fight for sport. If I'd had to box with him I wouldn't have lasted long."

Pike lifted his eyebrows and said, "Your feet?"

"I was trained to use everything I've got for maximum impact. The schooling was a lot different than what McClusky had had."

Pike was curious. "What schooling was that?" he asked.

Sage sat back in his chair. "I lived with a Buddhist monk for two years on one of the islands of Japan. His order didn't allow the use of weapons, so to stay alive in a land that had a lot of bandits, they developed a very effective form of unarmed combat over a period of centuries.

I can't say I learned anywhere near all of it, but I learned enough so that I have an advantage over those who haven't had that training, which is about everyone over here."

"How did you ever come to be in Japan?" asked Pike.

"I was a hand on a clipper, said Sage. "We went down in a typhoon off the Ryukyus. I spent four years there before I was picked up by an American vessel."

Pike stroked his beard and said, "I take it that you have the ability to integrate into a foreign culture, Mr. Sage, and I assume to pick up the language. Those are useful skills in this business.

"You are from the Southwest, so might you be conversant in Spanish?"

"I grew up speaking Spanish," replied Sage. "I spent two years in a school in Mexico when I was a kid and worked as a vaquero on a spread near Chihuahua for another two years."

Pike grinned widely and brought his hands together in a silent clap. He said, "Mr. Sage, I was thinking that I might have been a bit rash to offer you a position on my team, but now I'm thinking it was a fortuitous move.

"I've been tasked to join Ambassador Foster in Mexico City in April as his commerce officer. President Diaz has embarked on an ambitious development program with foreign investments, and the ambassador would like me to get around the country to provide some eyes and ears pertaining to American interests there. Foster and I served in the war together, and he would like my take on the business community.

"With your language skills, knowledge of the country, and, uh, other abilities, you may well be of valuable assistance."

Sage glanced at Nancy and said, "That sounds interesting, Mr. Pike, but I'm not too keen on the idea of leaving Nancy parked in Mexico City while I'm away on extended trips. We just got married, and I'm still working on getting used to her."

Pike grinned and said, "Mrs. Sage, I believe you will find the diplomatic community to be quite entertaining. However, not to worry, Mr. Sage. My wife and the wives of a couple of the other members of my team will be accompanying us on most of the excursions. We count the ladies as diplomats."

He addressed Nancy and asked, "Mrs. Sage, do you like traveling?"

"I haven't traveled very much," she replied. "Washington is the furthest I've been, but I've most certainly liked this trip. John has said he wanted to travel far and wide, and that did appeal to me. I'd like to do that, too."

"I've put in some long days with her on horseback," said Sage. "She travels mighty well. She only complains about half the time."

Nancy looked up at the ceiling and said, "Only because you can't keep up."

Amused, Pike said, "Do you speak Spanish as well?"

Nancy said, "You don't grow up in my part of the country without learning some Spanish, but not nearly as well as John."

"Where did you grow up?" asked Pike.

"My family had a ranch near Santa Fe," answered Nancy. "I moved to Rincon when I married my first husband. We had a ranch near there."

"After her husband was murdered, she managed the ranch herself," added Sage. "She's pretty handy. Got out and worked with her hands."

Pike raised his eyebrows. "Riding and roping?"

"And branding and digging and building," she said. "It was either that or go under. But I liked doing it. It was a lot better than sitting around and feeling sorry for myself."

Pike looked at her appraisingly and said, "Your husband was murdered?"

"A man wanted the ranch," she said. "We wouldn't sell. Jeffrey was bushwhacked, and one of our hands was murdered, too. Two other hands quit, so it was either get out and work or go broke."

"My word!" exclaimed Pike. "Were the murderers brought to justice?"

"Rincon wound up with a good deputy sheriff," said Nancy. "The best. Justice was done, all right. The three murderers and the man who ordered the murders are all dead. John shot two of them and executed the other two."

Pike nodded thoughtfully and said, "If you don't mind, I would like to get on a first name basis here. Next Saturday I am going to hold a social gathering at my home, and I would like you both to attend. You will meet the others who are going to Mexico with us as well as others who are in the Foreign Service.

"Are your current accommodations suitable?"

Nancy said, "The best we've ever been in. It's a magnificent hotel. Thank you."

Sage said, "I don't know how long you intended to cover our stay there, but we were thinking of staying through this month at our own expense. We want to explore Washington, and I have a lot of reading to do. Judge Bennett and a couple of others gave me a stack of books they thought would be useful, and I've only had time to get through one of them so far."

Pike said, "I'm putting you on the payroll for the next two weeks for familiarization, and the government will pay you per diem for that time. You'll mostly be familiarizing yourself, but I expect that you'll put the time to good use. I have another couple of books for you on our diplomatic service and diplomacy for you to get under your belt.

"After that you will be inactive and without pay until April first. The rest of us are mostly going to be studying Spanish. You won't need that. In April we'll be spending about a month attending briefings and other training. In early May we'll be taking a steamship to Veracruz, with a stop in Havana, then going on to Mexico City by train.

"How much education do you have, John?"

"I've only had two years of formal schooling beyond what I learned at home, but I intend to spend a lot of time studying," replied Sage. "Will that be a problem for me?"

"Your work for me won't be requiring a lot of education," replied Pike. "But you'll be the only one on the team without a college degree. I imagine that you will hear some remarks about that. I'll expect you to take them without tearing anyone's head off.

"On the other hand, they are mostly a young and inexperienced crew, and you will be doing some tutoring in the language and customs of the Mexicans.

"All four of them are about your age. How old are you, anyway?"

"I'll be twenty-five when we get underway," said Sage.

"Not having a degree will severely limit your access to advancement in the service if you choose to stay with it. You might think about getting one before long."

Sage gave Nancy a startled look. That had never occurred to him at all.

Pike Said, "What will you be doing for the four month interim, John?"

"We want to see some more of the country," replied Sage. "I'd like to see the North, but since it is this time of the year, we'll be seeing the South.

"And I'll be doing a lot of reading."

"You should at least get up to Philadelphia and New York," said Pike. "Do that before heading south.

"Do you have the resources to travel for four months?"

"Yes," said Sage.

After a tour of the State Department building, Nancy took a tram back to their hotel, and Sage was introduced to federal government paperwork.

-73-

Andrew Pike had a large home in Alexandria. The Sages were the first to arrive, and Pike introduced his wife Leona. She reminded Sage of the salty Maggie Morris—self-confident and direct.

Leona shook their hands and said to Nancy, "Andrew told me that you used to own and manage a cattle ranch. You look like a woman who could do that. You've got the socialites around here all beat to hell in my opinion."

"And if she has an opinion, you'll hear it," said Pike with a smile.

Over the next hour, the other four members of Pike's team arrived. Two of them had wives who accompanied them. Three friends of the Pikes also arrived with their wives. The three all worked in the Foreign Service.

Throughout the course of the dinner in the large dining room, the old hands regaled the young officers with tales of their experiences in foreign lands. Sage listened with interest while studying the four men that he would be working with.

David James Nemeth, who preferred to be called "Jim," had an advanced degree in political science. He spoke little, but when he did, Sage was impressed with his scholarly insights. He was the same height as Sage but apparently even more muscular. Sage learned later that Nemeth was an avid bodybuilder.

Richard Weeks, Michael Pilgreen, and Philip Nutzhorn all had business degrees. Weeks was tall, red-haired, and freckle-faced, and he had all the friendliness and eagerness of a puppy. His wife, Susan, could have been mistaken for his sister because she exhibited similar looks and traits.

Nutzhorn was somewhat short, muscular, and as reserved as Nemeth. Sage got the impression that he was someone who was well informed and had no need to demonstrate it. His wife, Constance, who Nutzhorn said liked to be called Connie, was a diminutive but exotic-looking woman with raven hair who never said a word all evening. Sage thought she was very attractive.

Pilgreen came across as highly intelligent and determined to let everyone know it. Sage was put off by the superior, haughty attitude. He was a handsome and well-formed man.

When he mentioned that he had captained the boxing team at Harvard, Pike said, "Well, don't box with John here. I'll want you to be in one piece when we get to Mexico."

Pike noticed Pilgreen's astonished look. "You've heard of Big Bill McClusky?"

"Of course," replied Pilgreen. "World champion bare-knuckle fighter. I saw him fight once in New York. I didn't think any man alive could beat him, but I heard some hick lawman out west whipped him."

Pilgreen shook his head. "That was hard to believe. McClusky is big, fast, and an incredibly good fighter. He'll still be champion when his jaw heals up enough—unless maybe that lawman takes him on in a sanctioned fight."

Pike waved a hand at Sage and said, "Meet ex-Deputy Sheriff John Sage, recently of New Mexico."

Sage cringed at the open-mouthed stares around the large table. Pike and Nancy looked amused.

Nemeth said, "I read about that. Your name sounded familiar. You took exception when McClusky beat up some cowboy in a saloon. You told him you were going to lay him out. Then you knocked him out and broke his jaw—and did it in a very short time. I don't think I'll be throwing any punches at you. How in the world did you get to be that good of a boxer?"

"I didn't," said Sage. "Michael here would take me in a minute in a ring if I had to fight by the boxing rules. I studied another form of fighting. I'm sorry that I broke McClusky's jaw. He didn't deserve that, but the man was so dangerous that I couldn't hold back. He was getting through my blocks, so I hit him as hard as I could with a front kick."

"What form of fighting was that?" asked one of Pike's friends. He'd been introduced as Nelson Mallory.

"It is known in Japan as "te", the empty hand or karate," said Sage. "It was developed on Okinawa from other disciplines used in China and other places."

"I know of that," said Mallory. "I was recently charge de affairs in Tokyo. I observed some demonstrations and contests when I visited Okinawa one time. The forces that can be generated by human hands and feet are quite amazing. How did you come to learn karate?"

"I was on Okinawa for four years," replied Sage. "I got stranded there by a shipwreck. I spent two of those years with a karate master."

"Recently?" asked Mallory.

"I was picked up by an American vessel almost four years ago," said Sage.

"Hmmm. That was before I was stationed there. You were fortunate," said Mallory. "We had just started trading on Okinawa at about that time.

"You speak Japanese, then?"

"I speak the dialect used on Okinawa. We made a stop in Tokyo, and I couldn't understand much of what was spoken there."

"Yes," said Mallory. "The dialect on Okinawa is different. There might be a future in the service for you there. We could use a man with your knowledge of the land and its language."

Sage thought about the overseer that he had killed and glanced at Nancy.

"I don't think I could go back there," he said. "I spent the first two years as a prisoner doing forced labor. My crime was being a foreigner. I escaped, and for all I know, I'm still a wanted man there."

"That could be worked out," said Mallory. "We have a better working relationship now."

Sage said, "Sir, I'm afraid not. I killed an overseer when I escaped. He was beating a friend of mine—a fellow prisoner. That overseer had beaten several prisoners to death while I was there.

"The prisoners weren't criminals. They were political prisoners who had been resisting the Japanese overlords."

Mallory raised his eyebrows and said, "My, my. That would make working things out a bit difficult. But perhaps not impossible. I think I'll look into that."

"Thank you, sir," said Sage. "But I don't have the education to be an officer in the Foreign Service."

"That could be remedied," said Mallory. "That's what colleges and universities are for. You're still young."

After dinner the men went into the living room to smoke cigars and talk while the women retired to the sitting room to sip tea and talk.

Pike outlined the political conditions in Mexico. President Porfirio Diaz had done wonders to improve the economy by suppressing the rampant banditry there and successfully campaigning for foreign investment. He had also begun a vigorous enforcement of laws that curbed the church, which had been swallowing up so many of Mexico's resources.

The man still had enemies, though—and not just the church and its conservative supporters. Ex-President Lerdo was holed up in New York, and he was fomenting yet another revolution. Diaz's term was about to expire, and Diaz had been a champion of one-term presidencies. Whether he intended to hold to that was yet to be seen.

The Europeans had been pretty sore at Mexico because of the execution of Maximilian, but they had eventually recognized Diaz's government, and most had embassies there now. America had taken longer because of troubles along the border, but it had finally given its recognition much to the relief of the current ambassador, John Foster.

Pike said, "John wants us to get around the country and talk to American businessmen and their Mexican counterparts. See how they're getting along. John wants to know any issues there are. It is a big country, and we can't get everywhere. We'll just be sampling some areas where there is a lot of American activity. The biggest ones are railroads and mining."

Weeks asked, "How safe is it to travel around down there?"

"Reasonably safe," replied Pike. "The Rurales have pretty much wiped out banditry, and the ambassador assures me that the people are generally friendly. He's traveled around with the womenfolk quite a lot."

Sage remarked, "Most of the bandits that were there now are the Rurales. A friend of mine is a Rurale, and he told me that when the bandits were offered respectable positions and adequate pay, there was a transformation in their behavior."

"Deputy Sheriff Sage's friend was a bandit?" Pilgreen said, sneering.

Sage gave Pilgreen a level look and said, "More like a brother, and no, he wasn't a bandit. Not all the Rurales were bandits. Diaz needed some trustworthy people in there. Turned out, though, that most of them were trustworthy.

"I lived in Mexico for about four years. I think you'll find the people there to be mostly like us. If you treat them right, they'll treat you right."

"That is true about anywhere," said Mallory. He looked around at the young officers and said, "Put that down as a basic assumption, and you'll do well in foreign relations."

Pilgreen looked at Sage and said, "Your brother is a Mexican? I was wondering about that dark skin of yours."

Sage was going to be working closely with these people, so he decided to lay it on the table.

"I grew up with him," said Sage. "But I'm not Mexican. My mother was an Apache."

Brandon Parker, one of Pike's friends, spoke up. "Now that is fascinating! I have a friend in the Bureau of Indian Affairs. The Apaches are driving him to distraction, what with Geronimo going off the reservation again. My friend says that the Apaches are the best guerilla fighters in the world, and trying to corral them has been a nightmare. Do you have any suggestions as to what would work?"

"Yes," said Sage, "If you treat them right, they'll treat you right. Indian Affairs never got that down. I've heard from Apaches that the agents and contractors are stealing most of the supplies that were promised to the tribes. I'm surprised that they all haven't gone off the reservations."

Parker said, "I don't know about the stealing. If they all went off the reservations, then we'd just do the Indian wars all over again, and the Indians would be beaten again. It's all so senseless."

"Of course," said Sage. "The Indians couldn't win. They'd rather fight each other than cooperate to whip the white man, and that's bringing about the end of them and their culture."

"How do you feel about that, John?" asked Pike.

Sage thought for a moment and said, "Man for man, the Indians are as good as anyone else, but a culture that values warfare over cooperation just can't compete with a culture that places a higher value on cooperation.

"I don't like what is happening to them. I don't like dust storms, either, but I'm not going to pick up a bucket of water and go out to fight one."

"Well said, John," said Pike.

He looked around the room and said, "I agree that cooperation is paramount. Those of us going to Mexico will work as a team. Do any of you have a problem with John's heritage that would preclude that?"

Weeks said, "I'm getting the impression that John is going to be a valuable resource for us. I've got no problem at all!"

Nemeth and Nutzhorn nodded in agreement.

Pike noted that Pilgreen stared at the floor and didn't say anything.

After another hour of discussion, Leona Pike brought the women into the room, and not long after, the party broke up.

When the other guests had left, Mallory said, "Andrew, your Mr. Sage is quite interesting and apparently quite lethal."

"You don't know the half of it," replied Pike. My friend out in New Mexico, Judge Will Bennett, gave me quite an earful. In addition to his skills in unarmed combat, he is superb with firearms. Probably better than Bill Hickok was. He's put a number of badmen in the ground.

"Thing is, Will says that Sage would much rather avoid a fight than get into one. He took down a criminal operation in Rincon by organizing a team of volunteer deputies that backed him up and kept the killing to a minimum, although there was some. I'm going to feel totally secure in Mexico with him around. There will be marines at the embassy, but there probably won't be any marines out in the field with us."

-74-

Sage reported for duty on the first of April. He and Nancy had rented a small house in Washington for the month; Sage had become a commuter and rode a horsecar to work.

They had visited Philadelphia and New York City and taken a train down along the coast to Florida. A highlight of the trip for both Nancy and Sage was a week they spent paddling a canoe around the everglades with an Indian guide. They had been fascinated with the display of exotic wildlife.

Then they took a train to New Orleans and spent a week exploring the city. They took an excursion on a paddle wheeler up the Mississippi. After that they went back to a location they had liked on the coast of North Carolina and rented a cottage on Albemarle Sound for a month.

The cottage had a dock, and Sage found a twenty-five-foot, single-masted yawl that he could rent for the length of their stay. The owner spent a morning familiarizing Sage with it, and after a couple of days of practice, he and Nancy were handling it with ease.

The small boat was a far cry from the clipper and schooner that Sage had sailed on, but the handling principles were the same, and it didn't take Sage long to become competent.

When a strong wind came up, they experienced the fright that all green sailors do when first encountering the formidable forces of the elements out on the water. Sage managed to furl the main sail and shorten the jib, and fright turned to exhilaration as the small boat proved capable of handling the wind and chop.

Nancy's exhilaration soon turned to extreme discomfort, though, and she spent a couple of hours heaving over the side and considering mutiny. After the wind calmed, she recovered, and Sage was silently forgiven.

The seasickness didn't recur, and Nancy became a pretty good sailor. They spent two weeks exploring the sheltered sounds. Then they ventured out into the Atlantic for a couple of days before an approaching late winter storm sent them scuttling back to safer waters.

Nancy spent a considerable amount of time piloting the boat while Sage was stretched out with a book.

During the train ride from Las Cruces to Washington, the subject of Indian sign language had come up. Nancy had been intrigued and insisted that Sage teach it to her. So while they were out on the water, Sage spent a great amount of time giving her instruction when he wasn't reading. She was a quick study, and by the time they returned the boat to its owner, she had developed a serviceable vocabulary.

They were reluctant to leave that pleasant existence but decided to get back to Washington two weeks early and spend more time exploring the nation's capital.

They found another house available for rent close to where they had been staying before.

Sage stopped by Pike's office to let him know they were in town and ran into Jim Nemeth and Richard Weeks, who offered to spend some time showing the Sage's more about how their government worked.

The men took them to the Capitol, along with Week's wife Susan, and they spent a day in the galleries, where Nemeth expounded the workings of Congress. Then they spent another day visiting the White House and Supreme Court.

Like countless other visitors to Washington, Sage came away with a deep feeling of pride for his country. He felt pretty damned lucky to be an American.

The rangy Weeks was a running enthusiast, and Sage joined him early just about every morning for a run along unpaved roads and through the parks. Weeks was astonished that Sage eschewed running shoes and preferred to run barefoot.

"I've spent a number of years barefoot, and they don't ever wear out," said Sage. "Why wear out a pair of good shoes?"

It took Sage a few days to get back in shape, but after that, Weeks marveled at the man's endurance. As fit as Weeks was, he just couldn't wear Sage out, and he'd tried.

Sage spent a few evenings in a gym with Nemeth, but he preferred to do his usual stretching and other exercises at home without an audience wondering just what in hell he was doing.

During the second week in April, Pike's team of five men went to an armory for firearms training. Sage had been told that the firearms would be provided at the armory, but he'd brought along his Colt in the hopes that he could use a gun he was familiar with.

Their instructor, a marine sergeant and a grizzled Civil War veteran, told them that U.S. Marines provided security at the embassy, but if they were going to be traveling around the country, they probably wouldn't be going with them. Best to be prepared.

After running through a lecture on firearms safety, the instructor had everyone plug their ears with cotton. Then he demonstrated the proper stance. He stood with his right side toward the target, his right arm extended straight out, and the revolver at eye level.

He demonstrated the proper way to squeeze off shots while holding the revolver on target with the sights properly aligned. There were paper targets set up thirty feet from the firing line, and he carefully put six bullets in the bull's eye of one of them.

The students then picked up the .38 caliber revolvers lying on stands, loaded them per instructions, and fired six rounds at their targets in the manner demonstrated.

The instructor shook his head. College kids didn't impress him much. Only one of the students had put all six on paper, and that one had even managed to put two rounds in the black. He was the only one that had kept his eyes open and didn't flinch with each shot.

That student put down his .38 and raised his hand.

"Sir, are we supposed to be learning how to shoot paper targets or how to be the one that walks away after a gunfight?"

"What's your name?" asked the instructor.

"John Sage."

"Well, Mr. Sage, first things first. The first thing is to learn how to handle a revolver properly and how to shoot straight. You aren't going to come away from here ready to take on the bad guys like some cowtown sheriff, but you should at least be able to use a revolver with some degree of accuracy."

The instructor wondered why that remark had caused so much amusement among the other students.

"Sir," said Sage, "if I took the time to stand properly and line up the sights properly, I'd be killed six times over before I was ready for the first shot."

"And just how do you think it should be done, Mr. Sage?" asked the instructor disdainfully.

Sage whirled around. A big Colt had appeared in his hand from somewhere, and with an almost unbroken roar the two-inch bull's eye on his target was nearly erased. Just the outer edge of it remained.

The instructor gaped at the target, and Nutzhorn said, "Holy shit!" while the others whooped.

The Marine turned and stared at Sage, and Nemeth said, "John here was recently a cowtown sheriff. I guess they shoot pretty well."

Sage ejected shells from his Colt and put them in a pocket. As he replaced them with bullets from another pocket, he said, "It takes a whole lot of years of practice to be really good with a handgun. We don't have a whole lot of years here.

"I think these men need to get a feel for pointing and shooting, but if we get into a close-up scrape, I'll want them to have shotguns handy. Rifles would be needed for long range if they can get some training with those. They wouldn't have to be so quick."

"We don't teach 'point and shoot,'" the instructor said through gritted teeth. "We teach the proper use of firearms, and you will all learn the proper use of firearms. We will be moving on to rifles, but we do not use shotguns in the military. Don't bring that Colt back here."

Sage nodded and replaced the Colt in the shoulder holster under his coat. He dutifully undertook the learning of the proper use of firearms.

Three days later the instructor took them out on the rifle range. Sage had thought better of bringing his Winchester and was handed a bolt action .303.

He tried using the sights for a while, but he was hitting all over the target, so he reverted to shooting shotgun style hoping the instructor wouldn't notice.

A target operator in the trench a hundred yards away would raise a marker on a pole after each shot to indicate where on the target the bullet had struck. A black disk on the end of the pole was held over each hole momentarily, and if the disk was waved back and forth, it indicated that the shot had missed the target completely.

Sage was startled when the operator waved the disk on his second and third shots without using the sights. Wondering if the bullets had gone through the same hole he started placing the rounds around the inside edge of the bull's eye. The marker then poked up satisfactorily after each shot.

The instructor came over and watched him shoot for a while. Then he said, "Dammit, Sage, close your left eye! Hell, you aren't even looking at the sights. Do like I instructed you, for Christ's sake!"

Sage went back to using the sights and kept missing the bull's eye.

The sergeant said, "Shit! Never mind. Just go on hitting the bull's eye like you were."

He stomped off in disgust.

At the end of the week, the captain in charge of the firearms training had the class gather around to review their scores. Andrew Pike showed up for the session.

The captain said, "I'd feel pretty safe with most of you shooting at me with revolvers, except for Sage. His scores weren't great, but pretty good. He'd be rated as proficient if he were a marine.

"Looks like some of you have spent some time hunting. Two of the rifle range scores, Pilgreen and Nutzhorn, rated as sharpshooters. One as expert. That was Sage again. Hell, he almost beat the range record."

The captain looked around and asked, "Which one of you is Sage?"

Sage lifted a hand, and the captain said, "If you hadn't had two clean misses, you'd have beat it. Nice shooting."

Sage looked at the ceiling, lifted his palms up, and shrugged.

The students thanked the captain and the sergeant and took a horsecar back to the State Department building with Pike.

In the car, Nemeth looked at Pike and said, "If the instructor had let John shoot in his own way, he wouldn't have missed a single bull's eye—not with either a rifle or revolver."

Pike chuckled and said, "The instructor told me that he'd never seen anyone shoot like John."

He looked at Sage and said, "He said you did a truly awesome demonstration with your Colt that belonged in a Wild West show, but not on a military range. He said if he'd had enough time, it might have been possible to teach you the proper use of firearms."

Sage said, "Well, their method apparently works for the military, but I wouldn't be here today if I'd been using it, and it doesn't suit our needs here.

"I don't think we're going to be in any kind of fight in Mexico, but if we're going to be carrying guns anywhere, I'd like to do some work with these men so that the guns would be of more use than just show."

Pike said, "Do you think they could be effective with handguns with the little time we'd have for training?"

"No," said Sage. "Might just as well not take any. But Mike and Phil aren't bad with rifles, and they could all learn to handle shotguns well enough to be effective in a tight spot."

"Very well," said Pike. "There is a sportsman's club here that has a trap range for shotguns. I'll arrange some time for you all there, and I'll go myself."

-75-

Pike and his team disembarked from the steamer at Veracruz near the end of May. The leg from Washington down the east coast to Havana had been rough. Most of the party had been violently seasick, although Sage and Nancy had not been affected.

Susan Weeks, a slender, pale woman, had been convinced that she was going to die, and for a while looked desperately forward to it. But much to Richard's relief, Sage told her that people just didn't die from seasickness.

Fortunately, the weather for the trip across the lower Gulf of Mexico from Cuba had been calm, and everyone was feeling good. Everyone was eager to see Veracruz and get on to Mexico City.

While on the final leg, Pike gathered the men on deck and informed them that they would be staying in Veracruz for two days of meetings with some American and Mexican businessmen.

Uh oh, thought Sage.

"Mr. Pike," said Sage. "Will anyone from a Garcia family or their associates be in those meetings?"

"Of course," said Pike. "There isn't much around Veracruz that the Garcias aren't involved in. Do you know them?"

"I don't know them," said Sage. "But I don't think I had better attend those meetings."

Pike raised his eyebrows and asked, "Why on earth not, John?"

"Um, I was in a posse out of Laredo a while back. We chased some bank robbers into Mexico and wound up in a shootout with a troop of Federales. The Federales rode in while we were fighting with the bandits, and a couple of the posse shot at them.

"Then the fight was on. I killed their officer. I learned later that he was a man named Gabriel Garcia, who was from a prominent family in Veracruz. His father, Aldolpho, is the family patriarch."

"Jesus Christ!" Pike exploded. "Have you killed someone in every port, John?"

Pike thought for a moment and said, "Would they know your name?"

"Yes sir," said Sage. "I was able to escape, but the sheriff and others in the posse were killed. Some must have been taken prisoner. I heard from my friend in the Rurales that my name was known. Someone in the posse must have told them."

Pike shook his head and said, "No, you hadn't better attend those meetings. I'm tempted to just send you back on this steamer."

Sage felt sick. The other men were looking at him in astonishment—except for Pilgreen, who was smirking.

"Mr. Pike," said Sage, "the Garcias are in opposition to Diaz. They have always been aligned with Lerdo. They have little power outside of Veracruz. If Diaz heard about this, I don't think it would be an issue with him.

Pike looked at Sage for a long moment while he considered the idea.

"All right," he said. "You wouldn't be a player in those meetings anyway. Just lay low while we're in Veracruz.

"I wasn't aware of the standing of the Garcia family. Is that valid information?"

"Yes," said Sage.

Sage didn't have any trouble in Veracruz. On the train to Mexico City, Nemeth sat with him for a while while Nancy sat in another seat deep in conversation with Leona Pike.

"One of the men we met with was Pedro Garcia, a son of Aldopho," said Nemeth. "He made it clear that he wasn't too fond of Americans, but he and Pilgreen seemed to hit it off. They had their heads together a lot, and Garcia invited him to his home.

"I took several classes at Harvard with Mike, and I was on the boxing team for a while. I socialized with him some. Mike's main interest is Mike. He's a lot more interested in making his fortune than he is in government service. I think the only reason he is here is to look for business opportunities, and if he comes across something good, that's the last we'll see of him."

"Is Andrew aware of that?" asked Sage.

"No. I haven't said anything," said Nemeth. "Not my business.

"That Pedro Garcia looked to me like one evil son of a bitch. There is a lot of resentment in Veracruz because Diaz has allowed the Americans there to pay Mexican workers a lot less for their labor than the American workers there are getting.

"I got the picture that Garcia is stoking that resentment in their struggle against Diaz. I'm glad you clued us in about the Garcia's position, and so is Pike. It helped us understand what is going on here.

"The revolution, if there is one, might start in Veracruz, the gateway to Mexico City. It's been done before. We did it, the French did it, and Diaz did it. Lerdo is in New York, but his top general, Escobedo, is up in Brownsville, and it wouldn't take him long to steam down with a force through the gulf.

"If we're backing Diaz, how come we're letting Escobedo sit up there in Brownsville?" asked Sage.

"I'm not sure," said Nemeth. "I know there has been some intrigue in Washington. There are some that would like to have an opportunity to annex more Mexican territory. Turmoil sometimes provides opportunity. That's making our relationship with Diaz a little uncomfortable to say the least."

After a while, Nemeth said, "Ever hear the Mexicans call us 'gringos'?"

"A time or two."

"That originated right along here," said Nemeth. "Back when Zachary Taylor was marching on Mexico City, his troops had a marching song, 'Green Grow the Lilacs.' The Mexicans picked the word 'gringo' out of that."

"At least they didn't wind up with 'lilacs,'" said Sage.

When the train steamed into Mexico City, carriages from the American embassy met it, and the group was taken to the American compound.

Sage remarked on the teeming population in Mexico city, Veracruz, and other towns they had passed through.

Nemeth said, "If Mexico had moved a lot more of their population north a hundred years ago, the United States would be a lot smaller than it is today. Americans can thank the Comanches, Navajos, Apaches, and other tribes that they didn't."

Sage and Nancy found that the quarters they were assigned to be very comfortable after they cleaned up, rearranged the furniture, and dispatched a few spiders and scorpions. The one-story adobe building had several apartments that shared a large central patio, and all of the team was quartered there except the Pikes. They had a house to themselves.

The compound had a corral with a number of horses for the use of embassy employees. While Pike met with the ambassador for the day, Sage and Nancy selected two of the animals and spent the day riding around the city. Sage was glad that they had brought their saddles.

They were awed by the massive stone buildings of the National Palace and the National Cathedral, and the proud Mexicans they encountered were delighted to give them impromptu tours.

Sage studied the stonework of the cathedral, and uncomfortable memories of his labors on Okinawa resurged. Their guide explained that all the work had been done by Indian laborers. The good fathers may have saved their souls, but they had certainly enslaved their bodies.

Sage didn't have to imagine how free-spirited Indians had been forced to do that kind of work.

While Sage and Nancy were admiring the huge painted murals in the palace, Nancy commented, "They sure go in for color and for gruesome scenes."

"They've had kind of a gruesome history," said Sage. "You'll find them to be generally friendly and easygoing, but they're not soft."

The meals they had been getting in Mexico were a lot more familiar than what they had been getting in the east. The waiter assured them the water had been boiled.

In her halting Spanish, Nancy said, "They kept saying that in Veracruz, too. Why is that?"

The waiter, a middle-aged man, said, "The plumbing here is over three hundred years old. The water and sewer lines were laid in the same trenches. Pipes that old...there are many leaks."

"Ever thought about laying new pipes?" she asked.

The waiter grinned and said, "We don't have Indian slaves to do that anymore. It is easier to boil the water."

After the waiter had left, Sage said, "They're sort of practical, too."

The team's first excursion took them by train to Morelia, the capitol of the state of Michoacan, which was about three hundred miles west of Mexico City. An American company based there was surveying for a new rail line westward to Guadalajara.

Sage was struck by the fact that just about every town they passed through, even ones that were fairly small and remote, had an enormous cathedral. He wondered how it would be in Mexico if all the effort that had gone into building them had gone into infrastructure and schools instead.

Sage attended all the meetings. He had been concerned that he was going to be mostly useless for the team, but it turned out that his language skills were valuable, and he had a talent for boiling the issues he was hearing down to their basics and contributed a number of insights that were appreciated to the discussions.

Morelia rivaled Mexico City in grand buildings and cathedrals, and Sage was impressed with the Roman-style aqueduct, which brought water into the city from a long distance away.

While having dinner in an outdoor restaurant on the edge of a magnificent plaza, Nancy said, "John, I did a good thing."

At Seeing his inquisitive look she said, "I married you. You've gotten me out into the big, wide world, and it's been wonderful. Your company hasn't been too bad, either. It's going to be hard to get this country girl back down on the farm."

"I don't think I'll try," grinned Sage. "I think I did a good thing, too. I never realized what I was missing before I met you. I just had a feeling down deep that something was missing.

"Not anymore. I'm feeling pretty complete. Maybe I'll feel totally complete if I can get a college education and establish my career. I'm thinking that this foreign service work in going to turn out to be...fulfilling."

Nancy grinned and reached across the table. Placing her hand on his, she said, "Leona told me that Andrew is pretty thankful that he didn't send us back on the steamer. She told me what that was all about when I asked her.

"She said that Andrew was truly impressed with your analytical abilities. He said that with an education you would be 'some kind of formidable.

"I thought you were some kind of formidable before. People tend to like you, but they'd rather step in front of a train than get into a fight with you. Same results, but faster and less painful."

Sage chuckled ruefully. "It has been nice lately not having to watch out all the time for someone trying to kill me. I'm starting to feel civilized.

Nancy said, "Well, our children are going to grow up in a more civilized world unless we wind up in some place like Africa. The boys probably won't even have to learn a fast draw."

Sage raised his eyebrows and said, "We haven't really talked a lot about that."

"No," said Nancy. "But we've been doing something about that. I think the first one is on the way."

Sage jerked upright and said, "What?"

"I haven't had my last two periods, and I feel different. A little sick in the mornings."

Sage jumped up, went around the table, and drew her to her feet. Mexicans around them watched in amusement as the crazy gringos made a display of themselves.

-76-

"We are going to be attending an interesting meeting today," said Pike. "You are all going to come along with Ambassador Foster and myself to confer with President Diaz."

The commerce team was in Pike's office after returning from Morelia.

Pike said, "John will be here shortly to meet with us before we go over to the National Palace. He wants to meet you all and to brief us on a situation of some concern to Diaz."

There was a tap on the door, and Ambassador Foster came in. He was a distinguished and fit-looking man with billowing muttonchop whiskers that were starting to go gray.

Pike introduced his men and related a few things about their backgrounds. Foster asked a few probing questions and seemed to be genuinely interested in the young men. When Pike mentioned that Sage had been a deputy sheriff in New Mexico, Foster was intrigued.

He said, "You appear to be pretty young. Were you a sheriff for long?"

"No," said Sage. "Just a few weeks before I took this job."

"Hmm. Then you probably weren't mixing it up with the gunfighters that I've heard about in that part of the country. I read an account where two lawmen out that way faced the Cummings Gang and killed all seven of them. Quite a remarkable feat. Did you hear about that?"

Pike choked down his mirth.

Sage said, "It wasn't a gang. A rancher named Cummings was trying to bust his son out of jail to keep him from getting hung. He had four of his hands with him, not six. Old man Cummings was fixing to let loose with a shotgun, so the Sheriff and I had to do."

Foster's eyes widened. "My God. That was you?"

"It sure was," said Pike. "Sage here is a real gunfighter. Maybe the best there is."

Foster studied Sage and then said, "That is quite interesting. Bear in mind, Mr. Sage, that we are here to establish good relationships with the Mexican people, not shoot them."

Sage nodded. "I understand, sir. I've lived in Mexico, I like the people, and I have no desire to shoot anyone."

Foster said, "My family and I have traveled extensively in this country, and not once have we been threatened even though there has been considerable anti-American sentiment due to problems along the border and other issues.

"Andrew, you are not to bear arms on your travels. The risk to you would be minimal and would be outweighed by the risk of creating an international incident."

Foster looked around the room and said, "If any of you are acutely adverse to personal risk, please return to the States forthwith."

Sage had reservations. He wasn't inclined to be an aggressor, but if he ran into aggression, he sure wanted to be able to respond with all the force he could bring. But the man was telling them and their wives to take a risk in the interest of the country. So be it.

Foster continued. "The United States has only recently recognized the Diaz government. I spent uncomfortable years working toward bringing that about. But there are still tensions. Our government has authorized armed military incursions into Mexico along the border when they are in pursuit of smugglers and raiders.

"Mexicans, no matter what their political leanings, are as patriotic as Americans. Understandably, Diaz has ordered his military to oppose any such incursions with force, but thankfully no conflicts have yet arisen.

"An even greater concern for Diaz is the activity of Lerdo's General Escobedo up in Texas to foment a revolution in the northern states of Mexico and possibly in Veracruz. As I mentioned, we are backing Diaz. He wishes to be on good terms with us, and we are all engaged in cooling off the tensions along the border. Bear that in mind when we meet with him this afternoon.

"President Diaz is an exemplary man, one of the truly great men of Mexico who has the respect of his people, and he has done a lot of good for those people. I have a great respect for the man, too. Our government has been at odds with him on some issues, but by and large, we are well off with him as president.

Foster paused and then said, "I am going to be traveling to Guanajuato, a major silver-mining town north of here. An American mining enterprise, the Silver King Company, is interested in partnering with Mexico to improve production and conduct more mineral exploration. This group will accompany me.

"We'll leave on the Monday after next by train to Queretaro and travel on horseback from there to Guanajuato, about a five-day ride through pretty rough and arid country. We'll use the old wagon road. It's shorter.

"My wife is fond of traveling, and I know Andrew's is also, so the three of you who have wives here are welcome to bring them along. Guanajuato is a fairly substantial city and has some good hotels.

"It has been good to meet you gentlemen. Please meet me in front of the National Palace at two o'clock. Good day."

On the way to the palace, Nemeth said, "Here we are, all highly trained in the proper use of firearms, armed to he teeth, and fierce as can be, and we are forbidden to bear the arms."

"Oh well," chuckled Sage. "I was a little leery about getting into a gunfight without you all having about two years of really intensive training under your belts. One week plus some practice with shotguns just made us a little less dangerous to each other."

After the team was shown to the large ornate meeting room in the palace, two of the president's guards entered the room. Sage was astonished and delighted that one of them was Miguel Vega. The other was one of the men who had accompanied Vega to Rincon.

Miguel was even more astonished to see Sage, and he came over quickly, clasped Sage's shoulders, and exclaimed in English, "John, this is wonderful! You're with the American embassy?"

"Yes," said Sage. "Not long after I saw you, I was offered a position in our foreign service."

Diaz came into the room with some aids and noticed Vega with Sage. He came over while everyone stood to welcome him.

In Spanish, Vega said, "Mr. President, this is John Sage, who I have spoken of."

Diaz shook Sage's hand and said, "Ahh, you grew up with Miguel and became an officer of the law. Miguel has told me that you are as good with weapons as he is. Miguel's skills are amazing. Now there are two formidable people in this room. Are you now a diplomat?"

"No, Mr. President," said Sage, "just a low-level aid on Ambassador Foster's commerce team. I am pleased to meet you, sir. The ambassador and my team leader, Andrew Pike, have spoken well of you."

"How diplomatic of you," said Diaz, grinning. "That is good to hear. I have spent a great deal of time with Ambassador Foster, and he is a true friend.

"I wish you well during your service here, John Sage."

Diaz spoke a few words with Foster and Pike and then convened the meeting. Foster introduced Pike, and Pike introduced his team.

The purpose of the meeting was to discuss American business affairs in general and mining and railroad interests in particular. It lasted until six o'clock.

As the Americans were preparing to leave, Vega approached Sage and said, "I'm a married man now, John. I'd like you to come to my home and meet my wife."

"Congratulations, Miguel," said Sage. "I'm married now, too. I would like to bring my wife along."

"Excellent," said Vega. "I had heard that you were."

Vega hurriedly gave Sage directions to his home before accompanying Diaz from the room.

Sage was puzzled about how Vega could have heard that he was married.

-77-

When he and Nancy arrived at Vega's home, they were both flabbergasted when Vega and his wife met them at the door.

"I believe that you have both met my wife," said Vega with a large grin.

"Welcome to our home, Mr. and Mrs. Sage," said the former Lupita Calderon.

"We aren't going to have to think too hard about a topic of conversation," said Sage.

Like most homes in the city, Vega's was packed along the street with many others. The huge varnished door in the bland exterior opened to a beautiful interior. Several rooms surrounded an open courtyard, where Lupita Vega led them.

Vega brought out drinks. "Are tequila and orange juice acceptable?" he asked.

"Very acceptable," said Sage. "Now I've got to hear how a beautiful and talented woman like Lupita fell into the clutches of an unsavory character like you."

"He is not unsavory!" piped Lupita. With a little grin she said, "He is very savory."

Vega said, "When I got back down here, I couldn't get her out of my mind. So after a while, I went back to Rincon. After about a thousand 'no's,' she said 'yes.' It only took that one."

"It was not a thousand," said Lupita. "How could I resist such a handsome man who worked for the president of Mexico?"

"When I got to Rincon, I was surprised to find that you weren't there anymore," said Vega. "Lupita told me that you had gotten married and gone to Washington. She told me about the wedding and about Nancy.

"Sounded like it was quite a wedding. Many important people there, along with about the whole town. I'm sorry I missed that."

Vega looked at Nancy and said, "All that for an unsavory character like John. How did he wind up with a beautiful woman like you?"

"He's very savory," said Nancy. "And I don't have to worry about any enemies. He's quite the warrior. But I love him because he is also kind, and he likes the things that I like. We're seeing the world, and I certainly enjoy seeing it with John."

"You know, we are warriors," mused Vega. "We were declared warriors by the Apaches back when we were sixteen, just before we parted ways. It wasn't all that long ago, but it sure seems like it.

"I've been seeing a lot of war ever since, and I don't expect that to change anytime soon. I'm grateful that John's father Nathan brought us up to be able to handle ourselves in any kind of fight."

Sage said, "Well, I've gotten a look at a civilized society in the east, and it does appeal to me. Folks don't have to go around wearing guns there. They've gotten to depend on law enforcement officers and the military to handle those that would harm them. And that's a good thing. It isn't that way in the West—yet—but it's headed that way.

"Maybe I'm not done with being a warrior, but I'd like to get headed in that direction. There are a lot of interesting things to do in the world that don't require a fast gun, and I want to do them. I guess I'll always have to do my part, though, if trouble comes up."

"You've done your part," said Nancy. "I'd like you to be able to hand trouble off. Maybe someday."

Lupita went in to heat up some enchiladas, and Nancy complimented Vega on his fine home.

Vega grinned and said, "I thank John for getting a price on his head. It went a long way toward paying for this place. Fortunately for John, I have a dishonest side and didn't insist on earning it."

"You earned it, Miguel," said Sage. "You were the key for getting to Lugo. A murderer paid for his own downfall. Now that's justice!"

"I spoke with Cody Miller," said Vega. "He told me about the trials and executions. You played your hand well.

"Cody said that Rincon has become very quiet. He is thinking about moving on."

"I hope he decides to stay around and enjoy it," said Sage. "But I've got to say that I wasn't looking forward to a mostly sedentary job. I guess being a warrior isn't all bad. Kind of stimulating."

"It was time to look for stimulation by other means," said Nancy. "I'd say your current position is pretty stimulating."

"It is," said Sage, "but I'm seeing that my options are limited. Those at a much higher level do the really fulfilling work. I need to get a better education. I'll be looking for a chance to go to college back in the States, but I'm not sure how I'll be able to stand the cost.

"I don't earn a great deal, and we pretty much used up what money we had on our trip through the South."

"We'll find a way," said Nancy.

Nancy excused herself and went in to help Lupita prepare the table.

Sage said, "Miguel, how has it been being married to Lupita?"

Vega grinned and said sheepishly, "I married Helen of Troy. Remember her from my aunt's school? Now I have to fight off the Greeks. When I bring her into a room, all the men there go crazy—even the ones with their women with them. I feel much pride, but it is kind of embarrassing."

"Well, if anyone can fight them off, you can," said Sage. "You're good with a bow and arrow. If Achilles shows up, you can handle him. Aim for the heel."

"Yes," said Vega. "Lupita enjoys the attention, but she is loyal to me. She does not flirt. I am very happy with her, and she seems to be happy with me.

"But I'll tell you, John, being her husband is a full-time job. I am consumed by that woman. Everything I do, I do with her in mind. I am always thinking, will this please Lupita? It is something of a burden.

"What will please Lupita is that I get promotions. I have become a Mexican citizen, and I am working to advance myself. That is why I am now in Diaz's personal bodyguard service."

Somewhat sadly he said, "I had thought about going back to raising horses, but that is no longer an option."

"I have some support from Diaz, but not so much with any others, so advancement is slow in coming. I don't have much education, either. There isn't much chance that I could get into the University of Mexico, and I am not fond of studying, anyway."

Sage said, "What is most important is that you do something that is fulfilling for you. Status isn't all that important."

"But status is important to Lupita," said Vega.

Sage hoped that his best friend would live a fulfilled and happy life, but he wasn't too confident that he would.

While they were eating Lupita's excellent enchiladas and side dishes, Sage talked about his team's upcoming trip to Guanajuato.

Vega said, "I don't think it is a very good idea that you are traveling unarmed. The countryside is peaceful these days, but it would be a disaster for Diaz if the American ambassador was harmed. The American government would hold him responsible, no matter what the circumstances.

"You should not only be armed but also accompanied by marines or Mexican troops."

"I take it that wouldn't be very diplomatic," said Sage.

-78-

As the sun was peeking up over the horizon, Sage and Weeks ran side by side through Chapultepec Park, near the embassy compound. No Mexicans were around at the early hour to laugh at the crazy Americans.

The effects of running at the high altitude diminished as they had become acclimated, and they were enjoying the feel of the crisp air. This would be their last run for a while. They were taking the train to Queretaro later in the morning.

"It sure surprised me when Mike resigned," said Weeks.

"Didn't surprise me too much," said Sage. "Although I was kind of surprised that he found a business opportunity so quickly."

"I don't think I'd like it too much in Veracruz," said Weeks. "Too damned hot and humid. I hope he doesn't get yellow fever. It's coming up on the season for it there."

"I'm not going to miss him," said Sage. "I was getting a little tired of his remarks about the uneducated, half-bred diplomat."

"Your restraint has been admirable," said Weeks. "You've got too many abilities, and you've gotten too much attention for Mike's liking. He thought he was the big fish, and you were using up too much of the pond."

"Not any money in our pond," said Sage. "I didn't expect him to stay around long."

The men loaded their saddle and pack animals onto stock cars. Then they joined the women in the coaches for the trip north. The party spent the night in Queretaro and then struck out westward for Guanajuato the following morning riding along the little-used wagon road through the broken, arid country.

The five women all wore ground-length divided skirts called culottes, which allowed them to ride their horses astride. Foster and Pike led off, and Sage trailed behind, leading the five packhorses. Nancy rode beside him, and they stayed far enough behind the rest to avoid the dust.

"If the scenery doesn't change, this is going to be a pretty boring ride," said Nancy.

Sage said, "This country reminds me of some I've seen in Arizona at elevations that were a little higher. It even has a lot of the same vegetation."

He pointed out a number of brush and cactus species and explained the uses that the Apaches had for them. To pass the time, they worked on Nancy's sign language vocabulary and Spanish.

Sage noted that a horse party had passed this way the day before traveling in the same direction.

They didn't meet anyone on their ride until the late afternoon on the third day, when they approached a group of men camped off to the side of the two ruts that passed for a road.

When the men saw Foster's party, they mounted their horses and rode to meet them.

Pike turned to Foster and said, "One of those men is Pedro Garcia. What in the world would he be doing out here?"

"That doesn't look like a group of businessmen," replied Foster. "Looks more like a gang of bandits. Eight of them. Must be a burden to haul all those guns and cartridge belts around. Are you on good terms with Garcia?"

"Our discussions went fairly well, but I can't say that he is particularly fond of Americans," said Pike. "He's an ally of Lerdo."

"That isn't good," said Foster.

Garcia led his men up to Pike and Foster. He pushed his sombrero back on his head and grinned at Pike. The grin showed an impressive array of white teeth under his flowing mustache. He said, "Good day, Mr. Pike. I hope that you have had a nice ride through our country. We are going to show you some more of it. You are coming with us."

Pike said, "No, we are not coming with you, Mr. Garcia. This is a diplomatic party, and this is the American ambassador, John Foster. We are authorized to travel freely in this country."

Garcia spat on the ground and said, "I am revoking that authorization in the name of the legitimate president of Mexico, Lerdo de Tejada."

He drew his revolver, and the rest of his men followed suit.

"If any of you have weapons, drop them on the ground, now!" he said.

"We are not armed," said Foster. "We are traveling under the assumption that this is a civilized country that respects international law. Your government will not tolerate your behavior. This is a disgrace to Mexico."

"This is a disgrace to Diaz," said Garcia, laughing. "But his government is already a disgrace."

Garcia looked around at the American party and said, "Which one of you is Mr. Sage?"

Sage had closed up with the packhorses. He sat quietly, and Nancy gave him a startled and frightened look.

Garcia looked at Sage and said, "You are the only one other than the ambassador that I have not met, so you must be Sage. I have been looking forward to meeting you ever since you murdered my brother."

Sage said, "It was an unfortunate incident. Your brother's troop got into a fight with an American posse that was chasing a band of bank robbers. It was the posse's fault that things got out of hand, and I regret that. I found myself in a position where I had to fight my way out. I'm sorry about your loss."

"It was a great loss," said Garcia. "And now you lose. Get off your horse."

Sage considered jumping his horse into Garcia's and going for his gun, but there were just too many of them, and Nancy might well catch a bullet.

Eyes venomous, Nancy started to stay something to Garcia, but Sage shook his head slightly, and she remained silent.

Sage gave Nancy a look that was a mixture of resignation and regret, swung out of the saddle, and faced Garcia.

"Take off your clothes," ordered Garcia. "All of them."

Sage gave Garcia an astonished look, hesitated a moment, and then complied. He stood straight, facing

Garcia, and waited for whatever was coming next. Maybe he wasn't going to be shot out of hand.

The women—except Nancy and Leonora Pike—averted their eyes.

Garcia called one of his men over to pick up Sage's clothing and boots and said, "We'll be leaving now, Mr. Sage. Enjoy your walk."

Sage looked around at the rugged land. It was about eighty miles back to Queretaro on the rough road, and they were almost that far from Guanajuato.

Sage limped gingerly around on his bare feet and said, "I'd rather take a bullet."

Garcia laughed and said, "You must mistake me for someone who is kind."

He waved his arm, pointed toward the north, and said, "Lets get moving."

Garcia led out across country, and his men herded the diplomatic party northward after him.

As his horse swung around, Pike looked back and said, "I am truly sorry, John. Go with God."

Nancy kept her eyes on Sage as her horse started to follow the others, and his hands moved in sign language. He watched the group until it disappeared in the distance, and then began to follow at a trot.

-79-

"Do you know what is up this way, John?" asked Pike.

"There is absolutely nothing before Delores Hidalgo, and that is a long way off," answered Foster.

"Silence!" commanded Garcia.

Trailing farther back, Leona Pike said, "Nancy, I am so sorry. I'm amazed that you are so calm."

"I'm not calm," said Nancy. "But that's John Sage back there."

She was silent for a minute and then said, "When John and I were in the South, we listened to a negro woman telling a story to a group of children. The story was about how a rabbit outfoxed a fox by getting the fox to throw the rabbit in a briar patch.

"The rabbit convinced the fox that being thrown into the briar patch was the worst kind of death imaginable. But the briar patch was its natural place of refuge.

"Well, John is in his briar patch, and he is coming."

"Your husband is no rabbit. He is a superb specimen of a man," said Leona, "but barefoot and naked. What can he do?"

"We'll see," said Nancy.

Leona shook her head hopelessly.

Nancy studied their guards as they rode. An hour after they'd left Sage, Nancy said that she had to stop to relieve herself, and Garcia reluctantly allowed the party to take a break.

Nancy moved next to Nemeth and whispered, "Jim, I need to get that man's knife. It's important. You've got to distract him while I go for it."

Nemeth regarded her for a moment and then nodded. With Nancy at his heels, he walked by the guard and stumbled into him, stepping hard on his boot.

The guard swore and swung a punch at Nemeth, and Nemeth wrapped his arms around the man, pinning his arms, and said, "Easy, easy, I'm very sorry. That was clumsy of me."

Nemeth released the man and stepped back, holding up his palms. The guard, awed by the power he'd felt in those arms, swore at him some more but didn't press the issue. Two of the other guards had drawn their guns but put them back in their holsters.

Nancy walked back the way they had come until she had a bit of privacy and relieved herself. The other women and a couple of the men had taken the opportunity to scatter out in the brush and do the same.

An hour later Jose Griego noticed that his sheath knife was missing. He wondered if it had fallen out when he was dancing with the stupid gringo, but he couldn't see how. He thought about riding back and looking for it but decided that would make him look foolish to Garcia.

Sage, following the tracks of his party and their captors, found the knife lying on the ground. Giving silent thanks to Nancy, he set about making other weapons.

Garcia kept the group moving until just before the sun set. They had covered about twenty miles from where he had taken them captive.

While the others set up camp and heated some tinned goods for a meal, Garcia went off with Ambassador Foster for a parley. They were gone for over an hour. When they came back, Garcia was looking angry. Foster was looking grim.

The Americans had set up tents for the women, but Garcia wouldn't let the men use tents. He wanted his men to be able to watch them through the night.

Foster and Pike bedded down next to each other, a little farther away from the other men.

In a low voice, Foster said, "Andrew, we are in serious trouble here. Garcia is convinced that General Escobedo and Lerdo will be successful in overthrowing Diaz. He gave me an ultimatum. Work with him and Escobedo against Diaz and have great influence with the new Lerdo government, or die out here. All of us will simply disappear from the face of the earth.

"That would put Diaz in an uncomfortable position vis-à-vis the American government. I refused to cooperate with him, of course. He told me to sleep on it. If I don't 'come to my senses,' we will be executed in the morning. All of us.

"I don't think I'll be sleeping much."

"Good Lord!" breathed Pike.

"I don't understand how Garcia knew where we were going to be," said Foster, "or about poor Sage being with us."

"I've been thinking about that," said Pike. "Pilgreen. He and Garcia seemed to be very friendly back in Veracruz, and he kept disappearing from time to time until he resigned. Said he had a business opportunity in Veracruz. I'm afraid that I badly misjudged the man."

"I'm afraid I misjudged when I forbade going armed here," said Foster, sighing.

"If all my boys were John Sages, I would have pushed back," said Pike. "That man could whip the devil with any kind of weapon, or without any weapon. But as it was, we wouldn't have been a match for Garcia and his men, no matter how well armed we were.

"Damn it, Garcia knew we weren't armed. Damn that Pilgreen!

"We've been soldiers, John," said Pike. "It sure does gall me to lie here knowing that we and our wives are facing certain death and we're helpless to do anything about it. Never was in a situation like this during all the war.

"Well, this soldier is going to go down fighting in the morning. Haven't got a prayer, but I'll go out feeling a little better. Maybe get a lick in."

"Amen," said Foster.

-80-

Limon Perez yawned and shook his head, fighting to stay awake. He'd been awakened at midnight, two hours before, to take his shift guarding the gringos. He envied their peaceful sleep. He looked up at the stars and wondered for the ten thousandth time just what in hell they were.

An arrow smacked into the front of his throat, burying the stone point in the vertebrae. Perez collapsed almost silently. The body made a low thump when it hit the ground.

Jose Griego, the other night guard, spun around when he heard noises that didn't belong to the night and took a lance sideways through his head. He too collapsed almost silently.

Sage drifted by Pike and Foster, and when they came up on their elbows, he motioned for them to remain still. They looked at the naked man holding a bow and arrow with a knife clamped in his teeth and froze. The hand that held the bow was also holding three other arrows.

Sage worked his way around the camp and returned to the men with an armload of rifles and revolvers. He faded into the dark and returned with more. Then he did it again.

Sage moved over to the smoldering campfire and heaped all the fuel piled near it on to the coals. He returned to Pike and Foster, who were now sitting up.

Sage whispered, "I'm going to try to get Nutzhorn, Nemeth, and Weeks over here, but if any of Garcia's bunch get up, let's get to it. All they'll have is rocks."

Sage moved over to Nemeth and touched him on the shoulder. Nemeth's eyes opened and then widened when he recognized Sage.

Sage touched a finger to his lips. Then he handed a revolver to Nemeth and waved him toward Pike's location. Nemeth rolled out of his blankets and quietly moved off.

Sage repeated the maneuver with Weeks and then moved on to Nutzhorn. When he touched Nutzhorn's shoulder, Nutzhorn yelped and shot up into a sitting position.

Garcia threw open his blanket and grabbed for his gun. It wasn't there, and he jackknifed up, staring wildly around the campsite. In the light of the brightly burning campfire, a naked figure raced at him, and as he started to get to his feet, a bare foot struck his jaw, knocking him senseless.

Sage fired his revolver into the ground and yelled in Spanish, "Lie still or die!"

One of the Mexicans rolled out of his blankets and frantically tried to locate his gun. Sage clipped his ear with a bullet. The man stretched out flat on his stomach and lay still.

Heads poked out of the women's tents as Pike, Foster, and the other men took control of the Mexicans.

Sage picked up a blanket and wrapped it around his waist. Nancy ran up and threw her arms around him, crying, "Oh John, oh John!"

Sage hugged her and said, "We're all right now. Good job getting me that knife. It came in handy.

"You wouldn't know what became of my clothes, would you?"

Foster and Pike came up to Sage, and Nancy went to look for the saddle that the Mexican had tied his bundled clothes and boots to.

Pike said, "Damn, John, you sure pulled our fat out of the fire. We'd written you off as a goner back there. Didn't think you could get anywhere the way you were limping around on your bare feet. I can't believe you made it all the way up here on that rough ground."

"I didn't want Garcia to think I could," said Sage. "He might have put a bullet in my leg. I've spent a lot of my life barefoot. Boots are just for show or for strapping spurs to."

Foster gripped Sage's hand and pumped it a couple of times. "Young man, during the war I saw a few men in action who made me very proud to be an American. I count you among their number. Garcia was fixing to execute us later this morning. All of us, including the women. Like Andrew said, you surely did pull our fat out of the fire."

Foster looked at Pike and said, "We'll take Garcia and his men back to Queretaro and telegraph Diaz. Guanajuato can wait.

"We won't be getting any more sleep tonight. The sun will be up before long. Let's go ahead and break camp."

Nancy brought Sage his clothes, and he went into a tent and put them on.

When the sun was full up, the party was ready to travel. The six prisoners sat on their horses with their hands tied behind their backs. Sage had their horses tied head to tail, and Nutzhorn took the job of leading them while Sage trailed behind with the packhorses.

Pike walked up to Sage holding an arrow in his hand. He held it up and said, "Strange-looking arrow."

Sage said, "I didn't have any feathers, so I just shaved up curls on the back quarter of the shaft like that so it would drag. That works if it doesn't have to travel far."

Pike looked over at Foster and said, "How in hell did we ever whip the Apaches?"

Foster said, "Apaches?"

"Sage here is half Apache. He grew up with them."

Foster stared at Sage. "I couldn't understand how you could possibly have the skills you just demonstrated. There are a lot of damn fools in our country who refuse to utilize the skills of many of our people just because they aren't purebred white like them. It weakens us."

-81-

The Americans had no authority to make arrests, so Foster had the men camp outside of Queretaro with the prisoners. He and Pike took the women into the city and checked them into a hotel before they went to a telegraph office.

Miguel Vega arrived on the train the next day with a contingent of Federales, who went out to the camp and took the prisoners into custody.

On the train ride south to Mexico City, Foster invited Sage to sit with him for a while.

“Have you thought about going to a university, John?” asked Foster.

“Yes, sir,” replied Sage. “But I don’t know how I could afford it. My wife is expecting a child. I’m happy about that, but it limits my options.”

“You are still under the age limit to enter a military academy,” mused Foster, “but they don’t accept married men.”

Sage grinned and said, “The military is out. I would have to learn the ‘proper use of firearms,’ and I don’t think I could get the hang of it.”

Foster looked puzzled but went on. “Andrew tells me that you have been devouring some heavy reading and that your reading comprehension is excellent. He has been impressed with your contributions to discussions. He hadn’t expected that when he hired you. I take it he did that on a whim, but it certainly worked out to our benefit.”

“Thank you, sir,” said Sage. “I would like to continue in the Foreign Service. I’ll try to find a way to improve my education.”

“Hmm,” murmured Foster.

-82-

Before being executed by firing squad, Garcia, under considerable duress, divulged information that enabled Diaz, with American assistance, to destroy the efforts of Lerdo and General Escobedo to start the revolution.

Diaz was all for having Pilgreen go to the wall with Garcia, but Foster convinced him that there would be too many unfortunate consequences. Pilgreen had influential connections in the East.

Pilgreen was declared an undesirable alien and unceremoniously ushered to the deck of the steamer for a ride back to the States.

Sage and Nancy continued to travel around Mexico, and Nancy enjoyed the diplomatic functions hosted by the various embassies. She became a good friend of Leona Pike and Ambassador Foster's wife.

Toward the middle of August, Ambassador Foster asked Sage to bring Nancy and meet with him in his office.

When they went in, Ambassador Foster and Andrew Pike stood and invited them to take chairs. Sage couldn't read their expressions.

After some pleasantries, Foster said, "John, your service here has been remarkable. You have contributed a great deal. Andrew and I wouldn't be alive today if it weren't for you. We're going to miss you."

Sage gave him a level look, waiting, and Nancy exclaimed, "What!?"

Foster smiled slightly and said, "I have been corresponding with my good friend Gordon Whaler, who is the president of Harvard University. You are enrolled there with a full scholarship, starting this fall. Class of '84, if that is satisfactory to you."

Sage was stunned. Nancy yelped and grabbed his hand.

Sage stood up, walked over to Foster's desk, and extended his hand across it.

"That was good of you," he said. "Of course it is satisfactory.

"I'm more apprehensive about taking on Harvard than I was about taking a deputy sheriff's job in New Mexico. I knew something about how to go about that. I'll do my best to do well at Harvard."

"Look out, Harvard," said Pike.

AFTERWORD

Santiago, Cuba - 1898

Colonel Roosevelt found General Shafter under a tarp that had been erected on poles for shade on the grounds of his headquarters.

Roosevelt saluted and said, "You sent for me, sir?"

"Yes, colonel. Thank you for coming promptly. I have a job for you and your Rough Riders. Do they have anything to ride yet?"

"Harrumph," said Roosevelt. "We've collected some serviceable Spanish mounts. We'll probably pass our own while we are on our way back to the States. Will our return be delayed greatly?"

"I don't believe so, colonel," replied Shafter. He indicated a man who had stood at Roosevelt's approach. "This man is our top civilian on the island, John Sage. He's the charge de affairs in Havana and was here in Santiago when hostilities commenced."

Roosevelt looked Sage over while he shook his hand. The man looked him steadily in the eye and appeared to be one cool customer. He also looked to be very fit. He was wearing a tan lightweight suit and a western-style, narrow-brimmed field hat. His jacket was draped over his chair, and Roosevelt was surprised that he was wearing a shoulder holster with a large Colt in it.

"Shouldn't you be at your post in Havana, Mr. Sage?" asked Roosevelt.

"When the Main blew up and it appeared that we would likely to be going to war, I came down here," said Sage. "I believe this is where I can best serve our interests.

"The Teller Amendment makes clear that with the defeat of Spain, Cuba will become an independent nation. It is in our best interests that the right people form the new government. A lot of the right people happen to be near here in a Spanish concentration camp. I'd like to see that those people survive the turnover. It could well be that the Spanish would like it if they didn't.

"While the Spanish army has surrendered to General Shafter, we haven't taken over the camp yet. That needs to be done before they decide to eliminate key prisoners. As far as I can determine, they haven't—yet."

"The Spanish are a civilized people," said Roosevelt. "I hardly think they would murder helpless prisoners."

"Those civilized people have many thousands of Cuban insurrectos in camps all over the island, and they have killed thousands of them over the years."

Roosevelt paused. "Who determined who the right people were?" he asked.

"While I've been here—three years now—I've made a point of meeting with people in the American business community and with the insurrectos in the Cuban community—those that have avoided the camps. I have a fair idea about which prisoners would be needed to help form a good government—a government that would generally have the support of the people and that we could work well with. Some of those prisoners are in that camp. I have reported my findings to Secretary of State Hay."

"Was that on your initiative?" queried Roosevelt.

"Yes, sir."

"Sounds like that could have rubbed the Spanish the wrong way. John let you do it?" asked Roosevelt.

"He didn't pull me out of here," replied Sage. "I was pretty damn careful that the Spanish didn't know about my inquiries."

Shafter spoke up. "Mr. Sage has requested my help to ensure the safety of the Cuban prisoners. There are about three hundred of them in the camp here. He has scouted the camp and has come up with an impressive strategy for accomplishing the mission. Your company has a lot of westerners in it. They may do very well with the unconventional maneuver that Mr. Sage has proposed.

"Please lay it out for the colonel, Mr. Sage."

Sage unrolled a large drawing he had made and proceeded to go over his proposal with Roosevelt."

"Bully!" said Roosevelt. "We'll go in tonight."

After Sage departed, Roosevelt turned to Shafter and said, "Rather unusual. Army people getting a battle plan from a civilian."

Shafter chuckled and said, "Before I came down here, Secretary Hay called me in. He said his man down here, a John Sage, was a piece of work. He said the man had a head on his shoulders and a real talent for figuring out what things needed to be done, and then getting them done. He said that if Sage communicated with me, I would be wise to pay attention.

"Hay said that Sage is Harvard-educated, but he is a western man. He was once a deputy sheriff in New Mexico. I take it he knows how to use that Colt."

Obie Tyler was a grizzled cowboy that Roosevelt had tapped to be one of his sergeants. He gathered with the other sergeants and officers in the evening for a briefing by a diplomat, a John Sage. The call to attend a briefing by a diplomat had him scratching his head.

He'd been up the Chisholm Trail way back with a John Sage. Funny coincidence.

When Tyler saw the diplomat arrive, his jaw dropped. Sage was wearing a dark shirt, jeans, and some kind of Indian moccasins. He had a belt gun strapped on, and there was a big sheath knife on the left side of the belt. Tyler recalled that he and Sage were forty-four now. Sage didn't look like he'd changed much. Still moved like a cat.

Tyler walked over and stood in front of Sage. "He said, "The Foreign Service must be scraping the bottom now, hiring a broke-down old cowboy for an important post like that."

Sage lifted his eyebrows, grinned, and said, "Hello, Obie. Looks like broke-down old cowboys are the thing now days. We'll just have to make do."

They shook hands warmly, and Tyler said, "Damn, John, it's sure good to see you—but a bit of a surprise."

"Well, I got me some book learning," said Sage. "Amazing what that can do."

Simon Ochoa finished digging the hole three feet wide, three feet long, and four feet deep. Ochoa was emaciated, and the work had exhausted him. He was out in the forest, away from the camp, and there had been one root after another, even in the clearing he was in. He struggled to climb out, but the nearest guard told him to stay where he was.

Nineteen other men had also finished similar holes. Their graves.

One of the young prisoners shouted, "You will kill us, but Cuba will be free of Spaniards at last!" Major Cortez promptly walked over to the young man, pulled his pistol, and shot him in the head.

As the dead man collapsed into his hole, a shout came from the trees, "You are all covered, raise your hands!"

Cortez and his nine guards spun toward the voice raising their weapons, and a volley from the trees cut five of them down. Cortez and the remaining guards dropped their guns and raised their hands.

A dozen Rough Riders and a diplomat moved out of the trees with guns leveled. Colonel Roosevelt's face was beet red, but no one noticed in the weak light from a number of kerosene lamps scattered on the ground. He marched up to Cortez and said, "You son of a bitch, that was murder. You are under arrest!"

Sage translated.

Roosevelt turned to Sage and said, "Thank God one of those prisoners knew what was going on out here and told us. Look at this! They've all dug their own graves!"

Roosevelt turned back to Cortez and said, "Here I was thinking that Spaniards were civilized. You've shown me to be wrong."

Sage translated.

Sage said, "It is a good thing we didn't make a lot of noise back there at the camp. All these men might be buried by now."

"Yes," said Roosevelt. "You took out those sentries like you were some kind of Indian. Not a peep out of them. The way you had the men placed, not a single Spaniard had a chance to resist. Jolly good show! Just Bully!

Sergeant Tyler and a squad of Rough Riders came thundering in with their rifles at the ready and looking for a fight, but the war was over.

On the way back to the camp, Roosevelt rode next to Tyler. He said, "Mr. Sage is apparently quite a formidable man. I'm curious about him. It appeared that you and Mr. Sage are old friends."

"We were on a trail drive together, back in '77," said Tyler. "He was some kind of a terror with guns and without them. He drew down on four would-be herd cutters and dropped them all before they could get off a shot. I heard later that he took on Big Bill McClusky, the world champion prizefighter, in a saloon. He laid him out cold with a broken jaw in all of a few seconds. Sage is just someone you don't want to get in a fight with. Not any kind of fight. He doesn't look like he's slowed down any, either."

Roosevelt looked appalled. "I heard about the McClusky fight! That was Sage? Good Lord! He must make people around him a little nervous."

"Not at all," said Tyler. "Sage was never one to pick a fight or even threaten anyone. I liked being around him. Made me feel kind of secure."

Roosevelt pondered that for a few moments and then said, "The man seems to be very good at scouting, too, and he certainly dispatched those sentries quite handily."

Tyler chuckled. "Didn't surprise me none. His mother was a Chiricahua Apache. He spent a lot of time with the Apaches growing up."

Roosevelt stared at Tyler and then muttered, "My word."

The colonel was uncharacteristically silent for the rest of the ride.

Majorca, Spain - 1906

Sage wriggled his toes in the sand and leaned back in his canvas chair. He took a pull on his cigar as he watched Nancy and oldest son Nathan splash around in the gently lapping Mediterranean. Nathan was getting as brown as he was under the bright sun. He was a little taller, slimmer, and blonder than his old man. More like his namesake. Sage was glad that Nathan had found some time on his summer break from Cambridge to visit.

His younger son, Jim, who looked like a pint-sized John Sage, grabbed the hands of his sisters, Cathy and Alicia, and dragged them squealing into the water. All three were on their break from the Embassy school in Madrid.

Sage spotted a man hiking up the beach. He was dressed in marine dress blues.

Uh oh, thought Sage.

The Marine paused and saluted as he approached and said, "Mr. Ambassador, I have a message from the President," and handed Sage an envelope.

Sage opened it and read.

JOHN

SINCE THEY WHIPPED THE RUSSIANS THE JAPANESE HAVE GOT THE BIT IN THEIR TEETH
HAVE REQUESTED THAT THE SECRETARY POST YOU TO JAPAN
YOUR UNIQUE TALENTS NEEDED THERE
FULL INSTRUCTIONS BEING SENT TO EMBASSY
SORRY ABOUT YOUR VACATION

TEDDY

Made in the USA
Charleston, SC
01 July 2011